MONSTRUM

MONSTRUM

CLASSIC TALES OF LEGENDARY, BEASTLY, AND GHASTLY CREATURES

Chad Arment, editor

COACHWHIP PUBLICATIONS
Landisville, Pennsylvania

CONTENTS

Henric Van Kaarten
or, The Valley of Spirits

Anonymous

Many of our millers may possibly not be aware that there are a number of secluded, yet ancient villages, whose population, thin as it is, is a medley of Portuguese, Mulattoes, New Yorkists, Virginians, and a few individuals whose parents were people of England, situate on the northwestern boundaries of Brazil,—with whom communication is uncertain and infrequent, and whose manners and mode of living, owing to their removal from the influence of modern improvement, are almost as simple as the patriarchal ages. One of these, named Rio-del-Nema, is the scene of the following narrative.

The inhabitants of this village were a nondescript kind of people, somewhat superstitious, but friendly in their intercourse with one another, and hospitable to the very few strangers that wandered in that direction. Half cultivators, half huntsmen, they wanted spirit and perseverance to become, or profit as either; a few plots of maize, and the raising a few vegetables that did not demand much experience, supplied them with the principal means of subsistence: inconstant by temperament, the spade was often relinquished for the rifle, and the reaping-hook for a gin. From the surpassing grandeur of the scenery around them, one might have expected to meet an admiration of the beauties of nature, an elevated tone of thinking and feeling, or at least a not total indifference to the refinement of mind. But this was not the case;—they seemed perfectly insensible to the hundred natural beauties, to which they could not avoid being daily witness; and plodded on with an apathetic equanimity, not certainly very enviable.

7

Among the inhabitants of the Rio-del-Nema, of best substance, about the middle of the past century, might be reckoned a wight, termed Henric Van Kaarten. His grandfather had, for some political reasons, migrated from New York somewhere about the year 1679; and, after roving through the coast towns of the Brazils, had wandered westwards, and at last had settled down at Rio. Sprung from an ancient Dutch family, he inherited the thrift and industry peculiar to the nation, and, in course of years, accumulated a tolerable property; not indeed in coin, but in grain, cattle, &c. This descended to his heirs with increase; and in 1734 Henric was able to look about him with complacency, and congratulate himself on possessions which were the envy of his neighbours, and a source of much satisfaction to himself. Never backward to relieve the deserving or undeserving, always jovial, familiar, and good-hearted, he was, as he ought to have been, extremely popular in the village: to him, as the most influential amongst them, were his neighbours accustomed to look for the administration of executive and distributive justice; to his opinion all were accustomed to defer; and representative and legislator of the little commonwealth, he might with justice have reckoned himself, had he been acquainted with the name, a Solon on a small scale.

His age was about forty-five; and, though stout, he was tall, and of a goodly presence: endowed with strong capabilities of supporting fatigue, and a mind not easily terrified by danger, it was often his practice to make long and extensive excursions into the surrounding country. A South American woodman has resources in himself calculated to surmount obstacles, and obviate what to others would appear insuperable inconveniences. When preparing for expeditious of this description, he would fit himself out in a species of Robinson Crusoe fashion: carrying, besides rifle, couteau, and powder horns, an axe to cut passages through brushwood, a bag containing provisions, a quilted cloak of ample volume to sleep upon, a flask of spirits, and sundry other necessaries of a similar kind. Attended by a dog of superior breed, that he called Alp, and apparently as well pleased with these sallies as his master, Henric was accustomed to range the forests and savannahs of that part of America; traversing long tracts of woodland, under the scorching beams of a tropical sun; swimming rivers, and crossing ridges of seemingly inaccessible mountains.

It happened that Henric had occasion to visit a Mynherr Bomstyck, an offset from the colony, at a distant point: and this coming in to aid his rambling disposition, he prepared for his journey. One tempting morning, properly accoutred, he set out, and walked stoutly forwards: masses of forest trees began to close around him, until the greater part of the lower country was shut in from view. On the brow of a grassy eminence, that sloped gently downwards, which he had now attained, Henric turned, and for the last time caught a fair glimpse of the village he had left behind him. It lay vaguely reposing in the early sunlight; its antique church tower peeping from the dark foliage that seemed to sheathe it in solitary peacefulness, and its few gilded roofs gracefully contrasted with the blueness of the country beyond.

Calling his dog to his side, Henric turned round, and strode valiantly forwards. Soon all traces of cultivation or inhabitants faded from his eye. A monotonous repetition of the same colour, green in all tints, from rich autumnal brown to the deepness of the olive, or the freshness of the emerald, seemed calculated to tire the eye. Forest succeeded forest in never-ending succession; and no sound broke the melancholy stillness of the scene, but now and then a strange and fitful whispering of the ocean of leaves that was spread before, and on either side of him; and, perhaps, the solitary cry of some bird of prey, rendering the silence more oppressive, by a momentary interruption of its reign.

Two days Henric spent in penetrating the forests that lay in the neighbourhood of his native settlement. Towards the approach of evening on the third, the country began to assume other and still more majestic aspects. Ho was approaching a towering ridge of mountains of unequal height and magnitude,—their bases clothed with luxuriant verdure abounding in birds of the most brilliant plumage, and broken with picturesque confusion into masses of rock, and partial breaks of water, and copsewood.

He threw himself on a soft green bank; and, taking off his cap, abandoned himself to a feeling of delicious listlessness; either watching the clouds, as they floated one after the other over the heavens; listening to the murmuring of a distant mountain eagle; or conjuring up shapes among the ancient trees before him, and

"Chewing the cud of sweet and bitter fancies;"

but night gradually began to creep on, and the scene to fade from his view. Rising hurriedly, and surprised at the length of time he had spent in rumination, he called Alp, and endeavoured to find some shelter for the night: his bag of provisions, too, ran low; and he hoped by encountering some eatable animal to be furnished with the means of replenishing it. Cautiously advancing, therefore, into a romantic glade that opened before him, and seemed to invite his footsteps,—rifle charged and primed, he peered before and about him, on the look-out for an object of attack. Fortune favoured him more than he could have hoped for: about forty paces before him a deer bounded across the sward. Casting a quick and terrific glance from his bright dark eye at the unwelcome intruder, it hastened forwards, and, after two or three ineffectual attempts to pierce the thicket of branches and leaves that formed an impenetrable barrier in many places beside it, leaped boldly upwards, flying like the wind over an almost perpendicular acclivity. Henric's rifle was, however, levelled in a moment—crack! the shot had told.

Thus supplied with fresh and wholesome provisions, Henric, after making a hearty woodland dinner, and washing it down with a copious draught of the clearest water, duly impregnated with the contents of his flask, now turned his thoughts upon constructing a temporary night shelter. Having, by the help of his friendly axe, cut a number of stakes from the branches of the trees about him, bending almost to the ground, he fixed them in a small circle in the earth and wrapping himself tightly in his cloak, carefully laying his weapons within instant reach, composed himself to sleep. His slumbers were undisturbed by the visit of any hairy wanderer, although he still conceived himself to be awake, and thus pursuing the dreadful adventures of his journey.

Ha thought that he had got far from the abodes of mankind, and to make the most of the day started quickly up, and drawing some refreshment from his wallet, ate hastily as he walked; the aspect of the country again changed, all seemed a wild and melancholy solitude. A disagreeable and overpowering feeling of utter loneliness stole over him, almost rising to something like terror; every minute, although he seemed to be the only inhabitant of the world, he caught himself looking furtively over his shoulder, but he strode boldly on, guiding himself by the sun; sometimes he was more than half tempted to think he had lost his way, as by this he had expected to see the country open towards districts more susceptible of cultivation, but traces of anything calculated to justify the expectation, were not to be discovered. Still mass after mass of foliage, covering steeps, sealing eminences, or declining into valleys, disclosed themselves one after the other. Henric was brought to a stand-still; he first became dubious of his route, then misgiving, and at last totally bewildered. He feared to proceed, through the suspicion that he might be increasing the distance between him and symptoms of civilization; he feared to retrace his steps, through the dread of still farther involving himself. In this state of indecision he sat himself down and night began to close around him. To heighten his perplexity and vexation, a violent thunder-storm came on, and roused the forest solitude into one wild roar of confusion. Sheltering himself as he best might, he waited for its subsidence; and after wringing his cloak, he walked a little way forward, but the discouraging consciousness that he knew not to which point of the compass to direct himself, made him stop, and look wistfully around.

At this moment a light in the distance attracted his attention. Henric laboured on, he now perceived that the ground rose rapidly; the woods became more gloomy, and had Henric been a believer in fays and goblins, this was a spot eminently calculated to recall all the tales and traditions of the kind to the reluctant memory; but Henric had never troubled himself with speculations as to their existence or non-existence, and had credence in nothing but what could be brought to the test of actual experience.

From what the light proceeded it was totally impassible to discover; it emitted a reddish misty glare upon the nearest objects, but left all in obscurity beyond. Henric would have shouted, but somehow or other his voice seemed to stick in his throat; an indefinable feeling of awe stole over him, his knees trembled, and unconsciously he stood for a moment still. At intervals there seemed to be something like faint peals of laughter borne to him on the breeze; laughter sounded strange in such a place; but it only confirmed his impression, namely, that there must be some human creature within hail. After much toiling, he attained the topmost edge of the ridge; but who can express his fright and astonishment at the scene that met his eye below!

A large fire of heaped up twigs and branches was kindled in the centre of the amphitheatre, whose craggy walls shot upwards to an immense height; here shelving into precipices, and there branching off into narrow rocky ledges, only practicable for animals of the surest feet. Above rose pyramids of foliage; trees bending horizontally inwards, and shutting out the moonlight clouds:—ponderous crags, which seemed as if a touch would hurl them on the sward below; and caverned blocks of fretted rock, fringed with intertwisted festoons of ivy. A dusky glare was profusely shed on every object, crimsoning leaf, branch, and trunk, and faintly irradiating the sky. Gathered around the fire was an assemblage of strange and hideous shapes, dwarf-like in proportion, and monstrous in features; their bodies were covered with hair, deformed, and uncouth in motion; from their shrivelled hands there extended claws of odious length; their heads, covered with long lank black hair, reaching down to their feet, were large and heavy looking, with "foreheads villanous low," ape-like ears, mouths resembling those of brutes, armed with yellow fangs, and fringed with shaggy beards; and the skin of their faces was withered and wrinkled.

Every now and then loud shouts of discordant laughter burst out from their lips, making the woods re-echo for miles round. A fawn, which they were devouring, lay torn and bleeding before them. But Henrie had scarcely leisure to observe all these particulars, his first thought, and a, horrible one it was, was that he beheld an assemblage of demons, revelling with satanic glee over the body of some lost mortal.

Henric had the ordinary courage of man, and would have feared nothing that had come before him in a human form; but this congregation completely mastered him. He lay gazing in a sort of fascination; while party after party of fresh comers descended into the valley, till the whole space was literally crowded with the strange and hideous looking creatures. Every jutting rock and branched tree were also occupied; and the fire seemed to glow brighter and fiercer, and to shed its glaring light with increased intensity. Roar and revelry, and shout and wild laughter, and still wilder antics, made the valley before him seem absolutely alive; and the cry was "Still they come!"—till so densely was the place peopled, that crowd was heaped upon crowd, and vast masses of these horrid beings were growing up like walls around the fire. Henric became utterly bewildered: he lay deprived of all power of locomotion, his head jutting over a ledge of the rock, the fierce light glowing in his face, and the struggling and yelling heaps of demons rising every moment higher and higher directly beneath him. Horrible were Henric's thoughts; and, stirred by the same feelings which make men inclined to throw themselves from lofty eminences, he swayed to and fro, every second losing his self-possession more and more completely; till at length, absolutely maddened, he toppled over the crag, dragging his dog with him; himself uttering a scream of horror, and his companion a howl of the same signification. As soon as his person was descried, whirling over the crag, a thousand arms were open to receive him, and a yell arose that drove consciousness from the mind of our unlucky traveller, who knew nothing farther till he awoke as from a dream, and found that the sun was almost in the meridian.

Shuddering at the recollection of the dreadful horrors of the past night, he arose, and gave one fearful glance around: all was now quite noiseless and deserted, and he strode as fast as possible

away. Anxious to escape from so horrible a neighbourhood, he travelled on with astonishing speed, and at evening had the satisfaction of perceiving that the country began to open. A little time
after he descried in the distance, the thrice welcome spire of the
ancient Portuguese village in which Mynherr Bomstyck resided.
When he arrived at it, the wonder with which his tale was received
may be easily imagined: some disbelieved it; but Mynherr
Bomstyck and a considerable portion of his neighbours, gave it the
fullest credence, aware of the irreproachable character for truth
which Henric had always maintained. From one thing to another,
it became a popular belief, through all the districts to the north-
westward of Brazil, that there was a valley inhabited by gnomes or
obscure spirits: and as Henric was never enabled to decide exactly
which was the precise one on which he had stumbled, a long range
of valleys were placed under ban, and as sedulously avoided by the
hunters and wayfarers as if certain destruction would have attended
the entering of the haunted district.

Not many years ago, circumstances placed the writer in the
vicinity of Henric Van Kaarten's gnome-valley. The story was told
me, and I was solemnly warned of the consequences which might
follow a visit to the secluded spot, which for nearly a century had
been untrodden by the foot of man; so universal was the tradition,
and so firmly was it believed by the primitive thinking inhabitants. Many fearful additions had, doubtless, been added to Henric's
original dream,—and the glare of fires and the roar of voices were
still seen and heard; whilst numbers of their herds were stolen away
for the nightly orgies of the gnomes. Not having much faith in
supernaturals, and placing the opinions of the secluded people to
the credit of superstition, I shouldered my rifle, and proceeded to
explore the haunted valleys. I was of course given up as a doomed
man. Like Henric I lost myself, and was benighted; but, unlike him,
I saw nothing in the shape of demons: I found the valleys rich in
picturesque scenery, and abounding in game: they had indeed been
the receptacles for all the stray cattle of the surrounding villages,
and hence were crowded with wild and half-tame animals. I had
excellent sport. I returned on the evening of the second day, greatly

to the surprise of the beholders. My tale was listened to, doubted, half believed,—and on the morrow a party accompanied me for the purpose of reclaiming the animals. The solitude was completely broken in upon, and the tradition of Henric Van Kaarten buried amongst other *reliquiae* of past times.

THE DEVIL OF THE MARSH

H. B. Marriott-Watson

It was nigh upon dusk when I drew close to the Great Marsh, and already the white vapours were about, riding across the sunken levels like ghosts in a churchyard. Though I had set forth in a mood of wild delight, I had sobered in the lonely ride across the moor and was now uneasily alert. As my horse jerked down the grassy slopes that fell away to the jaws of the swamp I could see thin streams of mist rise slowly, hover like wraiths above the long rushes, and then, turning gradually more material, go blowing heavily away across the flat. The appearance of the place at this desolate hour, so remote from human society and so darkly significant of evil presences, struck me with a certain wonder that she should have chosen this spot for our meeting. She was a familiar of the moors, where I had invariably encountered her; but it was like her arrogant caprice to test my devotion by some such dreary assignation. The wide and horrid prospect depressed me beyond reason, but the fact of her neighbourhood drew me on, and my spirits mounted at the thought that at last she was to put me in possession of herself. Tethering my horse upon the verge of the swamp, I soon discovered the path that crossed it, and entering struck out boldly for the heart. The track could have been little used, for the reeds, which stood high above the level of my eyes upon either side, straggled everywhere across in low arches, through which I dodged, and broke my way with some inconvenience and much impatience. A full half hour I was solitary

16

in that wilderness, and when at last a sound other than my own
footsteps broke the silence the dusk had fallen.

I was moving very slowly at the time, with a mind half disposed
to turn from the melancholy expedition, which it seemed to me
now must surely be a cruel jest she had played upon me. While
some such reluctance held me, I was suddenly arrested by a hoarse
croaking which broke out upon my left, sounding somewhere from
the reeds in the black mire. A little further it came again from close
at hand, and when I had passed on a few more steps in wonder and
perplexity, I heard it for the third time. I stopped and listened,
but the marsh was as a grave, and so taking the noise for the signal
of some raucous frog, I resumed my way. But in a little the croaking
was repeated, and coming quickly to a stand I pushed the reeds
aside and peered into the darkness. I could see nothing, but at the
immediate moment of my pause I thought I detected the sound of
some body trailing through the rushes. My distaste for the
adventure grew with this suspicion, and had it not been for my
delirious infatuation I had assuredly turned back and ridden home.
The ghastly sound pursued me at intervals along the track, until at
last, irritated beyond endurance by the sense of this persistent and
invisible company, I broke into a sort of run. This, it seemed, the
creature (whatever it was) could not achieve, for I heard no more
of it, and continued my way in peace. My path at length ran out
from among the reeds upon the smooth flat of which she had
spoken, and here my heart quickened, and the gloom of the
dreadful place lifted. The flat lay in the very centre of the marsh,
and here and there in it a gaunt bush or withered tree rose like a
spectre against the white mists. At the further end I fancied some
kind of building loomed up; but the fog which had been gathering
ever since my entrance upon the passage sailed down upon me at
that moment and the prospect went out with suddenness. As I stood
waiting for the clouds to pass, a voice cried to me out of its centre,
and I saw her next second with bands of mist swirling about her
body, come rushing to me from the darkness. She put her long arms
about me, and, drawing her close, I looked into her deep eyes. Far
down in them, it seemed to me, I could discern a mystic laughter

dancing in the wells of light, and I had that ecstatic sense of nearness to some spirit of fire which was wont to possess me at her contact.

"At last," she said, "at last, my beloved!" I caressed her.

"Why," said I, tingling at the nerves, "why have you put this dolorous journey between us? And what mad freak is your presence in this swamp?" She uttered her silver laugh, and nestled to me again.

"I am the creature of this place," she answered. "This is my home. I have sworn you should behold me in my native sin ere you ravished me away."

"Come, then," said I; "I have seen; let there be an end of this. I know you, what you are. This marsh chokes up my heart. God forbid you should spend more of your days here. Come."

"You are in haste," she cried. "There is yet much to learn. Look, my friend," she said, "you who know me, what I am. This is my prison, and I have inherited its properties. Have you no fear?"

For answer I pulled her to me, and her warm lips drove out the horrid humours of the night; but the swift passage of a flickering mockery over her eyes struck me as a flash of lightning, and I grew chill again.

"I have the marsh in my blood," she whispered: "the marsh and the fog of it. Think ere you vow to me, for I am the cloud in a starry night."

A lithe and lovely creature, palpable of warm flesh, she lifted her magic face to mine and besought me plaintively with these words. The dews of the nightfall hung on her lashes, and seemed to plead with me for her forlorn and solitary plight.

"Behold!" I cried, "witch or devil of the marsh, you shall come with me! I have known you on the moors, a roving apparition of beauty; nothing more I know, nothing more I ask. I care not what this dismal haunt means; not what these strange and mystic eyes. You have powers and senses above me; your sphere and habits are as mysterious and incomprehensible as your beauty. But that," I said, "is mine, and the world that is mine shall be yours also."

She moved her head nearer to me with an antic gesture, and her gleaming eyes glanced up at me with a sudden flash, the similitude (great heavens!) of a hooded snake. Starting, I fell away, but at that moment she turned her face and set it fast towards the fog that came rolling in thick volumes over the flat. Noiselessly the great cloud crept down upon us, and all dazed and troubled I watched her watching it in silence. It was as if she awaited some omen of horror, and I too trembled in the fear of its coming.

Then suddenly out of the night issued the hoarse and hideous croaking I had heard upon my passage. I reached out my arm to take her hand, but in an instant the mists broke over us, and I was groping in the vacancy. Something like panic took hold of me, and, beating through the blind obscurity, I rushed over the flat, calling upon her. In a little the swirl went by, and I perceived her upon the margin of the swamp, her arm raised as in imperious command. I ran to her, but stopped, amazed and shaken by a fearful sight. Low by the dripping reeds crouched a small squat thing, in the likeness of a monstrous frog, coughing and choking in its throat. As I stared, the creature rose upon its legs and disclosed a horrid human resemblance. Its face was white and thin, with long black hair; its body gnarled and twisted as with the ague of a thousand years. Shaking, it whined in a breathless voice, pointing a skeleton finger at the woman by my side.

"Your eyes were my guide," it quavered. "Do you think that after all these years I have no knowledge of your eyes? Lo, is there aught of evil in you I am not instructed in? This is the Hell you designed for me, and now you would leave me to a greater."

The wretch paused, and panting leaned upon a bush, while she stood silent, mocking him with her eyes, and soothing my terror with her soft touch.

"Hear!" he cried, turning to me, "hear the tale of this woman that you may know her as she is. She is the Presence of the marshes. Woman or Devil I know not, but only that the accursed marsh has crept into her soul and she herself is become its Evil Spirit; she herself, that lives and grows young and beautiful by it, has its full power to blight and chill and slay. I, who was once as you are, have this knowledge. What bones lie deep in this black swamp who can say but she? She has drained of health, she has drained of mind and of soul; what is between her and her desire that she should not drain also of life? She has made me a devil in her Hell, and now she would leave me to my solitary pain, and go search for another victim. But she shall not!" he screamed through his chattering teeth; "she shall not! My Hell is also hers! She shall not!"

Her smiling untroubled eyes left his face and turned to me: she put out her arms, swaying towards me, and so fervid and so great a light glowed in her face that, as one distraught of superhuman means, I took her into my embrace. And then the madness seized me.

"Woman or devil," I said, "I will go with you! Of what account this pitiful past? Blight me even as that wretch, so be only you are with me."

She laughed, and, disengaging herself, leaned, half-clinging to me, towards the coughing creature by the mire.

"Come," I cried, catching her by the waist. "Come!" She laughed again a silver-ringing laugh. She moved with me slowly across the flat to where the track started for the portals of the marsh. She laughed and clung to me.

But at the edge of the track I was startled by a shrill, hoarse screaming; and behold, from my very feet, that loathsome creature rose up and wound his long black arms about her shrieking and crying in his pain. Stooping I pushed him from her skirts, and with one sweep of my arm drew her across the pathway; as her face passed mine her eyes were wide and smiling. Then of a sudden the still mist enveloped us once more; but ere it descended I had a glimpse of that contorted figure trembling on the margin, the white face drawn and full of desolate pain. At the sight an icy shiver ran through me. And then through the yellow gloom the shadow of her darted past me to the further side. I heard the hoarse cough, the dim noise of a struggle, a swishing sound, a thin cry, and then the sucking of the slime over something in the rushes. I leapt forward: and once again the fog thinned, and I beheld her, woman or devil, standing upon the verge, and peering with smiling eyes into the foul and sickly bog. With a sharp cry wrung from my nerveless soul, I turned and fled down the narrow way from that accursed spot; and as I ran the thickening fog closed round me, and I heard far off and lessening still the silver sound of her mocking laughter.

The Basilisk

R. Murray Gilchrist

Marina gave no sign that she heard my protestation. The embroidery of Venus's hands in her silk picture of The Judgment of Paris was seemingly of greater import to her than the love which almost tore my soul and body asunder. In absolute despair I sat until she had replenished her needle seven times. Then impassioned nature cried aloud:— "You do not love me!"

She looked up somewhat wearily, as one debarred from rest. "Listen," she said. "There is a creature called a Basilisk, which turns men and women into stone. In my girlhood I saw the Basilisk—I am stone!"

And, rising from her chair, she departed the room, leaving me in amazed doubt as to whether I had heard aright. I had always known of some curious secret in her life: a secret which permitted her to speak of and to understand things to which no other woman had dared to lift her thoughts. But alas! it was a secret whose influence ever thrust her back from the attaining of happiness. She would warm, then freeze instantly; discuss the purest wisdom, then cease with contemptuous lips and eyes. Doubtless this strangeness had been the first thing to awaken my passion. Her beauty was not of the kind that smites men with sudden craving: it was pale and reposeful, the loveliness of a marble image. Yet, as time went on, so wondrous became her fascination that even the murmur of her swaying garments sickened me with longing. Not more than a year had passed since our first meeting, when I had found her laden with flaming tendrils in the thinned woods of my heritage. A very

Dryad, robed in grass colour, she was chanting to the sylvan deities. The invisible web took me, and I became her slave.

Her house lay two leagues from mine. It was a low-built mansion lying in a concave park. The thatch was gaudy with stonecrop and lichen. Amongst the central chimneys a foreign bird sat on a nest of twigs. The long windows blazed with heraldic devices; and paintings of kings and queens and nobles hung in the dim chambers. Here she dwelt with a retinue of aged servants, fantastic women and men half imbecile, who salaamed before her with eastern humility and yet addressed her in such terms as gossips use. Had she given them life they could not have obeyed with more reverence. Quaint things the women wrought for her— pomanders and cushions of thistledown; and the men were never happier than when they could tell her of the first thrush's egg in the thornbush or the sege of bitterns that haunted the marsh. She was their goddess and their daughter. Each day had its own routine. In the morning she rode and sang and played; at noon she read in the dusty library, drinking to the full of the dramatists and the platonists. Her own life was such a tragedy as an Elizabethan would have adored. None save her people knew her history, but there were wonderful stories of how she had bowed to tradition, and concentrated in herself the characteristics of a thousand wizard fathers. In the blossom of her youth she had sought strange knowledge, and had tasted thereof, and rued.

The morning after my declaration she rode across her park to the meditating walk I always paced till noon. She was alone, dressed in a habit of white lute-string with a loose girdle of blue. As her mare reached the yew hedge, she dismounted, and came to me with more lightness than I had ever beheld in her. At her waist hung a black glass mirror, and her half-bare arms were adorned with cabalistic jewels.

When I knelt to kiss her hand, she sighed heavily. "Ask me nothing," she said. "Life itself is too joyless to be more embittered by explanations. Let all rest between us as now. I will love coldly, you warmly, with no nearer approaching." Her voice rang full of a wistful expectancy: as if she knew that I should combat her half-explained decision. She read me well, for almost ere she had done I cried out loudly against it:— "It can never be so—I cannot breathe—I shall die!"

She sank to the low moss-covered wall. "Must the sacrifice be made?" she asked, half to herself. "Must I tell him all?" Silence prevailed a while, then turning away her face she said: "From the first I loved you, but last night in the darkness, when I could not sleep for thinking of your words, love sprang into desire."

I was forbidden to speak.

"And desire seemed to burst the cords that bound me. In that moment's strength I felt that I could give all for the joy of being once utterly yours."

I longed to clasp her to my heart. But her eyes were stern, and a frown crossed her brow.

"At morning light," she said, "desire died, but in my ecstasy I had sworn to give what must be given for that short bliss, and to lie in your arms and pant against you before another midnight. So I have come to bid you fare with me to the place where the spell may be loosed, and happiness bought."

She called the mare: it came whinnying, and pawed the ground until she had stroked its neck. She mounted, setting in my hand a tiny, satin-shod foot that seemed rather child's than woman's. "Let us go together to my house," she said. "I have orders to give and duties to fulfil. I will not keep you there long, for we must start soon on our errand." I walked exultantly at her side, but, the grange in view, I entreated her to speak explicitly of our mysterious journey. She stooped and patted my head. "'Tis but a matter of buying and selling," she answered.

When she had arranged her household affairs, she came to the library and bade me follow her. Then, with the mirror still swinging against her knees, she led me through the garden and the wilderness down to a misty wood. It being autumn, the trees were tinted gloriously in dusky bars of colouring. The rowan, with his amber leaves and scarlet berries, stood before the brown black-spotted sycamore; the silver beech flaunted his golden coins against my poverty; firs, green and fawn-hued, slumbered in hazy gossamer. No bird carolled, although the sun was hot. Marina noted the absence of sound, and without prelude of any kind began to sing from the ballad of the Witch Mother: about the nine enchanted knots, and the trouble-comb in the lady's knotted hair, and the master-kid that ran beneath her couch. Every drop of my blood froze in dread, for whilst she sang her face took on the majesty of one who traffics with infernal powers. As the shade of the trees fell over her, and we passed intermittently out of the light, I saw that her eyes glittered like rings of sapphires. Believing now that the ordeal she must undergo would be too frightful, I begged her to return. Supplicating on my knees— "Let me face the evil alone!" I said, "I will entreat the loosening of the bonds. I will compel and accept any penalty." She grew calm. "Nay," she said, very gently, "if aught can conquer, it is my love alone. In the fervour of my last wish I can dare everything."

By now, at the end of a sloping alley, we had reached the shores of a vast marsh. Some unknown quality in the sparkling water had stained its whole bed a bright yellow. Green leaves, of such a sour brightness as almost poisoned to behold, floated on the surface of the rush-girdled pools. Weeds like tempting veils of mossy velvet grew beneath in vivid contrast with the soil. Alders and willows hung over the margin. From where we stood a half-submerged path of rough stones, threaded by deep swift channels, crossed to the very centre. Marina put her foot upon the first step. "I must go first," she said. "Only once before have I gone this way, yet I know its pitfalls better than any living creature."

Before I could hinder her she was leaping from stone to stone like a hunted animal. I followed hastily, seeking, but vainly, to lessen the space between us. She was gasping for breath, and her heart-beats sounded like the ticking of a clock. When we reached a great pool, itself almost a lake, that was covered with lavender scum, the path turned abruptly to the right, where stood an isolated grove of wasted elms. As Marina beheld this, her pace slackened, and she paused in momentary indecision; but, at my first word of pleading that she should go no further, she went on, dragging her

silken mud-bespattered skirts. We climbed the slippery shores of
the island (for island it was, being raised much above the level of
the marsh), and Marina led the way over lush grass to an open
glade. A great marble tank lay there, supported on two thick pillars.
Decayed boughs rested on the crust of stagnancy within, and divers
frogs, bloated and almost blue, rolled off at our approach. To the
left stood the columns of a temple, a round, domed building, with
a closed door of bronze. Wild vines had grown athwart the portal;
rank, clinging herbs had sprung from the over-teeming soil;
astrological figures were enchiselled on the broad stairs.

Here Marina stopped. "I shall blindfold you," she said, taking
off her loose sash, "and you must vow obedience to all I tell you.
The least error will betray us." I promised, and submitted to the
bandage. With a pressure of the hand, and bidding me neither move
nor speak, she left me and went to the door of the temple. Thrice
her hand struck the dull metal. At the last stroke a hissing shriek
came from within, and the massive hinges creaked loudly. A breath
like an icy tongue leaped out and touched me, and in the terror my
hand sprang to the kerchief. Marina's voice, filled with agony, gave
me instant pause. *"Oh, why am I thus torn between the man and
the fiend? The mesh that holds life in will be ripped from end to
end! Is there no mercy?"*

My hand fell impotent. Every muscle shrank. I felt myself turn
to stone. After a while came a sweet scent of smouldering wood:
such an Oriental fragrance as is offered to Indian gods. Then the
door swung to, and I heard Marina's voice, dim and wordless, but
raised in wild deprecation. Hour after hour passed so, and still I
waited. Not until the sash grew crimson with the rays of the sinking
sun did the door open.

"Come to me!" Marina whispered. "Do not unblindfold. Quick—
we must not stay here long. He is glutted with my sacrifice."

Newborn joy rang in her tones. I stumbled across and was
caught in her arms. Shafts of delight pierced my heart at the first
contact with her warm breasts. She turned me round, and bidding
me look straight in front, with one swift touch untied the knot.
The first thing my dazed eyes fell upon was the mirror of black

glass which had hung from her waist. She held it so that I might gaze into its depths. And there, with a cry of amazement and fear, *I saw the shadow of the Basilisk.*

The Thing was lying prone on the floor, the presentment of a sleeping horror. Vivid scarlet and sable feathers covered its gold-crowned cocks-head, and its leathern dragon-wings were folded. Its sinuous tail, capped with a snake's eyes and mouth, was curved in luxurious and delighted satiety. A prodigious evil leaped in its atmosphere. But even as I looked a mist crowded over the surface of the mirror: the shadow faded, leaving only an indistinct and wavering shape. Marina breathed upon it, and, as I peered and pored, the gloom went off the plate and left, where the Chimera had lain, the prostrate figure of a man. He was young and stalwart, a dark outline with a white face, and short black curls that fell in tangles over a shapely forehead, and eyelids languorous and red. His aspect was that of a wearied demon-god.

When Marina looked sideways and saw my wonderment, she laughed delightedly in one rippling running tune that should have quickened the dead entrails of the marsh. "I have conquered!" she cried. "I have purchased the fulness of joy!" And with one outstretched arm she closed the door before I could turn to look; with the other she encircled my neck, and, bringing down my head, pressed my mouth to hers. The mirror fell from her hand, and with her foot she crushed its shards into the dank mould.

The sun had sunk behind the trees now, and glittered through the intricate leafage like a charcoal-burner's fire. All the nymphs of the pools arose and danced, grey and cold, exulting at the absence of the divine light. So thickly gathered the vapours that the path grew perilous. "Stay, love," I said. "Let me take you in my arms and carry you. It is no longer safe for you to walk alone." She made no reply, but, a flush arising to her pale cheeks, she stood and let me lift her to my bosom. She rested a hand on either shoulder, and gave no sign of fear as I bounded from stone to stone. The way lengthened deliciously, and by the time we reached the plantation the moon was rising over the further hills. Hope and fear fought in my heart: soon both were set at rest. When I set her on the dry ground she stood a-tiptoe, and murmured with exquisite shame: "To-night, then, dearest. My home is yours now."

So, in a rapture too subtle for words, we walked together, arm-enfolded, to her house. Preparations for a banquet were going on within: the windows were ablaze, and figures passed behind them bowed with heavy dishes. At the threshold of the hall we were met by a triumphant crash of melody. In the musician's gallery bald-pated veterans stood to it with flute and harp and viol-de-gamba. In two long rows the antic retainers stood, and bowed, and cried merrily: "Joy and health to the bride and groom!" And they kissed Marina's hands and mine, and, with the players sending forth that half-forgotten tenderness which threads through ancient song-books, we passed to the feast, seating ourselves on the dais, whilst the servants filled the tables below. But we made little feint of appetite. As the last dish of confections was removing, a weird pageant swept across the further end of the banqueting-room: Oberon and Titania with Robin Goodfellow and the rest, attired in silks and satins gorgeous of hue, and bedizened with such late flowers as were still with us. I leaned forward to commend, and saw that each face was brown and wizened and thin-haired: so that their motions and their wedding paean felt goblin and dis-comforting; nor could I smile till they departed by the further door. Then the tables were cleared away, and Marina, taking my finger-tips in hers, opened a stately dance. The servants followed, and in the second maze a shrill and joyful laughter proclaimed that the bride had sought her chamber. . . .

Ere the dawn I wakened from a troubled sleep. My dream had been of despair: I had been persecuted by a host of devils, thieves of a priceless jewel. So I leaned over the pillow for Marina's consolation; my lips sought hers, my hand crept beneath her head. My heart gave one mad bound—then stopped.

The Upper Berth

F. Marion Crawford

I

Somebody asked for the cigars. We had talked long, and the conversation as beginning to languish; the tobacco smoke had got into the heavy curtains, he wine had got into those brains which were liable to become heavy, and it was already perfectly evident that, unless somebody did something to rouse our oppressed spirits, the meeting would soon come to its natural conclusion, and we, the guests, would speedily go home to bed, and most certainly to sleep. No one had said anything very remarkable; it may be that no one had anything very remarkable to say. Jones had given us every particular of his last hunting adventure in Yorkshire. Mr. Tompkins, of Boston, had explained at elaborate length those working principles, by the due and careful maintenance of which the Atchison, Topeka, and Santa Fé Railroad not only extended its territory, increased its departmental influence, and transported live stock without starving them to death before the day of actual delivery, but, also, had for years succeeded in deceiving those passengers who bought its tickets into the fallacious belief that the corporation aforesaid was really able to transport human life without destroying it. Signor Tombola had endeavoured to persuade us, by arguments which we took no trouble to oppose, that the unity of his country in no way resembled the average modern torpedo, carefully planned, constructed with all the skill of the greatest European arsenals, but, when constructed, destined to be directed by feeble hands into a region where it must

29

undoubtedly explode, unseen, unfeared, and unheard, into the illimitable wastes of political chaos.

It is unnecessary to go into further details. The conversation had assumed proportions which would have bored Prometheus on his rock, which would have driven Tantalus to distraction, and which would have impelled Ixion to seek relaxation in the simple but instructive dialogues of Herr Ollendorff, rather than submit to the greater evil of listening to our talk. We had sat at table for hours; we were bored, we were tired, and nobody showed signs of moving.

Somebody called for cigars. We all instinctively looked towards the speaker. Brisbane was a man of five-and-thirty years of age, and remarkable for those gifts which chiefly attract the attention of men. He was a strong man. The external proportions of his figure presented nothing extraordinary to the common eye, though his size was above the average. He was a little over six feet in height, and moderately broad in the shoulder; he did not appear to be stout, but, on the other hand, he was certainly not thin; his small head was supported by a strong and sinewy neck; his broad, muscular hands appeared to possess a peculiar skill in breaking walnuts without the assistance of the ordinary cracker, and, seeing him in profile, one could not help remarking the extraordinary breadth of his sleeves, and the unusual thickness of his chest. He was one of those men who are commonly spoken of among men as deceptive; that is to say, that though he looked exceedingly strong he was in reality very much stronger than he looked. Of his features I need say little. His head was small, his hair is thin, his eyes are blue, his nose is large, he has a small moustache, and a square jaw. Everybody knows Brisbane, and when he asked for a cigar everybody looked at him.

"It is a very singular thing," said Brisbane.

Everybody stopped talking. Brisbane's voice was not loud, but possessed a peculiar quality of penetrating general conversation, and cutting it like a knife. Everybody listened. Brisbane, perceiving that he had attracted their general attention, lit his cigar with great equanimity.

"It is very singular," he continued, "that thing about ghosts. People are always asking whether anybody has seen a ghost. I have."

"Bosh! What, you? You don't mean to say so, Brisbane? Well, for a man of his intelligence!"

A chorus of exclamations greeted Brisbane's remarkable statement. Everybody called for cigars, and Stubbs, the butler, suddenly appeared from the depths of nowhere with a fresh bottle of dry champagne. The situation was saved; Brisbane was going to tell a story.

I am an old sailor, said Brisbane, and as I have to cross the Atlantic pretty often, I have my favourites. Most men have their favourites. I have seen a man wait in a Broadway bar for three-quarters of an hour for a particular car which he liked. I believe the bar-keeper made at least one-third of his living by that man's preference. I have a habit of waiting for certain ships when I am obliged to cross that duck-pond. It may be a prejudice, but I was never cheated out of a good passage but once in my life. I remember it very well; it was a warm morning in June, and the Custom House officials, who were hanging about waiting for a steamer already on her way up from the Quarantine, presented a peculiarly hazy and thoughtful appearance. I had not much luggage—I never have. I mingled with the crowd of passengers, porters, and officious individuals in blue coats and brass buttons, who seemed to spring up like mushrooms from the deck of a moored steamer to obtrude their unnecessary services upon the independent passenger. I have often noticed with a certain interest the spontaneous evolution of these fellows. They are not there when you arrive; five minutes after the pilot has called 'Go ahead!' they, or at least their blue coats and brass buttons, have disappeared from deck and gangway as completely as though they had been consigned to that locker which tradition ascribes to Davy Jones. But, at the moment of starting, they are there, clean shaved, blue coated, and ravenous for fees. I hastened on board. The *Kamtschatka* was one of my favourite ships. I saw was, because she emphatically no longer is. I cannot conceive of any inducement which could entice me to make

another voyage in her. Yes, I know what you are going to say. She
is uncommonly clean in the run aft, she has enough bluffing off in
the bows to keep her dry, and the lower berths are most of them
double. She has a lot of advantages, but I won't cross in her again.
Excuse the digression. I got on board. I hailed a steward, whose
red nose and redder whiskers were equally familiar to me.

"One hundred and five, lower berth," said I, in the businesslike
tone peculiar to men who think no more of crossing the Atlantic
than taking a whisky cocktail at down-town Delmonico's.

The steward took my portmanteau, greatcoat, and rug. I shall
never forget the expression on his face. Not that he turned pale. It
is maintained by the most eminent divines that even miracles
cannot change the course of nature. I have no hesitation in saying
that he did not turn pale; but, from his expression, I judged that
he was either about to shed tears, to sneeze, or to drop my portmanteau. As the latter contained two bottles of particularly fine
old sherry presented to me for my voyage by my old friend
Snigginson van Pickyns, I felt extremely nervous. But the steward
did none of these things.

"Well, I'm d—d!" said he in a low voice, and led the way.

I supposed my Hermes, as he led me to the lower regions, had
had a little grog, but I said nothing, and followed him. One hundred
and five was on the port side, well aft. There was nothing
remarkable about the state-room. The lower berth, like most of
those upon the *Kamtschatka*, was double. There was plenty of
room; there was the usual washing apparatus, calculated to convey
an idea of luxury to the mind of a North American Indian; there
were the usual inefficient racks of brown wood, in which it is more
easy to hand a large-sized umbrella than the common tooth-brush
of commerce. Upon the uninviting mattresses were carefully bolded
together those blankets which a great modern humorist has aptly
compared to cold buckwheat cakes. The question of towels was left
entirely to the imagination. The glass decanters were filled with a
transparent liquid faintly tinged with brown, but from which an
odour less faint, but not more pleasing, ascended to the nostrils,
like a far-off sea-sick reminiscence of oily machinery. Sad-coloured

curtains half-closed the upper berth. The hazy June daylight shed a faint illumination upon the desolate little scene. Ugh! how I hate that state-room!

The steward deposited my traps and looked at me, as though he wanted to get away—probably in search of more passengers and more fees. It is always a good plan to start in favour with those functionaries, and I accordingly gave him certain coins there and then.

"I'll try and make yer comfortable all I can," he remarked, as he put the coins in his pocket. Nevertheless, there was a doubtful intonation in his voice which surprised me. Possibly his scale of fees had gone up, and he was not satisfied; but on the whole I was inclined to think that, as he himself would have expressed it, he was "the better for a glass." I was wrong, however, and did the man injustice.

II

Nothing especially worthy of mention occurred during that day. We left the pier punctually, and it was very pleasant to be fairly under way, for the weather was warm and sultry, and the motion of the steamer produced a refreshing breeze. Everybody knows what the first day at sea is like. People pace the decks and stare at each other, and occasionally meet acquaintances whom they did not know to be on board. There is the usual uncertainty as to whether the food will be good, bad, or indifferent, until the first two meals have put the matter beyond a doubt; there is the usual uncertainty about the weather, until the ship is fairly off Fire Island. The tables are crowded at first, and then suddenly thinned. Pale-faced people spring from their seats and precipitate themselves towards the door, and each old sailor breathes more freely as his sea-sick neighbour rushes from his side, leaving him plenty of elbow-room and an unlimited command over the mustard.

One passage across the Atlantic is very much like another, and we who cross very often do not make the voyage for the sake of novelty. Whales and icebergs are indeed always objects of interest, but, after all, one whale is very much like another whale, and one rarely sees an iceberg at close quarters. To the majority of us the most delightful moment of the day on board an ocean steamer is when we have taken our last turn on deck, have smoked our last cigar, and having succeeded in tiring ourselves, feel at liberty to turn in with a clear conscience. On that first night of the voyage I felt particularly lazy, and went to bed in one hundred and five rather earlier than I usually do. As I turned in, I was amazed to see that I was to have a companion. A portmanteau, very like my own, lay in the opposite corner, and in the upper berth had been deposited a neatly-folded rug, with a stick and umbrella. I had hoped to be alone, and I was disappointed; but I wondered who my room-mate was to be, and I determined to have a look at him.

Before I had been long in bed he entered. He was, as far as I could see, a very tall man, very thin, very pale, with sandy hair and whiskers and colourless grey eyes. He had about him, I thought, an air of rather dubious fashion; the short of man you might see in Wall Street, without being able precisely to say what he was doing there—the sort of man who frequents the Café Anglais, who always seems to be alone and who drinks champagne; you might meet him on a racecourse, but he would never appear to be doing anything there either. A little over-dressed—a little odd. There are three or four of his kind on every ocean steamer. I made up my mind that I did not care to make his acquaintance, and I went to sleep saying to myself that I would study his habits in order to avoid him. If he rose early, I would rise late; if he went to bed late, I would go to bed early. I did not care to know him. If you once know people of that kind they are always turning up. Poor fellow! I need not have taken the trouble to come to so many decisions about him, for I never saw him again after that first night in one hundred and five.

I was sleeping soundly when I was suddenly waked by a loud noise. To judge from the sound, my room-mate must have sprung with a single leap from the upper berth to the floor. I heard him fumbling with the latch and bolt of the door, which opened almost immediately, and then I heard his footsteps as he ran at full speed down the passage, leaving the door open behind him. The ship was rolling a little, and I expected to hear him stumble or fall, but he ran as though he were running for his life. The door swung on its hinges with the motion of the vessel, and the sound annoyed me. I got up and shut it, and groped my way back to my berth in the darkness. I went to sleep again; but I have no idea how long I slept.

When I awoke it was still quite dark, but I felt a disagreeable sensation of cold, and it seemed to me that the air was damp. You know the peculiar smell of a cabin which has been wet with sea-water. I covered myself up as well as I could and dozed off again, framing complaints to be made the next day, and selecting the most powerful epithets in the language. I could hear my room-mate turn over in the upper berth. He had probably returned while I was asleep. Once I thought I heard him groan, and I argued that he was sea-sick. That is particularly unpleasant when one is below. Nevertheless I dozed off and slept till early daylight.

The ship was rolling heavily, much more than on the previous evening, and the grey light which came in through the porthole changed in tint with every movement according as the angle of the vessel's side turned the glass seawards or skywards. It was very cold—unaccountably so for the month of June. I turned my head and looked at the porthole, and saw to my surprise that it was wide open and hooked back. I believe I swore audibly. Then I got up and shut it. As I turned back I glanced at the upper berth. The curtains were drawn close together; my companion had probably felt cold as well as I. It struck me that I had slept enough. The state-room was uncomfortable, though, strange to say, I could not smell the dampness which had annoyed me in the night. My room-mate was still asleep—excellent opportunity for avoiding him, so I dressed at once and went on deck. The day was warm and cloudy, with an oily smell on the water. It was seven o'clock as I came out—much later than I had imagined. I came across the doctor, who was taking his first sniff of the morning air. He was a young man from the West of Ireland—a tremendous fellow, with black hair and blue eyes, already inclined to be stout; he had a happy-go-lucky, healthy look about him which was rather attractive.

"Fine morning," I remarked, by way of introduction.

"Well," said he, eyeing me with an air of ready interest, "it's a fine morning and it's not a fine morning. I don't think it's much of a morning."

"Well, no—it is not so very fine," said I.

"It's just what I call fuggly weather," replied the doctor.

"It was very cold last night, I thought," I remarked. "However, when I looked about, I found that the porthole was wide open. I had not noticed it when I went to bed. And the state-room was damp, too."

"Damp!" said he. "Whereabouts are you?"

"One hundred and five—"

To my surprise the doctor started visibly, and stared at me.

"What is the matter?" I asked.

"Oh—nothing," he answered; "only everybody has complained of that state-room for the last three trips."

"I shall complain too," I said. "It has certainly not been properly aired. It is a shame!"

"I don't believe it can be helped," answered the doctor. "I believe there is something—well, it is not my business to frighten passengers."

"You need not be afraid of frightening me," I replied. "I can stand any amount of damp. If I should get a bad cold I will come to you."

I offered the doctor a cigar, which he took and examined very critically.

"It is not so much the damp," he remarked. "However, I dare say you will get on very well. Have you a room-mate?"

"Yes; a deuce of a fellow, who bolts out in the middle of the night, and leaves the door open."

Again the doctor glanced curiously at me. Then he lit the cigar and looked grave. "Did he come back?" he asked presently.

"Yes. I was asleep, but I waked up, and heard him moving. Then I felt cold and went to sleep again. This morning I found the porthole open."

"Look here," said the doctor quietly, "I don't care much for this ship. I don't care a rap for her reputation. I tell you what I will do.

I have a good-sized place up here. I will share it with you, though I don't know you from Adam."

I was very much surprised at the proposition. I could not imagine why he should take such a sudden interest in my welfare. However, his manner as he spoke of the ship was peculiar.

"You are very good, doctor," I said. "But, really, I believe even now the cabin could be aired, or cleaned out, or something. Why do you not care for the ship?"

"We are not superstitious in our profession, sir," replied the doctor, "but the sea makes people so. I don't want to prejudice you, and I don't want to frighten you, but if you will take my advice you will move in here. I would as soon see you overboard," he added earnestly, "as know that you or any other man was to sleep in one hundred and five."

"Good gracious! Why?" I asked.

"Just because on the last three trips the people who have slept there actually have gone overboard," he answered gravely.

The intelligence was startling and exceedingly unpleasant, I confess. I looked hard at the doctor to see whether he was making game of me, but he looked perfectly serious. I thanked him warmly for his offer, but told him I intended to be the exception to the rule by which every one who slept in that particular state-room went overboard. He did not say much, but looked as grave as ever, and hinted that, before we got across, I should probably reconsider his proposal. In the course of time we went to breakfast, at which only an inconsiderable number of passengers assembled. I noticed that one or two of the officers who breakfasted with us looked grave. After breakfast I went into my state-room in order to get a book. The curtains of the upper berth were still closely drawn. Not a word was to be heard. My room-mate was probably still asleep.

As I came out I met the steward whose business it was to look after me. He whispered that the captain wanted to see me, and then scuttled away down the passage as if very anxious to avoid any questions. I went toward the captain's cabin, and found him waiting for me.

"Sir," said he, "I want to ask a favour of you."

I answered that I would do anything to oblige him.

"Your room-mate had disappeared," he said. "He is known to have turned in early last night. Did you notice anything extraordinary in his manner?"

The question coming, as it did, in exact confirmation of the fears the doctor had expressed half an hour earlier, staggered me.

"You don't mean to say he has gone overboard?" I asked.

"I fear he has," answered the captain.

"This is the most extraordinary thing—" I began.

"Why?" he asked.

"He is the fourth, then?" I exclaimed. In answer to another question from the captain, I explained, without mentioning the doctor, that I had heard the story concerning one hundred and five. He seemed very much annoyed at hearing that I knew of it. I told him what had occurred in the night.

"What you say," he replied, "coincides almost exactly with what was told me by the room-mates of two of the other three. They bolt out of bed and run down the passage. Two of them were seen to go overboard by the watch; we stopped and lowered boats, but they were not found. Nobody, however, saw or heard the man who was lost last night—if he is really lost. The steward, who is a superstitious fellow, perhaps, and expected something to go wrong, went to look for him, this morning, and found his berth empty, but his clothes lying about, just as he had left them. The steward was the only man on board who knew him by sight, and he has been searching everywhere for him. He has disappeared! Now, sir, I want to beg you not to mention the circumstance to any of the passengers; I don't want the ship to get a bad name, and nothing hangs about an ocean-goer like stories of suicides. You shall have your choice of any one of the officers' cabins you like, including my own, for the rest of the passage. Is that a fair bargain?"

"Very," said I; "and I am much obliged to you. But since I am alone, and have the state-room to myself, I would rather not move. If the steward will take out that unfortunate man's things, I would as leave stay where I am. I will not say anything about the matter, and I think I can promise you that I will not follow my room-mate."

The captain tried to dissuade me from my intention, but I preferred having a state-room alone to being the chum of any officer on board. I do not know whether I aced foolishly, but if I had taken his advice I should have had nothing more to tell. There would have remained the disagreeable coincidence of several suicides occurring among men who had slept in the same cabin, but that would have been all.

That was not the end of the matter, however, by any means. I obstinately made up my mind that I would not be disturbed by such tales, and I even went so far as to argue the question with the captain. There was something wrong about the state-room, I said. It was rather damp. The porthole had been left open last night. My room-mate might have been ill when he came on board, and he might have become delirious after he went to bed. He might even now be hiding somewhere on board, and might be found later. The place ought to be aired and the fastening on the port looked to. If the captain would give me leave, I would see that what I thought necessary were done immediately.

"Of course you have a right to stay where you are if you please," he replied, rather petulantly; "but I wish you would turn out and let me lock the place up, and be done with it."

I did not see it in the same light, and left the captain, after promising to be silent concerning the disappearance of my companion. The latter had had no acquaintances on board, and was not missed in the course of the day. Towards evening I met the doctor again, and he asked me whether I had changed my mind. I told him I had not.

"Then you will before long," he said, very gravely.

III

We played whist in the evening, and I went to bed late. I will confess now that I felt a disagreeable sensation when I entered my state-room. I could not help thinking of the tall man I had seen on the previous night, who was now dead, drowned, tossing about in the long swell, two or three hundred miles astern. His face rose very distinctly before me as I undressed, and I even went so far as to draw back the curtains of the upper berth, as though to persuade myself that he was actually gone. I also bolted the door of the stateroom. Suddenly I became aware that the porthole was open, and fastened back. This was more than I could stand. I hastily threw on my dressing-gown and went in search of Robert, the steward of my passage. I was very angry, I remember, and when I found him I dragged him roughly to the door of one hundred and five, and pushed him towards the open porthole.

"What the deuce do you mean, you scoundrel, by leaving that port open every night? Don't you know it is against the regulations? Don't you know that if the ship heeled and the water began to come in, ten men could not shut it? I will report you to the captain, you blackguard, for endangering the ship!"

I was exceedingly wroth. The man trembled and turned pale, and then began to shut the round glass plate with the heavy brass fittings.

"Why don't you answer me?" I said roughly.

"If you please, sir," faltered Robert, "there's nobody on board as can keep this 'ere port shut at night. You can try it yourself, sir. I ain't a-going to stop hany longer on board o' this vessel, sir; I ain't, indeed. But if I was you, sir, I'd just clear out and go and sleep with the surgeon, or something, I would. Look 'ere, sir, is that fastened what you may call securely, or not, sir? Try it, sir, see if it will move a hinch."

I tried the port, and found it perfectly tight.

"Well, sir," continued Robert triumphantly, "I wager my reputation as a A1 steward that in 'arf an hour it will be open again; fastened back, too, sir, that's the horful thing—fastened back!"

I examined the great screw and the looped nut that ran on it.

"If I find it open in the night, Robert, I will give you a sovereign. It is not possible. You may go."

"Soverin' did you say, sir? Very good, sir. Thank ye, sir. Goodnight, sir. Pleasant reepose, sir, and all manner of hinchantin' dreams, sir."

Robert scuttled away, delighted at being released. Of course, I thought he was trying to account for his negligence by a silly story, intended to frighten me, and I disbelieved him. The consequence was that he got his sovereign, and I spent a very peculiarly unpleasant night.

I went to bed, and five minutes after I had rolled myself up in my blankets the inexorable Robert extinguished the light that burned steadily behind the ground-glass pane near the door. I lay quite still in the dark trying to go to sleep, but I soon found that impossible. It had been some satisfaction to be angry with the steward, and the diversion had banished that unpleasant sensation I had at first experienced when I thought of the drowned man who had been my chum; but I was no longer sleepy, and I lay awake for some time, occasionally glancing at the porthole, which I could just see from where I lay, and which, in the darkness, looked like a faintly-luminous soup-plate suspended in blackness. I believe I must have lain there for an hour, and, as I remember, I was just dozing into sleep when I was roused by a draught of cold air, and by distinctly feeling the spray of the sea blown upon my face. I started to my feet, and not having allowed in the dark for the motion of the ship, I was instantly thrown violently across the state-room upon the couch which was placed beneath the port-hole. I recovered myself immediately, however, and climbed upon my knees. The port-hole was again wide open and fastened back!

Now these things are facts. I was wide awake when I got up, and I should certainly have been waked by the fall had I still been dozing. Moreover, I bruised my elbows and knees badly, and the bruises were there on the following morning to testify to the fact, if I myself had doubted it. The porthole was wide open and fastened back—a thing so unaccountable that I remember very well feeling astonishment rather that fear when I discovered it. I at once closed the plate again, and screwed down the loop nut with all my strength. It was very dark in the state-room. I reflected that the port had certainly been opened within an hour after Robert had at first shut it in my presence, and I determined to watch it, and see whether it would open again. Those brass fittings are very heavy and by no means easy to move; I could not believe that the clamp had been turned by the shaking of the screw. I stood peering out through the thick glass at the alternate white and grey streaks of the sea that foamed beneath the ship's side. I must have remained there a quarter of an hour.

Suddenly, as I stood, I distinctly heard something moving behind me in one of the berths, and a moment afterwards, just as I turned instinctively to look—though I could, of course, see nothing in the darkness—I heard a very faint groan. I sprang across the state-room, and tore the curtains of the upper berth aside, thrusting in my hands to discover if there were any one there. There was some one.

I remember that the sensation as I put my hands forward was as though I were plunging them into the air of a damp cellar, and from behind the curtains came a gust of wind that smelled horribly of stagnant sea-water. I laid hold of something that had the shape of a man's arm, but was smooth, and wet, and icy cold. But suddenly, as I pulled, the creature sprang violently forward against me, a clammy oozy mass, as it seemed to me, heavy and wet, yet endowed with a sort of supernatural strength. I reeled across the state-room, and in an instant the door opened and the thing rushed out. I had not had time to be frightened, and quickly recovering myself, I sprang through the door and gave chase at the top of my speed, but I was too late. Ten yards before me I could see—I am sure I saw it—a dark shadow moving in the dimly lighted passage, quickly as the shadow of a fast horse thrown before a dog-cart by the lamp on a dark night. But in a moment it had disappeared, and I found myself holding on to the polished rail that ran along the bulkhead where the passage turned towards the companion. My hair stood on end, and the cold perspiration rolled down my face. I am not ashamed of it in the least: I was very badly frightened.

Still I doubted my senses, and pulled myself together. It was absurd, I thought. The Welsh rare-bit I had eaten had disagreed with me. I had been in a nightmare. I made my way back to my state-room, and entered it with an effort. The whole place smelled of stagnant sea-water, as it had when I had waked on the previous evening. It required my utmost strength to go in, and grope among my things for a box of wax lights. As I lighted a railway reading lantern which I always carry in case I want to read after the lamps are out, I perceived that the porthole was again open, and a sort of creeping horror began to take possession of me which I never felt before, nor wish to feel again. But I got a light and proceeded to examine the upper berth, expecting to find it drenched with sea-water.

But I was disappointed. The bed had been slept in, and the smell of the sea was strong; but the bedding was as dry as a bone. I fancied that Robert had not had the courage to make the bed after the accident of the previous night—it had all been a hideous dream. I drew the curtains back as far as I could and examined the place very carefully. It was perfectly dry. But the porthole was open again. With a sort of dull bewilderment of horror I closed it and screwed it down, and thrusting my heavy stick through the brass loop, wrenched it with all my might, till the thick metal began to bend under the pressure. Then I hooked my reading lantern into the red velvet at the head of the couch, and sat down to recover my senses if I could. I sat there all night, unable to think of rest—hardly able to think at all. But the porthole remained closed, and I did not believe it would now open again without the application of a considerable force.

The morning dawned at last, and I dressed myself slowly, thinking over all that had happened in the night. It was a beautiful day and I went on deck, glad to get out into the early, pure sunshine, and to smell the breeze from the blue water, so different from the noisome, stagnant odour of my state-room. Instinctively I turned aft, towards the surgeon's cabin. There he stood, with a pipe in his mouth, taking his morning airing precisely as on the preceding day.

"Good-morning," said he quietly, but looking at me with evident curiosity.

"Doctor, you were quite right," said I. "There is something wrong about that place."

"I thought you would change your mind," he answered, rather triumphantly. "You have had a bad night, eh? Shall I make you a pick-me-up? I have a capital recipe."

"No, thanks," I cried. "But I would like to tell you what happened."

I then tried to explain as clearly as possible precisely what had occurred, not omitting to state that I had been scared as I had never been scared in my whole life before. I dwelt particularly on the phenomenon of the porthole, which was a fact to which I could testify, even if the rest had been an illusion. I had closed it twice in the night, and the second time I had actually bent the brass in wrenching it with my stick. I believe I insisted a good deal on this point.

"You seem to think I am likely to doubt the story," said the doctor, smiling at my detailed account of the state of the porthole. "I do not doubt in the least. I renew my invitation to you. Bring your traps here, and take half my cabin."

"Come and take half of mine for one night," I said. "Help me to get at the bottom of this thing."

"You will get to the bottom of something else if you try," answered the doctor.

"What?" I asked.

"The bottom of the sea. I am going to leave this ship. It is not canny."

"Then you will not help me to find out—"

"Not I," said the doctor quickly. "It is my business to keep my wits about me—not to go fiddling about with ghosts and things."

"Do you really believe it is a ghost?" I enquired, rather contemptuously. But as I spoke I remembered very well the horrible sensation of the supernatural which had got possession of me during the night. The doctor turned sharply on me—

"Have you any reasonable explanation of these things to offer?" he asked. "No; you have not. Well, you say you will find an explanation. I say that you won't, sir, simply because there is not any."

"But, my dear sir," I retorted, "do you, a man of science, mean to tell me that such things cannot be explained?"

"I do," he answered stoutly. "And, if they could, I would not be concerned in the explanation."

I did not care to spend another night alone in the state-room, and yet I was obstinately determined to get at the root of the disturbances. I do not believe there are many men who would have slept there alone, after passing two such nights. But I made up my mind to try it, if I could not get any one to share a watch with me. The doctor was evidently not inclined for such an experiment. He said he was a surgeon, and that in case any accident occurred on board he must be always in readiness. He could not afford to have his nerves unsettled. Perhaps he was quite right, but I am inclined to think that his precaution was prompted by his inclination. On enquiry, he informed me that there was no one on board who would be likely to join me in my investigations, and after a little more conversation I left him. A little later I met the captain, and told him my story. I said that, if no one would spend the night with me, I would ask leave to have the light burning all night, and would try it alone.

"Look here," said he, "I will tell you what I will do. I will share your watch myself, and we will see what happens. It is my belief that we can find out between us. There may be some fellow skulking on board, who steals a passage by frightening the passengers. It is just possible that there may be something queer in the carpentering of that berth."

I suggested taking the ship's carpenter below and examining the place; but I was overjoyed at the captain's offer to spend the night with me. He accordingly sent for the workman and ordered him to do anything I required. We went below at once. I had all the bedding cleared out of the upper berth, and we examined the place thoroughly to see if there was a board loose anywhere, or a panel which could be opened or pushed aside. We tried the planks everywhere, tapped the flooring, unscrewed the fittings of the lower berth and took it to pieces—in short, there was not a square inch of the state-room which was not searched and tested. Everything was in perfect order, and we put everything back in its place. As we were finishing our work, Robert came to the door and looked in.

"Well, sir—find anything, sir?" he asked, with a ghastly grin.

"You were right about the porthole, Robert," I said, and I gave him the promised sovereign. The carpenter did his work silently and skilfully, following my directions. When he had done he spoke.

"I'm a plain man, sir," he said. "But it's my belief you had better just turn out your things, and let me run half a dozen four-inch screws through the door of this cabin. There's no good never came o' this cabin yet, sir, and that's all about it. There's been four lives lost out o' here to my own remembrance, and that is four trips. Better give it up, sir—better give it up!"

"I will try it for one night more," I said.

"Better give it up, sir—better give it up! It's a precious bad job," repeated the workman, putting his tools in his bag and leaving the cabin.

But my spirits had risen considerably at the prospect of having the captain's company, and I made up my mind not to be prevented from going to the end of this strange business. I abstained from Welsh rare-bits and grog that evening, and did not even join in the customary game of whist. I wanted to be quite sure of my nerves, and my vanity made me anxious to make a good figure in the captain's eyes.

IV

The captain was one of those splendidly tough and cheerful specimens of seafaring humanity whose combined courage, hardihood, and calmness in difficulty leads them naturally into high positions of trust. He was not the man to be led away by an idle tale, and the mere fact that he was willing to join me in the investigation was proof that he thought there was something seriously wrong, which could not be accounted for on ordinary theories, nor laughed down as a common superstition. To some extent, too, his reputation was at stake, as well as the reputation of the ship. It is no light thing to lose passengers overboard, and he knew it.

About ten o'clock that evening, as I was smoking a last cigar, he came up to me, and drew me aside from the beat of the other passengers who were patrolling the deck in the warm darkness.

"This is a serious matter, Mr. Brisbane," he said. "We must make up our minds either way—to be disappointed or to have a pretty rough time of it. You see I cannot afford to laugh at the affair, and I will ask you to sign your name to a statement of whatever occurs. If nothing happens tonight we will try it again tomorrow and next day. Are you ready?"

So we went below, and entered the state-room. As we went in I could see Robert the steward, who stood a little further down the passage, watching us, with his usual grin, as though certain that something dreadful was about to happen. The captain closed the door behind us and bolted it.

"Supposing we put your portmanteau before the door," he suggested. "One of us can sit on it. Nothing can get out then. Is the port screwed down?"

I found it as I had left it in the morning. Indeed, without using a lever, as I had done, no one could have opened it. I drew back the curtains of the upper berth so that I could see well into it. By the captain's advice I lighted my reading lantern, and placed it so that it shone upon the white sheets above. He insisted upon sitting on the portmanteau, declaring that he wished to be able to swear that he had sat before the door.

Then he requested me to search the state-room thoroughly, an operation very soon accomplished, as it consisted merely in looking beneath the lower berth and under the couch below the porthole. The spaces were quite empty.

"It is impossible for any human being to get in," I said, "or for any human being to open the port."

"Very good," said the captain calmly. "If we see anything now, it must be either imagination or something supernatural."

I sat down on the edge of the lower berth.

"The first time it happened," said the captain, crossing his legs and leaning back against the door, "was in March. The passenger who slept here, in the upper berth, turned out have been a lunatic— at all events, he was known to have been a little touched, and he had taken his passage without the knowledge of his friends. He rushed out in the middle of the night, and threw himself overboard, before the officer who had the watch could stop him. We stopped and lowered a boat; it was a quiet night, just before that heavy weather came on; but we could not find him. Of course his suicide was afterwards accounted for on the ground of his insanity."

"I suppose that often happens?" I remarked, rather absently.

"Not often—no," said the captain; "never before in my experience, though I have heard of it happening on board of other ships. Well, as I was saying, that occurred in March. On the very next trip— What are you looking at?" he asked, stopping suddenly in his narration.

I believe I gave no answer. My eyes were riveted upon the porthole. It seemed to me that the brass loop-nut was beginning to turn very slowly upon the screw—so slowly, however, that I was not sure it moved at all. I watched it intently, fixing its position in my mind, and trying to ascertain whether it changed. Seeing where I was looking, the captain looked too.

"It moves!" he exclaimed, in a tone of conviction. "No, it does not," he added, after a minute.

"If it were the jarring of the screw," said I, "it would have opened during the day; but I found it this evening jammed tight as I left it this morning."

I rose and tried the nut. It was certainly loosened, for by an effort I could move it with my hands.

"The queer thing," said the captain, "is that the second man who was lost is supposed to have got through that very port. We had a terrible time over it. It was in the middle of the night, and the weather was very heavy; there was an alarm that one of the ports was open and the sea running in. I came below and found everything flooded, the water pouring in every time she rolled, and the whole port swinging from the top bolts—not the porthole in the middle. Well, we managed to shut it, but the water did some damage. Ever since that the place smells of sea-water from time to time. We supposed the passenger had thrown himself out, though the Lord only knows how he did it. The steward kept telling me that he cannot keep anything shut here. Upon my word—I can smell it now, cannot you?" he enquired, sniffing the air suspiciously.

"Yes—distinctly," I said, and I shuddered as that same odour of stagnant sea-water grew stronger in the cabin. "Now, to smell like this, the place must be damp," I continued, "and yet when I examined it with the carpenter this morning everything was perfectly dry. It is most extraordinary—hallo!"

My reading lantern, which had been placed in the upper berth, was suddenly extinguished. There was still a good deal of light from the pane of ground glass near the door, behind which loomed the regulation lamp. The ship rolled heavily, and the curtain of the upper berth swung far out into the state-room and back again. I rose quickly from my seat on the edge of the bed, and the captain at the same moment started to his feet with a loud cry of surprise. I had turned with the intention of taking down the lantern to examine it, when I heard his exclamation, and immediately afterwards his call for help. I sprang towards him. He was wrestling with all his might with the brass loop of the port. It seemed to turn against his hands in spite of all his efforts. I caught up my cane, a heavy oak stick I always used to carry, and thrust it through the ring and bore on it with all my strength. But the strong wood snapped suddenly and I fell upon the couch. When I rose again the port was wide open, and the captain was standing with his back against the door, pale to the lips.

"There is something in that berth!" he cried, in a strange voice, his eyes almost starting from his head. "Hold the door, while I look—it shall not escape us, whatever it is!"

But instead of taking his place, I sprang upon the lower bed, and seized something which lay in the upper berth.

It was something ghostly, horrible beyond words, and it moved in my grip. It was like the body of a man long drowned, and yet it moved, and had the strength of ten men living; but I gripped it with all my might—the slippery, oozy, horrible thing—the dead white eyes seemed to stare at me out of the dusk; the putrid odour of rank sea-water was about it, and its shiny hair hung in foul wet curls over its dead face. I wrestled with the dead thing; it thrust itself upon me and forced me back and nearly broke my arms; it wound its corpse's arms about my neck, the living death, and overpowered me, so that I, at last, cried aloud and fell, and left my hold.

As I fell the thing sprang across me, and seemed to throw itself upon the captain. When I last saw him on his feet his face was white and his lips set. It seemed to me that he struck a violent blow at the dead being, and then he, too, fell forward upon his face, with an inarticulate cry of horror.

The thing paused an instant, seeming to hover over his prostrate body, and I could have screamed again for very fright, but I had no voice left. The thing vanished suddenly, and it seemed to my disturbed senses that it made its exit through the open port, though how that was possible, considering the smallness of the aperture, is more than any one can tell. I lay a long time on the floor, and the captain lay beside me. At last I partially recovered my senses and moved, and instantly I knew that my arm was broken—the small bone of my left forearm near the wrist.

I got upon my feet somehow, and with my remaining hand I tried to raise the captain. He groaned and moved, and at last came to himself. He was not hurt, but he seemed badly stunned.

Well, do you want to hear any more? There is nothing more. That is the end of my story. The carpenter carried out his scheme of running half a dozen four-inch screws through the door of one hundred and five; and if ever you take a passage in the *Kamtschatka*, you may ask for a berth in that state-room. You will be told that it is engaged—yes—it is engaged by that dead thing.

I finished the trip in the surgeon's cabin. He doctored my broken arm, and advised me not to "fiddle about with ghosts and things" any more. The captain was very silent, and never sailed again in that ship, though it is still running. And I will not sail in her either. It was a very disagreeable experience, and I was very badly frightened, which is a thing I do not like. That is all. That is how I saw a ghost—if it was a ghost. It was dead, anyhow.

The Gorgon's Head

Gertrude Bacon

"They that go down to the sea in ships" see strange things, but what they tell is oft-times stranger still. A faculty for romancing is imparted by a seafaring life as readily and surely as a rolling gait and a weather-beaten countenance. A fine imagination is one of the gifts of the ocean—witness the surprising and unlimited power of expression and epithet possessed by the sailor. And a fine imagination will frequently manifest itself in other ways besides swear words.

Captain Brander is one of the most gifted men in this way in the whole merchant service. His officers say of him with pride that he possesses the largest vocabulary in the great steamship company of which he is one of the oldest and most respected skippers, and his yarns are only equalled in their utter impossibility by the genius he displays in furnishing them with minute detail and all the outward circumstance of truth.

I first learned this fact from the second engineer the evening of the sixth day of our voyage, as we leant across the bulwarks and watched the sunset. The second engineer was a bit of a liar—or I should say romancer —himself. The day he took me down into the engine-room he told me, as personal experiences, tales of mutinous Lascar firemen, unpopular officers who disappeared suddenly into the fiery maw of blazing furnaces, and so forth, which, whatever foundation of fact they may have possessed, certainly did not lose in the telling. As a humble aspirant in the same branch of art he naturally was quick to recognise the genius of that past master, the captain, and his admiration for his chief was as boundless as it was sincere.

"I say, Miss Baker," he said, *apropos* of nothing, "have you had the skipper 'on' yet?"

"Not that I am aware of," I said. "What do you mean?"

"Why, has he been spinning you any yarns yet? There isn't a man in the service can touch him for stories. I don't deny that he has seen some service, and been in some tight places, but for a real out-and-out lie, commend me to old Monkey Brand!" (It was by this sobriquet, I regret to say, suggested partly by his name, and mostly by his undoubted resemblance to a well-known advertisement, that the worthy captain was known in the unregenerate engine-room.)

"Oh, I should just love to hear him," I cried. "There is nothing I should like better. Do tell me how I can manage to draw him."

"Well, he doesn't want much drawing as a rule," said the engineer. "He likes to give vent to his imagination. Let me see," he continued; "to-morrow afternoon we shall be about passing the Grecian Islands. Ask him about them, and try and get him on the subject of Gorgons."

"Gorgons!" I said. "What a strange topic! Why, since I've left school I have almost forgotten what they were. Weren't they mythological creatures who turned people into stone when they looked at them?"

"That's about it, I believe," said the engineer, "and a fellow called Perseus cut off their heads, or something of that kind. It's a lie anyhow, but you ask the skipper."

It was the custom of Captain Brander every afternoon to make a kind of royal progress among his passengers. Going the entire circuit of the ship; passing slowly from group to group, with a joke here and a chat there, and bestowing his favours in lordly and impartial fashion—especially among the ladies. I have watched him often coming the whole length of the promenade deck, making some outrageous compliment to one girl, patting another on the shoulder, even chucking a third under the chin; a sense of supreme self-satisfaction animating his red cheeks, curling his grey hair, and suffusing his whole short, portly person. Eccentric he was; indifferent to his personal appearance—his battered old cap had seen almost as much service as he had—but a more popular man or an abler officer never walked the bridge. On this particular occasion I was at the end of the deck, and had so arranged that an inviting deck chair stood vacant beside me. Wearied by his progress by the time he reached me, he fell at once into my little trap, and sat down on the empty chair, leant back, and spread his legs. He and I were fast friends, and had been since the day when I tried to photograph him, and he had frustrated my design by unscrewing the front lens of my camera and keeping it in his pocket for the rest of the morning.

"Captain," I said, pointing to a cloudy grey outline faintly visible against the eastern horizon, "what land is that?"

"My dear young lady," said he, "I am quite sick of answering that question! If I have been asked it once I have been asked it twenty times in the last half-hour. That old Mrs. Matherson in the red shawl buttonholed me on the subject to such an extent that I thought I should never getaway again. Wonderful thirst for information that old party has! And she appears to think that because I'm captain I must have a complete knowledge of geography, geology, history, etymology, mythology, *and* navigation. Well, for the twenty-first time, then, we are passing the isles off the coast of Greece, and that one straight ahead is Zante."

"So that is Greece, is it?" I mused aloud. "Well, from here at least it looks old enough and romantic enough to-be the home of all those ancient heroes we read about—Alexander and Hercules and—and—Gorgons and those sort of things." I felt I had introduced the subject somewhat lamely, after all, and the captain looked me full in the face as if suspecting a plot. But if I am not very adroit in conversation, I can at least look innocent upon occasions, and he merely said. "And what do you know about Gorgons, pray?"

"Oh, as much as most people, I expect!" I answered. "They are only a sort of fairy tale, you know."

"I am not so sure of that," said Captain Brander. "Those fairy tales, as you call them, have often truth at the bottom of them.

And as to Gorgons, why, I could tell you a little incident that happened to me once—but it's rather a long story."

Then I urged my best persuasions—not that he needed much pressing—and pushing his old cap off his bald forehead, and speaking slowly and with that almost American accent peculiar to him, he unfolded his tale of wonder as follows:—

"It's nearly thirty years ago, Miss Baker—that's long before *you* were ever born or thought of—that I was fourth officer of the *Haslar,* 2,000-ton vessel of this same company I serve to this day. How times have altered, to be sure! The *Haslar* was reckoned a fine ship in those days, and if you had told me that I should presently command an 8,000-tonner, such as I do this day, with 11,000 horse-power engines, and more men for the crew alone than the *Haslar* could hold when she was packed her tightest, I very probably wouldn't have believed you. However, that is neither here nor there. But thirty years ago in the spring time—now I come to think of it, it was in the month of April—we were cruising in this very neighbourhood, and one thick foggy night our skipper lost his bearings a bit, got too near the coast, and ran us ashore off the south point of Zante.

"Of course there was a great fuss, and everybody came up on deck with life-belts, and all the girls screamed, and all the young fellows swore to save them or die in the attempt ; and the skipper turned as white as paper—not that he was afraid, for he was no coward—none of our officers are that—but because he knew his prospects were ruined, and he would be turned out of the company and perhaps lose his certificate, and he'd got a wife and a big family, poor chap! Of course that consideration didn't affect *me,* for I was in my bunk and asleep at the time, but it was certainly unfortunate for him.

"Well, it was very soon discovered that the ship wasn't going down in a hurry, and nobody got into the boats, though they were lowered ready. And when daylight came we saw we were fast on the rocks, with half the stern under water, and the saloon and a lot of the cabins flooded. But more than that the *Haslar* couldn't sink, and at low water you might almost walk dry-shod on to the shore.

There was no getting her off, however, and so all the passengers were landed and sent home as best they could across country, and a rough time they had of it, for Zante is not an over-hospitable sort of a place; while we officers had to stick to the ship till we could get help, and then till she was repaired sufficiently to work her into dock somewhere.

"It was a tedious job, for help was slow in coming; and then all her boilers had to be taken out before she would float, and we fellows got jolly sick of it, I ran tell you, for we were hard worked, and Zante is a wretched hole to spend more than half an hour in. Our one amusement, when we were off duty, was to go ashore on foot or row round the island in a boat, shooting wild fowl and exploring the country. There was precious little to see and not much to shoot, and it was slow fun altogether till, one day, the second officer came back from a tramp ashore and told us he had found his way to some very remote village on the eastern coast, where there was a cave among the hills which the villagers warned him not to enter. He could not gather for what reason, because he didn't understand enough of their outlandish tongue, but as it was then growing late he was obliged to return to the ship without further investigation.

"I was always one for adventure when I was a lad, and directly the second officer told his tale I made up my mind to go and explore that cave before any of the rest had a chance. It so happened that next day was my turn for going ashore, and I went and looked up one of the assistant engineers and persuaded him to come with me. I wanted him because he was a chum of mine, and also he was the only one of us who could talk the language a bit. He had been in those parts before, and generally acted as interpreter in our dealings with the natives. His name was Travers, a queer little dark chap, with black eyes and a hot temper, but a pleasant fellow enough if you did not rub him up the wrong way, and game for anything under the sun. He readily agreed to come with me, and we started as soon as we could get away, telling no one of our destination, for we had no wish to be forestalled.

"It was a long tramp, right across the island, to the village which Jenkins, the second officer, had indicated. But at last, after climbing a weary hill, we looked down on some clustering huts standing amid vineyards in the valley beneath, while another and much sheerer cliff rose on the opposite side, whose rugged scarp was all rent and riven as by an earthquake, and intersected by a deep ravine. Here and there among the rocks were dark shadows and black patches which might be the entrances to caverns in the crag. 'This must be the place,' I said, 'and one of those is the forbidden cave. How are we to find out which?'

"As if in answer to my question, at this moment there came along the hill-top towards us a burly countryman with a sunburned face and tattered garments. He regarded us with astonishment, as well he might, for they get few strangers in those parts, and he made some remark to us in his queer language, which, of course. I didn't understand, but Travers did and replied to it. Finding he was understood, the countryman stopped and talked.

"'Ah!' he said, or so Travers interpreted. 'So you have reached the valley of the Haunted Cavern! It is far to seek and hard to find, but it lies spread beneath you.'

"'But which is the Haunted Cavern, and why is it so called?' asked Travers.

"'It lies in yonder cleft of the hills,' answered the man, pointing to the opposite ravine, 'and it is called the Haunted Cavern because none who venture there return alive. Nay, they return not either alive or dead. They are seen no more!'

"'Tell that to the Marines!' said Travers, only he translated it into Greek, of course, or what the Zante people think is Greek. 'You don't expect me to believe such a yarn as that! Why, what is there up in that place?'

"'That is what none can tell,' replied the peasant; 'for none come back to say. And, indeed, it is the truth I speak. Many men have attempted to find the secret. In bygone days, I have heard, a whole party of soldiers were sent there to search for brigands supposed to be in hiding, but not one was seen again. The cavern has an evil name, and now is shunned by one and all, but every now and again there arises a youth venturesome beyond the rest; and he heeds not the warnings of the old, but hopes to break the spell and find the treasure that some say is hidden there, and he starts in high hope and courage, but never again do we behold his face!'

"'But what is the reason?' persisted Travers, the incredulous.

"'Nay, that we cannot say,' reiterated the man. 'A short distance can one go up the ravine that leads to the cavern. I have been there myself, and truly there is nothing that can be seen except a barren valley, scattered all over with big black stones. Nothing more, and farther than the entrance none must venture.'

"'Oh, I say!' exclaimed Travers, in delight, 'did you ever hear such an old liar? This beats anything I could have believed possible in the nineteenth century. Come on, Brander! We are in luck this time!' and the impetuous fellow dashed off down the hill, I at his heels, leaving the countryman dumb with amazement behind us.

"At the foot of the hill we entered the little village. An old, white-haired man of rather superior appearance was crossing the road before us. Travers accosted him and asked him the way to the Haunted Cavern. The old man turned quite pale with astonishment and apprehension.

"'The Haunted Cavern, my son!' he said, in quavering tones; 'surely you are not going thither?'

"'Yes, we are, though,' said Travers, his eyes dancing with excitement. It is wonderful what enterprise that boy—he was little more—had in him. 'And if you won't tell us, we'll find the way out for ourselves!' and he pushed past the old man, who held out his skinny hands as if to detain him.

"Before we had sot clear of the hamlet the news had somehow got circulated that we were about to explore the ravine, and the whole of the inhabitants turned out in the wildest excitement. Some were for staying us forcibly, till Travers began to get quite nasty, drew his revolver, and talked of firing. Many reiterated and emphasized alarming warnings and assurances that we should never return. All watched us with the most intense interest, and followed close on our footsteps until we began to near the fatal spot, when they fell off singly or in parties, till finally at the very entrance of the ravine we had left even the boldest spirits behind us.

"In truth, it was a strange spot to which we had penetrated. The narrow path had led us suddenly round the spur of the mountain, and now, look which way we might, the giant rocks towered up sheer above us, hundreds of feet high, in inaccessible grey walls. The sinking sun was now too low to shine within this well-like space, which his rays could only reach at midday, and the very air struck damp and chill. We were in an open valley, thus shut in by the cliffs, of considerable extent, but not to be reached by any path except that we had traversed. The ground was firm and smooth, but littered all over with the strangest black stones of all sorts of shapes, and in all positions, though of a fairly uniform size, and alike in material. There was something uncanny and weird about these queer black boulders, which strewed the valley the thicker the farther we advanced, till at the far end of the space, where a huge back hole yawned ominous in the cliff, they almost entirely blocked the way.

"The dark cavern looked terribly grim and forbidding in the fading light. A little stream issued from its mouth and trickled among the stones. It did not gurgle and glisten as most mountain streams, but flowed noiselessly, sluggish, and dull, and gathered in stagnant pools on its rocky bed. No birds sang in that dismal nook; no sound from without penetrated to its recesses. All was silent, dim, and chill as the tomb itself.

"Despite my utmost efforts, I felt the spell of the weird, wild spot stealing over me, and a cold shudder crept down my backbone. There was but room for one at a time in the ever-narrowing track, and I was at first leading. My steps became slower and slower, and finally I paused altogether and turned to look back on Travers to see if he too was feeling the oppressive sense of evil that seemed to hang heavy in the very air. But in his face was only visible an ecstasy almost of eagerness and delight. His dark eyes sparkled again, his cheeks were flushed, his breath came quick, and his whole body was quivering with excitement.

"'Go on, Brander!' he cried. 'What are you stopping for, man? This is grand! This is luck, indeed! Did you ever see such a place? Come on, I want to get to that cave!'

"I felt utterly ashamed to confess my weakness, but it was that cave that I had begun to dread more and more. Whatever else I may be, Miss Baker, it is not boasting to say I am no coward. I have seen danger, aye, and courted it all my life, and until that moment I doubt if I had known what fear was. But I knew then: the blind, unreasoning fear that saps the strength of mind and limb and melts the heart and paralyzes all thought save that one overpowering instinct to fly— somewhere. Yet, in face of Travers's eagerness, I could not bear to show the white feather. I turned my back therefore on the dark cavern, now just ahead of us, and endeavoured to temporize.

"'Travers,' I said, 'did you ever see such queer stones? How do you suppose they have got here? They are quite a different nature from these cliffs, so they could not have fallen from the sides.'

"'Oh, bother the stones!' said Travers. 'I can't look at them now, I want to get into the cave. Quick, before it gets dark!' and as I still hesitated, he pushed past me into a more open space beyond, almost at the cavern's mouth. I did not dare to leave him, and was scrambling after him as best I might, when I suddenly heard him cry out in a voice such as I had never heard before, and hope never to again. A shrill, high pitched cry in which there were surprise, wonder, disgust, alarm, and awful horror all combined in one: a cry of astonishment, a shriek of agony, a shout of dismay. 'Look, Brander! look! look!'

"I could have sworn that when he spoke my companion was in full view, close beside me, touching me almost, though at the exact moment my eyes were looking from him; but when I turned my head in answer to his cry he was gone.

"For one second only had my gaze been averted, but in that time he had utterly vanished from sight, disappeared in a flash, gone—whither? A large black stone stood close beside roe, similar to the rest in that ghostly valley; yet it struck me somehow that I had not noticed it there before. I placed my hand upon it as I peered round behind to see if Travers were there, and a shudder I could not explain ran up my arm, for the stone felt warm to the touch. I had not time then to analyze my unreasonable horror at this trivial circumstance; I was too eager to find my friend. I rushed madly among the stones, I yelled his name again and again, but the weird echoes of my cry, returned in countless reflections from cliff and cavern, alone answered me.

"In a frenzy of despair I continued my search, for certain was I that by no natural means could Travers have disappeared so utterly in so brief a space. Blind panic seized me, and I knew not what I did, till my eye suddenly fell on a shallow pool of water collected in a rocky hollow at my very feet. It was not more than a couple of inches deep, and scarce a yard across, but on its placid face were reflected the overhanging rock and opening of the cavern just behind it, and also something else that glued my eyes to it in horror and rooted my flying feet to the ground.

"Just above the cavern's mouth was a narrow ledge of rock, running horizontally, and of a few inches in width. On this natural shelf, reflected in the water, I saw, hanging downwards, a decayed fragment of goat-skin, rotten with age, but which might have been bound round something, long years before. Upon this, as if escaped from its folds, rested a Head.

"It was a human head, severed at the neck, but fresh and unfaded as if but newly dead. It bore the features of a woman—of a woman of more perfect loveliness than was ever told of in tile, or sculptured in marble, or painted on canvas. Every feature, every line, was of the truest beauty, cast in the noblest mould—the face of a goddess. But upon that perfect countenance was the mark of eternal pain, of deathless agony and suffering past words. The forehead was lined and knit, the death-white lips were tightly pressed in speechless torment; in the wide eyes seemed yet to lurk the flame of an unquenchable fire; while around the fair brows, in place of hair, curled and coiled the stark bodies of venomous serpents, stiff in death, but their loathsome forms still erect, their evil heads yet thrust forward as if to strike.

"My heart ceased beating, and the chill of death crept over my limbs, as with eyes starting from their sockets I stared at that awful head, reflected in the pool. For hours it seemed to me I gazed fascinated, as the bird by the eye of the snake that has charmed it. I was as incapable of thought as movement, till suddenly forgotten school-room learning began to cross my brain, and I knew that I looked at the reflection of Medusa, the Gorgon, fairest and foulest of living things, the unclean creature, half woman, half eagle, slain by the hero Perseus, and one glimpse of whose tortured face turned the luckless beholder into stone with the horror of it.

"If I once raised my eyes from the reflection to the actual head above I knew that I too should freeze in a moment into another black block, even as poor Travers, and every other who had entered the accursed valley had done before. And as this thought occurred to me, the longing to lift my eyes and look upon the real object became so overpowering that, in sheer self-preservation, I inclined my face closer and closer to the water till I seemed almost to touch it, when my senses fled and I knew no more.

"When I woke at last it was far on in the night, and a bright moon, riding high, shone full down upon the valley, revealing the ragged rocks and scattered stones with a cold brilliance that almost equalled the day. I was lying chilled and stiff beside the pool, and I started up in amazement, unable to recall to my mind, for a moment, where I was or what I was doing there. I had my back to the cavern, fortunately, and as I gazed over the ghostly and deserted scene the events of the day suddenly returned to my mind in a single flash of terror.

"To escape from this ghastly place was now my only thought, and in order to do this I resolved to look no more at the pool at my feet in case the terrible fascination should again take possession of me. What it cost me to adhere to this resolution I cannot tell you, but with the courage of despair I pressed blindly forward to the mouth of the ravine, only pausing a second to lay my hand upon the now ice-cold stone that once was Travers.

"Poor Travers! gay, light-hearted fellow! Ever in the forefront of mischief, of danger, of adventure. How eager he had been to solve the secret of the haunted valley, which now must be his tomb forever. How full of health and spirits he had scrambled a few hours before among those very boulders, one of which now, standing stiffly erect among its forest of brethren, was at once the monument and sole relic of a fearless lad, a cheery friend, and a gallant seaman. Dear old Travers! Brave, foolish boy! My heart was heavy, indeed, for his awful fate, as I reverently touched the stone and murmured to the night breeze, stealing around the rocks, 'Good-bye, old fellow; sleep sound!'

"It seemed to me, in my loneliness and terror, that my fearsome journey would never be ended: that, lost in a labyrinth, I should tread that valley for ever. But at last, after endless ages, I reached the mouth of the ravine, and once on open ground I stretched my cramped limbs and ran, without ceasing, till I once more reached the ship."

Here the captain paused, more from want of breath than anything else, I think.

"Go on, Captain Brander," I cried. "You haven't half finished yet. What did they say when you returned, and how did you explain about poor Travers?"

"Young lady," said Captain Brander, "don't ask any more questions. I think I have told you enough for one afternoon," and here, an officer coming up and summoning him, he left me.

Medusa

Phil Robinson

It was on the 17th of June that the world read in its morning paper that James Westerby had died suddenly in his office at Whitehall on the preceding day. The world may still, if its memory be jogged a little, be able to remember that the cause of death was said to have been heart disease, the crisis having been accelerated by overwork. As to the sadness of the event, the newspapers of all political shades agreed.

James Westerby would have been a prominent man, even if he had not been an Under Secretary and one of the pleasantest speakers in the House of Commons. He was of the Westerbys of Oxfordshire, the last, I fear, of a fine old line. "Hotspur" Westerby, of revolutionary fame, was one of his ancestors, and the Under Secretary prided himself not a little on his resemblance to the old hero, whom Cromwell hated so cordially. His father's place is secure in the world of letters. James Westerby promised to be worthy of his blood. Still young (he died when he was thirty-nine), he had borne himself admirably in public position; and when he died there were not wanting some who spoke of his loss as a national calamity.

To me his death was a personal sorrow. I was, and had been since his appointment, fifteen months before, his private secretary; and, previous to that again, for the twelve years since I came down from the 'Varsity we had been intimate friends, though he was some years my senior.

On the morning of that 16th day of June I was sitting at my desk as usual, between the ante-room and his private office. The last person who had been admitted to his presence was a lady, who, dressed in black and closely veiled, made at the time no distinct impression on my mind. The Under Secretary had refused admittance to some ten or twelve people that morning, but, on my handing him this lady's card, he told me to admit her. She was with him for, perhaps, half an hour. It must have been about 11 o'clock when she passed out. It was just 11.30 when I went into his office and found him dead in his chair.

Some of these facts—with many more or less imaginative details—were presented to the world by the morning papers, as already mentioned, of the 17th. But in no paper was any mention made of the veiled lady, for the altogether sufficient reason that no representative of any paper knew of the veiled lady's existence.

At about a quarter before twelve we were standing—two or three others of the higher employees of the department and myself—in my office, waiting for the arrival of the doctor. The door of the Under Secretary's private room was closed. In the excitement the doorkeeper in the ante-room had presumably deserted his post, for, seeing those to whom I was talking glance toward the outer door, I turned and found myself again confronting the veiled lady.

"Can I see Mr. Westerby once more?" she asked.

"Mr. Westerby, madam," I answered, "is dead."

She did not reply at once, but with both hands raised her veil as if to obtain a clearer view of my face, to see if I spoke the truth. In doing so, she showed me the most beautiful face that I have ever seen, or ever expect to see. One dreams of such eyes. Perhaps Endymion looked into them. But I had never hoped to see them in a woman's face. I scarcely remember that she murmured in a low, incredulous but very musical voice, the one word—

"Dead?"

"He died, madam, suddenly, less than an hour ago."

We had been standing, as we spoke, within earshot of the others. She now drew back to where my desk stood, in the further corner of the room, whither I followed her.

"Was any one with him after I left, can you remember?" she asked.

"No, madam, I had no occasion to go into his room for some little time after you went. When I did so, he was dead."

It was some time before she spoke again; then—

"Excuse me," she said, hesitatingly, "but I hope I shall not have to appear in connection with this. You can understand how very much I should dislike"—this with the faintest smile— "to have my name in all the newspapers. Of course, if there is an inquest, and if my evidence can be of service, I shall have to give it. But it does not seem to me that anything I can say could be of importance. He was well when I saw him—that is all."

Then, after a pause, during which I was silent: "If you can manage it so that my name will not be mentioned, I shall be very grateful to you," she said. As she spoke, she drew one of her cards from a small black card case and handed it to me, adding, "and I hope you will call and let me have the pleasure of thanking you."

I took the card and assured her that I would do what I could in her behalf. She lowered her veil again and left the room. I read the card now with more interest than I had the former one when taking it to my chief. It said:

MRS. WALTER F. TIERCE,
19, Grasmere Crescent, W.

Mrs. Tierce had hardly gone when the doctor came in, followed a moment later by a police inspector.

"Heart disease," the doctor said. The inspector asked me a few questions and said that no inquest would be necessary.

I was hardly conscious at the time, I think, that I was telling the officer that no one had been with the Under Secretary for an hour before his death. Nor when it was over and I recognised what I had done, did my conscience disturb me much. It was a mere courtesy to a woman, such as any man would do if he had it in his power. Why should she be made to suffer because he chanced to die about the time that she happened to call upon him?

So the world next morning heard nothing of the veiled lady.

Within a month I was back in my old chambers in Lincoln's Inn trying to gather up the interrupted threads of my legal studies— a task which would, perhaps, have progressed more rapidly if it had received my entire attention. As it was, however, work had to be content to divide my thoughts somewhat unequally with another subject—Mrs. Walter Tierce.

Mrs. Tierce was a widow. When I called at her home immediately after the funeral, she met me with delightful cordiality.

I called frequently after my first visit, and never met any other visitor at the house. It was difficult to understand how so charming a woman could live in a fashionable quarter of London in such complete isolation. But I had no desire that it should be otherwise.

At the age of thirty-five I had settled down, more or less reconciled to the belief that I should never marry. In theory, I have always maintained that it is the duty to himself and to society of every healthy man to take to himself a wife and assume the responsibilities of a householder before he is thirty years of age. A bachelor's life is an inchoate existence; a species of half-life at best— "like the odd half of a pair of scissors," as Benjamin Franklin said. It is as the head of a family alone, with the care of others on his shoulders, that a man arrives at the possibility of his best development. This was my loudly proclaimed belief. And still I was unmarried. If one could only wake some morning and find himself married—in his own house, with a charming and domestic wife— perhaps with children! But the necessary preliminaries to arriving at that state terrified me. The difficulty of a selection (in the face of an apparently incurable incapacity of falling seriously in love with any one individual) was appalling.

But now the picture of a home rose frequently before me, altogether pleasant to contemplate—a home in which two wonderful black eyes smiled at me across the breakfast table-cloth in the morning and were waiting to meet mine as I looked up from my reading in our library at night.

In fact, I was in love—at times. But there were also times when my condition seemed, on analysis, curiously unsatisfactory to myself, curiously contradictory. Especially was this the case immediately after being in Mrs. Tierce's presence, when there was a certain reaction. On leaving her home, I never failed to ask myself wonderingly, if I really loved her as a man should love a woman before asking her to be his wife. She filled all my thoughts by day and a large share of my dreams by night. Those eyes haunted me. In her presence I was helpless—intoxicated—a blind worshipper. I longed to touch her with my hands, to stroke the fabric of her dress or any object which her hands had recently touched. My whole being ached with very tenderness to approach more nearly to her— to be in contact with her—to caress her. The physical attraction of her presence was overmastering.

Fifteen minutes after leaving her, however, I would be dimly wondering if this was really love—the love that a husband should feel for a wife. This absolute submission of my individuality to hers—would it last through days and weeks and months of constant companionship? Through all the stress of years of wedded life? And if it did not, if my individuality asserted itself, and I became critical of her, what then?

Not that her beauty was her only attraction. On the contrary, few women whom I have ever met have impressed me more distinctly with their intellectuality.

But her most charming characteristic was a certain admirable self-possession and self-control. She seemed so thoroughly to understand herself and to know what was her right relation to things around her; and this without a suspicion of masculinity or of the business air. Never for a moment was there danger of her losing either her mental or emotional equilibrium.

In fact, she was adorable. But, though there was no point of view from which she did not seem to me to be entirely the most delightful thing that I had ever seen, I never failed to experience that same misgiving immediately after quitting her presence. It was as short-lived as it was regular in its recurrence. An hour later, as I sat in my chambers alone, her eyes haunted me once more.

Though I had never spoken of my love, she must have read it in my eyes a hundred times, nor apparently was the perusal distasteful to her.

I had been back in Lincoln's Inn now five months, and was sitting in my chambers one dark mid-afternoon in December. Had I been reading, I must have lit the gas. But there was light enough to sit and dream of her; light enough to see those eyes in the shadow of my book-case. My one clerk was away and would not return for an hour. So I dreamed uninterruptedly until a shuffling outside my office door recalled me to myself. It would have looked more business-like in the eyes of a client to have light enough in the room to work by, and I made a movement toward the matchbox. But there was no time. A knock at the door sounded and the door itself was thrown wide open. There was an interval of some seconds and then a figure entered, moving heavily and painfully with the aid of a crutch—a man and crippled, that was all that I could see.

The figure moved laboriously half way across the floor toward me. Then, standing on one foot, the visitor placed his crutch against the wall and allowed himself to drop heavily into a chair a few feet away from me, while I stood looking on, mutely anxious to render assistance but not knowing how to offer it.

After a short silence he spoke, simply pronouncing my name; not interrogatively, but as if to inform me that he knew to whom he was speaking and that his business was with me. I bowed in response, and with matter-of-fact business suavity asked what I could do for him.

He was silent for some moments, and as he sat fronting the window to which my back was turned, and through which came what small light there was in the office, I could see his face plainly enough. Not an old man, by any means, probably younger than myself, with features that must once have been handsome, and would be still but for the deep lines of sorrow or of pain. The figure, too, as he sat, looked full and healthy with nothing but a certain stiffness of pose to tell of its infirmity. At last he spoke, hurriedly, and in a hard, feverish-sounding voice.

"Nothing, thank you. You can do nothing for me. I have come to do something for you, instead." I bowed acknowledgment.

"I have come to warn you," he went on, still hurriedly and shifting uneasily in his seat, like one who has an unpleasant thing to tell and is anxious to be over with it The strangeness of his voice and manner, and the intentness—almost the fierceness—with which he looked at me, made me uneasy in my turn. I doubted his sanity, and wished that there was more light or that my clerk was present.

"I came to warn you," he said again, and I saw his hands moving nervously as he leaned toward me and spoke harshly and quickly. "You are in love with her—with Mrs. Tierce. No; don't deny it. I know, I know, and before heaven, if I can save you I will."

The heaviness of his breathing told the intensity of the excitement under which he was labouring as he went on, edging further forward on his chair and reaching out his hands toward me:

"She is not a woman; she is not human. Yes, I know how beautiful she is; how helpless a man must be before her. I have known it for six years; and had I not known it I should not now be what I am. You will think me mad," he said. "You probably think me so now. I do not wonder at it. What else should you think when a stranger comes into your chambers and tells you that in these matter-of-fact nineteenth-century days there exist beings who are not human—who have more than human attributes, and that one of these beings is the woman whom you love?"

He was quieter now, more serious, and spoke almost argumentatively, as one who seeks only to convince, while he almost despaired of doing it.

"You are laughing at me now—or pitying me; but I call the Almighty God to witness that I speak the truth—if a God can be almighty and let her live. I tell you, sir, that to know her is death. If you do not believe me you will become worse than I am—as her husband is who died at her feet here in London—as the American is who died before her in the *café* at Nice—as heaven only knows how many more are who have crossed her path."

Of course I had no doubt of his madness; but his earnestness—the utter strength of conviction with which he spoke—was strangely moving. That he, poor fellow, believed what he said, it was impossible to doubt.

"It is six years since I saw her first at Havre, in France. I chanced to be seated at the next table to her at Frascati's, and I knew that I loved her then. The American was with her. I followed her to Cannes, to Trouville, to Monaco, to Nice; and where she went the American went, too. There was no impropriety in their companionship, but he followed her as I did; only that he had her acquaintance and I had not. And I knew, or thought I knew, that it would be useless for me to try and win her while he was there. He evidently worshipped her, and she—for he was a handsome fellow (Reading was his name)—seemed to care for him. So I watched her from a distance, waiting and hoping; and as I have told you my turn came.

"It was in the Café Royal, and nobody saw it happen but herself. Suddenly she rushed out from the corner where they were sitting and called for help. Every one crowded around, and he was dead—dead in his chair, with his face upturned and his eyes fixed, staring like one suddenly terrified. They said it was heart disease. Heart disease!"

It had grown almost dark, and he drew his chair close to me. The paling light from the window just showed me the worn face and the sunken, feverish eyes.

"Then I came to know her," he continued, after a pause. "I hung upon her as he had done, and for three months I believed that I was the happiest man in Europe. In Venice, in Florence, in Paris, in London, I was constantly with her, day after day. She seemed to love me, and in the Bois or in Hyde Park how proud I was to be seen by her side! Then she went to stay for a month at Oxford, and I, with her permission, followed her there, and would call for her at the Mitre every morning. Under the shadow of the grey college walls and in the well-trimmed walks and gardens, it seemed that her face put on a new and holier beauty in keeping with the place. There it was that I told her that I loved her and asked her to be my wife, as we stood for a minute to rest in the cloisters of Christ Church."

His voice was very sad. It had lost its harshness, and as he remembered—or did he only imagine?—the sweetness of those days of love-making, there was more of a soft regretfulness than of anger in his tones.

"She did not refuse me," he said, "nor did she explicitly accept me. But I was idiotically happy—happy for three whole days—until that afternoon in the Magdalen Walks, when in ten minutes I became, from a healthy, strong man, the wreck you see me now."

The regretfulness was all gone, and the hard, fierce ring was in his voice again as he went on:

"It was on one of the benches in Addison's Walk, as they call it, and I pressed her for some more definite promise than she had yet given me. She did not seem to listen to me, to heed me, as she leaned back, her hands lying idly in her lap and her great, grave eyes looking out across the meadow. I grew more passionate; clasped her hands and begged for an answer. At last she turned her face towards me. I met her eyes—"

His voice broke and he stopped speaking. For a minute or more we sat in silence in the twilight, his face buried in his hands. Then he raised his head again, and in slow, unimpassioned accents, continued:

"As our eyes met, hers looked lustreless, hardly as if she saw me or was looking at me. But as I gazed into them they changed. Somewhere inside them, or behind them, a flame was lit. The pupils expanded, black and brilliant as eyes never shone before. What was it? Was it love? And leaning still closer, I gazed more intensely into the eyes that seemed now to blaze before me. And as I looked the spell came upon me. It was as though I swooned. Dimly I became aware that I was losing my power of motion, of speech, of thought. The eyes engulfed me. I was vaguely conscious that I must somehow disengage myself from the spell that was upon me; but I could not. I was powerless, and she—it was as if she fed upon my very life. I cannot phrase it otherwise. I was numb, and, though I tried to speak, could not move one muscle. Then consciousness began to leave me, and I was on the point of—God knows what— swoon or death—when the crunching of feet on the gravel path came sharply to my ears.

"Who it was that passed I do not know. I know not how long I sat there. I remember that she rose without a word and left me. When I moved it was evening. The sun was behind the college walls,

and the walk was dark. With my brain hardly awake and my lower
limbs still benumbed, slowly I made my way out of the college gates
and up the High Street to the Clarendon Hotel, where I was staying.
Next morning I awoke what you see me now—a cripple, a paralytic
for life."

During all this narrative I had sat silent, engrossed in the
madman's tale. As a piece of dramatic elocution, it was magnificent.
When he finished I cast about for some commonplace remark to
make, but in the state of my feelings it was not easy to find one,
and it was he who again broke the silence:

"Tierce, poor fool! I warned him as I am warning you. It was
two years afterward that she married him, and in two weeks more
he was dead—dead in their house in Park Lane—died of heart
disease! Heart disease!"

And as he said it, I could not help thinking of James Westerby.

My visitor was about to speak again when a footfall sounded
on the stairs outside, the door opened, and my clerk stood in the
entrance, astonished at the darkness.

"Come in, Jackson," I called, to let him know that I was there,
"and light the gas, please."

My visitor rose painfully, and again took his crutch.

"I have told you all that is vital to the case," he said in the
matter-of-fact voice of a client addressing his attorney, "and you
will, of course, do as you think best."

Jackson, about to light the gas, with a burning match in his
hand, held the door open for the stranger to pass out, and without
another word the cripple moved laboriously away. It was not until
he had gone that it occurred to me that I had not asked nor been
told his name.

"Has that gentleman ever called before, Jackson?"

"I think not, sir."

But probably I should meet him again.

And now, my thoughts reverted to her. He was mad, of course:
and his story was absurd. But as I walked home from the office,
those eyes were before me, blazing with the passion which he had
lit in them. What eyes they were in truth! How lovely, and how I

loved them! And how easy, too, it was to imagine them dilating and engulfing one's senses until he swooned!

I had not hoped to see her again that day, having spent part of the morning in "helping her to shop," and expecting to escort her to the theatre on the evening following. So after a solitary dinner at a restaurant, I climbed up to my chambers to dream away the evening alone.

The story which I had heard a few hours before certainly had not in any way altered my feelings towards Mrs. Tierce. Indeed, I hardly thought of the story, except to pity the poor fellow who told it and to speculate upon his history. Who was he? Had he loved her and gone mad for love of her? And should I tell her of his visit? It might pain her by bringing up unpleasant memories; but on the other hand I should like to know something more of the cripple's history.

But I was restless, and my rooms seemed more than ever lonely and unhomelike that evening; so about nine o'clock, I put on my hat and overcoat and went out into the street.

It was a cold night, damp and raw, with no sign of starlight or moonlight overhead, and a heavy, misty atmosphere through which the street lights shone blurred and twinkling.

Instinctively I turned westward, and, as a matter of course, set my face towards Grasmere Crescent, not with any intention of calling at the house, but with a lover's longing to see it and to be near to her. I passed the house on the opposite side of the street. No. 19 had a large bow-window in the drawing room, on the first floor, and as I approached, the blind of the narrow side-window facing me being raised some few inches gave a glimpse of the brightly lighted, daintily furnished room, with which I was so familiar, within. I had hoped to catch a glimpse of her, but in the small segment of the room that was visible through the aperture, no figure was to be seen.

After passing on to the end of the street I made a circuit round some by-streets and so back to Grasmere Crescent. As I approached now from the north the house looked dark, save for a narrowest chink of light which outlined the edge of the bow-window. When I had passed I turned to look back at the window of which the blind was raised; and doing so, I saw a curious thing.

It was only instantaneous; but just for that instant I saw two figures standing, herself and one of the servants, whom I recognised. They were facing one another, each, it seemed, leaning slightly forward. But even as I looked, the servant suddenly threw up her hands and fell—fell straight backward, rigidly, as if in a fit. Mrs. Tierce started towards the falling girl, as if to catch her. The movement took her out of my range of vision, the projecting woodwork of the window intervening.

It all happened so suddenly that I stood for a moment bewildered and irresolute. Had I really seen it? It was more like some tableau on a stage, or the flash of a slide from a magic lantern, than a reality.

Recovering my senses, my first impulse was to cross the street and offer my services. But why? The girl had but slipped suddenly upon the polished floor, and doubtless they were laughing over it now. It would be an impertinence for me to thrust myself in with a confession of having been playing spy. So, after standing and gazing at the window for a few moments, during which I once saw Mrs. Tierce pass quickly across the room and back, I moved on to my rooms.

The next morning as I sat at breakfast, a note was brought to me.

> "I am very sorry," she wrote, "to interfere with your theatre party this evening, but a dreadful thing happened here last night. One of my servants—Mary, you know her—died very suddenly. I was talking to her, when she simply threw up her hands and fell down before me, dead. Regretting that I must ask you to excuse me, I am,
> "Yours cordially,
> "Edith Tierce."

I wished now that I had obeyed my first impulse on the preceding evening and had rung at the door to volunteer my services. I would certainly go and see her immediately after breakfast.

Fortunately my theatre party included only two other persons besides Mrs. Tierce and myself, and I was on sufficiently intimate terms with John Bradstreet and his wife to have no fear of offending them. So I wrote Mrs. Bradstreet a short note explaining the situation briefly, enclosing the tickets and hoping she would use the box or not, as she saw fit. Then I drove at once to Grasmere Crescent.

In her quiet, self-possessed way Mrs. Tierce had already done all that was necessary, and I found that there was little excuse for thrusting my services upon her. Still I saw her frequently during the next two days, though never for any length of time and rarely to talk of things not associated immediately with the melancholy ceremony that was impending. The dead girl seemed to have had no family connections, and the funeral was conducted under Mrs. Tierce's directions. I accompanied her to the church and cemetery, and left her at her own door afterwards, accepting an invitation to call again that evening.

I have spoken before of the curious self-possession, an imperturbable self-reliance, which Mrs. Tierce possessed and which sat very becomingly upon her delicate grave face. Never had this quality in her seemed more admirably perfect to me than during those days when the shadow of death hung over her home.

On the evening of the day of the funeral, she was even more reposeful than usual, in a dreamy mood in which I had seen her before more than once, and in which she seemed hardly conscious of—or rather inattentive to—what passed around her. This mood of hers the cripple had recalled to me when describing the scene in the Oxford walk.

It may have been that the events and scenes of the last few days, with all their appeals to the emotions, had predisposed us both to tenderness. Certainly from the time of my entry when our greeting had been only a hand-clasp, with hardly an audible word on either side, we had spoken constrainedly, in undertones and on personal topics. Though more than once I strove desperately to be matter-of-fact, my voice in spite of myself would sink, and wherever the conversation started from, it ended in herself.

At last some chance word of hers made me broach a subject which I had never approached before, and which she rarely alluded to—her late husband. Before I was conscious of what I was doing, I had said:

"It is not, by any means, I know, your first contact with death. You have told me very little of Mr. Tierce."

"No," she said dreamily, "there is little to tell. We were only married a few weeks."

And then:

"And is it not possible that you might marry again? Could you not?" and I crossed from my chair to take a seat on the sofa by her side, "could you not—is there any hope for me?"

Instead of replying, she sat silent and inattentive, her large swimming eyes looking far into either the past or the future—I wondered which.

"Tell me," I urged, laying my hand on one of hers, as it rested in her lap, "tell me, is there any hope?"

She did not move, did not answer me. Again I implored her, and at last she spoke, but with seeming irrelevance.

"Did you ever hear of the Court of Love?" she asked, "the court over which the Countess Ermengarde presided in the tenth or eleventh century?"

No, I knew nothing of the Court of Love or the Countess Ermengarde, though I have since looked them up.

"The Court decided, and the decision was affirmed by a later Court composed of half the queens and duchesses of Europe, that true love could not exist between married persons."

"But you do not believe it? That was nine centuries ago; and how should queens and duchesses know anything of love?"

"I do not know whether I believe it or not," she murmured, and turned her head as it lay on the cushions of the sofa, to look at me with eyes that still seemed strangely dreamy and far away.

"But you do know," I urged impulsively, leaning forward till my face was dangerously close to hers. "You know that you do not believe it. You know that I should always love you—that I must always love you. And if I may love you as my wife—"

She smiled faintly, charmingly, but did not answer me.

"My darling," I whispered, "say something! Am I to be utterly happy?"

And still she did not answer; but leaned back with the faint half-smile on her lips, and her great inscrutable eyes looking into and through mine. Then in the silence and suspense, the cripple's story came into my mind. No wonder that he should believe that he had been fascinated in some mysterious way—spellbound, benumbed—by those eyes! No wonder! And still I looked into them; and still they looked through mine. I forgot the nearness of her lips; forgot that I held her hand. I thought only of, saw only, those eyes. And still I thought only of the cripple and vaguely pitied him.

But somehow—when it began I knew not—I found that the expression of the eyes had changed. They were no longer dreamy and far away, but intensely earnest, with a passion in them that was almost hunger.

"Yes," I thought to myself (and I must have smiled in thinking it), "this is what he described. No wonder that they seemed to him to flame. They are not looking at my eyes now, but through, into my brain, into me. My eyes are no more than two pieces of glass in the path of her vision." And I felt a curious, half-gratified recognition of the accuracy of the other's description. And still the eyes seemed to expand until they were many times larger than my own; till I could see nothing but them.

Have you ever, in a half-darkened room, set your face close against a mirror and looked into your own eyes and seen what terrible things they are; how the view of everything else is shut out and all your sense is drawn into the pupils confronting you? So I felt my whole being concentrating itself in—merging itself into—drowning in—her eyes. A strange feeling of intoxication possessed me, of ecstacy. I could have laughed aloud, but that it seemed as if to do it I would somehow have to summon my faculties from too far away.

At what point this strange calmness gave way to conscious fear, I do not know. I saw the pupils of her eyes expanding and contracting, as if with the regular beats of a passionate pulse behind them. I saw, or rather I was aware, that the colour flushed into her cheeks and died again, that her breath, which was warm on my face, came short and gasping. Her lips closed and parted, moist and glistening, suggesting to me somehow the craving of some animal in the presence of food which it could not reach. Her nostrils dilated, quivering, and her whole being strained with a passion which seemed carnivorous.

"It was as if she preyed upon my very life," he had said, and I understood him now. But the memory of the cripple was fading from me. I was conscious only of myself and of her; of the terror of her fierce hunger and my own helplessness. The power of motion was gone from me; even volition seemed slipping away. The burning of her eyes was in my brain which was as if laid open before her; as a hollow dish set open to the scorching sun. I was utterly at her mercy, without power of resistance; and as her breath grew yet more rapid and more heavy, I knew that she was in some way inhaling my very life.

Suddenly a flash of fear passed across her face—a spasm of agonised disappointment. For a moment it was as if she would, in one long, indrawn breath, draw the last of my strength from me; and then a man's voice sounded in my ear.

"I hope I am in time!"

She had fallen reclining against the cushions of the sofa. I looked up dazedly, and the cripple stood in the centre of the room, his hat in his hand.

"You had better let me take you away," he said, and I heard it half consciously. Turning to look at her, I saw her lie panting and exhausted. I cannot tell the horror of her appearance. Her eyes still sought mine hungrily as before. Her hands, lying in her lap, fumbled each other, her fingers knotting and intertwining. Her lips moved, and all her body quivered with passion. It was a dreadful fancy, but I could liken her to nothing but some bloodsucking thing; some human leech or vampire, torn from its prey, quivering dumbly with its unsated appetite.

At the time I only half understood what passed around me. I knew that the danger was over and that escape lay before me. I saw the cripple waiting for me to rise and was conscious of the horror with which she inspired me. But I was bewildered. My brain seemed numb, and when I endeavoured to stand up my limbs refused their office. Seeing my powerlessness the cripple moved forward and with his healthy arm assisted me. It was with difficulty that I stood, for there was no sensation in my feet or legs and it was only by leaning on my companion that I made my way laboriously to the door.

No word had been spoken beyond the two sentences which the cripple had uttered. Reaching the door of the room I turned to look at her once more, supporting myself against the door-post. She had not moved. Under the influence of the passion that was upon her she evidently had no other thought or emotion. There was no sign of shame or confusion on her face; nothing but the blind craving for the prey that was being taken from her. Even there, across the full width of the room, her eyes sought mine with the same despairing longing. But she only made me shudder now. The cripple still supporting me, we passed together from the house.

Of the remainder of that evening my memory is confused and faint. I know that I was helped to my chambers and that there, with the assistance of the cripple and some third person, though who, or whence or where he joined us, I know not, I was put to bed. That night was one long, half-waking swoon, and far into the next afternoon I lay motionless upon my back without speaking or wishing to speak, save only to tell the woman who took care of my rooms that I needed no help or food. As the twilight fell the same good woman came again, and yet again late at night. But I was scarcely conscious, and had no wishes. Even speech was an effort.

For seven days, all through the Christmas holidays, I lay in this state, taking little nourishment; hardly speaking, hardly thinking clearly. At last, on the day after Christmas, I found courage and strength to attack the mail which had been accumulating on my sick-room table. I had expected to find her handwriting on one at least of the envelopes. In this I was disappointed. But some instinct led me to open first one envelope the address of which was written in a hand that was strange to me. It contained nothing but a newspaper clipping:

"A sad accident occurred last night at 19 Grasmere Crescent, W. The house was inhabited by Mrs. Walter Tierce, the widow of the late Walter Tierce, Esq. Last evening Mrs. Tierce, who was twenty-six years of age, retired to rest as usual. This morning she failed to answer the knock of the servant at the door, and on the maid entering the room she noticed a strong and peculiar odour. She was frightened and went out and fetched another servant. The two entered the room and found Mrs. Tierce dead, and an overturned bottle of chloroform by the pillow. It was evidently an accident, and no inquest will be held. A curious coincidence in connection with the sad affair is that this is the second death in the same house within a week. On Monday last, a maid in the service of Mrs. Tierce died suddenly of heart disease. Her funeral occurred yesterday afternoon, when Mrs. Tierce attended it."

Attached to this clipping with a pin was the date line of the evening newspaper from which it was taken— "Friday, December 19th." That was the day after that terrible evening, and a week ago now. The funeral must have already taken place,

Though, as I have said, the handwriting on the envelope was unfamiliar to me, I had my conjecture as to whom the message was from, and after keeping the envelope for all these years, the clue has come which shows that the conjecture was correct. Six weeks ago I received information that I had been appointed executor of the estate of the late James Livingston, of Hereford. James Livingston? The name was unknown to me. Thinking that there might be some mistake, I called at the solicitor's office from which the intimation came. No, there was no mistake, the solicitor informed me; he had drawn up the will, and Mr. Livingston had given him special instructions how to communicate with me.

"And you say you never knew him at all?" he asked musingly, "that is certainly curious for he seemed to know you. But you could not well have forgotten him. He was a cripple—almost entirely paralysed in his right side."

THE MAN WHO WENT TOO FAR

E. F. Benson

The little village of St. Faith's nestles in a hollow of wooded till up on the north bank of the river Fawn in the country of Hampshire, huddling close round its grey Norman church as if for spiritual protection against the fays and fairies, the trolls and "little people," who might be supposed still to linger in the vast empty spaces of the New Forest, and to come after dusk and do their doubtful businesses. Once outside the hamlet you may walk in any direction (so long as you avoid the high road which leads to Brockenhurst) for the length of a summer afternoon without seeing sign of human habitation, or possibly even catching sight of another human being.

Shaggy wild ponies may stop their feeding for a moment as you pass, the white scuts of rabbits will vanish into their burrows, a brown viper perhaps will glide from your path into a clump of heather, and unseen birds will chuckle in the bushes, but it may easily happen that for a long day you will see nothing human. But you will not feel in the least lonely; in summer, at any rate, the sunlight will be gay with butterflies, and the air thick with all those woodland sounds which like instruments in an orchestra combine to play the great symphony of the yearly festival of June.

Winds whisper in the birches, and sigh among the firs; bees are busy with their redolent labour among the heather, a myriad birds chirp in the green temples of the forest trees, and the voice of the river prattling over stony places, bubbling into pools, chuckling and gulping round corners, gives you the sense that many presences and companions are near at hand.

Yet, oddly enough, though one would have thought that these benign and cheerful influences of wholesome air and spaciousness of forest were very healthful comrades for a man, in so far as Nature can really influence this wonderful human genus which has in these centuries learned to defy her most violent storms in its well-established houses, to bridle her torrents and make them light its streets, to tunnel her mountains and plough her seas, the inhabitants of St. Faith's will not willingly venture into the forest after dark. For in spite of the silence and loneliness of the hooded night it seems that a man is not sure in what company he may suddenly find himself, and though it is difficult to get from these villagers any very clear story of occult appearances, the feeling is widespread. One story indeed I have heard with some definiteness, the tale of a monstrous goat that has been seen to skip with hellish glee about the woods and shady places, and this perhaps is connected with the story which I have here attempted to piece together. It too is well-known to them; for all remember the young artist who died here not long ago, a young man, or so he struck the beholder, of great personal beauty, with something about him that made men's faces to smile and brighten when they looked on him. His ghost they will tell you "walks" constantly by the stream and through the woods which he loved so, and in especial it haunts a certain house, the last of the village, where he lived, and its garden in which he was done to death. For my part I am inclined to think that the terror of the forest dates chiefly from that day.

So, such as the story is, I have set it forth in connected form. It is based partly on the accounts of the villagers, but mainly on that of Darcy, a friend of mine and a friend of the man with whom these events were chiefly concerned.

The day had been one of untarnished midsummer splendour, and as the sun drew near to its setting, the glory of the evening grew every moment more crystalline, more miraculous.

Westward from St. Faith's the beechwood which stretched for some miles toward the heathery upland beyond already cast its veil of clear shadow over the red roofs of the village, but the spire of the grey church, over-topping all, still pointed a flaming orange finger into the sky. The river Fawn, which runs below, lay in sheets of sky-reflected blue, and wound its dreamy devious course round the edge of this wood, where a rough two-planked bridge crossed from the bottom of the garden of the last house in the village, and communicated by means of a little wicker gate with the wood itself. Then once out of the shadow of the wood the stream lay in flaming pools of the molten crimson of the sunset, and lost itself in the haze of woodland distances.

This house at the end of the village stood outside the shadow, and the lawn which sloped down to the river was still flecked with sunlight. Garden-beds of dazzling colour lined its gravel walks, and down the middle of it ran a brick pergola, half-hidden in clusters of rambler-rose and purple with starry clematis. At the bottom end of it, between two of its pillars, was slung a hammock containing a shirt-sleeved figure.

The house itself lay somewhat remote from the rest of the village, and a footpath leading across two fields, now tall and fragrant with hay, was its only communication with the high road.

It was low-built, only two stories in height, and like the garden, its walls were a mass of flowering roses. A narrow stone terrace ran along the garden front, over which was stretched an awning, and on the terrace a young silent-footed man-servant was busied with the laying of the table for dinner. He was neat-handed and quick with his job, and having finished it he went back into the house, and reappeared again with a large rough bath-towel on his arm. With this he went to the hammock in the pergola.

"Nearly eight, sir," he said.

"Has Mr. Darcy come yet?" asked a voice from the hammock.

"No, sir."

"If I'm not back when he comes, tell him that I'm just having a bathe before dinner."

The servant went back to the house, and after a moment or two Frank Halton struggled to a sitting posture, and slipped out on to the grass. He was of medium height and rather slender in build, but the supple ease and grace of his movements gave the impression of great physical strength: even his descent from the hammock was not an awkward performance. His face and hands were of very dark complexion, either from constant exposure to wind and sun, or, as his black hair and dark eyes tended to show, from some strain of southern blood. His head was small, his face of an exquisite beauty of modelling, while the smoothness of its contour would have led you to believe that he was a beardless lad still in his teens. But something, some look which living and experience alone can give, seemed to contradict that, and finding yourself completely puzzled as to his age, you would next moment probably cease to think about that, and only look at this glorious specimen of young manhood with wondering satisfaction.

He was dressed as became the season and the heat, and wore only a shirt open at the neck, and a pair of flannel trousers. His head, covered very thickly with a somewhat rebellious crop of short curly hair, was bare as he strolled across the lawn to the bathing-place that lay below. Then for a moment there was silence, then the sound of splashed and divided waters, and presently after, a great shout of ecstatic joy, as he swam up-stream with the foamed water standing in a frill round his neck. Then after some five minutes of limb-stretching struggle with the flood, he turned over on his back, and with arms thrown wide, floated down-stream, ripple-cradled and inert. His eyes were shut, and between half-parted lips he talked gently to himself.

"I am one with it," he said to himself, "the river and I, I and the river. The coolness and splash of it is I, and the water-herbs that wave in it are I also. And my strength and my limbs are not mine but the river's. It is all one, all one, dear Fawn."

A quarter of an hour later he appeared again at the bottom of the lawn, dressed as before, his wet hair already drying into its crisp short curls again. There he paused a moment, looking back at the stream with the smile with which men look on the face of a friend, then turned towards the house. Simultaneously his servant came to the door leading on to the terrace, followed by a man who appeared to be some half-way through the fourth decade of his years. Frank and he saw each other across the bushes and garden-beds, and each quickening his step, they met suddenly face to face round an angle of the garden walk, in the fragrance of syringa.

"My dear Darcy," cried Frank, "I am charmed to see you." But the other stared at him in amazement.

"Frank!" he exclaimed.

"Yes, that is my name," he said, laughing; "what is the matter?" Darcy took his hand.

"What have you done to yourself?" he asked.

"You are a boy again."

"Ah, I have a lot to tell you," said Frank.

"Lots that you will hardly believe, but I shall convince you—"

He broke off suddenly, and held up his hand.

"Hush, there is my nightingale," he said.

The smile of recognition and welcome with which he had greeted his friend faded from his face, and a look of rapt wonder took its place, as of a lover listening to the voice of his beloved.

His mouth parted slightly, showing the white line of teeth, and his eyes looked out and out till they seemed to Darcy to be focussed on things beyond the vision of man. Then something perhaps startled the bird, for the song ceased.

"Yes, lots to tell you," he said. "Really I am delighted to see you. But you look rather white and pulled down; no wonder after that fever. And there is to be no nonsense about this visit. It is June now, you stop here till you are fit to begin work again. Two months at least."

"Ah, I can't trespass quite to that extent."

Frank took his arm and walked him down the grass.

"Trespass? Who talks of trespass? I shall tell you quite openly when I am tired of you, but you know when we had the studio together, we used not to bore each other. However, it is ill talking of going away on the moment of your arrival. Just a stroll to the river, and then it will be dinner-time."

Darcy took out his cigarette case, and offered it to the other.

Frank laughed.

"No, not for me. Dear me, I suppose I used to smoke once. How very odd!"

"Given it up?"

"I don't know. I suppose I must have. Anyhow I don't do it now. I would as soon think of eating meat."

"Another victim on the smoking altar of vegetarianism?"

"Victim?" asked Frank. "Do I strike you as such?"

He paused on the margin of the stream and whistled softly. Next moment a moor-hen made its splashing flight across the river, and ran up the bank. Frank took it very gently in his hands and stroked its head, as the creature lay against his shirt.

"And is the house among the reeds still secure?" he half-crooned to it. "And is the missus quite well, and are the neighbours flourishing? There, dear, home with you," and he flung it into the air.

"That bird's very tame," said Darcy, slightly bewildered.

"It is rather," said Frank, following its flight.

During dinner Frank chiefly occupied himself in bringing himself up-to-date in the movements and achievements of this old friend whom he had not seen for six years. Those six years, it now appeared, had been full of incident and success for Darcy; he had made a name for himself as a portrait painter which bade fair to outlast the vogue of a couple of seasons, and his leisure time had been brief. Then some four months previously he had been through a severe attack of typhoid, the result of which as concerns this story was that he had come down to this sequestered place to recruit.

"Yes, you've got on," said Frank at the end. "I always knew you would. A.R.A. with more in prospect. Money? You roll in it, I suppose, and, O Darcy, how much happiness have you had all these years? That is the only imperishable possession. And how much have you learned? Oh, I don't mean in Art. Even I could have done well in that."

Darcy laughed.

"Done well? My dear fellow, all I have learned in these six years you knew, so to speak, in your cradle. Your old pictures fetch huge prices. Do you never paint now?"

Frank shook his head.

"No, I'm too busy," he said.

"Doing what? Please tell me. That is what everyone is for ever asking me."

"Doing? I suppose you would say I do nothing."

Darcy glanced up at the brilliant young face opposite him.

"It seems to suit you, that way of being busy," he said. "Now, it's your turn. Do you read? Do you study? I remember you saying that it would do us all—all us artists, I mean—a great deal of good if we would study any one human face carefully for a year, without recording a line."

"Have you been doing that?"

Frank shook his head again.

"I mean exactly what I say," he said. "I have been *doing* nothing. And I have never been so occupied. Look at me; have I not done something to myself to begin with?"

"You are two years younger than I," said Darcy, "at least you used to be. You therefore are thirty-five. But had I never seen you before I should say you were just twenty. But was it worth while to spend six years of greatly-occupied life in order to look twenty? Seems rather like a woman of fashion."

Frank laughed boisterously.

"First time I've ever been compared to that particular bird of prey," he said. "No, that has not been my occupation—in fact I am only very rarely conscious that one effect of my occupation has been that. Of course, it must have been if one comes to think of it. It is not very important."

"Quite true my body has become young. But that is very little; I have become young."

Darcy pushed back his chair and sat sideways to the table looking at the other.

"Has that been your occupation then?" he asked.

"Yes, that anyhow is one aspect of it. Think what youth means! It is the capacity for growth, mind, body, spirit, all grow, all get stronger, all have a fuller, firmer life every day. That is something, considering that every day that passes after the ordinary man reaches the full-blown flower of his strength, weakens his hold on life. A man reaches his prime, and remains, we say, in his prime for ten years, or perhaps twenty. But after his primest prime is reached, he slowly, insensibly weakens. These are the signs of age in you, in your body, in your art probably, in your mind. You are less electric than you were. But I, when I reach my prime—I am nearing it—ah, you shall see." The stars had begun to appear in the blue velvet of the sky, and to the east the horizon seen above the black silhouette of the village was growing dove-coloured with the approach of moon-rise.

White moths hovered dimly over the garden-beds, and the footsteps of night tip-toed through the bushes. Suddenly Frank rose.

"Ah, it is the supreme moment," he said softly. "Now more than at any other time the current of life, the eternal imperishable current runs so close to me that I am almost enveloped in it. Be silent a minute."

He advanced to the edge of the terrace and looked out, standing stretched with arms outspread. Darcy heard him draw a long breath into his lungs, and after many seconds expel it again. Six or eight times he did this, then turned back into the lamplight.

"It will sound to you quite mad, I expect," he said, "but if you want to hear the soberest truth I have ever spoken and shall ever speak, I will tell you about myself. But come into the garden if it is not damp for you. I have never told anyone yet, but I shall like to tell you. It is long, in fact, since I have even tried to classify what I have learned."

They wandered into the fragrant dimness of the pergola, and sat down. Then Frank began:

"Years ago, do you remember," he said, "we used often to talk about the decay of joy in the world. Many impulses, we settled, had contributed to this decay, some of which were good in themselves, others that were quite completely bad. Among the good things, I put what we may call certain Christian virtues, renunciation, resignation, sympathy with suffering, and the desire to relieve sufferers, but out of those things spring very bad ones,

useless renunciation, asceticism for its own sake, mortification of
the flesh with nothing to follow, no corresponding gain that is, and
that awful and terrible disease which devastated England some
centuries ago, and from which by heredity of spirit we suffer now,
Puritanism. That was a dreadful plague, the brutes held and taught
that joy and laughter and merriment were evil: it was a doctrine
the most profane and wicked. Why, what is the commonest crime
one sees? A sullen face. That is the truth of the matter. Now all my
life I have believed that we are intended to be happy, that joy is of
all gifts the most divine. And when I left London, abandoned my
career, such as it was, I did so because I intended to devote my life
to the cultivation of joy, and, by continuous and unsparing effort
to be happy. Among people, and in constant intercourse with
others, I did not find it possible; there were too many distractions
in towns and work-rooms, and also too much suffering. So I took
one step backwards or forwards, as you may choose to put it, and
went straight to Nature, to trees, birds, animals, to all those things
which quite clearly pursue one aim only, which blindly follow the
great native instinct to be happy without any care at all for morality,
or human law or divine law. I wanted, you understand, to get all
joy first-hand and unadulterated, and I think it scarcely exists
among men; it is obsolete."

Darcy turned in his chair.

"Ah, but what makes birds and animals happy?" he asked.
"Food, food and mating."

Frank laughed gently in the stillness.

"Do not think I became a sensualist," he said. "I did not make
that mistake. For the sensualist carries his miseries pick-a-back,
and round his feet is wound the shroud that shall soon enwrap him.
I may be mad, it is true, but I am not so stupid anyhow as to have
tried that. No, what is it that makes puppies play with their own
tails, that sends cats on their prowling ecstatic errands at night?"

He paused a moment.

"So I went to Nature," he said. "I sat down here in this New
Forest, sat down fair and square, and looked. That was my first
difficulty, to sit here quiet without being bored, to wait without

being impatient, to be receptive and very alert, though for a long time nothing particular happened. The change in fact was slow in those early stages."

"Nothing happened?" asked Darcy, rather impatiently, with the sturdy revolt against any new idea which to the English mind is synonymous with nonsense. "Why, what in the world *should* happen?"

Now Frank as he had known him was the most generous but most quick-tempered of mortal men; in other words his anger would flare to a prodigious beacon, under almost no provocation, only to be quenched again under a gust of no less impulsive kindliness. Thus the moment Darcy had spoken, an apology for his hasty question was half-way up his tongue. But there was no need for it to have travelled even so far, for Frank laughed again with kindly, genuine mirth.

"Oh, how I should have resented that a few years ago," he said. "Thank goodness that resentment is one of the things I have got rid of. I certainly wish that you should believe my story—in fact, you are going to—but that you at this moment should imply that you do not does not concern me."

"Ah, your solitary sojournings have made you inhuman," said Darcy, still very English.

"No, human," said Frank. "Rather more human, at least rather less of an ape."

"Well, that was my first quest," he continued, after a moment, "the deliberate and unswerving pursuit of joy, and my method, the eager contemplation of Nature. As far as motive went, I daresay it was purely selfish, but as far as effect goes, it seems to me about the best thing one can do for one's follow-creatures, for happiness is more infectious than small-pox. So, as I said, I sat down and waited; I looked at happy things, zealously avoided the sight of anything unhappy, and by degrees a little trickle of the happiness of this blissful world began to filter into me. The trickle grew more abundant, and now, my dear fellow, if I could for a moment divert from me into you one half of the torrent of joy that pours through me day and night, you would throw the world, art, everything aside, and just live, exist. When a man's body dies, it passes into trees and flowers. Well, that is what I have been trying to do with my soul before death."

The servant had brought into the pergola a table with syphons and spirits, and had set a lamp upon it. As Frank spoke he leaned forward towards the other, and Darcy for all his matter-of-fact common sense could have sworn that his companion's face shone, was luminous in itself. His dark brown eyes glowed from within, the unconscious smile of a child irradiated and transformed his face. Darcy felt suddenly excited, exhilarated.

"Go on," he said. "Go on. I can feel you are somehow telling me sober truth. I daresay you are mad; but I don't see that matters."

Frank laughed again.

"Mad?" he said. "Yes, certainly, if you wish. But I prefer to call it sane. However, nothing matters less than what anybody chooses to call things. God never labels his gifts; He just puts them into our hands; just as he put animals in the garden of Eden, for Adam to name if he felt disposed.

"So by the continual observance and study of things that were happy," continued he, "I got happiness, I got joy. But seeking it, as I did, from Nature, I got much more which I did not seek, but stumbled upon originally by accident. It is difficult to explain, but I will try.

"About three years ago I was sitting one morning in a place I will show you to-morrow. It is down by the river brink, very green, dappled with shade and sun, and the river passes there through some little clumps of reeds. Well, as I sat there, doing nothing, but just looking and listening, I heard the sound quite distinctly of some flute-like instrument playing a strange unending melody. I thought at first it was some musical yokel on the highway and did not pay much attention. But before long the strangeness and indescribable beauty of the tune struck me.

"It never repeated itself, but it never came to an end, phrase after phrase ran its sweet course, it worked gradually and inevitably up to a climax, and having attained it, it went on; another climax was reached and another and another. Then with a sudden gasp of wonder I localised where it came from. It came from the reeds and from the sky and from the trees. It was everywhere, it was the sound of life. It was, my dear Darcy, as the Greeks would have said, it was Pan playing on his pipes, the voice of Nature. It was the life-melody, the world-melody."

Darcy was far too interested to interrupt, though there was a question he would have liked to ask, and Frank went on:

"Well, for the moment I was terrified, terrified with the impotent horror of nightmare, and I stopped my ears and just ran from the place and got back to the house panting, trembling, literally in a panic. Unknowingly, for at that time I only pursued joy, I had begun, since I drew my joy from Nature, to get in touch with Nature. Nature, force, God, call it what you will, had drawn across my face a little gossamer web of essential life. I saw that when I emerged from my terror, and I went very humbly back to where I had heard the Pan-pipes. But it was nearly six months before I heard them again."

"Why was that?" asked Darcy.

"Surely because I had revolted, rebelled, and worst of all been frightened. For I believe that just as there is nothing in the world which so injures one's body as fear, so there is nothing that so much shuts up the soul. I was afraid, you see, of the one thing in the world which has real existence. No wonder its manifestation was withdrawn."

"And after six months?"

"After six months one blessed morning I heard the piping again. I wasn't afraid that time."

"And since then it has grown louder, it has become more constant. I now hear it often, and I can put myself into such an attitude towards Nature that the pipes will almost certainly sound. And never yet have they played the same tune, it is always something new, something fuller, richer, more complete than before."

"What do you mean by 'such an attitude towards Nature'?" asked Darcy.

"I can't explain that; but by translating it into a bodily attitude it is this."

Frank sat up for a moment quite straight in his chair, then slowly sunk back with arms outspread and head drooped.

"That;" he said, "an effortless attitude, but open, resting, receptive. It is just that which you must do with your soul."

Then he sat up again.

"One word more," he said, "and I will bore you no further. Nor unless you ask me questions shall I talk about it again. You will find me, in fact, quite sane in my mode of life. Birds and beasts you will see behaving somewhat intimately to me, like that moorhen, but that is all. I will walk with you, ride with you, play golf with you, and talk with you on any subject you like. But I wanted you on the threshold to know what has happened to me. And one thing more will happen."

He paused again, and a slight look of fear crossed his eyes.

"There will be a final revelation," he said, "a complete and blinding stroke which will throw open to me, once and for all, the full knowledge, the full realisation and comprehension that I am one, just as you are, with life. In reality there is no 'me,' no 'you,' no 'it.' Everything is part of the one and only thing which is life. I know that that is so, but the realisation of it is not yet mine.

"But it will be, and on that day, so I take it, I shall see Pan. It may mean death, the death of my body, that is, but I don't care. It may mean immortal, eternal life lived here and now and for ever.

"Then having gained that, ah, my dear Darcy, I shall preach such a gospel of joy, showing myself as the living proof of the truth, that Puritanism, the dismal religion of sour faces, shall vanish like a breath of smoke, and be dispersed and disappear in the sunlit air. But first the full knowledge must be mine."

Darcy watched his face narrowly.

"You are afraid of that moment," he said. Frank smiled at him.

"Quite true; you are quick to have seen that. But when it comes I hope I shall not be afraid."

For some little time there was silence; then Darcy rose. "You have bewitched me, you extraordinary boy," he said. "You have been telling me a fairy-story, and I find myself saying, 'Promise me it is true.'"

"I promise you that," said the other.

"And I know I shan't sleep," added Darcy.

Frank looked at him with a sort of mild wonder as if he scarcely understood.

"Well, what does that matter?" he said.

"I assure you it does. I am wretched unless I sleep."

"Of course I can make you sleep if I want," said Frank in a rather bored voice.

"Well, do."

"Very good: go to bed. I'll come upstairs in ten minutes."

Frank busied himself for a little after the other had gone, moving the table back under the awning of the verandah and quenching the lamp. Then he went with his quick silent tread upstairs and into Darcy's room. The latter was already in bed, but very wide-eyed and wakeful, and Frank with an amused smile of indulgence, as for a fretful child, sat down on the edge of the bed.

"Look at me," he said, and Darcy looked.

"The birds are sleeping in the brake," said Frank softly, "and the winds are asleep. The sea sleeps, and the tides are but the heaving of its breast. The stars swing slow, rocked in the great cradle of the Heavens, and—"

He stopped suddenly, gently blew out Darcy's candle, and left him sleeping.

Morning brought to Darcy a flood of hard common sense, as clear and crisp as the sunshine that filled his room. Slowly as he woke he gathered together the broken threads of the memories of the evening which had ended, so he told himself, in a trick of common hypnotism. That accounted for it all; the whole strange talk he had had was under a spell of suggestion from the extraordinary vivid boy who had once been a man; all his own excitement, his acceptance of the incredible had been merely the effect of a stronger, more potent will imposed on his own. How strong that will was, he guessed from his own instantaneous obedience to

Frank's suggestion of sleep. And armed with impenetrable common sense he came down to breakfast. Frank had already begun, and was consuming a large plateful of porridge and milk with the most prosaic and healthy appetite.

"Slept well?" he asked.

"Yes, of course. Where did you learn hypnotism?"

"By the side of the river."

"You talked an amazing quantity of nonsense last night," remarked Darcy, in a voice prickly with reason.

"Rather. I felt quite giddy. Look, I remembered to order a dreadful daily paper for you. You can read about money markets or politics or cricket matches." Darcy looked at him closely. In the morning light Frank looked even fresher, younger, more vital than he had done the night before, and the sight of him somehow dinted Darcy's armour of common sense.

"You are the most extraordinary fellow I ever saw," he said. "I want to ask you some more questions."

"Ask away," said Frank.

For the next day or two Darcy plied his friend with many questions, objections and criticisms on the theory of life, and gradually got out of him a coherent and complete account of his experience. In brief, then, Frank believed that "by lying naked," as he put it, to the force which controls the passage of the stars, the breaking of a wave, the budding of a tree, the love of a youth and maiden, he had succeeded in a way hitherto undreamed of in possessing himself of the essential principle of life. Day by day, so he thought, he was getting nearer to, and in closer union with, the great power itself which caused all life to be, the spirit of nature, of force, or the spirit of God. For himself, he confessed to what others would call paganism; it was sufficient for him that there existed a principle of life. He did not worship it, he did not pray to it, he did not praise it. Some of it existed in all human beings, just as it existed in trees and animals; to realise and make living to himself the fact that it was all one, was his sole aim and object.

Here perhaps Darcy would put in a word of warning.

"Take care," he said. "To see Pan meant death, did it not."

Frank's eyebrows would rise at this.

"What does that matter?" he said. "True, the Greeks were always right, and they said so, but there is another possibility. For the nearer I get to it, the more living, the more vital and young I become."

"What then do you expect the final revelation will do for you?"

"I have told you," said he. "It will make me immortal."

But it was not so much from speech and argument that Darcy grew to grasp his friend's conception, as from the ordinary conduct of his life. They were passing, for instance, one morning down the village street, when an old woman, very bent and decrepit, but with an extraordinary cheerfulness of face, hobbled out from her cottage. Frank instantly stopped when he saw her.

"You old darling! How goes it all?" he said.

But she did not answer, her dim old eyes were riveted on his face; she seemed to drink in like a thirsty creature the beautiful radiance which shone there. Suddenly she put her two withered old hands on his shoulders.

"You're just the sunshine itself," she said, and he kissed her and passed on.

But scarcely a hundred yards further a strange contradiction of such tenderness occurred. A child running along the path towards them fell on its face and set up a dismal cry of fright and pain. A look of horror came into Frank's eyes, and, putting his fingers in his ears, he fled at full speed down the street, and did not pause till he was out of hearing. Darcy, having ascertained that the child was not really hurt, followed him in bewilderment.

"Are you without pity then?" he asked. Frank shook his head impatiently.

"Can't you see?" he asked. "Can't you understand that that sort of thing, pain, anger, anything unlovely, throws me back, retards the coming of the great hour! Perhaps when it comes I shall be able to piece that side of life on to the other, on to the true religion of joy. At present I can't."

"But the old woman. Was she not ugly?"

Frank's radiance gradually returned.

"Ah, no. She was like me. She longed for joy, and knew it when she saw it, the old darling."

Another question suggested itself.

"Then what about Christianity?" asked Darcy.

"I can't accept it. I can't believe in any creed of which the central doctrine is that God who is Joy should have had to suffer. Perhaps it was so; in some inscrutable way I believe it may have been so, but I don't understand how it was possible. So I leave it alone; my affair is joy."

They had come to the weir above the village, and the thunder of riotous cool water was heavy in the air. Trees dipped into the translucent stream with slender trailing branches, and the meadow where they stood was starred with midsummer blossomings. Larks shot up carolling into the crystal dome of blue, and a thousand voices of June sang round them. Frank, bare-headed as was his wont, with his coat slung over his arm and his shirt sleeves rolled up above the elbow, stood there like some beautiful wild animal with eyes half-shut and mouth half-open, drinking in the scented warmth of the air. Then suddenly he flung himself face downwards on the grass at the edge of the stream, burying his face in the daisies and cowslips, and lay stretched there in wide-armed ecstasy, with his long fingers pressing and stroking the dewy herbs of the field. Never before had Darcy seen him thus fully possessed by his idea; his caressing fingers, his half-buried face pressed close to the grass, even the clothed lines of his figure were instinct with a vitality that somehow was different from that of other men. And some faint glow from it reached Darcy, some thrill, some vibration from that charged recumbent body passed to him, and for a moment he understood as he had not understood before, despite his persistent questions and the candid answers they received, how real, and how realised by Frank, his idea was.

Then suddenly the muscles in Frank's neck became stiff and alert, and he half-raised his head.

"The Pan-pipes, the Pan-pipes," he whispered. "Close, oh, so close."

Very slowly, as if a sudden movement might interrupt the melody, he raised himself and leaned on the elbow of his bent arm. His eyes opened wider, the lower lids drooped as if he focussed his eyes on something very far away, and the smile on his face broadened and quivered like sunlight on still water, till the exultance of its happiness was scarcely human. So he remained motionless and rapt for some minutes, then the look of listening died from his face, and he bowed his head, satisfied.

"Ah, that was good," he said. "How is it possible you did not hear? Oh, you poor fellow! Did you really hear nothing?"

A week of this outdoor and stimulating life did wonders in restoring to Darcy the vigour and health which his weeks of fever had filched from him, and as his normal activity and higher pressure of vitality returned, he seemed to himself to fall even more under the spell which the miracle of Frank's youth cast over him. Twenty times a day he found himself saying to himself suddenly at the end of some ten minutes silent resistance to the absurdity of Frank's idea: "But it isn't possible; it can't be possible," and from the fact of his having to assure himself so frequently of this, he knew that he was struggling and arguing with a conclusion which already had taken root in his mind. For in any case a visible living miracle confronted him, since it was equally impossible that this youth, this boy, trembling on the verge of manhood, was thirty-five.

Yet such was the fact.

July was ushered in by a couple of days of blustering and fretful rain, and Darcy, unwilling to risk a chill, kept to the house. But to Frank this weeping change of weather seemed to have no bearing on the behaviour of man, and he spent his days exactly as he did under the suns of June, lying in his hammock, stretched on the dripping grass, or making huge rambling excursions into the forest, the birds hopping from tree to tree after him, to return in the evening, drenched and soaked, but with the same unquenchable flame of joy burning within him.

"Catch cold?" he would ask; "I've forgotten how to do it, I think I suppose it makes one's body more sensible always to sleep out-of-doors. People who live indoors always remind me of something peeled and skinless."

"Do you mean to say you slept out-of-doors last night in that deluge?" asked Darcy. "And where, may I ask?"

Frank thought a moment.

"I slept in the hammock till nearly dawn," he said. "For I remember the light blinked in the east when I awoke. Then I went—where did I go—oh, yes, to the meadow where the Pan-pipes sounded so close a week ago. You were with me, do you remember? But I always have a rug if it is wet."

And he went whistling upstairs.

Somehow that little touch, his obvious effort to recall where he had slept, brought strangely home to Darcy the wonderful romance of which he was the still half-incredulous beholder. Sleep till close on dawn in a hammock, then the tramp—or probably scamper—underneath the windy and weeping heavens to the remote and lonely meadow by the weir! The picture of other such nights rose before him; Frank sleeping perhaps by the bathing-place under the filtered twilight of the stars, or the white blaze of moon-shine, a stir and awakening at some dead hour, perhaps a space of silent wide-eyed thought, and then awandering through the hushed woods to some other dormitory, alone with his happiness, alone with the joy and the life that suffused and enveloped him, without other thought or desire or aim except the hourly and never-ceasing communion with the joy of nature.

They were in the middle of dinner that night, talking on indifferent subjects, when Darcy suddenly broke off in the middle of a sentence.

"I've got it," he said. "At last I've got it."

"Congratulate you," said Frank. "But what?"

"The radical unsoundness of your idea. It is this: All Nature from highest to lowest is full, crammed full of suffering; every living organism in Nature preys on another, yet in your aim to get close to, to be one with Nature, you leave suffering altogether out; you run away from it, you refuse to recognise it. And you are waiting, you say, for the final revelation."

Frank's brow clouded slightly.

"Well," he asked, rather wearily.

"Cannot you guess then when the final revelation will be? In joy you are supreme, I grant you that; I did not know a man could be so master of it. You have learned perhaps practically all that Nature can teach. And if, as you think, the final revelation is coming to you, it will be the revelation of horror, suffering, death, pain in all its hideous forms. Suffering does exist: you hate it and fear it."

Frank held up his hand.

"Stop; let me think," he said.

There was silence for a long minute.

"That never struck me," he said at length. "It is possible that what you suggest is true. Does the sight of Pan mean that, do you think? Is it that Nature, take it altogether, suffers horribly, suffers to a hideous inconceivable extent? Shall I be shown all the suffering?" He got up and came round to where Darcy sat.

"If it is so, so be it," he said. "Because, my dear fellow, I am near, so splendidly near to the final revelation. To-day the pipes have sounded almost without pause. I have even heard the rustle in the bushes, I believe, of Pan's coming. I have seen, yes, I saw to-day, the bushes pushed aside as if by a hand, and piece of a face, not human, peered through. But I was not frightened, at least I did not run away this time."

He took a turn up to the window and back again.

"Yes, there is suffering all through," he said, "and I have left it all out of my search. Perhaps, as you say, the revelation will be that. And in that case, it will be good-bye. I have gone on one line. I shall have gone too far along one road, without having explored the other. But I can't go back now. I wouldn't if I could; not a step would I retrace! In any case, whatever the revelation is, it will be God. I'm sure of that."

The rainy weather soon passed, and with the return of the sun Darcy again joined Frank in long rambling days. It grew extraordinarily hotter, and with the fresh bursting of life, after the rain, Frank's vitality seemed to blaze higher and higher. Then, as is the habit of the English weather, one evening clouds began to bank themselves up in the west, the sun went down in a glare of coppery thunder-rack, and the whole earth broiling under an unspeakable oppression and sultriness paused and panted for the storm. After sunset the remote fires of lightning began to wink and flicker on the horizon, but when bed-time came the storm seemed to have moved no nearer, though a very low unceasing noise of thunder was audible. Weary and oppressed by the stress of the day, Darcy fell at once into a heavy uncomforting sleep.

He woke suddenly into full consciousness, with the din of some appalling explosion of thunder in his ears, and sat up in bed with racing heart. Then for a moment, as he recovered himself from the panic-land which lies between sleeping and waking, there was silence, except for the steady hissing of rain on the shrubs outside his window. But suddenly that silence was shattered and shredded into fragments by a scream from somewhere close at hand outside in the black garden, a scream of supreme and despairing terror. Again and once again it shrilled up, and then a babble of awful words was interjected. A quivering sobbing voice that he knew said, "My God, oh, my God; oh, Christ!" And then followed a little mocking, bleating laugh. Then was silence again; only the rain hissed on the shrubs.

All this was but the affair of a moment, and without pause either to put on clothes or light a candle, Darcy was already fumbling at his door-handle. Even as he opened it he met a terror-stricken face outside, that of the man-servant who carried a light.

"Did you hear?" he asked.

The man's face was bleached to a dull shining whiteness. "Yes, sir," he said. "It was the master's voice."

Together they hurried down the stairs and through the dining-room where an orderly table for breakfast had already been laid, and out on to the terrace. The rain for the moment had been utterly stayed, as if the tap of the heavens had been turned off, and under the lowering black sky, not quite dark, since the moon rode somewhere serene behind the conglomerated thunder-clouds, Darcy stumbled into the garden, followed by the servant with the candle. The monstrous leaping shadow of himself was cast before him on the lawn; lost and wandering odours of rose and lily and damp earth were thick about him, but more pungent was some sharp and acrid smell that suddenly reminded him of a certain chalet in which he had once taken refuge in the Alps. In the blackness of the hazy light from the sky, and the vague tossing of the candle behind him, he saw that the hammock in which Frank so often lay was tenanted. A gleam of white shirt was there, as if a man were sitting up in it, but across that there was an obscure dark shadow, and as he approached the acrid odour grew more intense.

He was now only some few yards away, when suddenly the black shadow seemed to jump into the air, then came down with tappings of hard hoofs on the brick path that ran down the pergola, and with frolicsome skippings galloped off into the bushes. When that was gone Darcy could see quite clearly that a shirted figure sat up in the hammock. For one moment, from sheer terror of the unseen, he hung on his step, and the servant joining him they walked together to the hammock.

It was Frank. He was in shirt and trousers only, and he sat up with braced arms. For one half-second he stared at them, his face a mask of horrible contorted terror. His upper lip was drawn back so that the gums of the teeth appeared, and his eyes were focussed not on the two who approached him, but on something quite close to him; his nostrils were widely expanded, as if he panted for breath, and terror incarnate and repulsion and deathly anguish ruled dreadful lines on his smooth cheeks and forehead. Then even as they looked the body sank backwards, and the ropes of the hammock wheezed and strained.

Darcy lifted him out and carried him indoors. Once he thought there was a faint convulsive stir of the limbs that lay with so dead a weight in his arms, but when they got inside, there was no trace of life. But the look of supreme terror and agony of fear had gone from his face, a boy tired with play but still smiling in his sleep was the burden he laid on the floor. His eyes had closed, and the beautiful mouth lay in smiling curves, even as when a few mornings ago, in the meadow by the weir, it had quivered to the music of the unheard melody of Pan's pipes. Then they looked further.

Frank had come back from his bathe before dinner that night in his usual costume of shirt and trousers only. He had not dressed, and during dinner, so Darcy remembered, he had rolled up the sleeves of his shirt to above the elbow. Later, as they sat and talked after dinner on the close sultriness of the evening, he had unbuttoned the front of his shirt to let what little breath of wind there was play on his skin. The sleeves were rolled up now, the front of the shirt was unbuttoned, and on his arms and on the brown skin of his chest were strange discolorations which grew momently more clear and defined, till they saw that the marks were pointed prints, as if caused by the hoofs of some monstrous goat that had leaped and stamped upon him.

AMINA

Edward Lucas White

Waldo, brought face to face with the actuality of the unbelievable—as he himself would have worded it—was completely dazed. In silence he suffered the consul to lead him from the tepid gloom of the interior, through the ruinous doorway, out into the hot, stunning brilliance of the desert landscape. Hassan followed, with never a look behind him. Without any word he had taken Waldo's gun from his nerveless hand and carried it, with his own and the consul's.

The consul strode across the gravelly sand, some fifty paces from the southwest corner of the tomb, to a bit of not wholly ruined wall from which there was a clear view of the doorway side of the tomb and of the side with the larger crevice.

"Hassan," he commanded, "watch here."

Hassan said something in Persian.

"How many cubs were there?" the consul asked Waldo. Waldo stared mute.

"How many young ones did you see?" the consul asked again.

"Twenty or more," Waldo made answer.

"That's impossible," snapped the consul.

"There seemed to be sixteen or eighteen," Waldo asserted. Hassan smiled and grunted. The consul took from him two guns, handed Waldo his, and they walked around the tomb to a point about equally distant from the opposite corner. There was another bit of ruin, and in front of it, on the side toward the tomb, was a block of stone mostly in the shadow of the wall.

"Convenient," said the consul. "Sit on that stone and lean against the wall, make yourself comfortable. You are a bit shaken, but you will be all right in a moment. You should have something to eat, but we have nothing. Anyhow, take a good swallow of this."

He stood by him as Waldo gasped over the raw brandy.

"Hassan will bring you his water-bottle before he goes," the consul went on; "drink plenty, for you must stay here for some time. And now, pay attention to me. We must extirpate these vermin. The male, I judge, is absent. If he had been anywhere about, you would not now be alive. The young cannot be as many as you say, but, I take it, we have to deal with ten, a full litter. We must smoke them out. Hassan will go back to camp after fuel and the guard. Meanwhile, you and I must see that none escape."

He took Waldo's gun, opened the breech, shut it, examined the magazine and handed it back to him.

"Now watch me closely," he said. He paced off, looking to his left past the tomb. Presently he stopped and gathered several stones together.

"You see these?" he called.

Waldo shouted an affirmation.

The consul came back, passed on in the same line, looking to his right past the tomb, and presently, at a similar distance, put up another tiny cairn, shouted again and was again answered. Again he returned.

"Now you are sure you cannot mistake those two marks I have made?"

"Very sure indeed," said Waldo.

"It is important, warned the consul. "I am going back to where I left Hassan, to watch there while he is gone. You will watch here. You may pace as often as you like to either of those stone heaps. From either you can see me on my beat. Do not diverge from the line from one to the other. For as soon as Hassan is out of sight I shall shoot any moving thing I see nearer. Sit here till you see me set up similar limits for my sentry—go on the farther side, then shoot any moving thing not on my line of patrol. Keep a lookout all around you. There is one chance in a million that the male might return in daylight—mostly, they are nocturnal, but this lair is evidently exceptional. Keep a bright lookout.

"And now listen to me. You must not feel any foolish sentimentalism about any fancied resemblance of these vermin to human beings. Shoot, and shoot to kill. Not only is it our duty, in general, to abolish them, but it will be very dangerous for us if we do not. There is little or no solidarity in Mohammedan communities, but on the comparatively few points upon which public opinion exists it acts with amazing promptitude and vigor. One matter as to which there is no disagreement is that it is incumbent upon every man to assist in eradicating these creatures. The good old Biblical custom of stoning to death is the mode of lynching indigenous hereabouts. These modern Asiatics are quite capable of applying it to anyone believed derelict against any of these inimical monsters. If we let one escape and the rumor of it gets about, we may precipitate an outburst of racial prejudice difficult to cope with. Shoot, I say, without hesitation or mercy."

"I understand," said Waldo.

"I don't care whether you understand or not," said the consul, "I want you to act. Shoot if needful, and shoot straight." And he tramped off.

Hassan presently appeared, and Waldo drank from his water-bottle as nearly all of its contents as Hassan would permit. After his departure Waldo's first alertness soon gave place to mere endurance of the monotony of watching and the intensity of the heat. His discomfort became suffering, and what with the fury of the dry glare, the pangs of thirst and his bewilderment of mind, Waldo was moving in a waking dream by the time Hassan returned with two donkeys and a mule laden with brushwood. Behind the beasts straggled the guard.

Waldo's trance became a nightmare when the smoke took effect and the battle began. He was, however, not only not required to join in the killing, but was enjoined to keep back. He did keep very much in the background, seeing only so much of the slaughter as his curiosity would not let him refrain from viewing. Yet he felt all a murderer as he gazed at the ten small carcasses laid out arow, and the memory of his vigil and its end, indeed of the whole day, though it was the day of his most marvelous adventure, remains to him as the broken recollections of a phantasmagoria.

On the morning of his memorable peril Waldo had waked early. The experiences of his sea-voyage, the sights at Gibraltar, at Port Said, in the canal, at Suez, at Aden, at Muscat, and at Basrah had formed an altogether inadequate transition from the decorous regularity of house and school life in New England to the breathless wonder of the desert immensities.

Everything seemed unreal, and yet the reality of its strangeness so besieged him that he could not feel at home in it, he could not sleep heavily in a tent. After composing himself to sleep, he lay long conscious and awakened early, as on this morning, just at the beginning of the false dawn.

The consul was fast asleep, snoring loudly. Waldo dressed quietly and went out; mechanically, without any purpose or forethought, taking his gun. Outside he found Hassan, seated, his gun across his knees, his head sunk forward, as fast asleep as the consul. Ali and Ibrahim had left the camp the day before for supplies. Waldo was the only waking creature about; for the guards, camped some little distance off, were but logs about the ashes of their fire. Meaning merely to enjoy, under the white glow of the false dawn, the magical reappearance of the constellations and the short last glory of the star-laden firmament, that brief coolness which compensated a trifle for the hot morning, the fiery day and the warmish night, he seated himself on a rock, some paces from the tent and twice as far from the guards. Turning his gun in his hands he felt an irresistible temptation to wander off by himself, to stroll alone through the fascinating emptiness of the arid landscape.

When he had begun camp life he had expected to find the consul, that combination of sportsman, explorer and archaeologist, a particularly easygoing guardian. He had looked forward to absolutely untrameled liberty in the spacious expanse of the limitless wastes. The reality he had found exactly the reverse of his preconceptions. The consul's first injunction was:

"Never let yourself get out of sight of me or of Hassan unless he or I send you off with Ali or Ibrahim. Let nothing tempt you to roam about alone. Even a ramble is dangerous. You might lose sight of the camp before you knew it."

At first Waldo acquiesced, later he protested. "I have a good pocket compass. I know how to use it. I never lost my way in the Maine woods."

"No Kourds in the Maine woods," said the consul.

Yet before long Waldo noticed that the few Kourds they encountered seemed simple-hearted, peaceful folk. No semblance of danger or even of adventure had appeared. Their armed guard of a dozen greasy tatterdemalions had passed their time in uneasy loafing.

Likewise Waldo noticed that the consul seemed indifferent to the ruins they passed by or encamped among, that his feeling for sites and topography was cooler than lukewarm, that he showed no ardor in the pursuit of the scanty and uninteresting game. He had picked up enough of several dialects to hear repeated conversations about "them." "Have you heard of any about here?" "Has one been killed?" "Any traces of them in this district?" And such queries he could make out in the various talks with the natives they met, as to what "they" were he received no enlightenment.

Then he had questioned Hassan as to why he was so restricted in his movements. Hassan spoke some English and regaled him with tales of Afrits, ghouls, specters and other uncanny legendary presences; of the jinn of the waste, appearing in human shape, talking all languages, ever on the alert to ensnare infidels; of the woman whose feet turned the wrong way at the ankles, luring the unwary to a pool and there drowning her victims; of the malignant ghosts of dead brigands, more terrible than their living fellows; of the spirit in the shape of a wild ass, or of a gazelle, enticing its pursuers to the brink of a precipice and itself seeming to run ahead upon an expanse of sand, a mere mirage, dissolving as the victim passed the brink and fell to death; of the sprite in the semblance of a hare feigning a limp, or of a ground bird feigning a broken wing, drawing its pursuer after it till he met death in an unseen pit or well shaft.

Ali and Ibrahim spoke no English. As far as Waldo could understand their long harangues, they told similar stories or hinted at dangers equally vague and imaginary. These childish bogy-tales merely whetted Waldo's craving for independence.

Now, as he sat on a rock, longing to enjoy the perfect sky, the clear, early air, the wide, lonely landscape, along with the sense of having it to himself, it seemed to him that the consul was merely innately cautious, overcautious. There was no danger. He would have a fine leisurely stroll, kill something perhaps, and certainly be back in camp before the sun grew hot. He stood up.

Some hours later he was seated on a fallen coping stone in the shadow of a ruined tomb. All the country they had been traversing is full of tombs and remains of tombs, prehistoric, Bactrian, old Persian, Parthian, Sassanian, or Mohammedan, scattered everywhere in groups or solitary. Vanished utterly are the faintest traces of the cities, towns, and villages, ephemeral houses or temporary huts, in which had lived the countless generations of mourners who had reared these tombs.

The tombs, built more durably than mere dwellings of the living, remained. Complete or ruinous, or reduced to mere fragments, they were everywhere. In that district they were all of one type. Each was domed and below was square, its one door facing eastward and opening into a large empty room, behind which were the mortuary chambers.

In the shadow of such a tomb Waldo sat. He had shot nothing, had lost his way, had no idea of the direction of the camp, was tired, warm, and thirsty. He had forgotten his water-bottle.

He swept his gaze over the vast, desolate prospect, the unvaried turquoise of the sky arched above the rolling desert. Far reddish hills along the skyline hooped in the less distant brown hillocks which, without diversifying it, hummocked the yellow landscape. Sand and rocks with a lean, starved bush or two made up the nearer view, broken here and there by dazzling white or streaked, grayish, crumbling ruins. The sun had not been long above the horizon, yet the whole surface of the desert was quivering with heat.

As Waldo sat viewing the outlook a woman came round the corner of the tomb. All the village women Waldo had seen had worn yashmaks or some other form of face covering or veil. This woman was bareheaded and unveiled. She wore some sort of yellowish-brown garment which enveloped her from neck to ankles, showing no waist line. Her feet, in defiance of the blistering sands, were bare.

At sight of Waldo she stopped and stared at him as he at her. He remarked the un-European posture of her feet, not at all turned out, but with the inner lines parallel. She wore no anklets, he observed, no bracelets, no necklace or earrings. Her bare arms he thought the most muscular he had ever seen on a human being. Her nails were pointed and long, both on her hands and feet. Her hair was black, short, and tousled, yet she did not look wild or uncomely. Her eyes smiled and her lips had the effect of smiling, though they did not part ever so little, not showing at all the teeth behind them.

"What a pity," said Waldo aloud, "that she does not speak English."

"I do speak English," said the woman, and Waldo noticed that as she spoke, her lips did not perceptibly open. "What does the gentleman want?"

"You speak English!" Waldo exclaimed, jumping to his feet. "What luck! Where did you learn it?"

"At the mission school," she replied, an amused smile playing about the corners of her rather wide, unopening mouth. "What can be done for you?" She spoke with scarcely any foreign accent, but very slowly and with a sort of growl running along from syllable to syllable.

"I am thirsty," said Waldo, "and I have lost my way."

"Is the gentleman living in a brown tent, shaped like half a melon?" she inquired, the queer, rumbling note drawling from one word to the next, her lips barely separated.

"Yes, that is our camp," said Waldo.

"I could guide the gentleman that way," she droned; "but it is far, and there is no water on that side."

"I want water first," said Waldo, "or milk."

"If you mean cow's milk, we have none. But we have goat's milk. There is to drink where I dwell," she said, sing-songing the words. "It is not far. It is the other way."

"Show me," said he.

She began to walk, Waldo, his gun under his arm, beside her. She trod noiselessly and fast. Waldo could scarcely keep up with her. As they walked he often fell behind and noted how her swathing garments clung to a lithe, shapely back, neat waist, and firm hips. Each time he hurried and caught up with her, he scanned her with intermittent glances, puzzled that her waist, so well-marked at the spine, showed no particular definition in front; that the outline of her from neck to knees, perfectly shapeless under her wrappings, was without any waistline or suggestion of firmness or undulation. Likewise he remarked the amused flicker in her eyes and the compressed line of her red, her too-red lips.

"How long were you in the mission school?" he inquired.

"Four years," she replied.

"Are you a Christian?" he asked.

"The Free-folk do not submit to baptism," she stated simply, but with rather more of the droning growl between her words.

He felt a queer shiver as he watched the scarcely moved lips through which the syllables edged their way.

"But you are not veiled," he could not resist saying.

"The Free-folk," she rejoined, "are never veiled."

"Then you are not a Mohammedan?" he ventured.

"The Free-folk are not Moslems."

"Who are the Free-folk?" he blurted out incautiously.

She shot one baleful glance at him. Waldo remembered that he had to do with an Asiatic. He recalled the three permitted questions.

"What is your name?" he inquired.

"Amina," she told him.

"That is a name from the 'Arabian Nights'," he hazarded.

"From the foolish tales of the believers," she sneered. "The Free-folk know nothing of such follies." The unvarying shutness of her speaking lips, the drawly burr between the syllables, struck him all the more as her lips curled but did not open.

"You utter your words in a strange way," he said.

"Your language is not mine," she replied.

"How is it that you learned my language at the mission school and are not a Christian?"

"They teach all at the mission school," she said, "and the maidens of the Free-folk are like the other maidens they teach, though the Free-folk when grown are not as town-dwellers are. Therefore they taught me as any town-bred girl, not knowing me for what I am."

"They taught you well," he commented.

"I have the gift of tongues," she uttered enigmatically, with an odd note of triumph burring the words through her unmoving lips.

Waldo felt a horrid shudder all over him, not only at her uncanny words, but also from mere faintness.

"Is it far to your home?" he breathed.

"It is there," she said, pointing to the doorway of a large tomb just before them.

The wholly open arch admitted them into a fairly spacious interior, cool with the abiding temperature of thick masonry. There was no rubbish on the floor. Waldo, relieved to escape the blistering glare outside, seated himself on a block of stone midway between the door and the inner partition wall, resting his gun butt on the floor. For the moment he was blinded by the change from the insistent brilliance of the desert morning to the blurred gray light of the interior.

When his sight cleared he looked about and remarked, opposite the door, the ragged hole which laid open the desecrated mausoleum. As his eyes grew accustomed to the dimness he was so startled that he stood up. It seemed to him that from its four corners the room swarmed with naked children. To his inexperienced conjecture they seemed about two years old, but they moved with the assurance of boys of eight or ten.

"Whose are these children?" he exclaimed.

"Mine," she said.

"All yours?" he protested.

"All mine," she replied, a curious suppressed boisterousness in her demeanor.

"But there are twenty of them," he cried.

"You count badly in the dark," she told him. "There are fewer."

"There certainly are a dozen," he maintained, spinning round as they danced and scampered about.

"The Free-people have large families," she said.

"But they are all of one age," Waldo exclaimed, his tongue dry against the roof of his mouth.

She laughed, an unpleasant, mocking laugh, clapping her hands. She was between him and the doorway, and as most of the light came from it he could not see her lips.

"Is not that like a man! No woman would have made that mistake."

Waldo was confuted and sat down again. The children circulated around him, chattering, laughing, giggling, snickering, making noises indicative of glee.

"Please get me something cool to drink," said Waldo, and his tongue was not only dry but big in his mouth.

"We shall have to drink shortly," she said, "but it will be warm."

Waldo began to feel uneasy. The children pranced around him, jabbering strange, guttural noises, licking their lips, pointing at him, their eyes fixed on him, with now and then a glance at their mother.

"Where is the water?"

The woman stood silent, her arms hanging at her sides, and it seemed to Waldo she was shorter than she had been.

"Where is the water?" he repeated.

"Patience, patience," she growled, and came a step near to him.

The sunlight struck upon her back and made a sort of halo about her hips. She seemed still shorter than before. There was a something furtive in her bearing, and the little ones sniggered evilly.

At that instant two rifle shots rang out almost as one. The woman fell face downward on the floor. The babies shrieked in a shrill chorus. Then she leapt up from all fours with an explosive suddenness, staggered in a hurled, lurching rush toward the hole in the wall, and, with a frightful yell, threw up her arms and whirled backward to the ground, doubled and contorted like a dying fish, stiffened, shuddered and was still. Waldo, his horrified eyes fixed on her face, even in his amazement noted that her lips did not open.

The children, squealing faint cries of dismay, scrambled through the hole in the inner wall, vanishing into the inky void beyond. The last had hardly gone when the consul appeared in the doorway, his smoking gun in his hand.

"Not a second too soon, my boy," he ejaculated. "She was just going to spring."

He cocked his gun and prodded the body with the muzzle.

"Good and dead," he commented. "What luck! Generally it takes three or four bullets to finish one. I've known one with two bullets through her lungs to kill a man.

"Did you murder this woman?" Waldo demanded fiercely.

"Murder?" the consul snorted. "Murder! Look at that."

He knelt down and pulled open the full, close lips, disclosing not human teeth, but small incisors, cusped grinders, wide-spaced; and long, keen, overlapping canines, like those of a greyhound: a fierce, deadly, carnivorous dentition, menacing and combative.

Waldo felt a qualm, yet the face and form still swayed his horrified sympathy for their humanness.

"Do you shoot women because they have long teeth?" Waldo insisted, revolted at the horrid death he had watched.

"You are hard to convince," said the consul sternly. "Do you call that a woman?"

He stripped the clothing from the carcass.

Waldo sickened all over. What he saw was not the front of a woman, but more like the underside of an old fox-terrier with puppies, or of a white sow, with her second litter; from collarbone to groin ten lolloping udders, two rows, mauled, stringy, and flaccid.

"What kind of a creature is it?" he asked faintly.

"A Ghoul, my boy," the consul answered solemnly, almost in a whisper.

"I thought they did not exist," Waldo babbled. "I thought they were mythical; I thought there were none.

"I can very well believe that there are none in Rhode Island," the consul said gravely. "This is in Persia, and Persia is in Asia."

Lukundoo

Edward Lucas White

"It stands to reason," said Twombly, "that a man must accept of his own eyes, and when eyes and ears agree, there can be no doubt. He has to believe what he has both seen and heard."

"Not always," put in Singleton, softly.

Every man turned toward Singleton. Twombly was standing on hearthrug, his back to the grate, his legs spread out, with his habitual air of dominating the room. Singleton, as usual, was as much as possible effaced in a corner. But when Singleton spoke he said something. We faced him in that flattering spontaneity of expectant silence which invites utterance.

"I was thinking," he said, after an interval, "of something I both saw and heard in Africa."

Now, if there was one thing we had found impossible, it had been to elicit from Singleton anything definite about his African experiences. As with the Alpinist in the story, who could tell only that he went up and came down, the sum of Singleton's revelations had been that he went there and came away. His words now riveted our attention at once. Twombly faded from the hearthrug, but not one of us could ever recall having seen him go. The room readjusted itself, focused on Singleton, and there was some hasty and furtive lighting of fresh cigars. Singleton lit one also, but it went out immediately, and he never relit it.

I

We were in the Great Forest, exploring for pigmies. Van Rieten had a theory that the dwarfs found by Stanley and others were a

117

mere cross-breed between ordinary negroes and the real pigmies. He hoped to discover a race of men three feet tall at most, or shorter. We had found no trace of any such beings.

Natives were few, game scarce; food, except game, there was none; and the deepest, dankest, drippingest forest all about. We were the only novelty in the country, no native we met had ever seen a white man before, most had never heard of white men. All of a sudden, late one afternoon, there came into our camp an Englishman, and pretty well used up he was, too. We had heard no rumor of him; he had not only heard of us but had made an amazing five-day march to reach us. His guide and two bearers were nearly as done up as he. Even though he was in tatters and had five days' beard on, you could see he was naturally dapper and neat and the sort of man to shave daily. He was small, but wiry. His face was the sort of British face from which emotion has been so carefully banished that a foreigner is apt to think the wearer of the face incapable of any sort of feeling; the kind of face which, if it has any expression at all, expresses principally the resolution to go through the world decorously, without intruding upon or annoying anyone.

His name was Etcham. He introduced himself modestly, and ate with us so deliberately that we should never have suspected, if our bearers had not had it from his bearers, that he had had but three meals in the five days, and those small. After we had lit up he told us why he had come.

"My chief is ve'y seedy," he said between puffs. "He is bound to go out if he keeps this way. I thought perhaps. . . ."

He spoke quietly in a soft, even tone, but I could see little beads of sweat oozing out on his upper lip under his stubby mustache, and there was a tingle of repressed emotion in his tone, a veiled eagerness in his eye, a palpitating inward solicitude in his demeanor that moved me at once. Van Rieten had no sentiment in him; if he was moved he did not show it. But he listened. I was surprised at that. He was just the man to refuse at once. But he listened to Etcham's halting, difficult hints. He even asked questions.

"Who is your chief?"

"Stone," Etcham lisped.

That electrified both of us.

"Ralph Stone?" we ejaculated together.

Etcham nodded.

For some minutes Van Rieten and I were silent. Van Rieten had never seen him, but I had been a classmate of Stone's, and Van Rieten and I had discussed him over many a campfire. We had heard of him two years before, south of Luebo in the Balunda country, which had been ringing with his theatrical strife against a Balunda witch-doctor, ending in the sorcerer's complete discomfiture and the abasement of his tribe before Stone. They had even broken the fetish-man's whistle and given Stone the pieces. It had been like the triumph of Elijah over the prophets of Baal, only more real to the Balunda.

We had thought of Stone as far off, if still in Africa at all, and here he turned up ahead of us and probably forestalling our quest.

II

Etcham's naming of Stone brought back to us all his tantalizing story, his fascinating parents, their tragic death; the brilliance of his college days; the dazzle of his millions; the promise of his young manhood; his wide notoriety, so nearly real fame; his romantic elopement with the meteoric authoress whose sudden cascade of fiction had made her so great a name so young, whose beauty and charm were so much heralded; the frightful scandal of the breach-of-promise suit that followed; his bride's devotion through it all; their sudden quarrel after it was all over; their divorce; the too much advertised announcement of his approaching marriage to the plaintiff in the breach-of-promise suit; his precipitate remarriage to his divorced bride; their second quarrel and second divorce; his departure from his native land; his advent in the dark continent. The sense of all this rushed over me and I believe Van Rieten felt it, too, as he sat silent.

Then he asked:

"Where is Werner?"

"Dead," said Etcham. "He died before I joined Stone."

"You were not with Stone above Luebo?"

"No," said Etcham, "I joined him at Stanley Falls."

"Who is with him?" Van Rieten asked.

"Only his Zanzibar servants and the bearers," Etcham replied.

"What sort of bearers?" Van Rieten demanded.

"Mang-Battu men," Etcham responded simply.

Now that impressed both Van Rieten and myself greatly. It bore out Stone's reputation as a notable leader of men. For up to that time no one had been able to use Mang-Battu as bearers outside of their own country, or to hold them for long or difficult expeditions.

"Were you long among the Mang-Battu?" was Van Rieten's next question.

"Some weeks," said Etcham. "Stone was interested in them and made up a fair-sized vocabulary of their words and phrases. He had a theory that they are an offshoot of the Balunda and he found much confirmation in their customs."

"What do you live on?" Van Rieten enquired.

"Game, mostly," Etcham lisped.

"How long has Stone been laid up?" Van Rieten next asked.

"More than a month," Etcham answered.

"And you have been hunting for the camp?" Van Rieten exclaimed.

Etcham's face, burnt and flayed as it was, showed a flush.

"I missed some easy shots," he admitted ruefully. "I've not felt ve'y fit myself."

"What's the matter with your chief?" Van Rieten enquired.

"Something like carbuncles," Etcham replied.

"He ought to get over a carbuncle or two," Van Rieten declared.

"They are not carbuncles," Etcham explained. "Nor one or two. He has had dozens, sometimes five at once. If they had been carbuncles he would have been dead long ago. But in some ways they are not so bad, though in others they are worse."

"How do you mean?" Van Rieten queried.

"Well," Etcham hesitated, "they do not seem to inflame so deep nor so wide as carbuncles, nor to be so painful, nor to cause so much fever. But then they seem to be part of a disease that affects his mind. He let me help him dress the first, but the others he has hidden most carefully, from me and from the men. He keeps his tent when they puff up, and will not let me change the dressings or be with him at all."

"Have you plenty of dressings?" Van Rieten asked.

"We have some," said Etcham doubtfully. "But he won't use them; he washes out the dressings and uses them over and over."

"How is he treating the swellings?" Van Rieten enquired.

"He slices them off clean down to flesh level, with his razor."

"What?" Van Rieten shouted.

Etcham made no answer but looked him steadily in the eyes.

"I beg pardon," Van Rieten hastened to say. "You startled me. They can't be carbuncles. He'd have been dead long ago."

"I thought I had said they are not carbuncles," Etcham lisped.

"But the man must be crazy!" Van Rieten exclaimed.

"Just so," said Etcham. "He is beyond my advice or control."

"How many has he treated that way?" Van Rieten demanded.

"Two, to my knowledge," Etcham said.

"Two?" Van Rieten queried.

Etcham flushed again.

"I saw him," he confessed, "through a crack in the hut. I felt impelled to keep a watch on him, as if he was not responsible."

"I should think not," Van Rieten agreed. "And you saw him do that twice?"

"I conjecture," said Etcham, "that he did the like with all the rest."

"How many has he had?" Van Rieten asked.

"Dozens," Etcham lisped.

"Does he eat?" Van Rieten enquired.

"Like a wolf," said Etcham. "More than any two bearers."

"Can he walk?" Van Rieten asked.

"He crawls a bit, groaning," said Etcham simply.

"Little fever, you say," Van Rieten ruminated.

"Enough and too much," Etcham declared.

"Has he been delirious?" Van Rieten asked.

"Only twice," Etcham replied; "once when the first swelling broke, and once later. He would not let anyone come near him then. But we could hear him talking, talking steadily, and it scared the natives.

"Was he talking their patter in delirium?" Van Rieten demanded.

"No," said Etcham, "but he was talking some similar lingo. Hamed Burghash said he was talking Balunda. I know too little Balunda. I do not learn languages readily. Stone learned more Mang-Battu in a week than I could have learned in a year. But I seemed to hear words like Mang-Battu words. Anyhow, the Mang-Battu bearers were scared."

"Scared?" Van Rieten repeated, questioningly.

"So were the Zanzibar men, even Hamed Burghash, and so was I," said Etcham, "only for a different reason. He talked in two voices."

"In two voices," Van Rieten reflected.

"Yes," said Etcham, more excitedly than he had yet spoken. "In two voices, like a conversation. One was his own, one a small, thin, bleaty voice like nothing I ever heard. I seemed to make out, among the sounds the deep voice made, something like Mang-Battu words I knew, as *nedru*, *metababa*, and *nedo*, their terms for 'head,' 'shoulder,' 'thigh,' and perhaps kudra and nekere ('speak' and 'whistle'); and among the noises of the shrill voice *matomipa*, *angunzi*, and *kamomami* ('kill,' 'death,' and 'hate'). Hamed Burghash said he also heard those words. He knew Mang-Battu far better than I."

"What did the bearers say?" Van Rieten asked.

"They said, 'Lukundoo, Lukundoo!'" Etcham replied. "I did not know the word; Hamed Burghash said it was Mang-Battu for 'leopard.'"

"It's Mang-Battu for 'witchcraft,'" said Van Rieten.

"I don't wonder they thought so," said Etcham. "It was enough to make one believe in sorcery to listen to those two voices."

"One voice answering the other?" Van Rieten asked perfunctorily.

Etcham's face went gray under his tan.

"Sometimes both at once," he answered huskily.

"Both at once!" Van Rieten ejaculated.

"It sounded that way to the men, too," said Etcham. "And that was not all."

He stopped and looked helplessly at us for a moment.

"Could a man talk and whistle at the same time?" he asked.

"How do you mean?" Van Rieten queried.

"We could hear Stone talking away, his big, deep-cheated baritone rumbling along, and through it all we could hear a high, shrill whistle, the oddest, wheezy sound. You know, no matter how shrilly a grown man may whistle, the note has a different quality from the whistle of a boy or a woman or a little girl. They sound more treble, somehow. Well, if you can imagine the smallest girl who could whistle keeping it up tunelessly right along, that whistle was like that, only even more piercing, and it sounded right through Stone's bass tones."

"And you didn't go to him?" Van Rieten cried.

"He is not given to threats," Etcham disclaimed. "But he had threatened, not volubly, nor like a sick man, but quietly and firmly, that if any man of us (he lumped me in with the men) came near him while he was in his trouble, that man should die. And it was not so much his words as his manner. It was like a monarch commanding respected privacy for a deathbed. One simply could not transgress."

"I see," said Van Rieten shortly.

"He's ve'y seedy," Etcham repeated helplessly. "I thought perhaps. . . ."

His absorbing affection for Stone, his real love for him, shone out through his envelope of conventional training. Worship of Stone was plainly his master passion.

Like many competent men, Van Rieten had a streak of hard selfishness in him. It came to the surface then. He said we carried our lives in our hands from day to day just as genuinely as Stone; that he did not forget the ties of blood and calling between any two explorers, but that there was no sense in imperiling one party for a very problematical benefit to a man probably beyond any help; that it was enough of a task to hunt for one party; that if two were united, providing food would be more than doubly difficult; that the risk of starvation was too great. Deflecting our march seven full days' journey (he complimented Etcham on his marching powers) might ruin our expedition entirely.

III

Van Rieten had logic on his side and he had a way with him. Etcham sat there apologetic and deferential, like a fourth-form schoolboy before a head master. Van Rieten wound up.

"I am after pigmies, at the risk of my life. After pigmies I go."

"Perhaps, then, these will interest you," said Etcham, very quietly.

He took two objects out of the side-pocket of his blouse, and handed them to Van Rieten. They were round, bigger than big plums, and smaller than small peaches, about the right size to enclose in an average hand. They were black, and at first I did not see what they were.

"Pigmies!" Van Rieten exclaimed. "Pigmies, indeed! Why, they wouldn't be two feet high! Do you mean to claim that these are adult heads?"

"I claim nothing," Etcham answered evenly. "You can see for yourself."

Van Rieten passed one of the heads to me. The sun was just setting and I examined it closely. A dried head it was, perfectly preserved, and the flesh as hard as Argentine jerked beef. A bit of a vertebra stuck out where the muscles of the vanished neck had shriveled into folds. The puny chin was sharp on a projecting jaw, the minute teeth white and even between the retracted lips, the tiny nose was flat, the little forehead retreating, there were inconsiderable clumps of stunted wool on the Lilliputian cranium. There was nothing babyish, childish or youthful about the head; rather it was mature to senility.

"Where did these come from?" Van Rieten enquired.

"I do not know," Etcham replied precisely. "I found them among Stone's effects while rummaging for medicines or drugs or anything that could help me to help him. I do not know where he got them. But I'll swear he did not have them when we entered this district."

"Are you sure?" Van Rieten queried, his eyes big and fixed on Etcham's.

"Ve'y sure," lisped Etcham.

"But how could he have come by them without your knowledge?" Van Rieten demurred.

"Sometimes we were apart ten days at a time hunting," said Etcham. "Stone is not a talking man. He gave me no account of his doings, and Hamed Burghash keeps a still tongue and a tight hold on the men."

"You have examined these heads?" Van Rieten asked.

"Minutely," said Etcham.

Van Rieten took out his notebook. He was a methodical chap. He tore out a leaf, folded it and divided it equally into three pieces. He gave one to me and one to Etcham.

"Just for a test of my impressions," he said, "I want each of us to write separately just what he is most reminded of by these heads. Then I want to compare the writings."

I handed Etcham a pencil and he wrote. Then he handed the pencil back to me and I wrote.

"Read the three," said Van Rieten, handing me his piece.

Van Rieten had written:

"An old Balunda witch-doctor."

Etcham had written:

"An old Mang-Battu fetish-man."

I had written:

"An old Katongo magician."

"There!" Van Rieten exclaimed. "Look at that! There is nothing Wagabi or Batwa or Wambuttu or Wabotu about these heads. Nor anything pigmy either."

"I thought as much," said Etcham.

"And you say he did not have them before?"

"To a certainty he did not," Etcham asserted.

"It is worth following up," said Van Rieten. "I'll go with you. And first of all, I'll do my best to save Stone."

He put out his hand and Etcham clasped it silently. He was grateful all over.

IV

Nothing but Etcham's fever of solicitude could have taken him in five days over the track. It took him eight days to retrace with full knowledge of it and our party to help. We could not have done it in seven, and Etcham urged us on, in a repressed fury of anxiety, no mere fever of duty to his chief, but a real ardor of devotion, a glow of personal adoration for Stone which blazed under his dry conventional exterior and showed in spite of him.

We found Stone well cared for. Etcham had seen to a good, high thorn *zareeba* round the camp, the huts were well built, and thatched and Stone's was as good as their resources would permit. Hamed Burghash was not named after two Seyyids for nothing. He had in him the making of a sultan. He had kept the Mang-Battu together, not a man had slipped off, and he had kept them in order. Also he was a deft nurse and a faithful servant.

The two other Zanzibaris had done some creditable hunting. Though all were hungry, the camp was far from starvation.

Stone was on a canvas cot and there was a sort of collapsible camp-stool-table, like a Turkish tabouret, by the cot. It had a water-bottle and some vials on it and Stone's watch, also his razor in its case.

Stone was clean and not emaciated, but he was far gone; not unconscious, but in a daze; past commanding or resisting anyone. He did not seem to see us enter or to know we were there. I should have recognized him anywhere. His boyish dash and grace had vanished utterly, of course. But his head was even more leonine; his hair was still abundant, yellow and wavy; the close, crisped blond beard he had grown during his illness did not alter him. He was big and big-cheated yet. His eyes were dull and he mumbled and babbled mere meaningless syllables, not words.

Etcham helped Van Rieten to uncover him and look him over. He was in good muscle for a man so long bedridden. There were no scars on him except about his knees, shoulders and chest. On each knee and above it he had a full score of roundish cicatrices, and a dozen or more on each shoulder, all in front. Two or three were open wounds and four or five barely healed. He had no fresh swellings, except two, one on each side, on his pectoral muscles, the one on the left being higher up and farther out than the other. They did not look like boils or carbuncles, but as if something blunt and hard were being pushed up through the fairly healthy flesh and skin, not much inflamed.

"I should not lance those," said Van Rieten, and Etcham assented.

They made Stone as comfortable as they could, and just before sunset we looked in at him again. He was lying on his back, and his chest showed big and massive yet, but he lay as if in a stupor. We left Etcham with him and went into the next hut, which Etcham had resigned to us. The jungle noises were no different than anywhere else for months past, and I was soon fast asleep.

V

Sometime in the pitch dark I found myself awake and listening. I could hear two voices, one Stone's, the other sibilant and wheezy. I knew Stone's voice after all the years that had passed since I heard it last. The other was like nothing I remembered. It had less volume than the wail of a new-born baby, yet there was an insistent carrying power to it, like the shrilling of an insect. As I listened I heard Van Rieten breathing near me in the dark; then he heard me and realized that I was listening, too. Like Etcham I knew little Balunda, but I could make out a word or two. The voices alternated, with intervals of silence between.

Then suddenly both sounded at once and fast. Stone's baritone basso, full as if he were in perfect health, and that incredibly stridulous falsetto, both jabbering at once like the voices of two people quarreling and trying to talk each other down.

"I can't stand this," said Van Rieten. "Let's have a look at him."

He had one of those cylindrical electric night-candles. He fumbled about for it, touched the button and beckoned me to come with him. Outside the hut he motioned me to stand still, and instinctively turned off the light, as if seeing made listening difficult.

Except for a faint glow from the embers of the bearers' fire we were in complete darkness, little starlight struggled through the trees, the river made but a faint murmur. We could hear the two voices together and then suddenly the creaking voice changed into a razor-edged, slicing whistle, indescribably cutting, continuing right through Stone's grumbling torrent of croaking words.

"Good God!" exclaimed Van Rieten.

Abruptly he turned on the light.

We found Etcham utterly asleep, exhausted by his long anxiety and the exertions of his phenomenal march, and relaxed completely now that the load was in a sense shifted from his shoulders to Van Rieten's. Even the light on his face did not wake him.

The whistle had ceased and the two voices now sounded together. Both came from Stone's cot, where the concentrated white ray showed him lying just as we had left him, except that he had tossed his arms above his head and had torn the coverings and bandages from his chest.

The swelling on his right breast had broken. Van Rieten aimed the center line of the light at it and we saw it plainly. From his flesh, grown out of it, there protruded a head, such a head as the dried specimens Etcham had shown us, as if it were a miniature of the head of a Balunda fetish-man. It was black, shining black as the blackest African skin; it rolled the whites of its wicked, wee eyes and showed its microscopic teeth between lips repulsively negroid in their red fullness, even in so diminutive a face. It had crisp, fuzzy wool on its minikin skull, it turned malignantly from side to side and chittered incessantly in that inconceivable falsetto. Stone babbled brokenly against its patter.

Van Rieten turned from Stone and waked Etcham, with some difficulty. When he was awake and saw it all, Etcham stared and said not one word.

"You saw him slice off two swellings?" Van Rieten asked.

Etcham nodded, chokingly.

"Did he bleed much?" Van Rieten demanded.

"Ve'y little," Etcham replied.

"You hold his arms," said Van Rieten to Etcham.

He took up Stone's razor and handed me the light. Stone showed no sign of seeing the light or of knowing we were there. But the little head mewled and screeched at us.

Van Rieten's hand was steady, and the sweep of the razor even and true. Stone bled amazingly little and Van Rieten dressed the wound as if it had been a bruise or scrape.

Stone had stopped talking the instant the excrescent head was severed. Van Rieten did all that could be done for Stone and then fairly grabbed the light from me. Snatching up a gun he scanned the ground by the cot and brought the butt down once and twice, viciously.

We went back to our hut, but I doubt if I slept.

VI

Next day, near noon, in broad daylight, we heard the two voices from Stone's hut. We found Etcham dropped asleep by his charge. The swelling on the left had broken, and just such another head was there miauling and spluttering. Etcham woke up and the three of us stood there and glared. Stone interjected hoarse vocables into the tinkling gurgle of the portent's utterance.

Van Rieten stepped forward, took up Stone's razor and knelt down by the cot. The atom of a head squealed a wheezy snarl at him.

Then suddenly Stone spoke English.

"Who are you with my razor?"

Van Rieten started back and stood up.

Stone's eyes were clear now and bright, they roved about the hut.

"The end," he said; "I recognize the end. I seem to see Etcham, as if in life. But Singleton! Ah, Singleton! Ghosts of my boyhood come to watch me pass! And you, strange specter with the black beard and my razor! Aroint ye all!"

"I'm no ghost, Stone," I managed to say. "I'm alive. So are Etcham and Van Rieten. We are here to help you."

"Van Rieten!" he exclaimed. "My work passes on to a better man. Luck go with you, Van Rieten."

Van Rieten went nearer to him.

"Just hold still a moment, old man," he said soothingly. "It will be only one twinge."

"I've held still for many such twinges," Stone answered quite distinctly. "Let me be. Let me die in my own way. The hydra was nothing to this. You can cut off ten, a hundred, a thousand heads, but the curse you can not cut off, or take off. What's soaked into the bone won't come out of the flesh, any more than what's bred there. Don't hack me any more. Promise!"

His voice had all the old commanding tone of his boyhood and it swayed Van Rieten as it always had swayed everybody.

"I promise," said Van Rieten.

Almost as he said the word Stone's eyes filmed again.

Then we three sat about Stone and watched that hideous, gibbering prodigy grow up out of Stone's flesh, till two horrid, spindling little black arms disengaged themselves. The infinitesimal nails were perfect to the barely perceptible moon at the quick, the pink spot on the palm was horridly natural. These arms gesticulated and the right plucked toward Stone's blond beard.

"I can't stand this," Van Rieten exclaimed and took up the razor again.

Instantly Stone's eyes opened, hard and glittering.

"Van Rieten break his word?" he enunciated slowly. "Never!"

"But we must help you," Van Rieten gasped.

"I am past all help and all hurting," said Stone. "This is my hour. This curse is not put on me; it grew out of me, like this horror here. Even now I go."

His eyes closed and we stood helpless, the adherent figure spouting shrill sentences.

In a moment Stone spoke again.

"You speak all tongues?" he asked quickly.

And the mergent minikin replied in sudden English:

"Yea, verily, all that you speak," putting out its microscopic tongue, writhing its lips and wagging its head from side to side. We could see the thready ribs on its exiguous flanks heave as if the thing breathed.

"Has she forgiven me?" Stone asked in a muffled strangle.

"Not while the moss hangs from the cypresses," the head squeaked. "Not while the stars shine on Lake Pontchartrain will she forgive."

And then Stone, all with one motion, wrenched himself over on his side. The next instant he was dead.

When Singleton's voice ceased the room was hushed for a space. We could hear each other breathing. Twombly, the tactless, broke the silence.

"I presume," he said, "you cut off the little minikin and brought it home in alcohol."

Singleton turned on him a stern countenance.

"We buried Stone," he said, "unmutilated as he died."

"But," said the unconscionable Twombly, "the whole thing is incredible."

Singleton stiffened.

"I did not expect you to believe it," he said; "I began by saying that although I heard and saw it, when I look back on it I cannot credit it myself."

THE WENDIGO

Algernon Blackwood

I

A considerable number of hunting parties were out that year without finding so much as a fresh trail; for the moose were uncommonly shy, and the various Nimrods returned to the bosoms of their respective families with the best excuses the facts of their imaginations could suggest. Dr. Cathcart, among others, came back without a trophy; but he brought instead the memory of an experience which he declares was worth all the bull moose that had ever been shot. But then Cathcart, of Aberdeen, was interested in other things besides moose—amongst them the vagaries of the human mind. This particular story, however, found no mention in his book on Collective Hallucination for the simple reason (so he confided once to a fellow colleague) that he himself played too intimate a part in it to form a competent judgment of the affair as a whole. . . .

Besides himself and his guide, Hank Davis, there was young Simpson, his nephew, a divinity student destined for the "Wee Kirk" (then on his first visit to Canadian backwoods), and the latter's guide, Défago. Joseph Défago was a French "Canuck," who had strayed from his native Province of Quebec years before, and had got caught in Rat Portage when the Canadian Pacific Railway was a-building; a man who, in addition to his unparalleled knowledge of wood-craft and bush-lore, could also sing the old *voyageur* songs and tell a capital hunting yarn into the bargain. He was deeply susceptible, moreover, to that singular spell which

132

the wilderness lays upon certain lonely natures, and he loved the wild solitudes with a kind of romantic passion that amounted almost to an obsession. The life of the backwoods fascinated him—whence, doubtless, his surpassing efficiency in dealing with their mysteries.

On this particular expedition he was Hank's choice. Hank knew him and swore by him. He also swore at him, "jest as a pal might," and since he had a vocabulary of picturesque, if utterly meaningless, oaths, the conversation between the two stalwart and hardy woodsmen was often of a rather lively description. This river of expletives, however, Hank agreed to dam a little out of respect for his old "hunting boss," Dr. Cathcart, whom of course he addressed after the fashion of the country as "Doc," and also because he understood that young Simpson was already a "bit of a parson." He had, however, one objection to Défago, and one only—which was, that the French Canadian sometimes exhibited what Hank described as "the output of a cursed and dismal mind," meaning apparently that he sometimes was true to type, Latin type, and suffered fits of a kind of silent moroseness when nothing could induce him to utter speech. Défago, that is to say, was imaginative and melancholy. And, as a rule, it was too long a spell of "civilization" that induced the attacks, for a few days of the wilderness invariably cured them.

This, then, was the party of four that found themselves in camp the last week in October of that "shy moose year" 'way up in the wilderness north of Rat Portage—a forsaken and desolate country. There was also Punk, an Indian, who had accompanied Dr. Cathcart and Hank on their hunting trips in previous years, and who acted as cook. His duty was merely to stay in camp, catch fish, and prepare venison steaks and coffee at a few minutes' notice. He dressed in the worn-out clothes bequeathed to him by former patrons, and, except for his coarse black hair and dark skin, he looked in these city garments no more like a real redskin than a stage Negro looks like a real African. For all that, however, Punk had in him still the instincts of his dying race; his taciturn silence and his endurance survived; also his superstition.

The party round the blazing fire that night were despondent, for a week had passed without a single sign of recent moose discovering itself. Défago had sung his song and plunged into a story, but Hank, in bad humor, reminded him so often that "he kep' mussing-up the fac's so, that it was 'most all nothin' but a petered-out lie," that the Frenchman had finally subsided into a sulky silence which nothing seemed likely to break. Dr. Cathcart and his nephew were fairly done after an exhausting day. Punk was washing up the dishes, grunting to himself under the lean-to of branches, where he later also slept. No one troubled to stir the slowly dying fire. Overhead the stars were brilliant in a sky quite wintry, and there was so little wind that ice was already forming stealthily along the shores of the still lake behind them. The silence of the vast listening forest stole forward and enveloped them.

Hank broke in suddenly with his nasal voice.

"I'm in favor of breaking new ground tomorrow, Doc," he observed with energy, looking across at his employer. "We don't stand a dead Dago's chance around here."

"Agreed," said Cathcart, always a man of few words. "Think the idea's good."

"Sure pop, it's good," Hank resumed with confidence. "S'pose, now, you and I strike west, up Garden Lake way for a change! None of us ain't touched that quiet bit o' land yet—"

"I'm with you."

"And you, Défago, take Mr. Simpson along in the small canoe, skip across the lake, portage over into Fifty Island Water, and take a good squint down that thar southern shore. The moose 'yarded' there like hell last year, and for all we know they may be doin' it agin this year jest to spite us."

Défago, keeping his eyes on the fire, said nothing by way of reply. He was still offended, possibly, about his interrupted story.

"No one's been up that way this year, an' I'll lay my bottom dollar on *that!*" Hank added with emphasis, as though he had a reason for knowing. He looked over at his partner sharply. "Better take the little silk tent and stay away a couple o' nights," he concluded, as though the matter were definitely settled. For Hank was recognized as general organizer of the hunt, and in charge of the party.

It was obvious to anyone that Défago did not jump at the plan, but his silence seemed to convey something more than ordinary disapproval, and across his sensitive dark face there passed a curious expression like a flash of firelight—not so quickly, however, that the three men had not time to catch it.

"He funked for some reason, *I* thought," Simpson said afterwards in the tent he shared with his uncle. Dr. Cathcart made no immediate reply, although the look had interested him enough at the time for him to make a mental note of it. The expression had caused him a passing uneasiness he could not quite account for at the moment.

But Hank, of course, had been the first to notice it, and the odd thing was that instead of becoming explosive or angry over the other's reluctance, he at once began to humor him a bit.

"But there ain't no *speshul* reason why no one's been up there this year," he said with a perceptible hush in his tone; "not the reason you mean, anyway! Las' year it was the fires that kep' folks out, and this year I guess—I guess it jest happened so, that's all!" His manner was clearly meant to be encouraging.

Joseph Défago raised his eyes a moment, then dropped them again. A breath of wind stole out of the forest and stirred the embers into a passing blaze. Dr. Cathcart again noticed the expression in the guide's face, and again he did not like it. But this time the nature of the look betrayed itself. In those eyes, for an instant, he caught the gleam of a man scared in his very soul. It disquieted him more than he cared to admit.

"Bad Indians up that way?" he asked, with a laugh to ease matters a little, while Simpson, too sleepy to notice this subtle by-play, moved off to bed with a prodigious yawn; "or—or anything wrong with the country?" he added, when his nephew was out of hearing.

Hank met his eye with something less than his usual frankness.

"He's jest skeered," he replied good-humouredly. "Skeered stiff about some ole feery tale! That's all, ain't it, ole pard?" And he gave Défago a friendly kick on the moccasined foot that lay nearest the fire.

Défago looked up quickly, as from an interrupted reverie, a reverie, however, that had not prevented his seeing all that went on about him.

"Skeered—*nuthin'!*" he answered, with a flush of defiance. "There's nuthin' in the Bush that can skeer Joseph Défago, and don't you forget it!" And the natural energy with which he spoke made it impossible to know whether he told the whole truth or only a part of it.

Hank turned towards the doctor. He was just going to add something when he stopped abruptly and looked round. A sound close behind them in the darkness made all three start. It was old Punk, who had moved up from his lean-to while they talked and now stood there just beyond the circle of firelight—listening.

"'Nother time, Doc!" Hank whispered, with a wink, "when the gallery ain't stepped down into the stalls!" And, springing to his feet, he slapped the Indian on the back and cried noisily, "Come up t' the fire an' warm yer dirty red skin a bit." He dragged him towards the blaze and threw more wood on. "That was a mighty good feed you give us an hour or two back," he continued heartily, as though to set the man's thoughts on another scent, "and it ain't Christian to let you stand out there freezin' yer ole soul to hell while we're gettin' all good an' toasted!" Punk moved in and warmed his feet, smiling darkly at the other's volubility which he only half understood, but saying nothing. And presently Dr. Cathcart, seeing that further conversation was impossible, followed his nephew's example and moved off to the tent, leaving the three men smoking over the now blazing fire.

It is not easy to undress in a small tent without waking one's companion, and Cathcart, hardened and warm-blooded as he was in spite of his fifty odd years, did what Hank would have described as "considerable of his twilight" in the open. He noticed, during the process, that Punk had meanwhile gone back to his lean-to, and that Hank and Défago were at it hammer and tongs, or, rather, hammer and anvil, the little French Canadian being the anvil. It was all very like the conventional stage picture of Western melodrama: the fire lighting up their faces with patches of alternate red and black; Défago, in slouch hat and moccasins in the part of the "badlands" villain; Hank, open-faced and hatless, with that reckless fling of his shoulders, the honest and deceived hero; and old Punk, eavesdropping in the background, supplying the atmosphere of mystery. The doctor smiled as he noticed the details; but at the same time something deep within him—he hardly knew what—shrank a little, as though an almost imperceptible breath of warning had touched the surface of his soul and was gone again before he could seize it. Probably it was traceable to that "scared expression" he had seen in the eyes of Défago; "probably"— for this hint of fugitive emotion otherwise escaped his usually so keen analysis. Défago, he was vaguely aware, might cause trouble somehow. . . . He was not as steady a guide as Hank, for instance. . . . Further than that he could not get. . . .

He watched the men a moment longer before diving into the stuffy tent where Simpson already slept soundly. Hank, he saw, was swearing like a mad African in a New York nigger saloon; but it was the swearing of "affection." The ridiculous oaths flew freely now that the cause of their obstruction was asleep. Presently he put his arm almost tenderly upon his comrade's shoulder, and they moved off together into the shadows where their tent stood faintly glimmering. Punk, too, a moment later followed their example and disappeared between his odorous blankets in the opposite direction.

Dr. Cathcart then likewise turned in, weariness and sleep still fighting in his mind with an obscure curiosity to know what it was that had scared Défago about the country up Fifty Island Water way,—wondering, too, why Punk's presence had prevented the completion of what Hank had to say. Then sleep overtook him. He would know tomorrow. Hank would tell him the story while they trudged after the elusive moose.

Deep silence fell about the little camp, planted there so audaciously in the jaws of the wilderness. The lake gleamed like a sheet of black glass beneath the stars. The cold air pricked. In the draughts of night that poured their silent tide from the depths of the forest, with messages from distant ridges and from lakes just beginning to freeze, there lay already the faint, bleak odors of coming winter. White men, with their dull scent, might never have divined them; the fragrance of the wood fire would have concealed from them these almost electrical hints of moss and bark and hardening swamp a hundred miles away. Even Hank and Défago, subtly in league with the soul of the woods as they were, would probably have spread their delicate nostrils in vain. . . .

But an hour later, when all slept like the dead, old Punk crept from his blankets and went down to the shore of the lake like a shadow—silently, as only Indian blood can move. He raised his head and looked about him. The thick darkness rendered sight of small avail, but, like the animals, he possessed other senses that darkness could not mute. He listened—then sniffed the air. Motionless as a hemlock stem he stood there. After five minutes again he lifted his head and sniffed, and yet once again. A tingling of the wonderful nerves that betrayed itself by no outer sign, ran through him as he tasted the keen air. Then, merging his figure into the surrounding blackness in a way that only wild men and animals understand, he turned, still moving like a shadow, and went stealthily back to his lean-to and his bed.

And soon after he slept, the change of wind he had divined stirred gently the reflection of the stars within the lake. Rising among the far ridges of the country beyond Fifty Island Water, it came from the direction in which he had stared, and it passed over the sleeping camp with a faint and sighing murmur through the tops of the big trees that was almost too delicate to be audible. With it, down the desert paths of night, though too faint, too high even for the Indian's hair-like nerves, there passed a curious, thin odor, strangely disquieting, an odor of something that seemed unfamiliar—utterly unknown.

The French Canadian and the man of Indian blood each stirred uneasily in his sleep just about this time, though neither of them woke. Then the ghost of that unforgettably strange odor passed away and was lost among the leagues of tenantless forest beyond.

II

In the morning the camp was astir before the sun. There had been a light fall of snow during the night and the air was sharp. Punk had done his duty betimes, for the odors of coffee and fried bacon reached every tent. All were in good spirits.

"Wind's shifted!" cried Hank vigorously, watching Simpson and his guide already loading the small canoe. "It's across the lake— dead right for you fellers. And the snow'll make bully trails! If there's any moose mussing around up thar, they'll not get so much as a tail-end scent of you with the wind as it is. Good luck, Monsieur Défago!" he added, facetiously giving the name its French pronunciation for once, "*bonne chance!*"

Défago returned the good wishes, apparently in the best of spirits, the silent mood gone. Before eight o'clock old Punk had the camp to himself, Cathcart and Hank were far along the trail that led westwards, while the canoe that carried Défago and Simpson, with silk tent and grub for two days, was already a dark speck bobbing on the bosom of the lake, going due east.

The wintry sharpness of the air was tempered now by a sun that topped the wooded ridges and blazed with a luxurious warmth upon the world of lake and forest below; loons flew skimming through the sparkling spray that the wind lifted; divers shook their dripping heads to the sun and popped smartly out of sight again; and as far as eye could reach rose the leagues of endless, crowding Bush, desolate in its lonely sweep and grandeur, untrodden by foot of man, and stretching its mighty and unbroken carpet right up to the frozen shores of Hudson Bay.

Simpson, who saw it all for the first time as he paddled hard in the bows of the dancing canoe, was enchanted by its austere beauty. His heart drank in the sense of freedom and great spaces just as his lungs drank in the cool and perfumed wind. Behind him in the stern seat, singing fragments of his native chanties, Défago steered the craft of birch bark like a thing of life, answering cheerfully all his companion's questions. Both were gay and light-hearted. On such occasions men lose the superficial, worldly distinctions; they become human beings working together for a common end.

Simpson, the employer, and Défago the employed, among these primitive forces, were simply—two men, the "guider" and the "guided." Superior knowledge, of course, assumed control, and the younger man fell without a second thought into the quasi-subordinate position. He never dreamed of objecting when Défago dropped the "Mr.," and addressed him as "Say, Simpson," or "Simpson, boss," which was invariably the case before they reached the farther shore after a stiff paddle of twelve miles against a head wind. He only laughed, and liked it; then ceased to notice it at all.

For this "divinity student" was a young man of parts and character, though as yet, of course, untraveled; and on this trip—the first time he had seen any country but his own and little Switzerland—the huge scale of things somewhat bewildered him. It was one thing, he realized, to hear about primeval forests, but quite another to see them. While to dwell in them and seek acquaintance with their wild life was, again, an initiation that no intelligent man could undergo without a certain shifting of personal values hitherto held for permanent and sacred.

Simpson knew the first faint indication of this emotion when he held the new .303 rifle in his hands and looked along its pair of faultless, gleaming barrels. The three days' journey to their headquarters, by lake and portage, had carried the process a stage farther. And now that he was about to plunge beyond even the fringe of wilderness where they were camped into the virgin heart of uninhabited regions as vast as Europe itself, the true nature of the situation stole upon him with an effect of delight and awe that his imagination was fully capable of appreciating. It was himself and Défago against a multitude—at least, against a Titan!

The bleak splendors of these remote and lonely forests rather overwhelmed him with the sense of his own littleness. That stern quality of the tangled backwoods which can only be described as merciless and terrible, rose out of these far blue woods swimming upon the horizon, and revealed itself. He understood the silent warning. He realized his own utter helplessness. Only Défago, as a symbol of a distant civilization where man was master, stood between him and a pitiless death by exhaustion and starvation.

It was thrilling to him, therefore, to watch Défago turn over the canoe upon the shore, pack the paddles carefully underneath, and then proceed to "blaze" the spruce stems for some distance on either side of an almost invisible trail, with the careless remark thrown in, "Say, Simpson, if anything happens to me, you'll find the canoe all correc' by these marks;—then strike doo west into the sun to hit the home camp agin, see?"

It was the most natural thing in the world to say, and he said it without any noticeable inflexion of the voice, only it happened to express the youth's emotions at the moment with an utterance that was symbolic of the situation and of his own helplessness as a factor in it. He was alone with Défago in a primitive world: that was all. The canoe, another symbol of man's ascendancy, was now to be left behind. Those small yellow patches, made on the trees by the axe, were the only indications of its hiding place.

Meanwhile, shouldering the packs between them, each man carrying his own rifle, they followed the slender trail over rocks and fallen trunks and across half-frozen swamps; skirting numerous lakes that fairly gemmed the forest, their borders fringed with mist; and towards five o'clock found themselves suddenly on the edge of the woods, looking out across a large sheet of water in front of them, dotted with pine-clad islands of all describable shapes and sizes.

"Fifty Island Water," announced Défago wearily, "and the sun jest goin' to dip his bald old head into it!" he added, with unconscious poetry; and immediately they set about pitching camp for the night.

In a very few minutes, under those skilful hands that never made a movement too much or a movement too little, the silk tent stood taut and cozy, the beds of balsam boughs ready laid, and a brisk cooking fire burned with the minimum of smoke. While the young Scotchman cleaned the fish they had caught trolling behind the canoe, Défago "guessed" he would "jest as soon" take a turn through the Bush for indications of moose. "*May* come across a trunk where they bin and rubbed horns," he said, as he moved off, "or feedin' on the last of the maple leaves"—and he was gone.

His small figure melted away like a shadow in the dusk, while Simpson noted with a kind of admiration how easily the forest absorbed him into herself. A few steps, it seemed, and he was no longer visible.

Yet there was little underbrush hereabouts; the trees stood somewhat apart, well spaced; and in the clearings grew silver birch and maple, spearlike and slender, against the immense stems of spruce and hemlock. But for occasional prostrate monsters, and the boulders of grey rock that thrust uncouth shoulders here and there out of the ground, it might well have been a bit of park in the Old Country. Almost, one might have seen in it the hand of man. A little to the right, however, began the great burnt section, miles in extent, proclaiming its real character—*brulé*, as it is called, where the fires of the previous year had raged for weeks, and the blackened stumps now rose gaunt and ugly, bereft of branches, like gigantic match heads stuck into the ground, savage and desolate beyond words. The perfume of charcoal and rain-soaked ashes still hung faintly about it.

The dusk rapidly deepened; the glades grew dark; the crackling of the fire and the wash of little waves along the rocky lake shore were the only sounds audible. The wind had dropped with the sun, and in all that vast world of branches nothing stirred. Any moment, it seemed, the woodland gods, who are to be worshipped in silence and loneliness, might stretch their mighty and terrific outlines among the trees. In front, through doorways pillared by huge straight stems, lay the stretch of Fifty Island Water, a crescent-shaped lake some fifteen miles from tip to tip, and perhaps five miles across where they were camped. A sky of rose and saffron, more clear than any atmosphere Simpson had ever known, still dropped its pale streaming fires across the waves, where the islands—a hundred, surely, rather than fifty—floated like the fairy barques of some enchanted fleet. Fringed with pines, whose crests fingered most delicately the sky, they almost seemed to move upwards as the light faded—about to weigh anchor and navigate the pathways of the heavens instead of the currents of their native and desolate lake.

And strips of colored cloud, like flaunting pennons, signaled their departure to the stars. . . .

The beauty of the scene was strangely uplifting. Simpson smoked the fish and burnt his fingers into the bargain in his efforts to enjoy it and at the same time tend the frying pan and the fire. Yet, ever at the back of his thoughts, lay that other aspect of the wilderness: the indifference to human life, the merciless spirit of desolation which took no note of man. The sense of his utter loneliness, now that even Défago had gone, came close as he looked about him and listened for the sound of his companion's returning footsteps.

There was pleasure in the sensation, yet with it a perfectly comprehensible alarm. And instinctively the thought stirred in him: "What should I—*could* I, do—if anything happened and he did not come back—?"

They enjoyed their well-earned supper, eating untold quantities of fish, and drinking unmilked tea strong enough to kill men who had not covered thirty miles of hard "going," eating little on the way. And when it was over, they smoked and told stories round the blazing fire, laughing, stretching weary limbs, and discussing plans for the morrow. Défago was in excellent spirits, though disappointed at having no signs of moose to report. But it was dark and he had not gone far. The *brulé*, too, was bad. His clothes and hands were smeared with charcoal. Simpson, watching him, realized with renewed vividness their position—alone together in the wilderness.

"Défago," he said presently, "these woods, you know, are a bit too big to feel quite at home in—to feel comfortable in, I mean! . . . Eh?" He merely gave expression to the mood of the moment; he was hardly prepared for the earnestness, the solemnity even, with which the guide took him up.

"You've hit it right, Simpson, boss," he replied, fixing his searching brown eyes on his face, "and that's the truth, sure. There's no end to 'em—no end at all." Then he added in a lowered tone as if to himself, "There's lots found out *that*, and gone plumb to pieces!"

But the man's gravity of manner was not quite to the other's liking; it was a little too suggestive for this scenery and setting; he was sorry he had broached the subject. He remembered suddenly how his uncle had told him that men were sometimes stricken with a strange fever of the wilderness, when the seduction of the uninhabited wastes caught them so fiercely that they went forth, half fascinated, half deluded, to their death. And he had a shrewd idea that his companion held something in sympathy with that queer type. He led the conversation on to other topics, on to Hank and the doctor, for instance, and the natural rivalry as to who should get the first sight of moose.

"If they went doo west," observed Défago carelessly, "there's sixty miles between us now—with ole Punk at halfway house eatin' himself full to bustin' with fish and coffee." They laughed together over the picture. But the casual mention of those sixty miles again made Simpson realize the prodigious scale of this land where they hunted; sixty miles was a mere step; two hundred little more than a step. Stories of lost hunters rose persistently before his memory. The passion and mystery of homeless and wandering men, seduced by the beauty of great forests, swept his soul in a way too vivid to be quite pleasant. He wondered vaguely whether it was the mood of his companion that invited the unwelcome suggestion with such persistence.

"Sing us a song, Défago, if you're not too tired," he asked; "one of those old *voyageur* songs you sang the other night." He handed his tobacco pouch to the guide and then filled his own pipe, while the Canadian, nothing loth, sent his light voice across the lake in one of those plaintive, almost melancholy chanties with which lumbermen and trappers lessen the burden of their labor. There was an appealing and romantic flavor about it, something that recalled the atmosphere of the old pioneer days when Indians and wilderness were leagued together, battles frequent, and the Old Country farther off than it is today. The sound traveled pleasantly over the water, but the forest at their backs seemed to swallow it down with a single gulp that permitted neither echo nor resonance.

It was in the middle of the third verse that Simpson noticed something unusual—something that brought his thoughts back with a rush from faraway scenes. A curious change had come into the man's voice. Even before he knew what it was, uneasiness caught him, and looking up quickly, he saw that Défago, though still singing, was peering about him into the Bush, as though he heard or saw something. His voice grew fainter—dropped to a hush—then ceased altogether. The same instant, with a movement amazingly alert, he started to his feet and stood upright—*sniffing the air*. Like a dog scenting game, he drew the air into his nostrils in short, sharp breaths, turning quickly as he did so in all directions, and finally "pointing" down the lake shore, eastwards. It was a performance unpleasantly suggestive and at the same time singularly dramatic. Simpson's heart fluttered disagreeably as he watched it.

"Lord, man! How you made me jump!" he exclaimed, on his feet beside him the same instant, and peering over his shoulder into the sea of darkness. "What's up? Are you frightened—?"

Even before the question was out of his mouth he knew it was foolish, for any man with a pair of eyes in his head could see that the Canadian had turned white down to his very gills. Not even sunburn and the glare of the fire could hide that.

The student felt himself trembling a little, weakish in the knees. "What's up?" he repeated quickly. "D'you smell moose? Or anything queer, anything—wrong?" He lowered his voice instinctively.

The forest pressed round them with its encircling wall; the nearer tree stems gleamed like bronze in the firelight; beyond that—blackness, and, so far as he could tell, a silence of death. Just behind them a passing puff of wind lifted a single leaf, looked at it, then laid it softly down again without disturbing the rest of the covey. It seemed as if a million invisible causes had combined just to produce that single visible effect. *Other* life pulsed about them—and was gone.

Défago turned abruptly; the livid hue of his face had turned to a dirty grey.

"I never said I heered—or smelt—nuthin'," he said slowly and emphatically, in an oddly altered voice that conveyed somehow a touch of defiance. "I was only—takin' a look round—so to speak. It's always a mistake to be too previous with yer questions." Then he added suddenly with obvious effort, in his more natural voice, "Have you got the matches, Boss Simpson?" and proceeded to light the pipe he had half filled just before he began to sing.

Without speaking another word they sat down again by the fire. Défago changing his side so that he could face the direction the wind came from. For even a tenderfoot could tell that. Défago changed his position in order to hear and smell—all there was to be heard and smelt. And, since he now faced the lake with his back to the trees it was evidently nothing in the forest that had sent so strange and sudden a warning to his marvelously trained nerves.

"Guess now I don't feel like singing any," he explained presently of his own accord. "That song kinder brings back memories that's troublesome to me; I never oughter've begun it. It sets me on t' imagining things, see?"

Clearly the man was still fighting with some profoundly moving emotion. He wished to excuse himself in the eyes of the other. But the explanation, in that it was only a part of the truth, was a lie, and he knew perfectly well that Simpson was not deceived by it. For nothing could explain away the livid terror that had dropped over his face while he stood there sniffing the air. And nothing— no amount of blazing fire, or chatting on ordinary subjects—could make that camp exactly as it had been before. The shadow of an unknown horror, naked if unguessed, that had flashed for an instant in the face and gestures of the guide, had also communicated itself, vaguely and therefore more potently, to his companion. The guide's visible efforts to dissemble the truth only made things worse. Moreover, to add to the younger man's uneasiness, was the difficulty, nay, the impossibility he felt of asking questions, and also his complete ignorance as to the cause . . . . Indians, wild animals, forest fires—all these, he knew, were wholly out of the question. His imagination searched vigorously, but in vain. . . .

Yet, somehow or other, after another long spell of smoking, talking and roasting themselves before the great fire, the shadow that had so suddenly invaded their peaceful camp began to shirt. Perhaps Défago's efforts, or the return of his quiet and normal attitude accomplished this; perhaps Simpson himself had exaggerated the affair out of all proportion to the truth; or possibly the vigorous air of the wilderness brought its own powers of healing. Whatever the cause, the feeling of immediate horror seemed to have passed away as mysteriously as it had come, for nothing occurred to feed it. Simpson began to feel that he had permitted himself the unreasoning terror of a child. He put it down partly to a certain subconscious excitement that this wild and immense scenery generated in his blood, partly to the spell of solitude, and partly to overfatigue. That pallor in the guide's face was, of course, uncommonly hard to explain, yet it *might* have been due in some way to an effect of firelight, or his own imagination. . . . He gave it the benefit of the doubt; he was Scotch.

When a somewhat unordinary emotion has disappeared, the mind always finds a dozen ways of explaining away its causes. . . . Simpson lit a last pipe and tried to laugh to himself. On getting home to Scotland it would make quite a good story. He did not realize that this laughter was a sign that terror still lurked in the recesses of his soul—that, in fact, it was merely one of the conventional signs by which a man, seriously alarmed, tries to persuade himself that he is *not* so.

Défago, however, heard that low laughter and looked up with surprise on his face. The two men stood, side by side, kicking the embers about before going to bed. It was ten o'clock—a late hour for hunters to be still awake.

"What's ticklin' yer?" he asked in his ordinary tone, yet gravely.

"I—I was thinking of our little toy woods at home, just at that moment," stammered Simpson, coming back to what really dominated his mind, and startled by the question, "and comparing them to—to all this," and he swept his arm round to indicate the Bush.

A pause followed in which neither of them said anything.

"All the same I wouldn't laugh about it, if I was you," Défago added, looking over Simpson's shoulder into the shadows. "There's places in there nobody won't never see into—nobody knows what lives in there either."

"Too big—too far off?" The suggestion in the guide's manner was immense and horrible.

Défago nodded. The expression on his face was dark. He, too, felt uneasy. The younger man understood that in a *hinterland* of this size there might well be depths of wood that would never in the life of the world be known or trodden. The thought was not exactly the sort he welcomed. In a loud voice, cheerfully, he suggested that it was time for bed. But the guide lingered, tinkering with the fire, arranging the stones needlessly, doing a dozen things that did not really need doing. Evidently there was something he wanted to say, yet found it difficult to "get at."

"Say, you, Boss Simpson," he began suddenly, as the last shower of sparks went up into the air, "you don't—smell nothing, do you— nothing pertickler, I mean?" The commonplace question, Simpson realized, veiled a dreadfully serious thought in his mind. A shiver ran down his back.

"Nothing but burning wood," he replied firmly, kicking again at the embers. The sound of his own foot made him start.

"And all the evenin' you ain't smelt—nothing?" persisted the guide, peering at him through the gloom; "nothing extrordiny, and different to anything else you ever smelt before?"

"No, no, man; nothing at all!" he replied aggressively, half angrily.

Défago's face cleared. "That's good!" he exclaimed with evident relief. "That's good to hear."

"Have *you?*" asked Simpson sharply, and the same instant regretted the question.

The Canadian came closer in the darkness. He shook his head. "I guess not," he said, though without overwhelming conviction. "It must've been just that song of mine that did it. It's the song they sing in lumber camps and godforsaken places like that, when they've skeered the Wendigo's somewhere around, doin' a bit of swift traveling—"

"And what's the Wendigo, pray?" Simpson asked quickly, irritated because again he could not prevent that sudden shiver of the nerves. He knew that he was close upon the man's terror and the cause of it. Yet a rushing passionate curiosity overcame his better judgment, and his fear.

Défago turned swiftly and looked at him as though he were suddenly about to shriek. His eyes shone, but his mouth was wide open. Yet all he said, or whispered rather, for his voice sank very low, was: "It's nuthin'—nuthin' but what those lousy fellers believe when they've bin hittin' the bottle too long—a sort of great animal that lives up yonder," he jerked his head northwards, "quick as lightning in its tracks, an' bigger'n anything else in the Bush, an' ain't supposed to be very good to look at—that's all!"

"A backwoods superstition—" began Simpson, moving hastily toward the tent in order to shake off the hand of the guide that clutched his arm. "Come, come, hurry up for God's sake, and get the lantern going! It's time we were in bed and asleep if we're going to be up with the sun tomorrow. . . ."

The guide was close on his heels. "I'm coming," he answered out of the darkness, "I'm coming." And after a slight delay he appeared with the lantern and hung it from a nail in the front pole of the tent. The shadows of a hundred trees shifted their places quickly as he did so, and when he stumbled over the rope, diving swiftly inside, the whole tent trembled as though a gust of wind struck it.

The two men lay down, without undressing, upon their beds of soft balsam boughs, cunningly arranged. Inside, all was warm and cozy, but outside the world of crowding trees pressed close about them, marshalling their million shadows, and smothering the little tent that stood there like a wee white shell facing the ocean of tremendous forest.

Between the two lonely figures within, however, there pressed another shadow that was *not* a shadow from the night. It was the Shadow cast by the strange Fear, never wholly exorcised, that had

leaped suddenly upon Défago in the middle of his singing. And
Simpson, as he lay there, watching the darkness through the open
flap of the tent, ready to plunge into the fragrant abyss of sleep,
knew first that unique and profound stillness of a primeval forest
when no wind stirs . . . and when the night has weight and substance
that enters into the soul to bind a veil about it. . . . Then sleep took
him. . . .

III

Thus, it seemed to him, at least. Yet it was true that the lap of
the water, just beyond the tent door, still beat time with his
lessening pulses when he realized that he was lying with his eyes
open and that another sound had recently introduced itself with
cunning softness between the splash and murmur of the little
waves.

And, long before he understood what this sound was, it had
stirred in him the centers of pity and alarm. He listened intently,
though at first in vain, for the running blood beat all its drums too
noisily in his ears. Did it come, he wondered, from the lake, or
from the woods? . . .

Then, suddenly, with a rush and a flutter of the heart, he knew
that it was close beside him in the tent; and, when he turned over
for a better hearing, it focused itself unmistakably not two feet
away. It was a sound of weeping; Défago upon his bed of branches
was sobbing in the darkness as though his heart would break, the
blankets evidently stuffed against his mouth to stifle it.

And his first feeling, before he could think or reflect, was the
rush of a poignant and searching tenderness. This intimate, human
sound, heard amid the desolation about them, woke pity. It was so
incongruous, so pitifully incongruous—and so vain! Tears—in this
vast and cruel wilderness: of what avail? He thought of a little child
crying in mid-Atlantic. . . . Then, of course, with fuller realization,
and the memory of what had gone before, came the descent of the
terror upon him, and his blood ran cold.

"Défago," he whispered quickly, "what's the matter?" He tried
to make his voice very gentle. "Are you in pain—unhappy—?" There

was no reply, but the sounds ceased abruptly. He stretched his hand out and touched him. The body did not stir.

"Are you awake?" for it occurred to him that the man was crying in his sleep. "Are you cold?" He noticed that his feet, which were uncovered, projected beyond the mouth of the tent. He spread an extra fold of his own blankets over them. The guide had slipped down in his bed, and the branches seemed to have been dragged with him. He was afraid to pull the body back again, for fear of waking him.

One or two tentative questions he ventured softly, but though he waited for several minutes there came no reply, nor any sign of movement. Presently he heard his regular and quiet breathing, and putting his hand again gently on the breast, felt the steady rise and fall beneath.

"Let me know if anything's wrong," he whispered, "or if I can do anything. Wake me at once if you feel—queer."

He hardly knew what to say. He lay down again, thinking and wondering what it all meant. Défago, of course, had been crying in his sleep. Some dream or other had afflicted him. Yet never in his life would he forget that pitiful sound of sobbing, and the feeling that the whole awful wilderness of woods listened. . . .

His own mind busied itself for a long time with the recent events, of which *this* took its mysterious place as one, and though his reason successfully argued away all unwelcome suggestions, a sensation of uneasiness remained, resisting ejection, very deep-seated—peculiar beyond ordinary.

IV

But sleep, in the long run, proves greater than all emotions. His thoughts soon wandered again; he lay there, warm as toast, exceedingly weary; the night soothed and comforted, blunting the edges of memory and alarm. Half an hour later he was oblivious of everything in the outer world about him.

Yet sleep, in this case, was his great enemy, concealing all approaches, smothering the warning of his nerves.

As, sometimes, in a nightmare events crowd upon each other's heels with a conviction of dreadfulest reality, yet some inconsistent detail accuses the whole display of incompleteness and disguise, so the events that now followed, though they actually happened, persuaded the mind somehow that the detail which could explain them had been overlooked in the confusion, and that therefore they were but partly true, the rest delusion. At the back of the sleeper's mind something remains awake, ready to let slip the judgment. "All this is not *quite* real; when you wake up you'll understand."

And thus, in a way, it was with Simpson. The events, not wholly inexplicable or incredible in themselves, yet remain for the man who saw and heard them a sequence of separate facts of cold horror, because the little piece that might have made the puzzle clear lay concealed or overlooked.

So far as he can recall, it was a violent movement, running downwards through the tent towards the door, that first woke him and made him aware that his companion was sitting bolt upright beside him—quivering. Hours must have passed, for it was the pale gleam of the dawn that revealed his outline against the canvas. This time the man was not crying; he was quaking like a leaf; the trembling he felt plainly through the blankets down the entire length of his own body. Défago had huddled down against him for protection, shrinking away from something that apparently concealed itself near the door flaps of the little tent.

Simpson thereupon called out in a loud voice some question or other—in the first bewilderment of waking he does not remember exactly what—and the man made no reply. The atmosphere and feeling of true nightmare lay horribly about him, making movement and speech both difficult. At first, indeed, he was not sure where he was—whether in one of the earlier camps, or at home in his bed at Aberdeen. The sense of confusion was very troubling.

And next—almost simultaneous with his waking, it seemed—the profound stillness of the dawn outside was shattered by a most uncommon sound. It came without warning, or audible approach; and it was unspeakably dreadful. It was a voice, Simpson declares, possibly a human voice; hoarse yet plaintive—a soft, roaring voice close outside the tent, overhead rather than upon the ground, of immense volume, while in some strange way most penetratingly and seductively sweet. It rang out, too, in three separate and distinct notes, or cries, that bore in some odd fashion a resemblance, farfetched yet recognizable, to the name of the guide: "*Dé-fa-go!*"

The student admits he is unable to describe it quite intelligently, for it was unlike any sound he had ever heard in his life, and combined a blending of such contrary qualities. "A sort of windy, crying voice," he calls it, "as of something lonely and untamed, wild and of abominable power. . . ."

And, even before it ceased, dropping back into the great gulfs of silence, the guide beside him had sprung to his feet with an answering though unintelligible cry. He blundered against the tent pole with violence, shaking the whole structure, spreading his arms out frantically for more room, and kicking his legs impetuously free of the clinging blankets. For a second, perhaps two, he stood upright by the door, his outline dark against the pallor of the dawn; then, with a furious, rushing speed, before his companion could move a hand to stop him, he shot with a plunge through the flaps of canvas—and was gone. And as he went—so astonishingly fast that the voice could actually be heard dying in the distance—he called aloud in tones of anguished terror that at the same time held something strangely like the frenzied exultation of delight—

"Oh! oh! My feet of fire! My burning feet of fire! Oh! oh! This height and fiery speed!"

And then the distance quickly buried it, and the deep silence of very early morning descended upon the forest as before.

It had all come about with such rapidity that, but for the evidence of the empty bed beside him, Simpson could almost have believed it to have been the memory of a nightmare carried over from sleep. He still felt the warm pressure of that vanished body against his side; there lay the twisted blankets in a heap; the very tent yet trembled with the vehemence of the impetuous departure. The strange words rang in his ears, as though he still heard them in the distance—wild language of a suddenly stricken mind.

Moreover, it was not only the senses of sight and hearing that reported uncommon things to his brain, for even while the man cried and ran, he had become aware that a strange perfume, faint yet pungent, pervaded the interior of the tent. And it was at this point, it seems, brought to himself by the consciousness that his nostrils were taking this distressing odor down into his throat, that he found his courage, sprang quickly to his feet—and went out.

The grey light of dawn that dropped, cold and glimmering, between the trees revealed the scene tolerably well. There stood the tent behind him, soaked with dew; the dark ashes of the fire, still warm; the lake, white beneath a coating of mist, the islands rising darkly out of it like objects packed in wool; and patches of snow beyond among the clearer spaces of the Bush—everything cold, still, waiting for the sun. But nowhere a sign of the vanished guide—still, doubtless, flying at frantic speed through the frozen woods. There was not even the sound of disappearing footsteps, nor the echoes of the dying voice. He had gone—utterly.

There was nothing; nothing but the sense of his recent presence, so strongly left behind about the camp; *and*—this penetrating, all-pervading odor.

And even this was now rapidly disappearing in its turn. In spite of his exceeding mental perturbation, Simpson struggled hard to detect its nature, and define it, but the ascertaining of an elusive scent, not recognized subconsciously and at once, is a very subtle operation of the mind. And he failed. It was gone before he could properly seize or name it. Approximate description, even, seems to have been difficult, for it was unlike any smell he knew. Acrid rather, not unlike the odor of a lion, he thinks, yet softer and not wholly unpleasing, with something almost sweet in it that reminded him of the scent of decaying garden leaves, earth, and the myriad, nameless perfumes that make up the odor of a big forest. Yet the "odor of lions" is the phrase with which he usually sums it all up.

Then—it was wholly gone, and he found himself standing by the ashes of the fire in a state of amazement and stupid terror that left him the helpless prey of anything that chose to happen. Had a muskrat poked its pointed muzzle over a rock, or a squirrel scuttled in that instant down the bark of a tree, he would most likely have collapsed without more ado and fainted. For he felt about the whole affair the touch somewhere of a great Outer Horror . . . and his scattered powers had not as yet had time to collect themselves into a definite attitude of fighting self-control.

Nothing did happen, however. A great kiss of wind ran softly through the awakening forest, and a few maple leaves here and there rustled tremblingly to earth. The sky seemed to grow suddenly much lighter. Simpson felt the cool air upon his cheek and uncovered head; realized that he was shivering with the cold; and, making a great effort, realized next that he was alone in the Bush—*and* that he was called upon to take immediate steps to find and succor his vanished companion.

Make an effort, accordingly, he did, though an ill-calculated and futile one. With that wilderness of trees about him, the sheet of water cutting him off behind, and the horror of that wild cry in his blood, he did what any other inexperienced man would have done in similar bewilderment: he ran about, without any sense of direction, like a frantic child, and called loudly without ceasing the name of the guide:

"Défago! Défago! Défago!" he yelled, and the trees gave him back the name as often as he shouted, only a little softened— "Défago! Défago! Défago!"

He followed the trail that lay a short distance across the patches of snow, and then lost it again where the trees grew too thickly for snow to lie. He shouted till he was hoarse, and till the sound of his own voice in all that unanswering and listening world began to frighten him. His confusion increased in direct ratio to the violence of his efforts. His distress became formidably acute, till at length his exertions defeated their own object, and from sheer exhaustion he headed back to the camp again. It remains a wonder that he ever found his way. It was with great difficulty, and only after numberless false clues, that he at last saw the white tent between the trees, and so reached safety.

Exhaustion then applied its own remedy, and he grew calmer. He made the fire and breakfasted. Hot coffee and bacon put a little sense and judgment into him again, and he realized that he had been behaving like a boy. He now made another, and more successful attempt to face the situation collectedly, and, a nature naturally plucky coming to his assistance, he decided that he must first make as thorough a search as possible, failing success in which, he must find his way into the home camp as best he could and bring help.

And this was what he did. Taking food, matches and rifle with him, and a small axe to blaze the trees against his return journey, he set forth. It was eight o'clock when he started, the sun shining over the tops of the trees in a sky without clouds. Pinned to a stake by the fire he left a note in case Défago returned while he was away.

This time, according to a careful plan, he took a new direction, intending to make a wide sweep that must sooner or later cut into indications of the guide's trail; and, before he had gone a quarter of a mile he came across the tracks of a large animal in the snow, and beside it the light and smaller tracks of what were beyond question human feet—the feet of Défago. The relief he at once experienced was natural, though brief; for at first sight he saw in these tracks a simple explanation of the whole matter: these big marks had surely been left by a bull moose that, wind against it, had blundered upon the camp, and uttered its singular cry of warning and alarm the moment its mistake was apparent. Défago, in whom the hunting instinct was developed to the point of uncanny perfection, had scented the brute coming down the wind hours before. His excitement and disappearance were due, of course, to— to his—

Then the impossible explanation at which he grasped faded, as common sense showed him mercilessly that none of this was true. No guide, much less a guide like Défago, could have acted in so irrational a way, going off even without his rifle . . . ! The whole affair demanded a far more complicated elucidation, when he remembered the details of it all—the cry of terror, the amazing language, the grey face of horror when his nostrils first caught the new odor; that muffled sobbing in the darkness, and—for this, too, now came back to him dimly—the man's original aversion for this particular bit of country. . . .

Besides, now that he examined them closer, these were not the tracks of a bull moose at all! Hank had explained to him the outline of a bull's hoofs, of a cow's or calf s, too, for that matter; he had drawn them clearly on a strip of birch bark. And these were wholly different. They were big, round, ample, and with no pointed outline as of sharp hoofs. He wondered for a moment whether bear tracks were like that. There was no other animal he could think of, for caribou did not come so far south at this season, and, even if they did, would leave hoof marks.

They were ominous signs—these mysterious writings left in the snow by the unknown creature that had lured a human being away from safety—and when he coupled them in his imagination with that haunting sound that broke the stillness of the dawn, a momentary dizziness shook his mind, distressing him again beyond belief. He felt the *threatening* aspect of it all. And, stooping down to examine the marks more closely, he caught a faint whiff of that sweet yet pungent odor that made him instantly straighten up again, fighting a sensation almost of nausea.

Then his memory played him another evil trick. He suddenly recalled those uncovered feet projecting beyond the edge of the tent, and the body's appearance of having been dragged towards the opening; the man's shrinking from something by the door when he woke later. The details now beat against his trembling mind with concerted attack. They seemed to gather in those deep spaces of the silent forest about him, where the host of trees stood waiting, listening, watching to see what he would do. The woods were closing round him.

With the persistence of true pluck, however, Simpson went forward, following the tracks as best he could, smothering these ugly emotions that sought to weaken his will. He blazed innumerable trees as he went, ever fearful of being unable to find the way back, and calling aloud at intervals of a few seconds the name of the guide. The dull tapping of the axe upon the massive trunks, and the unnatural accents of his own voice became at length sounds that he even dreaded to make, dreaded to hear. For they drew attention without ceasing to his presence and exact whereabouts, and if it were really the case that something was hunting himself down in the same way that he was hunting down another—

With a strong effort, he crushed the thought out the instant it rose. It was the beginning, he realized, of a bewilderment utterly diabolical in kind that would speedily destroy him.

Although the snow was not continuous, lying merely in shallow flurries over the more open spaces, he found no difficulty in following the tracks for the first few miles. They went straight as a ruled line wherever the trees permitted. The stride soon began to increase in length, till it finally assumed proportions that seemed absolutely impossible for any ordinary animal to have made. Like huge flying leaps they became. One of these he measured, and though he knew that "stretch" of eighteen feet must be somehow wrong, he was at a complete loss to understand why he found no signs on the snow between the extreme points. But what perplexed him even more, making him feel his vision had gone utterly awry, was that Défago's stride increased in the same manner, and finally covered the same incredible distances. It looked as if the great beast had lifted him with it and carried him across these astonishing intervals. Simpson, who was much longer in the limb, found that he could not compass even half the stretch by taking a running jump.

And the sight of these huge tracks, running side by side, silent evidence of a dreadful journey in which terror or madness had urged to impossible results, was profoundly moving. It shocked him in the secret depths of his soul. It was the most horrible thing his eyes had ever looked upon. He began to follow them mechanically, absentmindedly almost, ever peering over his shoulder to see if he, too, were being followed by something with a gigantic tread. . . . And soon it came about that he no longer quite realized what it was they signified—these impressions left upon the snow by something nameless and untamed, always

accompanied by the footmarks of the little French Canadian, his
guide, his comrade, the man who had shared his tent a few hours
before, chatting, laughing, even singing by his side. . . .

V

For a man of his years and inexperience, only a canny Scot,
perhaps, grounded in common sense and established in logic, could
have preserved even that measure of balance that this youth
somehow or other did manage to preserve through the whole
adventure. Otherwise, two things he presently noticed, while
forging pluckily ahead, must have sent him headlong back to the
comparative safety of his tent, instead of only making his hands
close more tightly upon the rifle stock, while his heart, trained for
the Wee Kirk, sent a wordless prayer winging its way to heaven.
Both tracks, he saw, had undergone a change, and this change, so
far as it concerned the footsteps of the man, was in some
undecipherable manner—appalling.

It was in the bigger tracks he first noticed this, and for a long
time he could not quite believe his eyes. Was it the blown leaves
that produced odd effects of light and shade, or that the dry snow,
drifting like finely ground rice about the edges, cast shadows and
high lights? Or was it actually the fact that the great marks had
become faintly colored? For round about the deep, plunging holes
of the animal there now appeared a mysterious, reddish tinge that
was more like an effect of light than of anything that dyed the
substance of the snow itself. Every mark had it, and had it
increasingly—this indistinct fiery tinge that painted a new touch
of ghastliness into the picture.

But when, wholly unable to explain or to credit it, he turned
his attention to the other tracks to discover if they, too, bore similar
witness, he noticed that these had meanwhile undergone a change
that was infinitely worse, and charged with far more horrible
suggestion. For, in the last hundred yards or so, he saw that they
had grown gradually into the semblance of the parent tread.
Imperceptibly the change had come about, yet unmistakably. It was
hard to see where the change first began. The result, however, was

beyond question. Smaller, neater, more cleanly modeled, they formed now an exact and careful duplicate of the larger tracks beside them. The feet that produced them had, therefore, also changed. And something in his mind reared up with loathing and with terror as he saw it.

Simpson, for the first time, hesitated; then, ashamed of his alarm and indecision, took a few hurried steps ahead; the next instant stopped dead in his tracks. Immediately in front of him all signs of the trail ceased; both tracks came to an abrupt end. On all sides, for a hundred yards and more, he searched in vain for the least indication of their continuance. There was—nothing.

The trees were very thick just there, big trees all of them, spruce, cedar, hemlock; there was no underbrush. He stood, looking about him, all distraught; bereft of any power of judgment. Then he set to work to search again, and again, and yet again, but always with the same result: *nothing*. The feet that printed the surface of the snow thus far had now, apparently, left the ground!

And it was in that moment of distress and confusion that the whip of terror laid its most nicely calculated lash about his heart. It dropped with deadly effect upon the sorest spot of all, completely unnerving him. He had been secretly dreading all the time that it would come—and come it did.

Far overhead, muted by great height and distance, strangely thinned and wailing, he heard the crying voice of Défago, the guide.

The sound dropped upon him out of that still, wintry sky with an effect of dismay and terror unsurpassed. The rifle fell to his feet. He stood motionless an instant, listening as it were with his whole body, then staggered back against the nearest tree for support, disorganized hopelessly in mind and spirit. To him, in that moment, it seemed the most shattering and dislocating experience he had ever known, so that his heart emptied itself of all feeling whatsoever as by a sudden draught.

"Oh! oh! This fiery height! Oh, my feet of fire! My burning feet of fire . . . !" ran in far, beseeching accents of indescribable appeal this voice of anguish down the sky. Once it called—then silence through all the listening wilderness of trees.

And Simpson, scarcely knowing what he did, presently found himself running wildly to and fro, searching, calling, tripping over roots and boulders, and flinging himself in a frenzy of undirected pursuit after the Caller. Behind the screen of memory and emotion with which experience veils events, he plunged, distracted and half-deranged, picking up false lights like a ship at sea, terror in his eyes and heart and soul. For the Panic of the Wilderness had called to him in that far voice—the Power of untamed Distance—the Enticement of the Desolation that destroys. He knew in that moment all the pains of someone hopelessly and irretrievably lost, suffering the lust and travail of a soul in the final Loneliness. A vision of Défago, eternally hunted, driven and pursued across the skiey vastness of those ancient forests fled like a flame across the dark ruin of his thoughts. . . .

It seemed ages before he could find anything in the chaos of his disorganized sensations to which he could anchor himself steady for a moment, and think. . . .

The cry was not repeated; his own hoarse calling brought no response; the inscrutable forces of the Wild had summoned their victim beyond recall—and held him fast.

Yet he searched and called, it seems, for hours afterwards, for it was late in the afternoon when at length he decided to abandon a useless pursuit and return to his camp on the shores of Fifty Island Water. Even then he went with reluctance, that crying voice still echoing in his ears. With difficulty he found his rifle and the homeward trail. The concentration necessary to follow the badly blazed trees, and a biting hunger that gnawed, helped to keep his mind steady. Otherwise, he admits, the temporary aberration he had suffered might have been prolonged to the point of positive disaster. Gradually the ballast shifted back again, and he regained something that approached his normal equilibrium.

But for all that the journey through the gathering dusk was miserably haunted. He heard innumerable following footsteps; voices that laughed and whispered; and saw figures crouching behind trees and boulders, making signs to one another for a concerted attack the moment he had passed. The creeping murmur of the wind made him start and listen. He went stealthily, trying to hide where possible, and making as little sound as he could. The shadows of the woods, hitherto protective or covering merely, had now become menacing, challenging; and the pageantry in his frightened mind masked a host of possibilities that were all the more ominous for being obscure. The presentiment of a nameless doom lurked ill-concealed behind every detail of what had happened.

It was really admirable how he emerged victor in the end; men of riper powers and experience might have come through the ordeal with less success. He had himself tolerably well in hand, all things considered, and his plan of action proves it. Sleep being absolutely out of the question and traveling an unknown trail in the darkness equally impracticable, he sat up the whole of that night, rifle in hand, before a fire he never for a single moment allowed to die down. The severity of the haunted vigil marked his soul for life; but it was successfully accomplished; and with the very first signs of dawn he set forth upon the long return journey to the home camp to get help. As before, he left a written note to explain his absence, and to indicate where he had left a plentiful *cache* of food and matches—though he had no expectation that any human hands would find them!

How Simpson found his way alone by the lake and forest might well make a story in itself, for to hear him tell it is to *know* the passionate loneliness of soul that a man can feel when the Wilderness holds him in the hollow of its illimitable hand—and laughs. It is also to admire his indomitable pluck.

He claims no skill, declaring that he followed the almost invisible trail mechanically, and without thinking. And this, doubtless, is the truth. He relied upon the guiding of the unconscious mind, which is instinct. Perhaps, too, some sense of orientation, known to animals and primitive men, may have helped as well, for through all that tangled region he succeeded in reaching the exact spot where Défago had hidden the canoe nearly three days before with the remark, "Strike doo west across the lake into the sun to find the camp."

There was not much sun left to guide him, but he used his compass to the best of his ability, embarking in the frail craft for the last twelve miles of his journey with a sensation of immense relief that the forest was at last behind him. And, fortunately, the water was calm; he took his line across the center of the lake instead of coasting round the shores for another twenty miles. Fortunately, too, the other hunters were back. The light of their fires furnished a steering point without which he might have searched all night long for the actual position of the camp.

It was close upon midnight all the same when his canoe grated on the sandy cove, and Hank, Punk and his uncle, disturbed in their sleep by his cries, ran quickly down and helped a very exhausted and broken specimen of Scotch humanity over the rocks toward a dying fire.

VI

The sudden entrance of his prosaic uncle into this world of wizardry and horror that had haunted him without interruption now for two days and two nights, had the immediate effect of giving to the affair an entirely new aspect. The sound of that crisp "Hulloa, my boy! And what's up *now*?" and the grasp of that dry and vigorous hand introduced another standard of judgment. A revulsion of feeling washed through him. He realized that he had let himself "go" rather badly. He even felt vaguely ashamed of himself. The native hard-headedness of his race reclaimed him.

And this doubtless explains why he found it so hard to tell that group round the fire—everything. He told enough, however, for the immediate decision to be arrived at that a relief party must start at the earliest possible moment, and that Simpson, in order to guide it capably, must first have food and, above all, sleep. Dr. Cathcart observing the lad's condition more shrewdly than his patient knew, gave him a very slight injection of morphine. For six hours he slept like the dead.

From the description carefully written out afterwards by this student of divinity, it appears that the account he gave to the astonished group omitted sundry vital and important details. He declares that, with his uncle's wholesome, matter-of-fact countenance staring him in the face, he simply had not the courage to mention them. Thus, all the search party gathered, it would seem, was that Défago had suffered in the night an acute and inexplicable attack of mania, had imagined himself "called" by someone or something, and had plunged into the bush after it without food or rifle, where he must die a horrible and lingering death by cold and starvation unless he could be found and rescued in time. "In time," moreover, meant *at once*.

In the course of the following day, however—they were off by seven, leaving Punk in charge with instructions to have food and fire always ready—Simpson found it possible to tell his uncle a good deal more of the story's true inwardness, without divining that it was drawn out of him as a matter of fact by a very subtle form of cross examination. By the time they reached the beginning of the trail, where the canoe was laid up against the return journey, he had mentioned how Défago spoke vaguely of "something he called a 'Wendigo'"; how he cried in his sleep; how he imagined an unusual scent about the camp; and had betrayed other symptoms of mental excitement. He also admitted the bewildering effect of "that extraordinary odor" upon himself, "pungent and acrid like the odor of lions." And by the time they were within an easy hour of Fifty Island Water he had let slip the further fact—a foolish avowal of his own hysterical condition, as he felt afterwards—that he had heard the vanished guide call "for help." He omitted the singular phrases used, for he simply could not bring himself to repeat the preposterous language. Also, while describing how the man's footsteps in the snow had gradually assumed an exact miniature likeness of the animal's plunging tracks, he left out the fact that they measured a *wholly* incredible distance. It seemed a question, nicely balanced between individual pride and honesty, what he should reveal and what suppress. He mentioned the fiery tinge in the snow, for instance, yet shrank from telling that body and bed had been partly dragged out of the tent. . . .

With the net result that Dr. Cathcart, adroit psychologist that he fancied himself to be, had assured him clearly enough exactly where his mind, influenced by loneliness, bewilderment and terror, had yielded to the strain and invited delusion. While praising his conduct, he managed at the same time to point out where, when, and how his mind had gone astray. He made his nephew think himself finer than he was by judicious praise, yet more foolish than he was by minimizing the value of the evidence. Like many another materialist, that is, he lied cleverly on the basis of insufficient knowledge, *because* the knowledge supplied seemed to his own particular intelligence inadmissible.

"The spell of these terrible solitudes," he said, "cannot leave any mind untouched, any mind, that is, possessed of the higher imaginative qualities. It has worked upon yours exactly as it worked upon my own when I was your age. The animal that haunted your little camp was undoubtedly a moose, for the 'belling' of a moose may have, sometimes, a very peculiar quality of sound. The colored appearance of the big tracks was obviously a defect of vision in your own eyes produced by excitement. The size and stretch of the tracks we shall prove when we come to them. But the hallucination of an audible voice, of course, is one of the commonest forms of delusion due to mental excitement—an excitement, my dear boy, perfectly excusable, and, let me add, wonderfully controlled by you under the circumstances. For the rest, I am bound to say, you have acted with a splendid courage, for the terror of feeling oneself lost in this wilderness is nothing short of awful, and, had I been in your place, I don't for a moment believe I could have behaved with one quarter of your wisdom and decision. The only thing I find it uncommonly difficult to explain is—that—damned odor."

"It made me feel sick, I assure you," declared his nephew, "positively dizzy!" His uncle's attitude of calm omniscience, merely because he knew more psychological formulae, made him slightly defiant. It was so easy to be wise in the explanation of an experience one has not personally witnessed. "A kind of desolate and terrible odor is the only way I can describe it," he concluded, glancing at the features of the quiet, unemotional man beside him.

"I can only marvel," was the reply, "that under the circumstances it did not seem to you even worse." The dry words, Simpson knew, hovered between the truth, and his uncle's interpretation of "the truth."

And so at last they came to the little camp and found the tent still standing, the remains of the fire, and the piece of paper pinned to a stake beside it—untouched. The cache, poorly contrived by inexperienced hands, however, had been discovered and opened— by musk rats, mink and squirrel. The matches lay scattered about the opening, but the food had been taken to the last crumb.

"Well, fellers, he ain't here," exclaimed Hank loudly after his fashion. "And that's as sartain as the coal supply down below! But whar he's got to by this time is 'bout as unsartain as the trade in crowns in t'other place." The presence of a divinity student was no barrier to his language at such a time, though for the reader's sake it may be severely edited. "I propose," he added, "that we start out at once an' hunt for'm like hell!"

The gloom of Défago's probable fate oppressed the whole party with a sense of dreadful gravity the moment they saw the familiar signs of recent occupancy. Especially the tent, with the bed of balsam branches still smoothed and flattened by the pressure of his body, seemed to bring his presence near to them. Simpson, feeling vaguely as if his world were somehow at stake, went about explaining particulars in a hushed tone. He was much calmer now, though overwearied with the strain of his many journeys. His uncle's method of explaining— "explaining away," rather—the details still fresh in his haunted memory helped, too, to put ice upon his emotions.

"And that's the direction he ran off in," he said to his two companions, pointing in the direction where the guide had vanished that morning in the grey dawn. "Straight down there he ran like a deer, in between the birch and the hemlock. . . ."

Hank and Dr. Cathcart exchanged glances.

"And it was about two miles down there, in a straight line," continued the other, speaking with something of the former terror in his voice, "that I followed his trail to the place where—it stopped—dead!"

"And where you heered him callin' an' caught the stench, an' all the rest of the wicked entertainment," cried Hank, with a volubility that betrayed his keen distress.

"And where your excitement overcame you to the point of producing illusions," added Dr. Cathcart under his breath, yet not so low that his nephew did not hear it.

It was early in the afternoon, for they had traveled quickly, and there were still a good two hours of daylight left. Dr. Cathcart and Hank lost no time in beginning the search, but Simpson was too exhausted to accompany them. They would follow the blazed marks on the trees, and where possible, his footsteps. Meanwhile the best thing he could do was to keep a good fire going, and rest.

But after something like three hours' search, the darkness already down, the two men returned to camp with nothing to report. Fresh snow had covered all signs, and though they had followed the blazed trees to the spot where Simpson had turned back, they had not discovered the smallest indication of a human being—or for that matter, of an animal. There were no fresh tracks of any kind; the snow lay undisturbed.

It was difficult to know what was best to do, though in reality there was nothing more they *could* do. They might stay and search for weeks without much chance of success. The fresh snow destroyed their only hope, and they gathered round the fire for supper, a gloomy and despondent party. The facts, indeed, were sad enough, for Défago had a wife at Rat Portage, and his earnings were the family's sole means of support.

Now that the whole truth in all its ugliness was out, it seemed useless to deal in further disguise or pretense. They talked openly of the facts and probabilities. It was not the first time, even in the experience of Dr. Cathcart, that a man had yielded to the singular seduction of the Solitudes and gone out of his mind; Défago, moreover, was predisposed to something of the sort, for he already had a touch of melancholia in his blood, and his fiber was weakened by bouts of drinking that often lasted for weeks at a time. Something on this trip—one might never know precisely what—had sufficed to push him over the line, that was all. And he had gone, gone off into the great wilderness of trees and lakes to die by starvation and exhaustion. The chances against his finding camp again were overwhelming; the delirium that was upon him would also doubtless have increased, and it was quite likely he might do violence to himself and so hasten his cruel fate. Even while they talked, indeed, the end had probably come. On the suggestion of Hank, his old pal, however, they proposed to wait a little longer and devote the whole of the following day, from dawn to darkness, to the most systematic search they could devise. They would divide the territory between them. They discussed their plan in great detail. All that men could do they would do. And, meanwhile, they talked about the particular form in which the singular Panic of the Wilderness had made its attack upon the mind of the unfortunate guide. Hank, though familiar with the legend in its general outline, obviously did not welcome the turn the conversation had taken. He contributed little, though that little was illuminating. For he admitted that a story ran over all this section of country to the effect that several Indians had "seen the Wendigo" along the shores of Fifty Island Water in the "fall" of last year, and that this was the true reason of Défago's disinclination to hunt there. Hank doubtless felt that he had in a sense helped his old pal to death by overpersuading him. "When an Indian goes crazy," he explained, talking to himself more than to the others, it seemed, "it's always put that he's 'seen the Wendigo.' An' pore old Défaygo was superstitious down to he very heels . . . !"

And then Simpson, feeling the atmosphere more sympathetic, told over again the full story of his astonishing tale; he left out no details this time; he mentioned his own sensations and gripping fears. He only omitted the strange language used.

"But Défago surely had already told you all these details of the Wendigo legend, my dear fellow," insisted the doctor. "I mean, he had talked about it, and thus put into your mind the ideas which your own excitement afterwards developed?"

Whereupon Simpson again repeated the facts. Défago, he declared, had barely mentioned the beast. He, Simpson, knew nothing of the story, and, so far as he remembered, had never even read about it. Even the word was unfamiliar.

Of course he was telling the truth, and Dr. Cathcart was reluctantly compelled to admit the singular character of the whole affair. He did not do this in words so much as in manner, however. He kept his back against a good, stout tree; he poked the fire into a blaze the moment it showed signs of dying down; he was quicker than any of them to notice the least sound in the night about them— a fish jumping in the lake, a twig snapping in the bush, the dropping of occasional fragments of frozen snow from the branches overhead where the heat loosened them. His voice, too, changed a little in quality, becoming a shade less confident, lower also in tone. Fear, to put it plainly, hovered close about that little camp, and though all three would have been glad to speak of other matters, the only thing they seemed able to discuss was this—the source of their fear. They tried other subjects in vain; there was nothing to say about them. Hank was the most honest of the group; he said next to nothing. He never once, however, turned his back to the darkness. His face was always to the forest, and when wood was needed he didn't go farther than was necessary to get it.

VII

A wall of silence wrapped them in, for the snow, though not thick, was sufficient to deaden any noise, and the frost held things pretty tight besides. No sound but their voices and the soft roar of the flames made itself heard. Only, from time to time, something soft as the flutter of a pine moth's wings went past them through the air. No one seemed anxious to go to bed. The hours slipped towards midnight.

"The legend is picturesque enough," observed the doctor after one of the longer pauses, speaking to break it rather than because he had anything to say, "for the Wendigo is simply the Call of the

Wild personified, which some natures hear to their own destruction."

"That's about it," Hank said presently. "An' there's no misunderstandin' when you hear it. It calls you by name right 'nough."

Another pause followed. Then Dr. Cathcart came back to the forbidden subject with a rush that made the others jump.

"The allegory *is* significant," he remarked, looking about him into the darkness, "for the Voice, they say, resembles all the minor sounds of the Bush—wind, falling water, cries of the animals, and so forth. And, once the victim hears *that*—he's off for good, of course! His most vulnerable points, moreover, are said to be the feet and the eyes; the feet, you see, for the lust of wandering, and the eyes for the lust of beauty. The poor beggar goes at such a dreadful speed that he bleeds beneath the eyes, and his feet burn."

Dr. Cathcart, as he spoke, continued to peer uneasily into the surrounding gloom. His voice sank to a hushed tone.

"The Wendigo," he added, "is said to burn his feet—owing to the friction, apparently caused by its tremendous velocity—till they drop off, and new ones form exactly like its own."

Simpson listened in horrified amazement; but it was the pallor on Hank's face that fascinated him most. He would willingly have stopped his ears and closed his eyes, had he dared.

"It don't always keep to the ground neither," came in Hank's slow, heavy drawl, "for it goes so high that he thinks the stars have set him all a-fire. An' it'll take great thumpin' jumps sometimes, an' run along the tops of the trees, carrying its partner with it, an' then droppin' him jest as a fish hawk'll drop a pickerel to kill it before eatin'. An' its food, of all the muck in the whole Bush is—moss!" And he laughed a short, unnatural laugh. "It's a moss-eater, is the Wendigo," he added, looking up excitedly into the faces of his companions. "Moss-eater," he repeated, with a string of the most outlandish oaths he could invent.

But Simpson now understood the true purpose of all this talk. What these two men, each strong and "experienced" in his own way, dreaded more than anything else was—silence. They were talking against time. They were also talking against darkness, against the invasion of panic, against the admission reflection might bring that they were in an enemy's country—against anything, in fact, rather than allow their inmost thoughts to assume control. He himself, already initiated by the awful vigil with terror, was beyond both of them in this respect. He had reached the stage where he was immune. But these two, the scoffing, analytical doctor, and the honest, dogged backwoodsman, each sat trembling in the depths of his being.

Thus the hours passed; and thus, with lowered voices and a kind of taut inner resistance of spirit, this little group of humanity sat in the jaws of the wilderness and talked foolishly of the terrible and haunting legend. It was an unequal contest, all things considered, for the wilderness had already the advantage of first attack—and of a hostage. The fate of their comrade hung over them with a steadily increasing weight of oppression that finally became insupportable.

It was Hank, after a pause longer than the preceding ones that no one seemed able to break, who first let loose all this pent-up emotion in very unexpected fashion, by springing suddenly to his feet and letting out the most ear-shattering yell imaginable into the night. He could not contain himself any longer, it seemed. To make it carry even beyond an ordinary cry he interrupted its rhythm by shaking the palm of his hand before his mouth.

"That's for Défago," he said, looking down at the other two with a queer, defiant laugh, "for it's my belief"—the sandwiched oaths may be omitted— "that my ole partner's not far from us at this very minute."

There was a vehemence and recklessness about his performance that made Simpson, too, start to his feet in amazement, and betrayed even the doctor into letting the pipe slip from between his lips. Hank's face was ghastly, but Cathcart's showed a sudden weakness—a loosening of all his faculties, as it were. Then a momentary anger blazed into his eyes, and he too, though with deliberation born of habitual self-control, got upon his feet and faced the excited guide. For this was unpermissible, foolish, dangerous, and he meant to stop it in the bud.

What might have happened in the next minute or two one may speculate about, yet never definitely know, for in the instant of profound silence that followed Hank's roaring voice, and as though in answer to it, something went past through the darkness of the sky overhead at terrific speed—something of necessity very large, for it displaced much air, while down between the trees there fell a faint and windy cry of a human voice, calling in tones of indescribable anguish and appeal—

"Oh, oh! This fiery height! Oh, oh! My feet of fire! My burning feet of fire!"

White to the very edge of his shirt, Hank looked stupidly about him like a child. Dr. Cathcart uttered some kind of unintelligible cry, turning as he did so with an instinctive movement of blind terror towards the protection of the tent, then halting in the act as though frozen. Simpson, alone of the three, retained his presence of mind a little. His own horror was too deep to allow of any immediate reaction. He had heard that cry before.

Turning to his stricken companions, he said almost calmly—

"That's exactly the cry I heard—the very words he used!"

Then, lifting his face to the sky, he cried aloud, "Défago, Défago! Come down here to us! Come down—!"

And before there was time for anybody to take definite action one way or another, there came the sound of something dropping heavily between the trees, striking the branches on the way down, and landing with a dreadful thud upon the frozen earth below. The crash and thunder of it was really terrific.

"That's him, s'help me the good Gawd!" came from Hank in a whispering cry half choked, his hand going automatically toward the hunting knife in his belt. "And he's coming! He's coming!" he added, with an irrational laugh of horror, as the sounds of heavy footsteps crunching over the snow became distinctly audible, approaching through the blackness towards the circle of light.

And while the steps, with their stumbling motion, moved nearer and nearer upon them, the three men stood round that fire, motionless and dumb. Dr. Cathcart had the appearance of a man suddenly withered; even his eyes did not move. Hank, suffering shockingly, seemed on the verge again of violent action; yet did nothing. He, too, was hewn of stone. Like stricken children they seemed. The picture was hideous. And, meanwhile, their owner still invisible, the footsteps came closer, crunching the frozen snow. It was endless—too prolonged to be quite real—this measured and pitiless approach. It was accursed.

VIII

Then at length the darkness, having thus laboriously conceived, brought forth—a figure. It drew forward into the zone of uncertain light where fire and shadows mingled, not ten feet away; then halted, staring at them fixedly. The same instant it started forward again with the spasmodic motion as of a thing moved by wires, and coming up closer to them, full into the glare of the fire, they perceived then that—it was a man; and apparently that this man was—Défago.

Something like a skin of horror almost perceptibly drew down in that moment over every face, and three pairs of eyes shone through it as though they saw across the frontiers of normal vision into the Unknown.

Défago advanced, his tread faltering and uncertain; he made his way straight up to them as a group first, then turned sharply and peered close into the face of Simpson. The sound of a voice issued from his lips—

"Here I am, Boss Simpson. I heered someone calling me." It was a faint, dried up voice, made wheezy and breathless as by immense exertion. "I'm havin' a reg'lar hellfire kind of a trip, I am." And he laughed, thrusting his head forward into the other's face.

But that laugh started the machinery of the group of waxwork figures with the wax-white skins. Hank immediately sprang forward with a stream of oaths so farfetched that Simpson did not recognize them as English at all, but thought he had lapsed into Indian or some other lingo. He only realized that Hank's presence,

thrust thus between them, was welcome—uncommonly welcome.
Dr. Cathcart, though more calmly and leisurely, advanced behind
him, heavily stumbling.

Simpson seems hazy as to what was actually said and done in
those next few seconds, for the eyes of that detestable and blasted
visage peering at such close quarters into his own utterly
bewildered his senses at first. He merely stood still. He said
nothing. He had not the trained will of the older men that forced
them into action in defiance of all emotional stress. He watched
them moving as behind a glass that half destroyed their reality; it
was dreamlike; perverted. Yet, through the torrent of Hank's
meaningless phrases, he remembers hearing his uncle's tone of
authority—hard and forced—saying several things about food and
warmth, blankets, whisky and the rest . . . and, further, that whiffs
of that penetrating, unaccustomed odor, vile yet sweetly
bewildering, assailed his nostrils during all that followed.

It was no less a person than himself, however—less experienced
and adroit than the others though he was—who gave instinctive
utterance to the sentence that brought a measure of relief into the
ghastly situation by expressing the doubt and thought in each one's
heart.

"It *is—you*, isn't it, Défago?" he asked under his breath, horror
breaking his speech.

And at once Cathcart burst out with the loud answer before the
other had time to move his lips. "Of course it is! Of course it is!
Only—can't you see—he's nearly dead with exhaustion, cold and
terror! Isn't *that* enough to change a man beyond all recognition?"
It was said in order to convince himself as much as to convince the
others. The overemphasis alone proved that. And continually, while
he spoke and acted, he held a handkerchief to his nose. That odor
pervaded the whole camp.

For the "Défago" who sat huddled by the big fire, wrapped in
blankets, drinking hot whisky and holding food in wasted hands,
was no more like the guide they had last seen alive than the picture
of a man of sixty is like a daguerreotype of his early youth in the
costume of another generation. Nothing really can describe that

ghastly caricature, that parody, masquerading there in the firelight as Défago. From the ruins of the dark and awful memories he still retains, Simpson declares that the face was more animal than human, the features drawn about into wrong proportions, the skin loose and hanging, as though he had been subjected to extraordinary pressures and tensions. It made him think vaguely of those bladder faces blown up by the hawkers on Ludgate Hill, that change their expression as they swell, and as they collapse emit a faint and wailing imitation of a voice. Both face and voice suggested some such abominable resemblance. But Cathcart long afterwards, seeking to describe the indescribable, asserts that thus might have looked a face and body that had been in air so rarified that, the weight of atmosphere being removed, the entire structure threatened to fly asunder and become—*incoherent*. . . .

It was Hank, though all distraught and shaking with a tearing volume of emotion he could neither handle nor understand, who brought things to a head without much ado. He went off to a little distance from the fire, apparently so that the light should not dazzle him too much, and shading his eyes for a moment with both hands, shouted in a loud voice that held anger and affection dreadfully mingled:

"You ain't Défaygo! You ain't Défaygo at all! I don't give a—damn, but that ain't you, my ole pal of twenty years!" He glared upon the huddled figure as though he would destroy him with his eyes. "An' if it is I'll swab the floor of hell with a wad of cotton wool on a toothpick, s'help me the good Gawd!" he added, with a violent fling of horror and disgust.

It was impossible to silence him. He stood there shouting like one possessed, horrible to see, horrible to hear—*because it was the truth*. He repeated himself in fifty different ways, each more outlandish than the last. The woods rang with echoes. At one time it looked as if he meant to fling himself upon "the intruder," for his hand continually jerked towards the long hunting knife in his belt.

But in the end he did nothing, and the whole tempest completed itself very shortly with tears. Hank's voice suddenly broke, he collapsed on the ground, and Cathcart somehow or other persuaded him at last to go into the tent and lie quiet. The remainder of the affair, indeed, was witnessed by him from behind the canvas, his white and terrified face peeping through the crack of the tent door flap.

Then Dr. Cathcart, closely followed by his nephew who so far had kept his courage better than all of them, went up with a determined air and stood opposite to the figure of Défago huddled over the fire. He looked him squarely in the face and spoke. At first his voice was firm.

"Défago, tell us what's happened—just a little, so that we can know how best to help you?" he asked in a tone of authority, almost of command. And at that point, it *was* command. At once afterwards, however, it changed in quality, for the figure turned up to him a face so piteous, so terrible and so little like humanity, that the doctor shrank back from him as from something spiritually unclean. Simpson, watching close behind him, says he got the impression of a mask that was on the verge of dropping off, and that underneath they would discover something black and diabolical, revealed in utter nakedness. "Out with it, man, out with it!" Cathcart cried, terror running neck and neck with entreaty. "None of us can stand this much longer . . . !" It was the cry of instinct over reason.

And then "Défago," smiling *whitely*, answered in that thin and fading voice that already seemed passing over into a sound of quite another character—

"I seen that great Wendigo thing," he whispered, sniffing the air about him exactly like an animal. "I been with it too—"

Whether the poor devil would have said more, or whether Dr. Cathcart would have continued the impossible cross examination cannot be known, for at that moment the voice of Hank was heard yelling at the top of his voice from behind the canvas that concealed all but his terrified eyes. Such a howling was never heard.

"His feet! Oh, Gawd, his feet! Look at his great changed—feet!"

Défago, shuffling where he sat, had moved in such a way that for the first time his legs were in full light and his feet were visible. Yet Simpson had no time, himself, to see properly what Hank had seen. And Hank has never seen fit to tell. That same instant, with a leap like that of a frightened tiger, Cathcart was upon him, bundling the folds of blanket about his legs with such speed that the young student caught little more than a passing glimpse of something dark and oddly massed where moccasined feet ought to have been, and saw even that but with uncertain vision.

Then, before the doctor had time to do more, or Simpson time to even think a question, much less ask it, Défago was standing upright in front of them, balancing with pain and difficulty, and upon his shapeless and twisted visage an expression so dark and so malicious that it was, in the true sense, monstrous.

"Now *you* seen it too," he wheezed, "you seen my fiery, burning feet! And now—that is, unless you kin save me an' prevent—it's 'bout time for—"

His piteous and beseeching voice was interrupted by a sound that was like the roar of wind coming across the lake. The trees overhead shook their tangled branches. The blazing fire bent its flames as before a blast. And something swept with a terrific, rushing noise about the little camp and seemed to surround it entirely in a single moment of time. Défago shook the clinging blankets from his body, turned towards the woods behind, and with the same stumbling motion that had brought him—was gone: gone, before anyone could move muscle to prevent him, gone with an amazing, blundering swiftness that left no time to act. The darkness positively swallowed him; and less than a dozen seconds later, above the roar of the swaying trees and the shout of the sudden wind, all three men, watching and listening with stricken hearts, heard a cry that seemed to drop down upon them from a great height of sky and distance—

"Oh, oh! This fiery height! Oh, oh! My feet of fire! My burning feet of fire . . . !" then died away, into untold space and silence.

Dr. Cathcart—suddenly master of himself, and therefore of the others—was just able to seize Hank violently by the arm as he tried to dash headlong into the Bush.

"But I want ter know,—you!" shrieked the guide. "I want ter see! That ain't him at all, but some—devil that's shunted into his place . . . !"

Somehow or other—he admits he never quite knew how he accomplished it—he managed to keep him in the tent and pacify him. The doctor, apparently, had reached the stage where reaction had set in and allowed his own innate force to conquer. Certainly he "managed" Hank admirably. It was his nephew, however, hitherto so wonderfully controlled, who gave him most cause for anxiety, for the cumulative strain had now produced a condition of lachrymose hysteria which made it necessary to isolate him upon a bed of boughs and blankets as far removed from Hank as was possible under the circumstances.

And there he lay, as the watches of that haunted night passed over the lonely camp, crying startled sentences, and fragments of sentences, into the folds of his blanket. A quantity of gibberish about speed and height and fire mingled oddly with biblical memories of the classroom. "People with broken faces all on fire are coming at a most awful, awful, pace towards the camp!" he would moan one minute; and the next would sit up and stare into the woods, intently listening, and whisper, "How terrible in the wilderness are—are the feet of them that—" until his uncle came across the change the direction of his thoughts and comfort him.

The hysteria, fortunately, proved but temporary. Sleep cured him, just as it cured Hank.

Till the first signs of daylight came, soon after five o'clock, Dr. Cathcart kept his vigil. His face was the color of chalk, and there were strange flushes beneath the eyes. An appalling terror of the soul battled with his will all through those silent hours. These were some of the outer signs. . . .

At dawn he lit the fire himself, made breakfast, and woke the others, and by seven they were well on their way back to the home camp—three perplexed and afflicted men, but each in his own way having reduced his inner turmoil to a condition of more or less systematized order again.

IX

They talked little, and then only of the most wholesome and common things, for their minds were charged with painful thoughts that clamoured for explanation, though no one dared refer to them. Hank, being nearest to primitive conditions, was the first to find himself, for he was also less complex. In Dr. Cathcart "civilization" championed his forces against an attack singular enough. To this day, perhaps, he is not *quite* sure of certain things. Anyhow, he took longer to "find himself."

Simpson, the student of divinity, it was who arranged his conclusions probably with the best, though not most scientific, appearance of order. Out there, in the heart of unreclaimed wilderness, they had surely witnessed something crudely and essentially primitive. Something that had survived somehow the advance of humanity had emerged terrifically, betraying a scale of life still monstrous and immature. He envisaged it rather as a glimpse into prehistoric ages, when superstitions, gigantic and uncouth, still oppressed the hearts of men; when the forces of nature were still untamed, the Powers that may have haunted a primeval universe not yet withdrawn. To this day he thinks of what he termed years later in a sermon "savage and formidable Potencies lurking behind the souls of men, not evil perhaps in themselves, yet instinctively hostile to humanity as it exists."

With his uncle he never discussed the matter in detail, for the barrier between the two types of mind made it difficult. Only once, years later, something led them to the frontier of the subject—of a single detail of the subject, rather—

"Can't you even tell me what—*they* were like?" he asked; and the reply, though conceived in wisdom, was not encouraging, "It is far better you should not try to know, or to find out."

"Well—that odour . . . ?" persisted the nephew. "What do you make of that?"

Dr. Cathcart looked at him and raised his eyebrows.

"Odours," he replied, "are not so easy as sounds and sights of telepathic communication. I make as much, or as little, probably, as you do yourself."

He was not quite so glib as usual with his explanations. That was all.

At the fall of day, cold, exhausted, famished, the party came to the end of the long portage and dragged themselves into a camp that at first glimpse seemed empty. Fire there was none, and no Punk came forward to welcome them. The emotional capacity of all three was too over-spent to recognize either surprise or annoyance; but the cry of spontaneous affection that burst from the lips of Hank, as he rushed ahead of them towards the fire-place, came probably as a warning that the end of the amazing affair was not quite yet. And both Cathcart and his nephew confessed afterwards that when they saw him kneel down in his excitement and embrace something that reclined, gently moving, beside the extinguished ashes, they felt in their very bones that this "something" would prove to be Défago—the true Défago, returned.

And so, indeed, it was.

It is soon told. Exhausted to the point of emaciation, the French Canadian—what was left of him, that is—fumbled among the ashes, trying to make a fire. His body crouched there, the weak fingers obeying feebly the instinctive habit of a lifetime with twigs and matches. But there was no longer any mind to direct the simple operation. The mind had fled beyond recall. And with it, too, had fled memory. Not only recent events, but all previous life was a blank.

This time it was the real man, though incredibly and horribly shrunken. On his face was no expression of any kind whatever— fear, welcome, or recognition. He did not seem to know who it was that embraced him, or who it was that fed, warmed and spoke to him the words of comfort and relief. Forlorn and broken beyond all reach of human aid, the little man did meekly as he was bidden. The "something" that had constituted him "individual" had vanished for ever.

In some ways it was more terribly moving than anything they had yet seen—that idiot smile as he drew wads of coarse moss from his swollen cheeks and told them that he was "a damned moss-eater"; the continued vomiting of even the simplest food; and, worst of all, the piteous and childish voice of complaint in which he told them that his feet pained him— "burn like fire"—which was natural enough when Dr. Cathcart examined them and found that both were dreadfully frozen. Beneath the eyes there were faint indications of recent bleeding.

The details of how he survived the prolonged exposure, of where he had been, or of how he covered the great distance from one camp to the other, including an immense detour of the lake on foot since he had no canoe—all this remains unknown. His memory had vanished completely. And before the end of the winter whose beginning witnessed this strange occurrence, Défago, bereft of mind, memory and soul, had gone with it. He lingered only a few weeks.

And what Punk was able to contribute to the story throws no further light upon it. He was cleaning fish by the lake shore about five o'clock in the evening—an hour, that is, before the search party returned—when he saw this shadow of the guide picking its way weakly into camp. In advance of him, he declares, came the faint whiff of a certain singular odour.

That same instant old Punk started for home. He covered the entire journey of three days as only Indian blood could have covered it. The terror of a whole race drove him. He knew what it all meant. Défago had "seen the Wendigo."

The Derelict

William Hope Hodgson

"It's the *material*," said the old ship's doctor— "the *material* plus the conditions—and, maybe," he added slowly, "a third factor— yes, a third factor; but there, there—" He broke off his half-meditative sentence and began to charge his pipe.

"Go on, doctor," we said encouragingly, and with more than a little expectancy. We were in the smoke-room of the Sand-a-lea, running across the North Atlantic; and the doctor was a character. He concluded the charging of his pipe, and lit it; then settled himself, and began to express himself more fully.

"The *material*," he said with conviction, "is inevitably the medium of expression of the life-force—the fulcrum, as it were; lacking which it is unable to exert itself, or, indeed, to express itself in any form or fashion that would be intelligible or evident to us. So potent is the share of the *material* in the production of that thing which we name life, and so eager the life-force to express itself, that I am convinced it would, if given the right conditions, make itself manifest even through so hopeless seeming a medium as a simple block of sawn wood; for I tell you, gentlemen, the life-force is both as fiercely urgent and as indiscriminate as fire—the destructor; yet which some are now growing to consider the very essence of life rampant. There is a quaint seeming paradox there," he concluded, nodding his old grey head.

"Yes, doctor," I said. "In brief, your argument is that life is a thing, state, fact, or element, call it what you like, which requires the *material* through which to manifest itself, and that given the *material*, plus the conditions, the result is life. In other words, that life is an evolved product, manifested through matter and bred of conditions—eh?"

"As we understand the word," said the old doctor. "Though, mind you, there may be a third factor. But, in my heart, I believe that it is a matter of chemistry—conditions and a suitable medium; but given the conditions, the brute is so almighty that it will seize upon anything through which to manifest itself. It is a force generated by conditions; but, nevertheless, this does not bring us one iota nearer to its explanation, any more than to the explanation of electricity or fire. They are, all three, of the outer forces— monsters of the void. Nothing we can do will *create* any one of them, our power is merely to be able, by providing the conditions, to make each one of them manifest to our physical senses. Am I clear?"

"Yes, doctor, in a way, you are," I said. "But I don't agree with you, though I think I understand you. Electricity and fire are both what I might call natural things, but life is an abstract something— a kind of all-permeating wakefulness. Oh, I can't explain it! Who could? But it's spiritual, not just a thing bred out of a condition, like fire, as you say, or electricity. It's a horrible thought of yours. Life's a kind of spiritual mystery —"

"Easy, my boy!" said the old doctor, laughing gently to himself. "Or else I may be asking you to demonstrate the spiritual mystery of life of the limpet, or the crab, shall we say." He grinned at me with ineffable perverseness. "Anyway," he continued, "as I suppose you've all guessed, I've a yarn to tell you in support of my impression that life is no more a mystery or a miracle than fire or electricity. But, please to remember, gentlemen, that because we've succeeded in naming and making good use of these two forces, they're just as much mysteries, fundamentally as ever. And, anyway, the thing I'm going to tell you won't explain the mystery of life, but only give you one of my pegs on which I hang my feeling that life is as I have said, a force made manifest through con- ditions—that is to say, natural chemistry—and that it can take for its purpose and need, the most incredible and unlikely matter; for without matter it cannot come into existence—it cannot become manifest —"

"I don't agree with you, doctor," I interrupted. "Your theory would destroy all belief in life after death. It would —"

"Hush, sonny," said the old man, with a quiet little smile of comprehension. "Hark to what I've to say first; and, anyway, what objection have you to material life after death? And if you object to a material framework, I would still have you remember that I am speaking of life, as we understand the word in this our life. Now do be a quiet lad, or I'll never be done:

"It was when I was a young man, and that is a good many years ago, gentlemen. I had passed my examinations, but was so run down with overwork that it was decided that I had better take a trip to sea. I was by no means well off, and very glad in the end to secure a nominal post as doctor in the sailing passenger clipper running out to China.

"The name of the ship was the Bheospse, and soon after I had got all my gear aboard she cast off, and we dropped down the Thames, and next day were well away out in the Channel.

"The captain's name was Gannington, a very decent man, though quite illiterate. The first mate, Mr. Berlies, was a quiet, sternish, reserved man, very well-read. The second mate, Mr. Selvern, was, perhaps, by birth and upbringing, the most socially cultured of the three, but he lacked the stamina and indomitable pluck of the two others. He was more of a sensitive, and emotionally and even mentally, the most alert man of the three.

"On our way out, we called at Madagascar, where we landed some of our passengers; then we ran eastward, meaning to call at North-West Cape; but about a hundred degrees east we encountered very dreadful weather, which carried away all our sails, and sprung the jibboom and foret'gallantmast.

"The storm carried us northward for several hundred miles, and when it dropped us finally, we found ourselves in a very bad state. The ship had been strained, and had taken some three feet of water through her seams; the maintopmast had been sprung, in addition to the jibboom and foret'gallantmast, two of our boats had gone, as also one of the pigstys, with three fine pigs, these latter having been washed overboard but some half-hour before the wind began to ease, which it did very quickly, though a very ugly sea ran for some hours after.

"The wind left us just before dark, and when morning came it brought splendid weather—a calm, mildly undulating sea, and a brilliant sun, with no wind. It showed us also that we were not alone, for about two miles away to the westward was another vessel, which Mr. Selvern, the second mate, pointed out to me.

"'That's a pretty rum-looking, packet, doctor,' he said, and handed me his glass.

"I looked through it at the other vessel, and saw what he meant; at least, I thought I did.

"'Yes, Mr. Selvern,' I said. 'She's got a pretty old-fashioned look about her.'

"He laughed at me in his pleasant way.

"'It's easy to see you're not a sailor, doctor,' he remarked. 'There's a dozen rum things about her. She's a derelict, and has been floating round, by the look of her, for many a score of years. Look at the shape of her counter, and the bows and cutwater. She's as old as the hills, as you might say, and ought to have gone down to Davy Jones a good while ago. Look at the growths on her, and the thickness of her standing rigging; that's all salt encrustations, I fancy, if you notice the white colour. She's been a small barque; but, don't you see, she's not a yard left aloft. They've all dropped out of the slings; everything rotted away; wonder the standing rigging hasn't gone, too. I wish the old man would let us take the boat and have a look at her. She'd be well worth it.'

"'There seemed little chance, however, of this, for all hands were turned to and kept hard at it all day long repairing the damage to the masts and gear; and this took a long while, as you may think. Part of the time I gave a hand heaving on one of the deck capstans, for the exercise was good for my liver. Old Captain Gannington approved, and I persuaded him to come along and try some of the same medicine, which he did; and we got very chummy over the job.

"We got talking about the derelict, and he remarked how lucky we were not to have run full tilt on to her in the darkness, for she lay right away to leeward of us, according, to the way that we had been drifting in the storm. He also was of the opinion that she had a strange look about her, and that she was pretty old; but on this latter point he plainly had far less knowledge than the second mate, for he was, as I have said, an illiterate man, and knew nothing of seacraft beyond what experience had taught him. He lacked the book knowledge which the second mate had of vessels previous to his day, which it appeared the derelict was.

"'She's an old 'un, doctor,' was the extent of observations in this direction.

"Yet, when I mentioned to him that it would be interesting to go aboard and give her a bit of an overhaul, he nodded his head as if the idea had been already in his mind and accorded with his own inclinations.

"'When the work's over, doctor,' he said. 'Can't spare the men now, ye know. Got to get all shipshape an' ready as smart as we can. But, we'll take my gig, an' go off in the second dog-watch. The glass is steady, an' it'll be a bit of gam for us.'

"That evening, after tea, the captain gave orders to clear the gig and get her overboard. The second mate was to come with us, and the skipper gave him word to see that two or three lamps were put into the boat, as it would soon fall dark. A little later we were pulling across the calmness of the sea with a crew of six at the oars, and making very good speed of it.

"Now, gentlemen, I have detailed to you with great exactness all the facts, both big and little, so that you can follow step by step each incident in this extraordinary affair, and I want you now to pay the closest attention. I was sitting in the stern-sheets with the second mate and the captain, who was steering, and as we drew nearer and nearer to the stranger I studied her with an ever-growing attention, as, indeed, did Captain Gannington and the second mate. She was, as you know, to the west-ward of us, and the sunset was making a great flame of red light to the back of her, so that she showed a little blurred and indistinct by reason of the halation of the light, which almost defeated the eye in any attempt to see her rotting spars and standing rigging, submerged, as they were, in the fiery glory of the sunset.

"It was because of this effect of the sunset that we had come quite close, comparatively, to the derelict before we saw that she was all surrounded by a sort of curious scum, the colour of which was difficult to decide upon by reason of the red light that was in the atmosphere, but which afterwards we discovered to be brown. This scum spread all about the old vessel for many hundreds of yards in a huge, irregular patch, a great stretch of which reached out to the eastward, upon the starboard side of the boat some score or so fathoms away.

"'Queer stuff,' said Captain Gannington, leaning to the side and looking over. 'Something in the cargo as 'as gone rotten, and worked out through 'er seams.'

"'Look at her bows and stern,' said the second mate. 'Just look at the growth on her!'

"There were, as he said, great clumpings of strange-looking sea-fungi under the bows and the short counter astern. From the stump of her jibboom and her cutwater great beards of rime and marine growths hung downward into the scum that held her in. Her blank starboard side was presented to us—all a dead, dirtyish white, streaked and mottled vaguely with dull masses of heavier colour.

"'There's a steam or haze rising off her,' said the second mate, speaking again. 'You can see it against the light. It keeps coming and going. Look!'

"I saw then what he meant—a faint haze or steam, either suspended above the old vessel or rising from her. And Captain Gannington saw it also.

"'Spontaneous combustion!' he exclaimed. 'We'll 'ave to watch when we lift the 'atches, 'nless it's some poor devil that's got aboard of 'er. But that ain't likely.'

"We were now within a couple of hundred yards of the old derelict, and had entered into the brown scum. As it poured off the lifted oars I heard one of the men mutter to himself, 'Dam' treacle!' And, indeed, it was not something unlike it. As the boat continued to forge nearer and nearer to the old ship the scum grew thicker and thicker, so that, at last, it perceptibly slowed us.

"'Give way, lads! Put some beef to it!' sang out Captain Gannington. And thereafter there was no sound except the panting of the men and the faint, reiterated suck, suck of the sullen brown scum upon the oars as the boat was forced ahead. As we went, I was conscious of a peculiar smell in the evening air, and whilst I had no doubt that the puddling of the scum by the oars made it rise, I could give no name to it; yet, in a way, it was vaguely familiar.

"We were now very close to the old vessel, and presently she was high about us against the dying light. The captain called out then to 'in with the bow oars and stand by with the boat-hook,' which was done.

"'Aboard there! Ahoy! Aboard there! Ahoy!' shouted Captain Gannington; but there came no answer, only the dull sound his voice going lost into the open sea, each time he sung out.

"'Ahoy! Aboard there! Ahoy!' he shouted time after time, but there was only the weary silence of the old hulk that answered us; and, somehow as he shouted, the while that I stared up half expectantly at her, a queer little sense of oppression, that amounted almost to nervousness, came upon me. It passed, but I remember how I was suddenly aware that it was growing dark. Darkness comes fairly rapidly in the tropics, though not so quickly as many fiction writers seem to think; but it was not that the coming dusk had perceptibly deepened in that brief time of only a few moments, but rather that my nerves had made me suddenly a little hypersensitive. I mention my state particularly, for I am not a nervy man normally, and my abrupt touch of nerves is significant, in the light of what happened.

"'There's no one on board there!' said Captain Gannington. 'Give way, men!' For the boat's crew had instinctively rested on their oars, as the captain hailed the old craft. The men gave way again; and then the second mate called out excitedly, 'Why, look there, there's our pigsty! See, it's got Bheospse painted on the end. It's drifted down here and the scum's caught it. What a blessed wonder!'

"It was, as he had said, our pigsty that had been washed overboard in the storm; and most extraordinary to come across it there.

"'We'll tow it off with us, when we go,' said the captain, and shouted to the crew to get down to their oars; for they were hardly moving the boat, because the scum was so thick, close in around the old ship, that it literally clogged the boat from moving. I remember that it struck me, in a half-conscious sort of way, as curious that the pigsty, containing our three dead pigs, had managed to drift in so far unaided, whilst we could scarcely manage to force the boat in, now that we had come right into the scum. But the thought passed from my mind, for so many things happened within the next few minutes.

"The men managed to bring the boat in alongside, within a couple of feet of the derelict, and the man with the boat-hook hooked on.

"''Ave ye got 'old there, forrard?' asked Captain Gannington.

"'Yessir!' said the bowman; and as he spoke there came a queer noise of tearing.

"'What's that?' asked the Captain.

"'It's tore, sir. Tore clean away!' said the man, and his tone showed that he had received something of a shock.

"'Get a hold again, then!' said Captain Gannington irritably. 'You don't s'pose this packet was built yesterday! Shove the hook into the main chains' The man did so gingerly, as you might say, for it seemed to me, in the growing dusk, that he put no strain on to the hook, though, of course there was no need—you see the boat could not go very far of herself, in the stuff in which she was imbedded. I remember thinking this, also as I looked up at the bulging side of the old vessel. Then I heard Captain Gannington's voice:

"'Lord, but she s old! An' what a colour, doctor! She don't half want paint, do she? Now then, somebody, one of them oars.' An oar was passed to him, and he leant it up against the ancient, bulging side; then he paused, and called to the second mate to light a couple of the lamps, and stand by to pass them up, for darkness had settled down now upon the sea.

"The second mate lit two of the lamps, and told one of the men to light a third, and keep it handy in the boat; then he stepped across, with a lamp in each hand, to where Captain Gannington stood by the oar against the side of the ship.

"'Now, my lad,' said the captain to the man who had pulled stroke, 'up with you, an' we'll pass ye up the lamps.'

"The man jumped to obey, caught the oar, and put his weight upon it; and as he did so, something seemed to give way a little.

"'Look!' cried out the second mate, and pointed, lamp in hand. 'It's sunk in!'

"This was true. The oar had made quite an indentation into the bulging, somewhat slimy side of the old vessel.

"'Mould, I reckon,' said Captain Gannington, bending towards the derelict to look. Then to the man:

"'Up you go, my lad, and be smart! Don't stand there waitin'!'

"At that the man, who had paused a moment as he felt the oar give beneath his weight began to shin' up, and in a few seconds he was aboard, and leant out over the rail for the lamps. These were passed up to him, and the captain called to him to steady the oar. Then Captain Gannington went, calling to me to follow, and after me the second mate.

"As the captain put his face over the rail, he gave a cry of astonishment.

"'Mould, by gum! Mould—tons of it. Good lord!'

"As I heard him shout that I scrambled the more eagerly after him, and in a moment or two I was able to see what he meant— everywhere that the light from the two lamps struck there was nothing but smooth great masses and surfaces of a dirty white coloured mould. I climbed over the rail, with the second mate close behind, and stood upon the mould covered decks. There might have been no planking beneath the mould, for all that our feet could feel. It gave under our tread with a spongy, puddingy feel. It covered the deck furniture of the old ship, so that the shape of each article and fitment was often no more than suggested through it.

"Captain Gannington snatched a lamp from the man and the second mate reached for the other. They held the lamps high, and we all stared. It was most extraordinary, and somehow most abominable. I can think of no other word, gentlemen, that so much describes the predominant feeling that affected me at the moment.

"'Good lord!' said Captain Gannington several times. 'Good lord!' But neither the second mate nor the man said anything, and, for my part I just stared, and at the same time began to smell a little at the air, for there was a vague odour of something half familiar, that somehow brought to me a sense of half-known fright.

"I turned this way and that, staring, as I have said. Here and there the mould was so heavy as to entirely disguise what lay beneath, converting the deck-fittings into indistinguishable mounds of mould all dirty-white and blotched and veined with irregular, dull, purplish markings.

"There was a strange thing about the mould which Captain Gannington drew attention to—it was that our feet did not crush into it and break the surface, as might have been expected, but merely indented it.

"'Never seen nothin' like it before! Never!' said the captain after having stooped with his lamp to examine the mould under our feet. He stamped with his heel, and the mould gave out a dull, puddingy sound. He stooped again, with a quick movement, and stared, holding the lamp close to the deck. 'Blest if it ain't a reg'lar skin to it!'

"The second mate and the man and I all stooped and looked at it. The second mate progged it with his forefinger, and I remember I rapped it several times with my knuckles, listening to the dead sound it gave out, and noticing the close, firm texture of the mould.

"'Dough!' the second mate. 'It's just like blessed dough! Pouf!' He stood up with a quick movement. 'I could fancy it stinks a bit,' he said.

"As he said this I knew, suddenly, what the familiar thing was in the vague odour that hung about us—it was that the smell had something animal-like in it; something of the same smell, only *heavier*, that you would smell in any place that is infested with mice. I began to look about with a sudden very real uneasiness. There might be vast numbers of hungry rats aboard. They might prove exceedingly dangerous, if in a starving condition; yet, as you will understand, somehow I hesitated to put forward my idea as a reason for caution, it was too fanciful.

"Captain Gannington had begun to go aft along the mould-covered main-deck with the second mate, each of them holding their lamps high up, so as to cast a good light about the vessel. I turned quickly and followed them, the man with me keeping close to my heels, and plainly uneasy. As we went, I became aware that there was a feeling of moisture in the air, and I remembered the slight mist, or smoke, above the hulk, which had made Captain Gannington suggest spontaneous combustion in explanation.

"And always, as we went, there was that vague, animal smell; suddenly I found myself wishing we were well away from the old vessel.

"Abruptly, after a few paces, the captain stopped and pointed at a row of mould-hidden shapes on each side of the maindeck. 'Guns,' he said. 'Been a privateer in the old days, I guess—maybe worse! We'll 'ave a look below, doctor; there may be something worth touchin'. She's older than I thought. Mr. Selvern thinks she's about two hundred years old; but I scarce think it.'

"We continued our way aft, and I remember that I found myself walking as lightly and gingerly as possible, as if I were sub-consciously afraid of treading through the rotten, mould-hid decks. I think the others had a touch of the same feeling, from the way that they walked. Occasionally the soft stuff would grip our heels, releasing them with a little sullen suck.

"The captain forged somewhat ahead of the second mate; and I know that the suggestion he had made himself, that perhaps there might be something below worth carrying away, had stimulated his imagination. The second mate was, however, beginning to feel somewhat the same way that I did; at least I have that impression. I think, if it had not been for what I might truly describe as Captain Gannington's sturdy courage, we should all of us have just gone back over the side very soon, for there was most certainly an unwholesome feeling abroad that made one feel queerly lacking in pluck; and you will soon see that this feeling was justified.

"Just as the captain reached the few mould-covered steps leading up on to the short half-poop, I was suddenly aware that the feeling of moisture in the air had grown very much more definite. It was perceptible now, intermittently, as a sort of thin, moist, fog-like vapour, that came and went oddly, and seemed to make the decks a little indistinct to the view, this time and that. Once an odd puff of it beat up suddenly from somewhere, and caught me in the face, carrying a queer, sickly, heavy odour with it that somehow frightened me strangely with a suggestion of a waiting and half-comprehended danger.

"We had followed Captain Gannington up the three mould covered steps, and now went slowly along the raised after-deck. By the mizzenmast Captain Gannington paused, and held his lantern near to it. 'My word, mister,' he said to the second mate, 'it's fair thickened up with mould! Why, I'll g'antee it's close on four foot thick.' He shone the light down to where it met the deck. 'Good lord!' he said. 'Look at the sea-lice on it!' I stepped up, and it was as he had said; the sea-lice were thick upon it, some of them huge, not less than the size of large beetles, and all a clear, colourless shade, like water, except where there were little spots of grey on them.

"'I've never seen the like of them, 'cept on a live cod,' said Captain Gannington, in an extremely puzzled voice. 'My word! But they're whoppers!' Then he passed on; but a few paces farther aft he stopped again, and held his lamp near to the mould-hidden deck.

"'Lord bless me, doctor,' he called out, in a low voice, 'did ye ever see the like of that? Why, it's a foot long, if it's a hinch!'

"I stooped over his shoulder, and saw what he meant; it was a clear, colourless creature about a foot long, and about eight inches high, with a curved back that was extraordinarily narrow. As we stared, all in a group, it gave a queer little flick, and was gone.

"'Jumped!' said the captain. 'Well, if that ain't a giant of all the sea-lice that ever I've seen. I guess it's jumped twenty foot clear.' He straightened his back, and scratched his head a moment, swinging the lantern this way and that with the other hand, and staring about us. 'Wot are *they* doin' aboard 'ere?' he said. 'You'll see 'em—little things—on fat cod an' such-like. I'm blowed, doctor, if I understand.'

"He held his lamp towards a big mound of the mould that occupied part of the after portion of the low poop-deck, a little foreside of where there came a two-foot high 'break' to a kind of second and loftier poop, that ran away aft to the taffrail. The mound was pretty big, several feet across, and more than a yard high. Captain Gannington walked up to it.

"'I reck'n this's the scuttle,' he remarked, and gave it a heavy kick. The only result was a deep indentation into the huge, whiteish hump of mould, as if he had driven his foot into a mass of some doughy substance. Yet I am not altogether correct in saying that this was the only result, for a certain other thing happened. From the place made by the captain's foot there came a sudden gush of a purplish fluid, accompanied by a peculiar smell, that was, and was not, half familiar. Some of the mould-like substance had stuck to the toe of the captain's boot, and from this likewise there issued a sweat, as it were, of the same colour.

"'Well?' said Captain Gannington, in surprise, and drew back his foot to make another kick at the hump of mould. But he paused at an exclamation from the second mate:

"'Don't sir,' said the second mate.

"I glanced at him, and the light from Captain Gannington's lamp showed me that his face had a bewildered, half-frightened look, as if he were suddenly and unexpectedly half afraid of something, and as if his tongue had given away his sudden fright, without any intention on his part to speak. The captain also turned and stared at him.

"'Why, mister?' he asked, in a somewhat puzzled voice, through which there sounded just the vaguest hint of annoyance. 'We've got to shift this muck, if we're to get below.'

"I looked at the second mate, and it seemed to me that, curiously enough he was listening less to the captain than to some other sound. Suddenly he said, in a queer voice, 'Listen, everybody!'

"Yet we heard nothing, beyond the faint murmur of the men talking together in the boat alongside.

"'I don't, hear nothing,' said Captain Gannington, after a short pause. 'Do you, doctor?'

"'No,' I said.

"'Wot was it you thought you heard?' the captain, turning again to the second mate. But the second mate shook his head in a curious, almost irritable way, as if the captain's question interrupted his listening. Captain Gannington stared a moment at him, then held his lantern up and glanced about him almost uneasily. I know I felt a queer sense of strain. But the light showed nothing beyond the greyish dirty-white of the mould in all directions.

"'Mister Selvern,' said the captain, at last, looking at him, 'don't get fancying, things. Get hold of your bloomin' self. Ye know ye heard nothin'?'

"'I'm quite sure I heard something, sir,' said the second mate. 'I seemed to hear—' He broke off sharply, and appeared to listen with an almost painful intensity.

"'What did it sound like?' I asked.

"'It's all right, doctor,' said Captain Gannington, laughing gently. 'Ye can give him a tonic when we get back. I'm goin' to shift this stuff.' He drew back, and kicked for the second time at the ugly mass which he took to hide the companionway. The result of his kick was startling, for the whole thing wobbled sloppily, like a mound of unhealthy-looking jelly.

"He drew his foot out of it quickly, and took a step backward, staring, and holding his lamp towards it. 'By gum,' he said, and it was plain that he was generally startled, 'the blessed thing's gone soft!'

"The man had run back several steps from the suddenly flaccid mound, and looking horribly frightened. Though of what, I am sure he had not the least idea. The second mate stood where he was, and stared. For my part, I know I had a most hideous uneasiness upon me. The captain continued to hold his light towards the wobbling mound and stare.

"'It's gone squashy all through,' he said. 'There's no scuttle there. There's no bally woodwork inside that lot! Phoo! What a rum smell!'

"He walked round to the after side of the strange mound, to
see whether there might be some signs of an opening, into the hull
at the back of the great heap of mould-stuff. And then:

"'Listen!' said the second mate again, in the strangest sort of
voice.

"Captain Gannington straightened himself upright, and there
succeeded a pause of the most intense quietness, in which there
was not even the hum of talk from the men alongside in the boat.
We all heard it—a kind of dull, soft thud, thud, thud, thud, somewhere in the hull under us, yet so vague as to make me half doubtful
I heard it, only that the others did so, too.

"Captain Gannington turned suddenly to where the man stood.

"'Tell them—' he began. But the fellow cried out something, and
pointed. There had come a strange intensity into his somewhat
unemotional face, so that the captain's glance followed his action
instantly. I stared also as you may think. It was the great mound at
which the man was pointing. I saw what he meant. From the two
gapes made in the mould-like stuff by Captain Gannington's boot,
the purple fluid was jetting out in a queerly regular fashion, almost
as if it were being forced out by a pump. My word! But I stared!
And even as I stared a larger jet squirted out, and splashed as far
as the man, spattering his boots and trouser legs.

"The fellow had been pretty nervous before, in a stolid, ignorant
sort of way, and his funk had been growing steadily; but at this he
simply let out a yell, and turned about to run. He paused an
instant,as if a sudden fear of the darkness that held the decks,
between him and the boat, had taken him. He snatched at the
second mate's lantern, tore it out of his hand, and plunged heavily
away over the vile stretch of mould.

"Mr. Selvern, the second mate, said not a word; he was just
staring, staring at the strange-smelling twin-streams of dull purple
that were jetting out from the wobbling mound. Captain
Gannington, however, roared an order to the man to come back,
but the man plunged on and on across the mould, his feet seeming
to be clogged by the stuff, as if it had grown suddenly soft. He
zigzagged as he ran, the lantern swaying, in wild circles as he

wrenched his feet free with a constant plop, plop; and I could hear his frightened gasps even from where I stood.

"'Come back with that lamp!' roared the captain again; but still the man took no notice.

"And Captain Gannington was silent an instant, his lips working in a queer, inarticulate fashion, as if he were stunned momentarily by the very violence of his anger at the man's insubordination. And in the silence I heard the sounds again—thud, thud, thud, thud! Quite distinctly now, beating, it seemed suddenly to me, right down under my feet, but deep.

"I stared down at the mould on which I was standing, with a quick, disgusting sense of the terrible all about me; then I looked at the captain, and tried to say something, without appearing frightened. I saw that he had turned again to the mound, and all the anger had gone out of his face. He had his lamp out towards the mound, and was listening. There was another moment of absolute silence, at least, I knew that I was not conscious of any sound at all in all the world, except that extraordinary thud, thud, thud, thud, down somewhere in the huge bulk under us.

"The captain shifted his feet with a sudden, nervous movement, and as he lifted them the mould went plop, plop! He looked quickly at me, trying to smile, as if he were not thinking anything very much about it.

"'What do you make of it, doctor?' he said.

"'I think—' I began. But the second mate interrupted with a single word, his voice pitched a little high, in a tone that made us both stare instantly at him.

"'Look!' he said, and pointed at the mound. The thing was all of a slow quiver. A strange ripple ran outward from it, along the deck, like you will see a ripple run inshore out of a calm sea. It reached a mound a little foreside of us, which I had supposed to be the cabin skylight, and in a moment the second mound sank nearly level with the surrounding decks, quivering floppily in a most extraordinary fashion. A sudden quick tremor took the mould right under the second mate, and he gave out a hoarse little cry, and held his arms out on each side of him, to keep his balance. The tremor in the mould spread, and Captain Gannington swayed, and spread out his feet with a sudden curse of fright. The second mate jumped across to him, and caught him by the wrist.

"'The boat, sir!' he said, saying the very thing that I had lacked the pluck to say. 'For God's sake—'

"But he never finished, for a tremendous hoarse scream cut off his words. They hove themselves round and looked. I could see without turning. The man who had run from us was standing in the waist of the ship, about a fathom from the starboard bulwarks. He was swaying from side to side, and screaming, in a dreadful fashion. He appeared to be trying to lift his feet, and the light from his swaying lantern showed an almost incredible sight. All about him the mould was in active movement. His feet had sunk out of sight. The stuff appeared to be *lapping* at his legs and abruptly his bare flesh showed. The hideous stuff had rent his trouser-leg away as if it were paper. He gave out a simply sickening scream, and, with a vast effort, wrenched one leg free. It was partly destroyed. The next instant he pitched face downward, and the stuff heaped itself upon him, as if it were actually alive, with a dreadful, severe life. It was simply infernal. The man had gone from sight. Where he had fallen was now a writhing, elongated mound, in constant and horrible increase, as the mould appeared to move towards it in strange ripples from all sides.

"Captain Gannington and the second mate were stone silent, in amazed and incredulous horror, but I had begun to reach towards a grotesque and terrific conclusion, both helped and hindered by my professional training.

"From the men in the boat alongside there was a loud shouting. and I saw two of their faces appear suddenly above the rail. They showed clearly a moment in the light from the lamp which the man had snatched from Mr. Selvern; for, strangely enough, this lamp was standing upright and unharmed on the deck, a little way foreside of that dreadful, elongated, growing mound, that still swayed and writhed with an incredible horror. The lamp rose and fell on the passing ripples of the mould, just—for all the world—as you will see a boat rise and fall on little swells. It is of some interest to me now, psychologically, to remember how that rising and falling lantern brought home to me more than anything the incomprehensible dreadful strangeness of it all.

"The men's faces disappeared with sudden yells, as if they had slipped, or been suddenly hurt; and there was a fresh uproar of shouting from the boat. The men were calling to us to come away—to come away. In the same instant I felt my left boot drawn suddenly and forcibly downward, with a horrible, painful grip. I wrenched it free, with a yell of angry fear. Forrard of us, I saw that the vile surface was all amove, and abruptly I found myself shouting in a queer, frightened voice, 'The boat, captain! The boat, captain!'

"Captain Gannington stared round at me, over his right shoulder, in a peculiar, dull way, that told me he was utterly dazed with bewilderment and the incomprehensibleness of it all. I took a quick, clogged, nervous step towards him, and gripped his arm, and shook it fiercely. 'The boat!' I shouted at him. 'The boat! For God's sake, tell the men to bring the boat aft!'

"Then the mound must have drawn his feet down, for abruptly he bellowed fiercely with terror, his momentary apathy giving place to furious energy. His thickset, vastly muscular body doubled and writhed with his enormous effort, and he struck out madly dropping the lantern. He tore his feet free, something ripping as he did so. The *reality* and necessity of the situation had come upon him brutishly real, and he was roaring to the men in the boat, 'Bring the boat aft! Bring 'er aft! Bring 'er aft!' The second mate and I were shouting the same thing madly.

"'For God's sake, be smart, lads!' roared the captain, and stooped quickly for his lamp, which still burned. His feet were gripped again, and he hove them out, blaspheming breathlessly, aud leaping a yard high with his effort. Then he made a run for the side, wrenching his feet free at each step. In the same instant the second mate cried out something, and grabbed at the captain.

"'It's got hold of my feet! It's got hold of my feet!' he screamed. His feet, had disappeared up to his boot-tops, and Captain Gannington caught him round the waist with his powerful left arm, gave a mighty heave, and the next instant had him free; but both his boot-soles had gone. For my part, I jumped madly from foot to foot, to avoid the plucking of the mould; and suddenly I made a run for the ship's side. But before I could get there, a queer gape came in the mould between us and the side, at least a couple of feet wide, and how deep I don't know. It closed up in an instant, and all the mould where the cape had been vent into a sort of flurry of horrible ripplings, so that I ran back from it; for I did not dare to put my foot upon it. Then the captain was shouting to me:

"'Aft, doctor! Aft, doctor! This way, doctor! Run!' I saw then that he had passed me, and was up on the after raised portion of the poop. He had the second mate, thrown like a sack, all loose and quiet, over his left shoulder; for Mr. Selvern had fainted, and his long legs flogged limp and helpless against the captain's massive knees as he ran. I saw, with a queer, unconscious noting of minor details, how the torn soles of the second mate's boots flapped and jigged as the captain staggered aft.

"'Boat ahoy! Boat ahoy! Boat ahoy!' shouted the captain; and then I was beside him, shouting also. The men were answering with loud yells of encouragement, and it was plain they were working desperately to force the boat aft through the thick scum about the ship.

"We reached the ancient, mould-hid taffrail, and slewed about breathlessly in the half-darkness to see what was happening. Captain Gannington had left his lantern by the big mound when he picked up the second mate; and as we stood, gasping we discovered suddenly that all the mould between us and the light was full of movement. Yet, the part on which we stood, for about six or eight feet forrard of us, was still firm.

"Every couple of seconds we shouted to the men to hasten, and they kept on calling to us that they would be with us in an instant. And all the time we watched the deck of that dreadful hulk, feeling, for my part, literally sick with mad suspense, and ready to jump overboard into that filthy scum all about us.

"Down somewhere in the huge bulk of the ship there was all the time that extraordinary dull, ponderous thud, thud, thud, thud growing ever louder. I seemed to feel the whole hull of the derelict, beginning to quiver and thrill with each dull beat. And to me, with the grotesque and hideous suspicion of what made that noise, it was at once the most dreadful and incredible sound I have ever heard.

"As we waited desperately for the boat, I scanned incessantly so much of the grey white bulk as the lamp showed. The whole of the decks seemed to be in strange movement. Forrard of the lamp, I could see indistinctly the moundings of the mould swaying and nodding hideously beyond the circle of the brightest rays. Nearer, and full in the glow of the lamp, the mound which should have indicated the skylight, was swelling steadily. There were ugly, purple veinings on it, and as it swelled, it seemed to me that the veinings and mottlings on it were becoming plainer, rising as though embossed upon it, like you will see the veins stand out on the body of a powerful, full-blooded horse. It was most extraordinary. The mound that we had supposed to cover the companionway had sunk flat with the surrounding mould, and I could not see that it jetted out any more of the purplish fluid.

"A quaking movement of the mound began away forrard of the lamp, and came flurrying away aft towards us, and at the sight of that I climbed up on to the spongy-feeling taffrail, and yelled afresh for the boat. The men answered with a shout, which told me they were nearer, but the beastly scum was so thick that it was evidently a fight to move the boat at all. Beside me, Captain Gannington was shaking the second mate furiously, and the man stirred and began to moan. The captain shook him again, 'Wake up! Wake up, mister!' he shouted.

"The second mate staggered out of the captain's arms, and collapsed suddenly, shrieking: 'My feet! Oh, God! My feet!' The captain and I lugged him off the mound, and got him into a sitting position upon the taffrail, where he kept up a continual moaning.

"'Hold 'im, doctor,' said the captain. And whilst I did so, he ran forrard a few yards, and peered down over the starboard quarter rail. 'For God's sake, be smart, lads! Be smart! Be smart!' he shouted down to the men, and they answered him, breathless, from close at hand, yet still too far away for the boat to be any use to us on the instant.

"I was holding the moaning, half-unconscious officer, and staring forrard along the poop decks. The flurrying of the mould was coming aft, slowly and noiselessly. And then, suddenly, I saw something closer:

"'Look out, captain!' I shouted. And even as I shouted, the mould near to him gave a sudden, peculiar slobber. I had seen a ripple stealing towards him through the mould. He gave an enormous, clumsy leap, and landed near to us on the sound part of the mould, but the movement followed him. He turned and faced it, swearing fiercely. All about his feet there came abruptly little gapings, which made horrid sucking noises. 'Come back, captain!' I yelled. 'Come back, *quick!*' As I shouted, a ripple came at his feet— lipping at them; and he stamped insanely at it, and leaped back, his boot torn half off his foot. He swore madly with pain and anger, and jumped swiftly for the taffrail.

"'Come on, doctor! Over we go!' he called. Then he remembered the filthy scum, and hesitated, and roared out desperately to the men to hurry. I stared down, also.

"'The second mate?' I said.

"'I'll take charge doctor,' said Captain Gannington, and caught hold of Mr. Selvern. As he spoke, I thought I saw something beneath us, outlined against the scum. I leaned out over the stern, and peered. There was something under the port-quarter.

"'There's something down there, captain!' I called, and pointed in the darkness. He stooped far over, and stared.

"'A boat, by gum! A *boat!*' he yelled, and began to wriggle swiftly along the taffrail, dragging the second mate after him. I followed. 'A boat it is, sure!' he exclaimed a few moments later, and, picking up the second mate clear of the rail, he hove him down into the boat, where he fell with a crash into the bottom.

"'Over ye go, doctor!' he yelled at me, and pulled me bodily off the rail and dropped me after the officer. As he did so, I felt the whole of the ancient, spongy rail give a peculiar, sickening quiver, and begin to wobble. I fell on to the second mate, and the captain came after, almost in the same instant, but, fortunately, he landed clear of us, on to the fore thwart, which broke under his weight, with a loud crack and splintering of wood.

"'Thank God!' I heard him mutter. 'Thank God! I guess that was a mighty near thing to going to Hades.'

"He struck a match, just as I got to my feet, and between us we got the second mate straightened out on one of the after fore-and-aft thwarts. We shouted to the men in the boat, telling them where we were, and saw the light of their lantern shining round the starboard counter of the derelict. They called back to us to tell us they were doing their best, and then, whilst we waited, Captain Gannington struck another match, and began to overhaul the boat we had dropped into. She was a modern, two-bowed boat, and on the stern there was painted 'Cyclone, Glasgow.' She was in pretty fair condition, and had evidently drifted into the scum and been held by it.

"Captain Gannington struck several matches, and went forrard towards the derelict. Suddenly he called to me, and I jumped over the thwarts to him. 'Look, doctor,' he said, and I saw what he meant—a mass of bones up in the bows of the boat. I stooped over them, and looked; there were the bones of at least three people, all mixed together in an extraordinary fashion, and quite clean and dry. I had a sudden thought concerning the bones, but I said nothing, for my thought was vague in some ways, and concerned the grotesque and incredible suggestion that had come to me as to the cause of that ponderous, dull thud, thud, thud thud, that beat on so infernally within the hull, and was plain to hear even now that we had got off the vessel herself. And all the while, you know, I had a sick, horrible mental picture of that frightful, wriggling mound aboard the hulk.

"As Captain Gannington struck a final match, I saw something that sickened me and the captain saw it in the same instant. The match went out, and he fumbled clumsily for another, and struck it. We saw the thing again. We had not been mistaken. A great lip of grey-white was protruding in over the edge of the boat—a great lappet of the mould was coming stealthily towards us—a live mass of *the very hull itself!* And suddenly Captain Gannington yelled out in so many words the grotesque and incredible thing I was thinking: '*She's alive!*'

"I never heard such a sound of comprehension and terror in a man's voice. The very horrified assurance of it made actual to me the thing that before had only lurked in my subconscious mind. I knew he was right; I knew that the explanation my reason and my training both repelled and reached towards was the true one. Oh, I wonder whether anyone can possibly understand our feelings in that moment? The unmitigated horror of it and the incredibleness!

"As the light of the match burned up fully, I saw that the mass of living matter coming towards us was streaked and veined with purple, the veins standing out, enormously distended. The whole thing quivered continuously to each ponderous thud, thud, thud, thud, of that gargantuan organ that pulsed within the huge grey-white bulk. The flame of the match reached the captain's fingers, and there came to me a little sickly whiff of burned flesh, but he seemed unconscious of any pain. Then the flame went out in a brief sizzle, yet at the last moment I had seen an extraordinary raw look become visible upon the end of that monstrous, protruding lappet. It had become dewed with a hideous, purplish sweat. And with the darkness there came a sudden charnel-like stench.

"I heard the matchbox split in Captain Gannington's hands as he wrenched it open. Then he swore, in a queer frightened voice, for he had come to the end of his matches. He turned clumsily in the darkness, and tumbled over the nearest thwart, in his eagerness to get to the stern of the boat; and I after him. For we knew that thing was coming towards us through the darkness, reaching over that piteous mingled heap of human bones all jumbled together in the bows. We shouted madly to the men, and for answer saw the bows of the boat emerge dimly into view round the starboard counter of the derelict.

"'Thank God!' I gasped out. But Captain Gannington roared to them to show a light. Yet this they could not do, for the lamp had just been stepped on in their desperate efforts to force the boat round to us.

"'Quick! Quick!' I shouted.

"'For God's sake, be smart, men!' roared the captain.

"And both of us faced the darkness under the port-counter, out of which we knew—but could not see—the thing was coming to us.

"'An oar! Smart, now—pass me an oar!' shouted the captain; and reached out his hands through the gloom towards the on-coming boat. I saw a figure stand up in the bows, and hold something out to us across the intervening yards of scum. Captain Gannington swept his hands through the darkness, and encountered it.

"'I've got it! Let go there!' he said, in a quick, tense voice.

"In the same instant the boat we were in was pressed over suddenly to starboard by some tremendous weight. Then I heard the captain shout, 'Duck y'r head, doctor!' And directly afterwards he swung the heavy, fourteen-foot oar round his head, and struck into the darkness. There came a sudden squelch, and he struck again, with a savage grunt of fierce energy. At the second blow the boat righted with a slow movement, and directly afterwards the other boat bumped gently into ours.

"Captain Gannington dropped the oar, and, springing across to the second mate, hove him up off the thwart, and pitched him with knee and arms clear in over the bows among the men; then he shouted to me to follow, which I did, and he came after me, bringing the oar with him. We carried the second mate aft, and the captain shouted to the men to back the boat a little; then they got her bows clear of the boat we had just left, and so headed out through the scum for the open sea.

"'Where's Tom 'Arrison?" gasped one of the men, in the midst of his exertions. He happened to be Tom Harrison's particular chum, and Captain Gannington answered him briefly enough:

"'Dead! Pull! Don't talk!"

"Now, difficult as it had been to force the boat through the scum to our rescue, the difficulty to get clear seemed tenfold. After some five minutes pulling, the boat seemed hardly to have moved a fathom, if so much, and a quite dreadful fear took me afresh, which one of the panting men put suddenly into words, 'It's got us!' he gasped out. 'Same as poor Tom!' It was the man who had inquired where Harrison was.

"'Shut y'r mouth an' *pull!*' roared the captain. And so another few minutes passed. Abruptly, it seemed to me that the dull, ponderous thud, thud, thud, thud came more plainly through the dark, and I stared intently over the stern. I sickened a little, for I could almost swear that the dark mass of the monster was actually *nearer*—that it was coming nearer to us through the darkness. Captain Gannington must have had the same thought, for, after a brief look into the darkness, he jumped forrard, and began to double-bank the stroke-oar.

"'Get forrid under the oars, doctor,' he said to me rather breathlessly. 'Get in the bows, an' see if you can't free the stuff a bit round the bows.'

"I did as he told me, and a minute later I was in the bows of the boat, puddling the scum from side to side, and trying to break up the viscid, clinging muck. A heavy almost animal-like smell rose off it, and all the air seemed full of the deadening, heavy smell. I shall never find words to tell anyone on earth the whole horror of it all—the threat that seemed to hang in the very air around us, and but a little astern that incredible thing, coming, as I firmly believed, nearer, and scum holding us, like half-melted glue.

"The minutes passed in a deadly, eternal fashion, and I kept staring back astern into the darkness but never ceasing to puddle that filthy scum, striking at it and switching it from side to side until I sweated.

"Abruptly Captain Gannington sang out: 'We're gaining, lads. Pull!' And I felt the boat forge ahead perceptibly, as they gave way with renewed hope and energy. There was soon no doubt of it, for presently that hideous thud, thud, thud, thud had grown quite dim and vague somewhere astern and I could no longer see the derelict, for the night had come down tremendously dark and all the sky was thick, overset with heavy clouds. As we drew nearer and nearer to the edge of the scum, the boat moved more and more perceptibly, until suddenly we emerged with a clean, sweet, fresh sound into the open sea.

"'Thank God!' I said aloud, and drew in the boathook, and made my way aft again to where Captain Gannington now sat once more at the tiller. I saw him looking anxiously up at the sky and across to where the lights of our vessel burned, and again he would seem to listen intently, so that I found myself listening also.

"'What's that, Captain?' I said sharply; for it seemed to me that I heard a sound far astern, something, between a queer whine and a low whistling. 'What's that?'

"'It's wind, doctor.' he said in a low voice. 'I wish to God we were aboard.' Then to the men: 'Pull! Put y'r backs into it, or ye'll never put y'r teeth through good bread again!' The men obeyed nobly, and we reached the vessel safely, and had the boat safely stowed before the storm came, which it did in a furious white smother out of the west. I could see it for some minutes beforehand, tearing the sea in the gloom into a wall of phosphorescent foam; and as it came nearer, that peculiar whining, piping sound grew louder and louder, until it was like a vast steam whistle rushing towards us. And when it did come, we got it very heavy indeed, so that the morning showed us nothing but a welter of white seas, with that grim derelict many a score of miles away in the smother, lost as utterly as our hearts could wish to lose her.

"When I came to examine the second mate's feet, I found them in a very extraordinary condition. The soles of them had the appearance of having been partly digested. I know of no other word that so exactly describes their condition, and the agony the man suffered must have been dreadful.

"Now," concluded the doctor, "that is what I call a case in point. If we could know exactly what the old vessel had originally been loaded with, and the juxtaposition of the various articles of her cargo, plus the heat and time she had endured, plus one or two other only guessable quantities, we should have solved the chemistry of the life-force, gentlemen. Not necessarily the *origin*, mind you; but, at least, we should have taken a big step on the way. I've often regretted that gale, you know—in a way, that is, in a way. It was a most amazing discovery, but at the same time I had nothing but thankfulness to be rid of it. A most amazing chance. I often think of the way the monster woke out of its torpor. And that scum! The dead pigs caught in it! I fancy that was a grim kind of a net, gentlemen. It caught many things. It—"

The old doctor sighed and nodded.

"If I could have had her bill of lading," he said, his eyes full of regret. "If— It might have told me something to help. But, anyway—" He began to fill his pipe again. "I suppose," he ended, looking round at us gravely, "I s'pose we humans are an ungrateful lot of beggars at the best! But—but, what a chance? What a, chance, eh?"

Fishhead

Irvin S. Cobb

It goes past the powers of my pen to try to describe Reelfoot Lake for you so that you, reading this, will get the picture of it in your mind as I have it in mine.

For Reelfoot Lake is like no other lake that I know anything about. It is an after-thought of Creation.

The rest of this continent was made and had dried in the sun for thousands of years-millions of years, for all I know-before Reelfoot came to be. It's the newest big thing in nature on this hemisphere, probably, for it was formed by the great earthquake of 1811.

That earthquake of 1811 surely altered the face of the earth on the then far frontier of this country.

It changed the course of rivers, it converted hills into what are now the sunk lands of three states, and it turned the solid ground to jelly and made it roll in waves like the sea.

And in the midst of the retching of the land and the vomiting of the waters it depressed to varying depths a section of the earth crust sixty miles long, taking it down—trees, hills, hollows, and all, and a crack broke through to the Mississippi River so that for three days the river ran up stream, filling the hole.

The result was the largest lake south of the Ohio, lying mostly in Tennessee, but extending up across what is now the Kentucky line, and taking its name from a fancied resemblance in its outline to the splay, reeled foot of a cornfield negro. Niggerwool Swamp, not so far away, may have got its name from the same man who christened Reelfoot: at least so it sounds.

Reelfoot is, and has always been, a lake of mystery.

In places it is bottomless. Other places the skeletons of the cypress-trees that went down when the earth sank, still stand upright so that if the sun shines from the right quarter, and the water is less muddy than common, a man, peering face downward into its depths, sees, or thinks he sees, down below him the bare top-limbs upstretching like drowned men's fingers, all coated with the mud of years and bandaged with pennons of the green lake slime.

In still other places the lake is shallow for long stretches, no deeper than breast high to a man, but dangerous because of the weed growths and the sunken drifts which entangle a swimmer's limbs. Its banks are mainly mud, its waters are muddied, too, being a rich coffee color in the spring and a copperish yellow in the summer, and the trees along its shore are mud colored clear up their lower limbs after the spring floods, when the dried sediment covers their trunks with a thick, scrofulous-looking coat.

There are stretches of unbroken woodland around it, and slashes where the cypress knees rise countlessly like headstones and footstones for the dead snags that rot in the soft ooze.

There are deadenings with the lowland corn growing high and rank below and the bleached, fire-blackened girdled trees rising above, barren of leaf and limb.

There are long, dismal flats where in the spring the clotted frog-spawn cling like patches of white mucus among the weed-stalks, and at night the turtles crawl out to lay clutches of perfectly, round, white eggs with tough, rubbery shells in the sand.

There are bayous leading off to nowhere, and sloughs that wind aimlessly, like great, blind worms, to finally join the big river that rolls its semi-liquid torrents a few miles to the westward.

So Reelfoot lies there, flat in the bottoms, freezing lightly in the winter, steaming torridly in the summer, swollen in the spring when the woods have turned a vivid green and the buffalo-gnats by the million and the billion fill the flooded hollows with their pestilential buzzing, and in the fall, ringed about gloriously with all the colors which the first frost brings-gold of hickory, yellow-russet of sycamore, red of dogwood and ash, and purple-black of sweet-gum.

But the Reelfoot country has its uses. It is the best game and fish country, natural or artificial, that is left in the South today.

In their appointed seasons the duck and the geese flock in, and even semi-tropical birds, like the brown pelican and the Florida snake-bird, have been known to come there to nest.

Pigs, gone back to wildness, range the ridges, each razor-backed drove captained by a gaunt, savage, slab-sided old boar. By night the bullfrogs, inconceivably big and tremendously vocal, bellow under the banks.

It is a wonderful place for fish—bass and crappie, and perch, and the snouted buffalo fish.

How these edible sorts live to spawn, and how their spawn in turn live to spawn again is a marvel, seeing how many of the big fish-eating cannibal-fish there are in Reelfoot.

Here, bigger than anywhere else, you find the garfish, all bones and appetite and horny plates, with a snout like an alligator, the nearest link, naturalists say, between the animal life of today and the animal life of the Reptilian Period.

The shovel-nose cat, really a deformed kind of fresh-water sturgeon, with a great fan-shaped membranous plate jutting out from his nose like a bowsprit, jumps all day in the quiet places with mighty splashing sounds, as though a horse had fallen into the water.

On every stranded log the huge snapping turtles lie on sunny days in groups of four and six, baking their shells black in the sun, with their little snaky heads raised watchfully, ready to slip noiselessly off at the first sound of oars grating in the row-locks. But the biggest of them all are the catfish!

These are monstrous creatures, these catfish of Reelfoot—scaleless,slick things, with corpsy, dead eyes and poisonous fins, like javelins, and huge whiskers dangling from the sides of their cavernous heads.

Six and seven feet long they grow to be, and weigh 200 pounds or more, and they have mouths wide enough to take in a man's foot or a man's fist, and strong enough to break any hook save the strongest, and greedy enough to eat anything, living or dead or putrid, that the horny jaws can master.

Oh, but they are wicked things, and they tell wicked tales of them down there. They call them man-eaters, and compare them, in certain of their habits, to sharks.

Fishhead was of a piece with this setting.

He fitted into it as an acorn fits its cup. All his life he had lived on Reelfoot, always in the one place, at the mouth of a certain slough.

He had been born there, of a negro father and a half-breed Indian mother, both of them now dead, and the story was that before his birth his mother was frightened by one of the big fish, so that the child came into the world most hideously marked.

Anyhow, Fishhead was a human monstrosity, the veritable embodiment of nightmare!

He had the body of a man—a short, stocky sinewy body—but his face was as near to being the face of a great fish as any face could be and yet retain some trace of human aspect.

His skull sloped back so abruptly that he could hardly be said to have a have a forehead at all; his chin slanted off right into nothing. His eyes were small and round with shallow, glazed, pale-yellow pupils, and they were set wide apart in his head, and they were unwinking and staring, like a fish's eyes.

His nose was no more than a pair of tiny slits in the middle of the yellow mask. His mouth was the worst of all. It was the awful mouth of a catfish, lipless and almost inconceivably wide, stretching from side to side.

Also when Fishhead became a man grown his likeness to a fish increased, for the hair upon his face grew out into two tightly kinked slender pendants that drooped down either side of the mouth like the beards of a fish!

If he had another name than Fishhead, none excepting he knew it. As Fishhead he was known, and as Fishhead he answered.

Because he knew the waters and the woods of Reelfoot better than any other man there, he was valued as a guide by the city men who came every year to hunt or fish; but there were few such jobs that Fishhead would take.

Mainly he kept to himself, tending his corn patch, netting the lake, trapping a little, and in season pot hunting for the city markets. His neighbors, ague-bitten whites and malaria-proof negroes alike, left him to himself

Indeed, for the most part they had a superstitious fear of him. So he lived alone, with no kith nor kin, nor even a friend, shunning his kind and shunned by them.

His cabin stood just below the State line, where Mud Slough runs into the lake. It was a shack of logs, the only human habitation for four miles up or down.

Behind it the thick timber came shouldering right up to the edge of Fishhead's small truck patch, enclosing it in thick shade except when the sun stood just overhead.

He cooked his food in a primitive fashion, outdoors, over a hole in the soggy earth or upon the rusted red ruin of an old cookstove, and he drank the saffron water of the lake out of a dipper made of a gourd, faring and fending for himself, a master hand at skiff and net, competent with duck gun and fishspear, yet a creature of affliction and loneliness, part savage, almost amphibious, set apart from his fellows, silent and suspicious.

In front of his cabin jutted out a long fallen cottonwood trunk, lying half in and half out of the water, its top side burnt by the sun and worn by the friction of Fishhead's bare feet until it showed countless patterns of tiny scrolled lines, its underside black and rotted, and lapped at unceasingly by little waves like tiny licking tongues.

Its farther end reached deep water. And it was a part of Fishhead, for no matter how far his fishing and trapping might take him in the daytime, sunset would find him back there, his boat drawn up on the bank, and he on the other end of this log.

From a distance men had seen him there many times, sometimes squatted motionless as the big turtles that would crawl upon its dipping tip in his absence, sometimes erect and motionless like a creek crane, his misshapen yellow form outlined against the yellow sun, the yellow water, the yellow banks—all of them yellow together.

If the Reelfooters shunned Fishhead by day they feared him by night and avoided him as a plague, dreading even the chance of a casual meeting. For there were ugly stories about Fishhead—stories which all the negroes and some of the whites believed.

They said that a cry which had been heard just before dusk and just after, skittering across the darkened waters, was his calling cry to the big cats, and at his bidding they came trooping in, and that in their company he swam in the lake on moonlight nights, sporting with them, diving with them, even feeding with them on what manner of unclean things they fed.

The cry had been heard many times, that much was certain, and it was certain also that the big fish were noticeably thick at the mouth of Fishhead's slough. No native Reelfooter, white or black, would willingly wet a leg or an arm there.

Here Fishhead had lived, and here he was going to die. The Baxters were going to kill him, and this day in late summer was to be the time of the killing.

The two Baxters—Jake and Joel—were coming in their dugout to do it!

This murder had been a long time in the making. The Baxters had to brew their hate over a slow fire for months before it reached the pitch of action.

They were poor whites, poor in everything, repute, and worldly goods, and standing—a pair of fever-ridden squatters who lived on whiskey and tobacco when they could get it, and on fish and cornbread when they couldn't.

The feud itself was of months' standing. Meeting Fishhead one day, in the spring on the spindly scaffolding of the skiff landing at Walnut Log, and being themselves far overtaken in liquor and vainglorious with a bogus alcoholic substitute for courage, the brothers had accused him, wantonly and without proof, of running their trout-line and stripping it of the hooked catch—an unforgivable sin among the water dwellers and the shanty boaters of the South.

Seeing that he bore this accusation in silence, only eyeing them steadfastly, they had been emboldened then to slap his face, whereupon he turned and gave them both the beating of their lives—bloodying their noses and bruising their lips with hard blows against their front teeth, and finally leaving them, mauled and prone, in the dirt.

Moreover, in the onlookers a sense of the everlasting fitness of things had triumphed over race prejudice and allowed them—two freeborn, sovereign whites—to be licked by a nigger! Therefore they were going to get the nigger!

The whole thing had been planned out amply. They were going to kill him on his log at sundown. There would be no witnesses to see it, no retribution to follow after it. The very ease of the undertaking made them forget even their inborn fear of the place of Fishhead's habitation.

For more than an hour they had been coming from their shack across a deeply indented arm of the lake.

Their dugout, fashioned by fire and adz and draw-knife from the bole of a gum-tree, moved through the water as noiselessly as a swimming mallard, leaving behind it a long, wavy trail on the stilled waters.

Jake, the better oarsman, sat flat in the stern of the round-bottomed craft, paddling with quick, splashless strokes, Joel, the better shot, was squatted forward. There was a heavy, rusted duck gun between his knees.

Though their spying upon the victim had made them certain sure he would not be about the shore for hours, a doubled sense of caution led them to hug closely the weedy banks. They slid along the shore like shadows, moving so swiftly and in such silence that the watchful mudturtles barely turned their snaky heads as they passed.

So, a full hour before the time, they came slipping around the mouth of the slough and made for a natural ambuscade which the mixed-breed had left within a stone's jerk of his cabin to his own undoing.

Where the slough's flow joined deeper water a partly uprooted tree was stretched, prone from shore, at the top still thick and green with leaves that drew nourishment from the earth in which the half uncovered roots yet held, and twined about with an exuberance of trumpet vines and wild fox-grapes. All about was a huddle of drift— last year's cornstalks, shreddy strips of bark, chunks of rotted weed, all the riffle and dunnage of a quiet eddy.

Straight into this green clump glided the dugout and swung, broadside on, against the protecting trunk of the tree, hidden from the inner side by the intervening curtains of rank growth, just as the Baxters had intended it should be hidden when days before in their scouting they marked this masked place of waiting and included it, then and there, in the scope of their plans.

There had been no hitch or mishap. No one had been abroad in the late afternoon to mark their movements—and in a little while Fishhead ought to be due. Jake's woodman's eye followed the downward swing of the sun speculatively.

The shadows, thrown shoreward, lengthened and slithered on the small ripples. The small noises of the day died out; the small noises of the coming night began to multiply.

The green-bodied flies went away and big mosquitoes with speckled gray legs, came to take the places of the flies.

The sleepy lake sucked at the mud banks with small mouthing sounds, as though it found the taste of the raw mud agreeable. A monster crawfish, big as a chicken lobster, crawled out of the top of his dried mud chimney and perched himself there, an armored sentinel on the watchtower.

Bull bats began to flitter back and forth, above the tops of the trees. A pudgy muskrat, swimming with head up, was moved to sidle off briskly as he met a cotton-mouth moccasin snake, so fat and swollen with summer poison that it looked almost like a legless lizard as it moved along the surface of the water in a series of slow torpid S's. Directly above the head of either of the waiting assassins a compact little swarm of midges hung, holding to a sort of kite-shaped formation.

A little more time passed and Fishhead came out of the woods at the back, walking swiftly, with a sack over his shoulder.

For a few seconds his deformities showed in the clearing, then the black inside of the cabin swallowed him up.

By now the sun was almost down. Only the red nub of it showed above the timber line across the lake, and the shadows lay inland a long way. Out beyond, the big cats were stirring, and the great smacking sounds as their twisting bodies leaped clear and fell back in the water, came shoreward in a chorus.

But the two brothers, in their green covert, gave heed to nothing except the one thing upon which their hearts were set and their nerves tensed. Joel gently shoved his gun barrels across the log, cuddling the stock to his shoulder and slipping two fingers caressingly back and forth upon the triggers. Jake held the narrow dugout steady by a grip upon a fox-grape tendril.

A little wait and then the finish came!

Fishhead emerged from the cabin door and came down the narrow footpath to the water and out upon the water on his log.

He was barefooted and bareheaded, his cotton shirt open down the front to show his yellow neck and breast, his dungaree trousers held about his waist by a twisted tow string.

His broad splay feet, with the prehensile toes outspread, gripped the polished curve of the log as he moved along its swaying, dipping surface until he came to its outer end, and stood there erect, his chest filling, his chinless face lifted up, and something of mastership and dominion in his poise.

And then—his eye caught what another's eyes might have missed—the round, twin ends of the gun barrels, the fixed gleam of Joel's eyes, aimed at him through the green tracery! In that swift passage of time, too swift almost to be measured by seconds, realization flashed all through him, and he threw his head still higher and opened wide his shapeless trap of a mouth, and out across the lake he sent skittering and rolling his cry.

And in his cry was the laugh of a loon, and the croaking bellow of a frog, and the bay of a hound, all the compounded night noises of the lake. And in it, too, was a farewell, and a defiance, and an appeal!

The heavy roar of the duck gun came!

At twenty yards the double charge tore the throat out of him. He came down, face forward, upon the log and clung there, his trunk twisting distortedly, his legs twitching and kicking like the legs of a speared frog; his shoulders hunching and lifting spasmodically as the life ran out of him all in one swift coursing flow.

His head canted up between the heaving shoulders, his eyes looked full on the staring face of his murderer, and then the blood came out of his mouth, and Fishhead, in death still as much fish as man, slid, flopping, head first, off the end of the log, and sank, face downward slowly, his limbs all extended out.

One after another a string of big bubbles came up to burst in the middle of a widening reddish stain on the coffee-colored water.

The brothers watched this, held by the horror of the thing they had done, and the cranky dugout, having been tipped far over by the recoil of the gun, took water steadily across its gunwale; and now there was a sudden stroke from below upon its careening bottom and it went over and they were in the lake.

But shore was only twenty feet away, the trunk of the uprooted tree only five. Joel, still holding fast to his shot gun, made for the log, gaining it with one stroke. He threw his free arm over it and clung there, treading water, as he shook his eyes free.

Something gripped him—some great, sinewy, unseen thing gripped him fast by the thigh, crushing down on his flesh!

He uttered no cry, but his eyes popped out, and his mouth set in a square shape of agony, and his fingers gripped into the bark of the tree like grapples. He was pulled down and down, by steady jerks, not rapidly but steadily, so steadily, and as he went his fingernails tore four little white strips in the tree-bark. His mouth went under, next his popping eyes, then his erect hair, and finally his clawing, clutching hand, and that was the end of him.

Jake's fate was harder still, for he lived longer—long enough to see Joel's finish. He saw it through the water that ran down his face, and with a great surge of his whole body, he literally flung himself across the log and jerked his legs up high into the air to save them. He flung himself too far, though, for his face and chest hit the water on the far side.

And out of this water rose the head of a great fish, with the lake slime of years on its flat, black head, its whiskers bristling, its corpsy eyes alight. Its horny jaws closed and clamped in the front of Jake's flannel shirt. His hand struck out wildly and was speared on a poisoned fin, and, unlike Joel, he went from sight with a great yell, and a whirling and churning of the water that made the cornstalks circle on the edges of a small whirlpool.

But the whirlpool soon thinned away, into widening rings of ripples, and the corn stalks quit circling and became still again, and only the multiplying night noises sounded about the mouth of the slough.

The bodies of all three came ashore on the same day near the same place. Except for the gaping gunshot wound where the neck met the chest, Fishhead's body was unmarked.

But the bodies of the two Baxters were so marred and mauled that the Reelfooters buried them together on the bank without ever knowing which might be Jake's and which might be Joel's.

The Mollmeit of the Mountain

Cynthia Stockley

When the number of coloured pupils attending the Friend for
Little Children School reached one hundred and fifty, it was
decided that Sister Joanna ought to have the assistance of a white
pupil-teacher as well as the three half-caste young girls she had
already trained. The several High-Dutch ladies of Brandersberg
who interested themselves in Sister Joanna's good work, both by
collecting subscriptions for it abroad and helping to place the young
girls in domestic service after they had left school, determined to
advertise in the Free State newspapers for a girl who would not
only teach in the school, but also live with Sister Joanna at the
school cottage, and help with the simple domestic arrangements.
For Sister Joanna kept no servant; she would have considered it
extravagant to do so while she had health and strength; besides,
she had lived so long in the Colony that there was nothing in the
way of domestic and everyday housework she was not able for. She
was a good cook, could make her own soap, smoke her own legs of
mutton, and grow her own vegetables. She had a neat little garden
round the cottage (which stood some hundred and fifty yards from
the school), and a corner of it was devoted to herbs, for she was
deeply learned in the science of herbal healing, and could cure a
headache, a varicose vein, a black eye, or supply you with a sleeping
draught that would make you forget you had ever known neuralgia;
all out of one little corner of her garden. Besides this, she managed

* *Mollmeit* = Dutch for madwoman or witch.

with great skill and discipline the large school of coloured boys and girls which she had started herself with half a dozen children, some fifteen or sixteen years before; and yet found time to tend the sick, harass the lazy, and manage the affairs generally of everyone in the native Location. However, though she would not admit it, she was beginning to look old and worn, and it was certainly a good idea to get someone to help her in her busy life.

The advertisement brought several answers, but none of them so satisfactory as that of a young Bloemhof girl called Mary Russel. Mary it seemed had not only received a good education and passed her "Matric" (a rather unusual thing in a girl of seventeen), but being the eldest of a large and not at all wealthy family was also extremely domesticated. The Brandersberg ladies thought well of her letter of application, and better still of Mary herself when she arrived, pretty and fresh and kind, with a firm mouth and a courageous glance in her grey eyes. Though of English extraction she was colonial born, a further qualification for the place, for Colonials though kind and just do not spoil natives by making too much of them as English people are apt to do. No sooner was Mary Russel installed than she became a great favourite with the children, and the Brandersberg ladies feeling that they had done well by so popular a character as Sister Joanna thereafter turned their attention to their own affairs. The large and flourishing town of Brandersberg lay within the shadow of a mighty *berg* that in any other country would be called a mountain, and that even in Africa was considered worthy of a title. Thaba Inkosisan it was called, and when the sun set, its great jagged shadow was flung far across the veld, just missing Brandersberg, but falling full and black upon the native Location; and this was considered a curious and sinister thing by the coloured population, for it was upon their village and in their hearts that the mountain had cast sorrow and fear.

The Friend for Little Children School was close at the foot of the *berg,* and a road ran direct from it to the Location, so that the children could go to and fro between their homes and the school without approaching the Dutch town; and perhaps this was one of

the reasons why Sister Joanna's work was as popular with the
whites as with the natives, for in the Free State the whites did not
care for their children to mix with the natives, and any arrangement
to keep the two races apart was greatly favoured. But the situation
of the school was a cause of inquietude amongst the coloured
parents; not because it was too far from the town, but because it
was too near the *berg*. For Thaba Inkosisan was haunted by a
mollmeit, and a mollmeit is no friend to little children.

The haunting of the mountain dated from many years back.
When Mary Russel heard the story, she knew that the horrible
tragedy in which it originated must have occurred about the time
she was born, for it was in that year that the Basutoes fought in
the Free State, surrounding and putting many a town into a state
of siege. Brandersberg had been among the beleaguered towns, and
the inhabitants of several farms near by had been put to the assegai
by the fierce Basuto warriors.

Now, on the other side of the mountain, about thirty miles from
the town, there had stood a little stone farmhouse which an old
Boer had built with an eye to defence in case of war. Its windows
were small and high, its doors and shutters of iron, and there was
nothing inflammable anywhere in its outer structure. When the
Boer died, the place was bought by an Englishman with a pretty
wife and little daughter. Just before the trouble with the Basutoes,
another woman came to supplement the little family, a certain
Janet Fink, middle-aged, well-educated, and recently arrived in
Africa on an emigrant ship. She had been engaged by an agent at
the Cape to come to the farm as a sort of combined nursery
governess and mother's Help. The people of Brandersberg who
knew the Englishman and his wife and liked them, had not had
time to make the acquaintance of the Help before the war with the
natives broke out and the town went into *laager*. Unfortunately
this family was one of those cut off from the town. The Englishman
had indeed been warned, but he pooh-poohed the idea of war, or
only heeded it enough to postpone going in as usual to the town to
get the monthly supply of provisions. But eventually supplies ran
so low that he was obliged one day to set forth after giving careful

instructions for the defence of the farm in case of attack. He had, however, delayed too long, and on his way into the town he was met by the Basutoes out for killing, and put to the assegai. A contingent of the main *impi* then went to the farmhouse and tried to take it, but the women had seen them coming, and received them so resolutely, and with such well-aimed shots from the high windows that having more important things on hand than the taking of two women they presently proceeded on their way, leaving two men behind with instructions to watch the house and kill the women if possible; if not, to starve them out. Being well informed (as Kaffirs always are at such times), they were aware that though there was water in the house there was no meat or meal to speak of, and that the little garrison could not hold out for more than a few days. It held out, however, for ten days, during which time smoke went up every morning from the chimney, and whenever the Basutoes made a feint of approaching they were received with rifle fire. On the eleventh day, however, there was no smoke, and towards evening the two Basutoes feeling pretty sure of their prey crept close, meaning to try for the chimney. Within ten yards of the house one of them was picked off with a bullet through his head, and the other turning to run got a shot in his leg that put him out of business, but in spite of which he managed to crawl away into the bush, where a day or two later he was found by a troop of Dutch Artillery. Under the lash of the *sjambok* he was induced to tell all he knew about the farmhouse, and the Dutchmen, at length convinced that the place was not an ambush but really contained the two white women and child, rode up to it and found, not what they expected, but many surprising things. First of all, instead of signs of famine there was every evidence that many meals had been eaten; plates with remains of meat and gravy were scattered about, and a saucepan contained the leavings of a stew that had been curried and flavoured with onions. Plainly fuel had given out, for every wooden thing in the scantily furnished kitchen had been chopped up and burned. The Boers were deeply puzzled until in an adjoining room the body of the farmer's wife was found lying in a corner covered with old sacks. She had been dead for many days, and the manner of her dying was swift and sudden; there was a knife deeply imbedded in her back. When later the charred skull and thigh bones of a little child were raked out of the ashes in the fireplace the dark tragedy was made clearer still, and the rough men turned from the scene with sick hearts and grim mouths. There were husbands and fathers amongst them, and it would have gone hard with her if in that hour they had come across the mother's Help who in so hideous a fashion had helped herself. But they never found her. Whether after escaping from the house she was caught and killed by the Basutoes, or, lost in the bush had been eaten by wild beasts, or wandering on had reached some town and under an assumed name told a plausible tale and been taken in and cared for, had never been discovered. Only, presently in some strange way a story got about that she had fled to Thaba Inkosisan, and was living there in a cave, subsisting on wild roots and rock rabbits.

The tale first got credence among others besides the natives on the disappearance from some transport waggons outspanned near the mountain of a little Kaffir child. It was declared by the Kaffirs that the "flesh-eating woman" from the farm had turned into a mollmeit with cravings for human flesh, and that the children of Brandersberg would never be safe again while she lived in the mountain. Mollmeits, according to them, were like tigers which having once tasted human blood find no other so much to their liking; and, though other food must of needs be eaten, the evil craving comes upon them at times like a madness and must be satisfied. Most of the Dutch people scoffed at this ghoulish tale, saying that it was more likely that the Kaffir child had fallen down a ravine, and thereafter been eaten by jackals. But some there were who believed in the mollmeit theory, and spoke of searching the mountain. However, the idea came to nothing. There are too many little *piccannins* in Africa for one more or less to make any difference except to its mother; and the sorrows of a Kaffir woman do not count for much in some parts of the world. Moreover, the searching of Thaba Inkosisan was not an affair to be lightly undertaken; its sides were steep and rough, with great inaccessible cliffs in some parts, and masses of bush growing thick and close as moss. There were known to be caves too, and cracks and fissures that led far into the mountainside; but the notion of anyone living in such places seemed to the Dutch impracticable and ridiculous. At any rate, nothing was done, and with the passing of months and years, the legend of the mollmeit had almost died out when another child disappeared—a little orphan this time, whom no one missed at first because it was no one's business to look after her; thus some days passed before her loss was realised and then it seemed rather late to make more than a perfunctory search, for if she was lost in the bush (and it must be remembered that the bush grows right up to the outskirts of many South African towns) she was probably already dead from starvation or sunstroke. A search was made in a half-hearted sort of way, and mainly because Sister Joanna agitated for it; but no one bothered for long about a little half-caste orphan child. Besides, the coloured people, whom the matter mostly concerned, said that it was no use looking for what was already eaten and digested up in the caves of Thaba Inkosisan; which clearly showed what their solution of the problem was.

It was long before the mollmeit was heard of again. True, the superstitious and fearful tried to make out that little Anna Blaine, the youngest of a large coloured family, had fallen a victim to the witch; but to all sensible people it was plain that the child had been drowned at the Sunday-school picnic. She was not missed until the children got I home, and then it was remembered that when last seen she was throwing stones into the *spruit* swollen with recent rains near whose banks the picnic had been held. Sister Joanna, with whom the child had been a special favourite, worried the police until they consented to drag the *spruit* for some six miles; but the body was never recovered.

The fourth disappearance created more stir than any of the others. For one thing it *was* the fourth, and when four children have mysteriously disappeared within the space of fourteen years it is time to be up and doing, said both the Dutch and the coloured population of Brandersberg. Further, it was no orphan or unwanted child this time, but Susie Brown, the pet child of a highly respec-table coloured carpenter. The little thing had started for school one morning, and had just simply never arrived. From the time she set out, an hour late, on the long empty road that skirted the foot of the *berg* no one had seen her. It was as though some great *asvogel* had swooped down from the skies and carried her off. Indeed some people were inclined to think this the answer to the riddle. Possibly, they said, a great bird of prey had its nest in a secret place of the mountain, and fed its young thus! At any rate it was time for the mountain to be searched and the mystery made an end of. And the mountain *was* searched, from end to end, by a large band of men. It is true that all the inner crevices could not be explored, nor the highest cliffs, but the searchers were satisfied if others were not, that neither monstrous bird nor human monster occupied Thaba Inkosisan.

So again with the passing of years, the weird legend died away, and at the time of Mary Russel's coming to the school it was almost forgotten, except by loving mothers who warned their children to keep as far away from the mountain as possible, and the children themselves who never wearied of embroidering and embellishing the fearsome tale, handing it on to one another, and sometimes frightening a timid child into a fit with it.

Mary one day in the schoolyard came upon a little group who having finished their tiffin were seated in a ring listening with scared eyes and parted lips to the story (with variations and improvements) of Susie Brown's disappearance.

". . . and the mollmeit chose her because she had such nice, fat, round arms and legs . . . just like Rosalie Paton's there," announced the historian, and a chubby pale-brown maiden of five gave a howl of terror. Mary sat down and took the child in her arms, roundly scolding the story-teller while she cuddled the soft fuzzy head against her breast. For it must not be supposed that these little coloured children are not just as sweet and pretty and attractive as white children. Hardly any of the inhabitants of the Brandersberg native Location were real negroes. The negro races mostly live in kraals far from the towns, speaking no language but that of their tribe, and being classed under the general heading of "Kaffirs." The scholars of the Friend for Little Children School were mostly the offspring of pale brown people— "Cape folks" who have long hair and Malay blood in them, and natives of St. Helena, who are also long-haired, but rather dusky; some were of Koranna or Hottentot breed (and these were not beautiful), but many were the children of mixed marriages between "poor whites" and Cape natives, and these were nearly always pretty and charming-looking. The language used generally amongst themselves was a kind of Low-Dutch patois, but all spoke English well, and were taught in that language.

Little Rosalie Paton's mother was a Cape woman, and a very disreputable one, the drunkard of the village, in fact; but it was probable that the child's father was a white man, for except for the fuzziness of her long black hair and the brilliance of her great dark eyes, she was as like a pretty little white child as she could be.

When Mary had thoroughly scolded the children for talking about the mollmeit, she carried the still weeping Rosalie with her up to the cottage and her own room there. A little petting soon dispersed the tears, and then Mary produced her trinket-box, and allowed the child to look at its contents. A poorly brought-up colonial girl possesses little in the way of jewellery beyond a necklace and bracelet or two made by her own clever fingers from the seeds of the *sponspeck* melon and a few imitation pearls; but Mary had been a favourite wherever she went and had received many little presents. There was a necklace of jagged red corals which her mother had put round her neck as a baby, and that Rosalie gurgled so joyously over that Mary, after a moment's hesitation, clasped it round the little dusky neck and told the child that she might wear it that night at the magic-lantern entertainment. For the Michaelmas holidays were approaching, and Sister Joanna was going to celebrate the break in the school term by giving one of her frequent little entertainments, only this time a new and up-to-date magic lantern, sent by admiring friends across the sea, was to make its *debut,* and all the children were wildly excited about it. In the midst of Rosalie's joyful caperings, the voice of Sister Joanna was heard calling:

"Mary, Mary, where are you, my child? Isn't it time for the school bell?" And Mary jumped up guiltily (she had forgotten that the bell was to be rung a quarter of an hour earlier that day), just as Sister appeared in the doorway filling it with her plump, large presence. She was a short woman who in spite of her great activity could not keep down stoutness. Her large round face was pallid with the dead pallor peculiar to people who have lived long in hot climates, but lighted by an unfailing smile of cheerfulness and sky-blue eyes. She wore a quaint garb of black alpaca made in somewhat monk-like fashion, long and full, and confined by a cord at the waist, while on her head was an arrangement that resembled a cross between a coal-scuttle and a Turkish woman's *yashma*. She belonged to no Order, but was an Order unto herself, and made her uniform with her own hands; and if it was a quaint and funny one no one laughed, for Sister Joanna was both liked and respected.

When Mary had told the tale of Rosalie's trouble, Sister burst into her jolly laugh.

"The poor little thing! Was it afraid for its nice little fat brown body," she said tenderly, and taking Rosalie on her knee rolled up the child's cotton sleeves, looked at the plump pale arms, and pinched the soft neck.

"Let me catch any old mollmeit trying to eat my Rosalie!" she said fondly. "Run along, Mary, and ring the bell. Get lessons over early. Tell the children I am letting them off an hour earlier so that they may have time to curl their hair for to-night." She laughed merrily at her own little jest, well knowing, that hair curling is an unnecessary item in a coloured child's toilette. She was always full of merry little jokes of this kind, and the natives being a laughter-loving lot rejoiced in them as much as she did.

Mary hurried away leaving Rosalie sitting happily on the old woman's knees, and did not see her again until during the afternoon Sister carried her into the schoolroom fast asleep.

"Oh, Sister! How can you carry that great fat thing! You'll be tired out before to-night," said Mary reproachfully, for she thought Sister looked even paler than usual. And sure enough that night the old lady was too tired to eat any supper before starting for the

entertainment. She looked as haggard as death, though her sky-
blue eyes were brighter than ever and full of excitement; but the
beautifully broiled mutton chop Mary had prepared, with potatoes
baked in their skins lay on her plate untouched. Even when Mary
made a cup of foamy coffee according to Sister's own famous receipt
it was wasted. Mary, in all the months she had been at the cottage,
had never known Sister with anything but an excellent appetite,
and was troubled, and before leaving for the school she cut the
meat from the uneaten chop and made it into a sandwich, while
the potatoes she sliced into a nice salad with a tiny onion chopped
over it. This little repast she put on a table in Sister's room. They
were simple in their ways at the cottage.

Down at the school, the children were buzzing like bees outside
the closed door, while Sister and the pupil-teachers within put the
final touches to the magic-lantern arrangements. Mary fished
Rosalie out of the crowd, and found that though she was still
wearing her torn, school frock, she had been washed, her hair was
braided, and she was proudly sporting the coral necklace. She still
seemed more than half asleep, but she blinked happily at Mary.

The entertainment was an enormous success.

The magic lantern worked like magic indeed, and there were
howls of regret when at nine o'clock the last slide was shown. Sister
Joanna made an announcement that during holiday week she would
give another exhibition for the parents, and the children then
danced and partook of the back to where she had been since
breakfast time in the village, egging on the search and agitating
for a party to be sent into the bush even up the mountain, if
necessary.

During afternoon school, Mary's neuralgia became so acute that
she determined to go to the cottage for some painkiller, and having
set her class a task, she put the eldest pupil-teacher in charged
and slipped away.

A short-cut to the cottage was over a broken-down place in the
school-yard wall, through the cottage garden, and in by the kitchen
door which stood open. Fingo whined as she passed, but she took
no notice, being intent on the matter of relieving her pain. Gaining

her room, she reached for the painkiller from a shelf and began to apply the medicament to her gums with the tip of her finger. At the same moment, she heard Sister Joanna going through the kitchen to the back door, and was on the point of getting up and making her presence known when the sound of Sister's voice speaking to Fingo arrested her.

"What are *you* snivelling about, you dirty cur?"

Mary could hardly believe her ears. Not only the coarse words astonished her, but the indescribably vicious way in which they were spoken, the harsh voice so utterly unlike the genial tones day morning she was to leave by a carrier's cart and would reach her home by Saturday afternoon.

During the night, she was much disturbed by the howling of her dog Fingo who was fastened in the yard. She had been allowed to bring Fingo from Bloemhof, and he had always slept in the kitchen, and been allowed the run of the house, but that very afternoon Sister had accused him of rooting in the garden, and insisted on his being kept tied up in future. Whether it was the curtailing of his freedom that desolated Fingo, it is hard to say, but certainly Mary had never before heard him make such tragic and doleful sounds. He at last left off, and she got to sleep, but it seemed only a moment later that she was awakened by a loud thumping on the front door, and sleepily putting out her hand for the matches, she suddenly realised that the light of early dawn was already in the room. Jumping out of bed, she threw a cloak over her nightdress and went to open the door. As she passed through the dining-room, she heard Sister also hurrying out of bed.

"Someone must be ill, Mary," she called through her door, and as if in answer came another loud knocking and a voice crying in bitter trouble.

"Sister Joanna— Oh! Sister Joanna!"

"What, my poor thing? What?" called back the old woman, and came floundering half-dressed from her room as Mary opened the door.

A coloured woman was standing there, haggard and dishevelled, her hair hanging in streaks about her wild face, fear in her bloodshot eyes. Her clothes were rumpled as though they had been slept in, and she was panting and covered with dust. A picture of misery!

"Is my little Rosalie here?" she gasped, and with the question came a sickening odour of stale brandy. It was then they recognised her for Rosalie Paton's mother.

"Here! Why, of course not, Mrs. Paton," cried Mary.

"What do you mean?" said Sister in astonishment.

"Then the mollmeit's got her," wailed the woman distractedly. *"Oh, Jesus! The mollmeit's got my child!"*

"But what do you mean?" repeated Sister in a sterner voice, for she saw that the woman was on the verge of hysteria. "Rosalie went home with all the other children last night, I suppose! Do you mean to say they didn't bring her to you?"

"No!" said the woman, and in her voice was dreadful despair, "God forgive me, Sister, I was drunk—and asleep—it was not till this morning that I knew she hadn't been home—at least she wasn't in the house—since then I've been to a dozen houses, and no one knows anything, but some of the children say that on their way home they were frightened by something that jumped out from behind a rock down there where the *berg* comes near the road—"

"Stuff and nonsense!" broke in Sister scornfully. "Listening to children's tales! You just go back to the village, Sarah Paton, and look for your child. She's there right enough. Someone has kept her for the night, knowing the state you were in. You ought to be ashamed of yourself, my woman. Be off now and find her, and when you have found her come straight back here and tell me, and see if you can turn over a new leaf after this."

Thus with good-natured scoldings she waved the more than half-comforted woman from the door.

"Get back to your bed, Mary, child, and sleep a little longer. It's not five o'clock yet, and we've earned a little lie-abed after the tiring day yesterday. That child's all right—safely tucked up in some kind soul's bed, you may be sure. It will be a lesson to that good-for-nothing hussy."

But Mary though she went back to bed was too disturbed to sleep. She was haunted by the fear of harm having come to little Rosalie, and could not rid herself of foreboding. Why had she not gone down the road herself with the children? She had indeed watched them for awhile from the school door, and had adjured the elders to take the hands of the little ones and see them all safely to their doors. But well she knew the careless, irresponsible nature of the coloured race! No doubt the little ones had soon been allowed to lag behind. Even so, what harm *could* befall them on that straight road not three quarters of a mile long? Of course the talk of a mollmeit was silly and yet—and yet— Oh! it was no use staying in bed, worrying and fretting. She jumped out and busied herself getting breakfast, making the coffee on a little oil-stove, so that she might have the wood coals for the toast. She then looked into the larder, set the rest of yesterday's milk in soup plates to thicken for dessert at the mid-day meal; put a little more pepper and salt on the neck of mutton that was for dinner, and turned it in its dish, and placed fresh wet cloths round the big lump of butter that must last till the end of the week. By that time, Sister also was dressed, and together according to custom, they went into the Oratory and said Matins before the small altar. Although she was not a real nun, Sister Joanna never missed saying any of the daily Offices, and at the morning and evening ones Mary always joined her.

It was a nice little Oratory, the floor covered with a soft hand-made rug of red and brown woollen scraps like little autumn leaves, sewn one above the other; several chairs with kneeling-stools before them, and an altar-table that no one would have guessed was made of rough packing-case wood for it was hidden by a scarlet cloth and linen embroidered by the school children, and there were flowers and candles upon it. The many small panes of the one window had been glorified by means of scarlet and purple tissue paper, which cut in sheets and pasted on alternate panes made an excellent substitute for stained glass, and when the sun shone through and fell in a flood of colour upon the patch-work rug, Mary felt a subtle pleasure woven amongst her prayers. Under the

window, a large dark oaken chest lent a further air of ecclesi-
asticism to the little room. It was worm-eaten and full of cracks
and holes, but was reputed to have been part of the furniture of a
church, and Sister loved it, and kept the altar cloths and holy books
in it.

As the two finished their orisons, the sound of voices broke in
upon them, followed by a knocking on the door. Once more Sarah
Paton stood without, but now several women were with her, and a
scattering of children with scared faces and eyes ready to jump
out of their heads. There was ill news to tell. Rosalie was not to be
found in the village or out of it. No one had seen her since last
night, but some of the elder children remembered calling out to
her to "Come on" as she loitered sleepily behind. Other smaller
children averred that as they were capering along in the rear,
"something white" had darted out from behind a rock, and "made
noises like a mollmeit" They were quite unable to describe said
noises, but declared that they had all run screaming down the road.
Evidently in the pleasurable excitement of this adventure sleepy,
lagging Rosalie had been forgotten; and no one thought of her again
until with the morning came the weeping mother.

"And I tell you the mollmeit's got her," shrieked the unhappy
woman once more, while the others gazed apprehensively at Sister
Joanna.

"How long is that witch going to be left up in the mountain?"
they muttered. "You must write to the Government, Sister. None
of our children are safe—"

Sister Joanna did not conceal her impatience with them.

"It is all nonsense and silly superstition," she said. "The child
will be found all right. I'll find her." And she pulled Sarah Paton
indoors and made her eat the breakfast Mary had prepared,
scolding, comforting, and lecturing the poor woman all at once.
She herself ate nothing so anxious was she to be off and start the
search.

"Lock up, Mary," she said briskly, "and come along. I'll find
the little *schelm,* see if I don't, and give her a good shaking for
causing all this trouble."

However, a thorough search in every nook and corner of the
village, and inquiry at every house, elicited no result, and at the
end of the morning, Sister began to look as blank as the muttering
women and much more weary. There was no question of school;
the children were given a holiday and told to join in the search.
The Dutch police were then communicated with, and the afternoon
was spent going through Brandersberg. Sister Joanna was on her
feet all day, but at five o'clock Mary persuaded her to return home,
begging her to eat something and go straight to bed. Mary herself
stayed some time later in the Location wandering about,
questioning, and trying to comfort Sarah Paton with words of hope
that had no response in her own breast. It was sundown before
she got home tired and dispirited, and it was just as well that she
had accepted a cup of tea in the village, for of course Sister had
been too tired to prepare a meal and there was not even a fire in
the kitchen. Knowing that Sister would be anxious to hear if there
was any news, Mary went at once to her bedroom, but there was
no one there; only a cloud of flies buzzing and crawling over the
sandwich and potato salad which stood untouched by the bedside.
That meant that Sister had eaten nothing since midday the day
before, and Mary was worried. However, in the kitchen she found
a cup with the remains of some herbal brew Sister had evidently
been making for herself and a moment later Sister herself came
out of the Oratory. Fresh hope and courage, gained perhaps in
prayer, showed in her face, for though still pale, she looked
extraordinarily excited, and her blue eyes gleamed with some inner
fire that Mary's news could not quench.

"We shall find her—we shall find her, never fear," she
prophesied.

But Mary went to bed cold and miserable, and trying to stave
off a bout of neuralgia that had its origin in a tooth she could not
afford to have stopped. The doleful howling of Fingo throughout
the night further depressed her, and drove away all hope of sleep.
In the morning, Sister Joanna decreed that Fingo must return to
Bloemhof.

"I can quite understand your fondness for him, Mary, he's a dear little dog, but we can't be kept awake like this night after night. You must take him back with you to-morrow. By the way, I've made all arrangements for Tom Jackson to call for you."

"But, Sister, I don't want to go. I feel I can't, unless Rosalie is found."

"Nonsense, my dear, what good can you do? If she is to be found I'll find her. While if you miss Jackson's cart you miss your holiday, and I'm not going to have that." There was resolution in the old woman's voice and Mary made no further remark, only ate her breakfast and hurried off to school, for work had to go on whatever befell. It was the last day before the holidays and should have been a bright and merry one, but gloom hung over everyone. The children spoke in hushed voices, and at tiffin time instead of playing sat whispering in groups. Sister Joanna came in for a few moments in the morning and wished the children pleasant holidays; then went saw that the carving knife with a fresh edge to it lay upon the table.

When school was over at last, and the children gone, there was still much to be done, and it was dusk before Mary approached the house again, walking slowly, for she felt a strange reluctance to meet Sister Joanna. But the house was empty. Sister had not returned from her sick visit. Mary made the fire and put on the kettle for a cup of tea; then turned her attention to the matter of supper. Since Sarah Paton had first knocked on the door, no regular meal had been sat down to in the cottage; and after she had visited the larder, the bread-tin, and the egg-jar, Mary's simple calculations told her that if she had eaten little during the two troubled days Sister Joanna had eaten absolutely nothing at all. Apparently another cup of herbal tea had been brewed and drunk, for the empty cup, giving out a faint peculiarly bitter odour, was on the table; herbal tea, however, is poor sustenance, and it behoved Mary to see about getting a good meal ready. The neck of mutton in the larder was two days' old and no good to anyone but Fingo, but fortunately the butcher had left some stewing mutton that morning, and this Mary cut up and put into a sauce-pan with onions and a lump of butter, browned it over a fierce fire, added a cupful of cold water, and put it to simmer. Then she sat down to peel potatoes. She was going to make an Irish stew. As she sat there, her mind wrestled persistently with the problem of little Rosalie, and when she had finished the potatoes, she determined she would go into the Oratory and pray. She had often prayed for things, as the young do, with fervour and faith, and her prayers had sometimes been answered in a wonderful way. The thought of going to God, now, in the quiet house appealed to her. She stepped softly into the Oratory and kneeling down, not in her usual place but right before the altar, she prayed with all her heart that Rosalie might be found. When she had finished, the tears were streaming down her cheeks, so ardently and pleadingly like a child in trouble had she called upon God. Immediately her heart was lighter, her courage higher. It was as though she had passed a burden from her into other hands—very safe sure Hands.

As she rose, she felt a brittle, crunching sensation under her boot, and stooping picked out something from under the red and brown leaves of the rug, and a thrill of amazement ran suddenly through her. The chapel was by now so dark that she could only dimly see what it was she had found, but not for a moment did she mistake the familiar feel of a thing she had possessed all her life. It was her own little coral necklace! The necklace Rosalie was wearing when she disappeared!

No sound broke from the girl's lips, but a cry went up from her heart at this strange answer to her prayer. She realised that if she had not gone to the altar step to pray, her foot would never have found the necklace. Bewildered, amazed, *frightened* as she was, she suddenly felt strong and secure,— God was at work.

As she opened the door that led back into the kitchen, lighted only by the flickering firelight, she collided heavily with someone, and her arm was gripped as by a hand of iron.

"What were you doing in there?" Sister Joanna, breathing heavily as if she had been running, barked the question hoarsely at her. Mary stared a moment, a sort of terror creeping over her at that harsh brutal voice heard twice in the same day. Some swift instinct warned her to conceal what she felt.

"I have been praying, Sister," she answered quietly. "Praying that our little Rosalie may be found."

Slowly the grip on her arm relaxed, and as though nothing untoward had happened, she moved across to the fire and lifted the saucepan.

"I'm afraid my Irish stew is burning! I hope it won't taste."

She was talking to hide something. A terrible inspiration had come to her that she must not share with Sister Joanna the discovery she had just made; and as she shook the saucepan with one hand, with the other she slipped the necklace into her pocket. Then she lighted the kitchen lamp, and got out the teapot.

"I'm just going to make you a cup of tea, Sister," she said cheerfully. "I expect you are dead beat."

The old woman had sunk into a chair by the table, but her eyes had a strange glare in them as she watched Mary, who affecting not to notice, bustled about rattling the tea-things.

"I can see you are just tired out, and as nervous and worried as ever you can be." Mary's arm was still tingling with pain, and that may have had something to do with her newly discovered powers of acting; but the sky-blue eyes still glared. At last, the tea was made and poured out.

"And now tell me, Sister dear,—is there any news yet?"

Sister Joanna gave a sigh as if some tight band round her had suddenly been loosened and she had breathing space once more.

"No, child," and it was almost her old genial voice. "The men have come back from the bush. But to-morrow they are going up the mountain. I've worked them up to *that*."

"I'm glad," said Mary thoughtfully. "For do you know, Sister, I am beginning to believe as the children do, that there really *is* a mollmeit up there and that she is at the bottom of all the disappearances."

The blue eyes fastened themselves keenly on the girl's face, then, "I have always believed it myself," said Sister Joanna solemnly.

The Irish stew had only a faintly burnt flavour, and looked appetising enough in its dish; but the sight of it had a curious effect on Sister Joanna. She looked at it almost ravenously, then turned away as though the sight sickened her.

"No—no, I couldn't eat any," she muttered half to herself. "I'm not hungry, but to-morrow—to-morrow I will make myself a little curry. Curry always brings back my appetite and bucks me up when I am tired out."

Mary's own appetite had taken wings since that curious scene in the kitchen. Nevertheless she made a great pretence of hunger. Fortunately, Sister did not stay to see whether the large helping of stew was eaten, but rose and stumbled towards her room which was next to the dining-room. It was easy to see that she was dropping with fatigue. How could it be otherwise after two days of ceaseless activity during which she had eaten nothing? Her heavy pallid cheeks hung in haggard rolls about her jaws, and with the glare gone out of them, her eyes resembled two large blue beads stuck in a fat doll's face.

"I'll go to bed, Mary," she said heavily. "I must get rest."

"Yes, do, Sister. No Compline in the Oratory to-night, I suppose."

Like a flash, energy came back into the old woman's glance, and the haggard muscles of her face seemed to tighten; but Mary, though her heart had come bounding up into her throat, ate on placidly.

"No," said Sister slowly, "I shall say the Office in my room, and I advise you, my dear, to get to bed as soon as possible, for Jackson will be here for you at five in the morning. Have you got your things ready?"

"Not yet," said Mary, and secretly repeated to herself, "*Not yet!*" She was dazed, bewildered, and terrified; creeping, creeping terror of she knew not what was in her veins. But not for nothing had she prayed and felt answering faith and courage poured into her heart! Definitely, she knew that after that prayer and its answer she had no right to go yet—until Rosalie was found—

Though she could not eat, she sat for some little time at the table, making sounds with her knife and fork. Her idea was to prolong the evening as much as possible. She did not wish to go to bed until Sister Joanna slept. She could hear the latter undressing, and presently murmuring the words of the Office; later, the iron bed creaked, but sleep was as yet far from that bed. Long ago, Mary had observed in Sister Joanna an intense, almost foxlike acuteness, that in one less kind and genial would have alarmed the girl; now it did alarm her, for from the silent bedroom, through the closed door she felt it directed upon her; those unfortunate last words about Compline had aroused it!

At last, Mary rose and softly cleared the table, went out to the yard and fed Fingo, made one or two little preparations for the morning, then bolted the back door, and retired to her room. With her door carefully ajar, as she often left it, she then began to shake out and fold up her holiday things and pack them in a carpet bag. In all she did, she was careful to be perfectly natural and make no sound more or less than she would any ordinary night, for she was still aware of that acute attention piercing through the very walls about her. At last, she washed her face, brushed and plaited her hair, and got into bed. But under her night-dress she was fully dressed.

There in the darkness she lay thinking, thinking, and while she thought, she practised breathing regularly and evenly as she had often done when a child. What was the meaning of it all?—the strange words in the kitchen—the abuse flung at the dog—the screeching knife—the grip on her arm—the watching eyes—the coral necklace in the Oratory? Mary had no clear idea; only, when she tried to piece the strange puzzle together, she was afraid with a deadly fear that froze the blood in her veins and paralysed her heart.

It seemed as though years instead of hours passed before that happened which she had known must happen—very gently Sister Joanna's door opened, and feet came padding softly to the kitchen; beside Mary's door they paused; it was for this moment Mary had practised her regular breathing, and the practise stood her in good stead. After some frightful moments, the longest it seemed to Mary she had ever lived through, the stealthy feet crossed the kitchen, and the Oratory door was opened. It was then that Mary sat up in bed straining her ear-drums until she thought they would crack; but the only sound that reached her was a little soft *creaking* sound. A moment later, she was lying flat again, breathing regularly, for the feet were returning to pause by her door and the light of a candle flickered in. At last the gentle opening and shutting of another door, and the creak of the iron bed under a heavy body told that Sister Joanna had finished her midnight prowlings. It was Mary's turn to get up.

For a full hour, she stood listening in the darkness and in the end she heard the stertorous breathing of a stout, tired woman fallen heavily asleep. To strike a sulphur match without noise was no simple task, and only accomplished by making a cave of the bed-clothes. This time it was Mary who stole, candle in hand, to the Oratory. Drops of cold sweat stood on her forehead and round her mouth, as without a sound she opened the door of that silent room to seek there that which Sister Joanna had hidden and feared for another to find. Whatever and wherever it was, there was no time to lose. At any moment the old woman might wake! Fearfully the girl stole to the altar, and lifting the heavy red cloth stared beneath. Nothing!

The only other possible place was the oak chest. With faltering hands she lifted the lid (which gave a little creak) and looked in, and at what she saw the candle all but fell from her hand. White and still upon the folded altar-cloths lay the body of little Rosalie. Mary turned faint and sick, but the Power that had sustained her throughout the terrible night did not fail her in that moment. She put out her hand to touch the child, and at the same moment a faint bitter odour of herbs came towards her, and she recognised it as the same she had smelled in the cup in the kitchen. There was a brown stain on the child's lips, and drops of liquid on her dress. Like a flash Mary realised the truth, and touching the little hands found them still warm. The child was not dead, but under the influence of a sleeping herb. Plenty of air came through the holes and cracks of the old chest. She was being kept asleep until—until what. The sinister words muttered in the kitchen came back to memory.

"No, no, I mustn't—I mustn't—I must wait till to-morrow!"

Until to-morrow when Mary would be gone. Was that it? Then, in the silent house—what?

"To-morrow I will make a curry!"

Ah, God! What terrible thoughts! They almost unnerved Mary, but she found strength to catch up the child's still form, and turning fled from the accursed place. The lid of the chest fell with a loud bang, and as she gained the back door and fumbled with the bolt, she heard Sister Joanna leap like a tiger from her lair.

Ah! What a race was that through the black night! Over garden beds to the gate mercifully open, and down the long, lonely road. Far, far in front lay the native village and a single point of light glimmering out from a sick woman's hut; and behind was a wild beast balked of its prey, snarling, and panting. Mary ran until a glaze came over her eyes and the blood burst from her nostrils. The rush of the air woke the child in her arms to weak but piercing crying, and only then did the padding shambling feet behind begin to falter and fall back. But Mary ran staggering on toward the light burning in Sarah Paton's hut, and only stopped to fall fainting on the doorstep.

Within half an hour the tale was told, and men with lanterns in their hands and black fury in their hearts were out on the road. But they found no one and the school and cottage were both empty.

The mollmeit had fled to the mountain at last.

Sewn into the mattress of Sister Joanna's bed were discovered the emigration papers of Janet Fink, and later, from under the bed of herbs in the garden men dug out the skulls and bones of four little children. Then, raging, they burned the Cottage and school of the Friend for Little Children, and with brands from the fire set alight the thick bush of the mountain. For four days the flames roared and crackled, sending down great gusts of heat to the town below, and by night lighting up the veld for miles. The rock rabbits and mountain buck came scudding down to the safety of the bush, but the men, deployed in a wide circle round the base of the *berg,* never raised a gun to them so intent were they on their grim vigil.

At length the flames died down, and Thaba Inkosisan blackened and bare, with no leaf or flower or branch, nor any living thing left upon it, gloomed silent above the town.

The Yarn of Lanky Job

John Masefield

Lanky Job was a lazy Bristol sailor, notorious for his sleepiness throughout the seven seas. And though many captains had taken him in hand, none had ever made him spryer, or got more than a snail's work out of him. Perhaps he would have been more wakeful had he not been born with a caul, which preserved him at sea from any danger of drowning. Often he had fallen from aloft or from the forecastle rail while dreaming during his work or look-out. But his captains had always paused to pick him up, and to all his captains he had made a graceful speech of thanks which ended with a snore at the ninth or tenth word.

One day he was lolling on a bollard on the quay at Bristol as fast asleep as man could wish. He had fallen asleep in the forenoon, but when he woke the sun was setting, and right in front of him, moored to the quay, was the most marvellous ship that ever went through water. She was bluff-bowed and squat, with a great castle in her bows and five poops, no less, one above the other, at her starn. And outside her bulwarks there were painted screens, all scarlet and blue and green, with ships painted on them, and burning birds and ladies in cloth of gold. And then above them were rows of hammocks covered with a white piece of linen. And every little poop had a rail. And her buckets were green, and in every bucket there were roses growing. And the masts were of ebony with mast-rings of silver. And her decks were all done in parquet-work in green and white woods, and the man who did the caulking had caulked the deck-seams with red tar, for he was a master of his trade. And the cabins was all glorious to behold with carving, and sweet to smell, like oranges. And right astern she carried a great gold lantern with a big blue banner underneath it, and an ivory staff to the whole, all carved by a Chinaman.

So Job looks at the ship, and he thinks he never see a finer, so he ups alongside, and along a gangway, and there he sees a little sea captain with a big red hat and feather, and a silver whistle to him, walking on the quarter-deck.

"Good morning, Job," says the little sea captain, "and how dy'ye like my ship?"

"Sir," says Job, "I never see a finer."

So the little sea captain takes Job forrard and gives him a bite in the forecastle, and then takes him aft and gives him a sup in the cabin.

"And Job," he says, "how would ye like to sail aboard this beautiful ship?"

So Job, who was all wide awake with the beauty of her, he says:

"Oh, sir, I'd like it of all things; she be so comely to see."

And immediately he said that, Job see the little captain pipe his whistle, and a lot of little sailors in red hats ran up and cast her hawsers off. And then the sheets sheeted home of themselves and the ship swung away from Bristol, and there was Job nodding on the quarter-deck, a mile out to sea, the ship running west like a deer.

"You'll be in the port watch," said the little captain to him, "and woe betide you, Lanky Job, if we catch you asleep in your watch."

Now Job never knowed much about that trip of his among them little men in red hats, but he knowed he slept once, and they stuck needles in him. And he knowed he slept twice, and they stuck hot pokers in him. And he knowed he slept a third time, and "Woe betide you, Lanky Job," they said, and they set him on the bowsprit end, with bread in one hand and a sup of water in the other. "And stay you there, Lanky Job," they said, "till you drop into the sea and drown."

Now pitiful was his case truly, for if he looked behind there was little red men to prick him, and if he looked before he got giddy, and if he looked down he got sick, and if he looked up he got dazzled. So he looked all four ways and closed his eyes, and down he toppled from his perch, going splash into the wash below the bows. "And now for a sleep," he says, "since there's no water wet enough to drown me." And asleep he falls, and long does he drift in the sea.

Now, by and by, when he had floated for quite a while, he sees a big ship, black as pitch, with heavy red sails, come sailing past him in the dawn. And although he had a caul and couldn't be drowned, he was glad enough to see that ship, and right glad indeed to clutch her braces as she rolled. She came swooping down on him, and he caught her main brace as she lay down to leeward from a gust. And with her windward roll and a great heave, he just managed to reach her deck before he fell asleep again. He noticed as he scrambled up the side that she was heavily barnacled, and that she had forty boats to a broadside, all swinging on ivory davits.

But when he woke from his sleep, lo and behold, the ship was manned by nothing but great rats, and they were all in blue clothes like sailors, and snarling as they swung the yards. And as soon as they saw Lanky Job they came around him, gnashing their long yellow teeth and twirling their hairy whiskers. And the multitude of them was beyond speech, and at every moment it seemed to Job that a boat came alongside with more of them, till the decks were ropy with their tails. Six or seven of them seized hold of him and dragged him aft to where a big bone tiller swung, with a helmsman on each side of it, seated in heavy golden chairs. These helmsmen were half men, half rats, and they were hairy like rats, and grey like rats, and they had rats' eyes. But they had the minds of men, and they were the captains of that hooker, and right grim they were to look at. Now when he sees those grim things sitting there, Job knew that he'd come aboard the rat flag-ship, whose boats row every sea, picking up the rats as they leave ships going to sink. And he gave a great scream and punched out at the gang who held him, and over the side he bounded. And he drifted a day and a night, till the salt-cracks were all over his body, and he came ashore half dead at Avonmouth, having been a week away. But always after that Lanky Job was a spry sailor, as smart as you could find anywheres.

The People of the Pit

A. Merritt

North of us a shaft of light shot half way to the zenith. It came from behind the five peaks. The beam drove up through a column of blue haze whose edges were marked as sharply as the rain that streams from the edges of a thunder cloud. It was like the flash of a searchlight through an azure mist. It cast no shadows.

As it struck upward, the summits were outlined hard and black and I saw that the whole mountain was shaped like a hand. As the light silhouetted it, the gigantic fingers stretched, the hand seemed to thrust itself forward. It was exactly as though it moved to push something back. The shining beam held steady for a moment; then broke into myriad little luminous globes that swung to and fro and dropped gently. They seemed to be searching.

The forest had become very still. Every wood noise held its breath. I felt the dogs pressing against my legs. They, too, were silent; but every muscle in their bodies trembled, their hair was stiff along their backs and their eyes, fixed on the falling lights, were filmed with the terror glaze.

I looked at Anderson. He was staring at the north where once more the beam had pulsed upward.

"It can't be the aurora," I spoke without moving my lips. My mouth was as dry as though Lao T'zai had poured his fear dust down my throat.

"If it is I never saw one like it," he answered in the same tone. "Besides, who ever heard of an aurora at this time of the year?"

He voiced the thought that was in my own mind.

"It makes me think something is being hunted up there," he said, "an unholy sort of hunt—it's well for us to be out of range."

"The mountain seems to move each time the shaft shoots up," I said. "What's it keeping back, Starr? It makes me think of the frozen hand of cloud that Shan Nadour set before the Gate of Ghouls to keep them in the lairs that Eblis cut for them."

He raised a hand—listening.

From the north and high overhead there came a whispering. It was not the rustling of the aurora, that rushing, crackling sound like the ghosts of winds that blew at Creation racing through the skeleton leaves of ancient trees that sheltered Lilith. It was a whispering that held in it a demand. It was eager. It called us to come up where the beam was flashing. It drew. There was in it a note of inexorable insistence. It touched my heart with a thousand tiny fear-tipped fingers and it filled me with a vast longing to race on and merge myself in the light. It must have been so that Ulysses felt when he strained at the mast and strove to obey the crystal sweet singing of the Sirens.

The whispering grew louder.

"What the hell's the matter with those dogs?" cried Anderson savagely. "Look at them!"

The malamutes, whining, were racing away toward the light. We saw them disappear among the trees. There came back to us a mournful howling. Then that too died away and left nothing but the insistent murmuring overhead.

The glade we had camped in looked straight to the north. We had reached, I suppose, three hundred miles above the first great bend of the Koskokwim toward the Yukon. Certainly we were in an untrodden part of the wilderness. We had pushed through from Dawson at the breaking of the spring, on a fair lead to the lost five peaks between which, so the Athabascan medicine man had told us, the gold streams out like putty from a clenched fist. Not an Indian were we able to get to go with us. The land of the Hand Mountain was accursed, they said. We had sighted the peaks the night before, their tops faintly outlined against a pulsing glow. And now we saw the light that had led us to them.

Anderson stiffened. Through the whispering had broken a curious pad-pad and a rustling. It sounded as though a small bear were moving toward us. I threw a pile of wood on the fire and, as it blazed up, saw something break through the bushes. It walked on all fours, but it did not walk like a bear. All at once it flashed upon me—it was like a baby crawling upstairs. The forepaws lifted themselves in grotesquely infantile fashion. It was grotesque but it was—terrible. It drew closer. We reached for our guns—and dropped them. Suddenly we knew that this crawling thing was a man!

It was a man. Still with the high climbing pad-pad he swayed to the fire. He stopped.

"Safe," whispered the crawling man, in a voice that was an echo of the murmur overhead. "Quite safe here. They can't get out of the blue, you know. They can't get you—unless you go to them—"

He fell over on his side. We ran to him. Anderson knelt.

"God's love!" he said. "Frank, look at this!"

He pointed to the hands. The wrists were covered with torn rags of a heavy shirt. The hands themselves were stumps! The fingers had been bent into the palms and the flesh had been worn to the bone. They looked like the feet of a little black elephant! My eyes traveled down the body. Around the waist was a heavy band of yellow metal. From it fell a ring and a dozen links of shining white chain!

"What is he? Where did he come from?" said Anderson. "Look, he's fast asleep—yet even in his sleep his arms try to climb and his feet draw themselves up one after the other! And his knees—how in God's name was he ever able to move on them?"

It was even as he said. In the deep sleep that had come upon the crawler, arms and legs kept raising in a deliberate, dreadful climbing motion. It was as though they had a life of their own—they kept their movement independently of the motionless body. They were semaphoric motions. If you have ever stood at the back of a train and had watched the semaphores rise and fall you will know exactly what I mean.

Abruptly the overhead whispering ceased. The shaft of light dropped and did not rise again. The crawling man became still. A gentle glow began to grow around us. It was dawn, and the short Alaskan summer night was over. Anderson rubbed his eyes and turned to me a haggard face.

"Man!" he exclaimed. "You look as though you have been through a spell of sickness!"

"No more than you, Starr," I said. "What do you make of it all?"

"I'm thinking our only answer lies there," he answered, pointing to the figure that lay so motionless under the blankets we had thrown over him. "Whatever it was—that's what it was after. There was no aurora about that light, Frank. It was like the flaring up of some queer hell the preacher folk never frightened us with."

"We'll go no further today," I said. "I wouldn't wake him for all the gold that runs between the fingers of the five peaks—nor for all the devils that may be behind them."

The crawling man lay in a sleep as deep as the Styx. We bathed and bandaged the pads that had been his hands. Arms and legs were as rigid as though they were crutches. He did not move while we worked over him. He lay as he had fallen, the arms a trifle raised, the knees bent.

"Why did he crawl?" whispered Anderson. "Why didn't he walk?"

I was filing the band about the waist. It was gold, but it was like no gold I had ever handled. Pure gold is soft. This was soft, but it had an unclean, viscid life of its own. It clung to the file. I gashed through it, bent it away from the body and hurled it far off. It was— loathsome!

All that day he slept. Darkness came and still he slept. That night there was no shaft of light, no questing globes, no whispering. Some spell of horror seemed lifted from the land. It was noon when the crawling man awoke. I jumped as the pleasant, drawling voice sounded.

"How long have I slept?" he asked. His pale blue eyes grew quizzical as I stared at him.

"A night—and almost two days," I said.

"Was there any light up there last night?" He nodded to the north eagerly. "Any whispering?"

"Neither," I answered. His head fell back and he stared up at the sky.

"They've given it up, then?" he said at last.

"Who have given it up?" asked Anderson.

"Why, the people of the pit," replied the crawling man quietly. We stared at him.

"The people of the pit," he said. "Things that the Devil made before the Flood and that somehow have escaped God's vengeance. You weren't in any danger from them—unless you had followed their call. They can't get any further than the blue haze. I was their prisoner," he added simply. "They were trying to whisper me back to them!"

Anderson and I looked at each other, the same thought in both our minds.

"You're wrong," said the crawling man. "I'm not insane. Give me a very little to drink. I'm going to die soon, but I want you to take me as far south as you can before I die, and afterwards I want you to build a big fire and burn me. I want to be in such shape that no infernal spell of theirs can drag my body back to them. You'll do it too, when I've told you about them—" He hesitated. "I think their chain is off me?" he said.

"I cut it off," I answered shortly.

"Thank God for that, too," whispered the crawling man.

He drank the brandy and water we lifted to his lips.

"Arms and legs quite dead," he said. "Dead as I'll be soon. Well, they did well for me. Now I'll tell you what's up there behind that hand. Hell!

"Now listen. My name is Stanton—Sinclair Stanton. Class of 1900, Yale. Explorer. I started away from Dawson last year to hunt for five peaks that rise like a hand in a haunted country and run pure gold between them. Same thing you were after? I thought so. Late last fall my comrade sickened. Sent him back with some Indians. Little later all my Indians ran away from me. I decided I'd stick, built a cabin, stocked myself with food and lay down to winter it. In the spring I started off again. Little less than two weeks ago I sighted the five peaks. Not from this side, though—the other. Give me some more brandy.

"I'd made too wide a detour," he went on. "I'd gotten too far north. I beat back. From this side you see nothing but forest straight up to the base of the Hand Mountain. Over on the other side—"

He was silent for a moment.

"Over there is forest, too. But it doesn't reach so far. No! I came out of it. Stretching miles in front of me was a level plain. It was as worn and ancient looking as the desert around the ruins of Babylon. At its end rose the peaks. Between me and them—far off—was what looked like a low dike of rocks. Then—I ran across the road!"

"The road!" cried Anderson incredulously.

"The road," said the crawling man. "A fine smooth stone road. It ran straight on to the mountain. Oh, it was road all right—and worn as though millions and millions of feet had passed over it for thousands of years. On each side of it were sand and heaps of stones. After a while, I began to notice these stones. They were cut, and the shape of the heaps somehow gave me the idea that a hundred thousand years ago they might have been houses. I sensed man about them and at the same time they smelled of immemorial antiquity. Well—

"The peaks grew closer. The heaps of ruins thicker. Something inexpressibly desolate hovered over them; something reached from them that struck my heart like the touch of ghosts so old that they could be only the ghosts of ghosts. I went on.

"And now I saw that what I had thought to be the low rock range at the base of the peaks was a thicker litter of ruins. The Hand Mountain was really much farther off. The road passed between two high rocks that raised themselves like a gateway."

The crawling man paused.

"They were a gateway," he said. "I reached them. I went between them. And then I sprawled and clutched the earth in sheer awe! I was on a broad stone platform. Before me was—sheer space! Imagine the Grand Canyon five times as wide and with the bottom dropped out. That is what I was looking into. It was like peeping over the edge of a cleft world down into the infinity where the planets roll! On the far side stood the five peaks. They looked like a gigantic warning hand stretched up to the sky. The lip of the abyss curved away on each side of me.

"I could see down perhaps a thousand feet. Then a thick blue haze shut out the eye. It was like the blue you see gather on the high hills at dusk. And the pit—it was awesome; awesome as the Maori Gulf of Ranalak, that sinks between the living and the dead and that only the freshly released soul has strength to leap—but never strength to cross again.

"I crept back from the verge and stood up, weak. My hand rested against one of the pillars of the gateway. There was carving upon it. It bore in still sharp outlines the heroic figure of a man. His back was turned. His arms were outstretched. There was an odd, peaked headdress upon him. I looked at the opposite pillar. It bore a figure exactly similar. The pillars were triangular and the carvings were on the side away from the pit. The figures seemed to be holding something back. I looked closer. Behind the outstretched hands I seemed to see other shapes.

"I traced them out vaguely. Suddenly I felt unaccountably sick. There had come to me an impression of enormous upright slugs. Their swollen bodies were faintly cut—all except the heads which were well-marked globes. They were—unutterably loathsome. I turned from the gates back to the void. I stretched myself upon the slab and looked over the edge.

"A stairway led down into the pit!"

"A stairway!" we cried.

"A stairway," repeated the crawling man as patiently as before. "It seemed not so much carved out of the rock as built into it. The slabs were about six feet long and three feet wide. It ran down from the platform and vanished into the blue haze."

"But who could build such a stairway as that?" I said. "A stairway built into the wall of a precipice and leading down into a bottomless pit!"

"Not bottomless," said the crawling man quietly. "There was a bottom. I reached it!"

"Reached it?" we repeated.

"Yes, by the stairway," answered the crawling man. "You see— I went down it!

"Yes," he said. "I went down the stairway. But not that day. I made my camp back of the gates. At dawn I filled my knapsack with food, my two canteens with water from a spring that wells up there by the gateway, walked between the carved monoliths and stepped over the edge of the pit.

"The steps ran along the side of the rock at a forty-degree pitch. As I went down and down I studied them. They were of a greenish rock quite different from the granitic porphyry that formed the wall of the precipice. At first I thought that the builders had taken advantage of an outcropping stratum, and had carved from it their gigantic flight. But the regularity of the angle at which it fell made me doubtful of this theory.

"After I had gone perhaps half a mile I stepped out upon a landing. From this landing the stairs made a V-shaped turn and ran on downward, clinging to the cliff at the same angle as the first flight; it was a zigzag, and after I had made three of these turns I knew that the steps dropped straight down in a succession of such angles. No strata could be so regular as that. No, the stairway was built by hands! But whose? The answer is in those ruins around the edge, I think—never to be read.

"By noon I had lost sight of the five peaks and the lip of the abyss. Above me, below me, was nothing but the blue haze. Beside me, too, was nothingness, for the further breast of rock had long since vanished. I felt no dizziness, and any trace of fear was swallowed in a vast curiosity. What was I to discover? Some ancient and wonderful civilization that had ruled when the Poles were tropical gardens? Nothing living, I felt sure—all was too old for life. Still, a stairway so wonderful must lead to something quite as wonderful, I knew. What was it? I went on.

"At regular intervals I had passed the mouths of small caves. There would be two thousand steps and then an opening, two thousand more steps and an opening—and so on and on. Late that afternoon I stopped before one of these clefts. I suppose I had gone then three miles down the pit, although the angles were such that I had walked in all fully ten miles. I examined the entrance. On each side were carved the figures of the great portal above, only now they were standing face forward, the arms outstretched as though to hold something back from the outer depths. Their faces were covered with veils. There were no hideous shapes behind them. I went inside. The fissure ran back for twenty yards like a burrow. It was dry and perfectly light. Outside I could see the blue haze rising upward like a column, its edges clearly marked. I felt an extraordinary sense of security, although I had not been conscious of any fear. I felt that the figures at the entrance were guardians—but against what?

"The blue haze thickened and grew faintly luminescent. I fancied that it was dusk above. I ate and drank a little and slept. When I awoke the blue had lightened again, and I fancied it was dawn above. I went on. I forgot the gulf yawning at my side. I felt no fatigue and little hunger or thirst, although I had drunk and eaten sparingly. That night I spent within another of the caves, and at dawn I descended again.

"It was late that day when I first saw the city—"

He was silent for a time.

"The city," he said at last; "there is a city, you know. But not such a city as you have ever seen—nor any other man who has lived to tell of it. The pit, I think, is shaped like a bottle; the opening before the five peaks is the neck. But how wide the bottom is I do not know—thousands of miles maybe. I had begun to catch little glints of light far down in the blue. Then I saw the tops of—trees, I suppose they are. But not our kind of trees—unpleasant, snaky kind of trees. They reared themselves on high thin trunks and their tops were nests of thick tendrils with ugly little leaves like arrow heads. The trees were red, a vivid angry red. Here and there I glimpsed spots of shining yellow. I knew these were water because I could see things breaking through their surface or at least I could see the splash and ripple, but what it was that disturbed them I never saw.

"Straight beneath me was the—city. I looked down upon mile after mile of closely packed cylinders. They lay upon their sides in pyramids of three, of five—of dozens—piled upon each other. It is hard to make you see what that city is like—look, suppose you have water pipes of a certain length and first you lay three of them side by side and on top of them you place two and on these two one; or suppose you take five for a foundation and place on these four and then three, then two and then one. Do you see? That was the way they looked. But they were topped by towers, by minarets, by flares, by fans and twisted monstrosities. They gleamed as though coated with pale rose flame. Beside them the venomous red trees raised themselves like the heads of hydras guarding nests of gigantic, jeweled and sleeping worms!

"A few feet beneath me the stairway jutted out into a titanic arch, unearthly as the span that bridges Hell and leads to Asgard. It curved out and down straight through the top of the highest pile of carven cylinders and then it vanished through it. It was appalling—it was demonic—"

The crawling man stopped. His eyes rolled up into his head. He trembled and his arms and legs began their horrible crawling movement. From his lips came a whispering. It was an echo of the high murmuring we had heard the night he came to us. I put my hands over his eyes. He quieted.

"The Things Accursed!" he said. "The People of the Pit! Did I whisper? Yes—but they can't get me now—they can't!"

After a time he began as quietly as before.

"I crossed the span. I went down through the top of that—building. Blue darkness shrouded me for a moment and I felt the steps twist into a spiral. I wound down and then—I was standing high up in—I can't tell you in what, I'll have to call it a room. We have no images for what is in the pit. A hundred feet below me was the floor. The walls sloped down and out from where I stood in a series of widening crescents. The place was colossal—and it was filled with a curious mottled red light. It was like the light inside a green and gold flecked fire opal. I went down to the last step. Far in front of me rose a high, columned altar. Its pillars were carved in monstrous scrolls—like mad octopuses with a thousand drunken tentacles; they rested on the backs of shapeless monstrosities carved in crimson stone. The altar front was a gigantic slab of purple covered with carvings.

"I can't describe these carvings! No human being could—the human eye cannot grasp them any more than it can grasp the shapes that haunt the fourth dimension. Only a subtle sense in the back of the brain sensed them vaguely. They were formless things that gave no conscious image, yet pressed into the mind like small hot seals—ideas of hate—of combats between unthinkable monstrous things—victories in a nebulous hell of steaming, obscene jungles—aspirations and ideals immeasurably loathsome—

"And as I stood I grew aware of something that lay behind the lip of the altar fifty feet above me. I knew it was there—I felt it with every hair and every tiny bit of my skin. Something infinitely malignant, infinitely horrible, infinitely ancient. It lurked, it brooded, it threatened and it—was invisible!

"Behind me was a circle of blue light. I ran for it. Something urged me to turn back, to climb the stairs and make away. It was impossible. Repulsion for that unseen Thing raced me onward as though a current had my feet. I passed through the circle. I was out on a street that stretched on into dim distance between rows of the carven cylinders.

"Here and there the red trees arose. Between them rolled the stone burrows. And now I could take in the amazing ornamentation that clothed them. They were like the trunks of smooth-skinned trees that had fallen and had been clothed with high-reaching noxious orchids. Yes—those cylinders were like that—and more. They should have gone out with the dinosaurs. They were— monstrous. They struck the eyes like a blow and they passed across the nerves like a rasp. And nowhere was there sight or sound of living thing.

"There were circular openings in the cylinders like the circle in the Temple of the Stairway. I passed through one of them. I was in a long, bare vaulted room whose curving sides half closed twenty feet over my head, leaving a wide slit that opened into another vaulted chamber above. There was absolutely nothing in the room save the same mottled reddish light that I had seen in the Temple. I stumbled. I still could see nothing, but there *was* something on the floor over which I had tripped. I reached down—and my hand touched a thing cold and smooth—that moved under it. I turned and ran out of that place—I was filled with a loathing that had in it something of madness—I ran on and on blindly—wringing my hands—weeping with horror—

"When I came to myself I was still among the stone cylinders and red trees. I tried to retrace my steps; to find the Temple. I was more than afraid. I was like a new-loosed soul panic-stricken with the first terrors of Hell. I could not find the Temple! Then the haze began to thicken and glow; the cylinders to shine more brightly. I knew that it was dusk in the world above and I felt that with dusk my time of peril had come; that the thickening of the haze was the signal for the awakening of whatever things lived in this pit.

"I scrambled up the sides of one of the burrows. I hid behind a twisted nightmare of stone. Perhaps, I thought, there was a chance of remaining hidden until the blue lightened, and the peril passed. There began to grow around me a murmur. It was everywhere—and it grew and grew into a great whispering. I peeped from the side of the stone down into the street. I saw lights passing and repassing. More and more lights—they swam out of the circular doorways and they thronged the street. The highest were eight feet above the pave; the lowest perhaps two. They hurried, they sauntered, they bowed, they stopped and whispered—and there was nothing under them!"

"Nothing under them!" breathed Anderson.

"No," he went on, "that was the terrible part of it—there was nothing under them. Yet certainly the lights were living things. They had consciousness, volition, thought—what else I did not know. They were nearly two feet across—the largest. Their center was a bright nucleus—red, blue, green. This nucleus faded off, gradually, into a misty glow that did not end abruptly. It, too, seemed to fade off into nothingness—but a nothingness that had under it a—somethingness. I strained my eyes trying to grasp this

body into which the lights merged and which one could only feel
was there, but could not see.

"And all at once I grew rigid. Something cold, and thin like a
whip, had touched my face. I turned my head. Close behind were
three of the lights. They were a pale blue. They looked at me—if
you can imagine lights that are eyes. Another whiplash gripped my
shoulder. Under the closest light came a shrill whispering. I
shrieked. Abruptly the murmuring in the street ceased. I dragged
my eyes from the pale blue globe that held them and looked out—
the lights in the streets were rising by myriads to the level of where
I stood! There they stopped and peered at me. They crowded and
jostled as though they were a crowd of curious people—on
Broadway. I felt a score of the lashes touch me—

"When I came to myself I was again in the great Place of the
Stairway, lying at the foot of the altar. All was silent. There were
no lights—only the mottled red glow. I jumped to my feet and ran
toward the steps. Something jerked me back to my knees. And then
I saw that around my waist had been fastened a yellow ring of
metal. From it hung a chain and this chain passed up over the lip
of the high ledge. I was chained to the altar!

"I reached into my pockets for my knife to cut through the ring.
It was not there! I had been stripped of everything except one of
the canteens that I had hung around my neck and which I suppose
They had thought was—part of me. I tried to break the ring. It
seemed alive. It writhed in my hands and it drew itself closer
around me! I pulled at the chain. It was immovable. There came to
me the consciousness of the unseen Thing above the altar. I
groveled at the foot of the slab and wept. Think—alone in that place
of strange light with the brooding ancient Horror above me—a
monstrous Thing, a Thing unthinkable—an unseen Thing that
poured forth horror—

"After a while I gripped myself. Then I saw beside one of the
pillars a yellow bowl filled with a thick white liquid. I drank it. If it
killed I did not care. But its taste was pleasant and as I drank,
strength came back to me with a rush. Clearly I was not to be

starved. The lights, whatever they were, had a conception of human needs.

"And now the reddish mottled gleam began to deepen. Outside arose the humming and through the circle that was the entrance came streaming the globes. They ranged themselves in ranks until they filled the Temple. Their whispering grew into a chant, a cadenced whispering chant that rose and fell, rose and fell, while to its rhythm the globes lifted and sank, lifted and sank.

"All that night the lights came and went—and all that night the chant sounded as they rose and fell. At the last I felt myself only an atom of consciousness in a sea of cadenced whispering; an atom that rose and fell with the bowing globes. I tell you that even my heart pulsed in unison with them! The red glow faded, the lights streamed out; the whispering died. I was again alone and I knew that once again day had broken in my own world.

"I slept. When I awoke I found beside the pillar more of the white liquid. I scrutinized the chain that held me to the altar. I began to rub two of the links together. I did this for hours. When the red began to thicken there was a ridge worn in the links. Hope rushed up within me. There was, then, a chance to escape.

"With the thickening the lights came again. All through that night the whispering chant sounded, and the globes rose and fell. The chant seized me. It pulsed through me until every nerve and muscle quivered to it. My lips began to quiver. They strove like a man trying to cry out in a nightmare. And at last they, too, were whispering the chant of the people of the pit. My body bowed in unison with the lights—I was, in movement and sound, one with the nameless things while my soul sank back sick with horror and powerless. While I whispered I—saw them!"

"Saw the lights?" I asked stupidly.

"Saw the Things under the lights," he answered. "Great transparent snail-like bodies—dozens of waving tentacles stretching from them—round gaping mouths under the luminous seeing globes. They were like the ghosts of inconceivably monstrous slugs! I could see through them. And as I stared, still bowing and whispering, the dawn came and they streamed to and through the entrance. They did not crawl or walk—they floated! They floated and were—gone!

"I did not sleep. I worked all that day at my chain. By the thickening of the red I had worn it a sixth through. And all that night I whispered and bowed with the pit people, joining in their chant to the Thing that brooded above me!

"Twice again the red thickened and the chant held me—then on the morning of the fifth day I broke through the worn links of the chain. I was free! I drank from the bowl of white liquid and poured what was left in my flask. I ran to the Stairway. I rushed up and past that unseen Horror behind the altar ledge and was out upon the Bridge. I raced across the span and up the Stairway.

"Can you think what it is to climb straight up the verge of a cleftworld—with hell behind you? Hell was behind me and terror rode me. The city had long been lost in the blue haze before I knew that I could climb no more. My heart beat upon my ears like a sledge. I fell before one of the little caves feeling that here at last was sanctuary. I crept far back within it and waited for the haze to thicken. Almost at once it did so. From far below me came a vast and angry murmur. At the mouth of the rift I saw a light pulse up through the blue; die down, and as it dimmed I saw myriads of the globes that are the eyes of the pit people swing downward into the abyss. Again and again the light pulsed and the globes fell. They were hunting me. The whispering grew louder, more insistent.

"There grew in me the dreadful desire to join in the whispering as I had done in the Temple. I bit my lips through and through to still them. All that night the beam shot up through the abyss, the globes swung and the whispering sounded—and now I knew the purpose of the caves and of the sculptured figures that still had power to guard them. But what were the people who had carved them? Why had they built their city around the verge and why had they set that Stairway in the pit? What had they been to those Things that dwelt at the bottom and what use had the Things been to them that they should live beside their dwelling place? That there had been some purpose was certain. No work so prodigious as the Stairway would have been undertaken otherwise. But what was the purpose? And why was it that those who had dwelt about the abyss had passed away ages gone, and the dwellers in the abyss still lived? I could find no answer—nor can I find any now. I have not the shred of a theory.

"Dawn came as I wondered and with it silence. I drank what was left of the liquid in my canteen, crept from the cave and began to climb again. That afternoon my legs gave out. I tore off my shirt, made from it pads for my knees and coverings for my hands. I crawled upward. I crawled up and up. And again I crept into one of the caves and waited until again the blue thickened, the shaft of light shot through it and the whispering came.

"But now there was a new note in the whispering. It was no longer threatening. It called and coaxed. It drew. A new terror gripped me. There had come upon me a mighty desire to leave the cave and go out where the lights swung; to let them do with me as they pleased, carry me where they wished. The desire grew. It gained fresh impulse with every rise of the beam until at last I vibrated with the desire as I had vibrated to the chant in the Temple. My body was a pendulum. Up would go the beam and I would swing toward it! Only my soul kept steady. It held me fast to the floor of the cave. And all that night it fought with my body against the spell of the pit people.

"Dawn came. Again I crept from the cave and faced the Stairway. I could not rise. My hands were torn and bleeding; my knees an agony. I forced myself upward step by step. After a while my hands became numb, the pain left my knees. They deadened. Step by step my will drove my body upward upon them.

"And then—a nightmare of crawling up infinite stretches of steps—memories of dull horror while hidden within caves with the lights pulsing without and whisperings that called and called me—memory of a time when I awoke to find that my body was obeying the call and had carried me halfway out between the guardians of the portals while thousands of gleaming globes rested in the blue haze and watched me. Glimpses of bitter fights against sleep and always, always—a climb up and up along infinite distances of steps that led from Abaddon to a Paradise of blue sky and open world!

"At last a consciousness of the clear sky close above me, the lip of the pit before me—memory of passing between the great portals of the pit and of steady withdrawal from it—dreams of giant men with strange peaked crowns and veiled faces who pushed me onward and onward and held back Roman-candle globules of light that sought to draw me back to a gulf wherein planets swam between the branches of red trees that had snakes for crowns.

"And then a long, long sleep—how long God alone knows—in a cleft of rocks; an awakening to see far in the north the beam still rising and falling, the lights still hunting, the whispering high above me calling.

"Again crawling on dead arms and legs that moved—that moved—like the Ancient Mariner's ship—without volition of mine, but that carried me from a haunted place. And then—your fire—and this—safety!"

The crawling man smiled at us for a moment. Then swiftly life faded from his face. He slept.

That afternoon we struck camp and carrying the crawling man started back south. For three days we carried him and still he slept. And on the third day, still sleeping, he died. We built a great pile of wood and we burned his body as he had asked. We scattered his ashes about the forest with the ashes of the trees that had consumed him. It must be a great magic indeed that could disentangle those ashes and draw him back in a rushing cloud to the pit he called Accursed. I do not think that even the People of the Pit have such a spell. No.

But we did not return to the five peaks to see.

THE SONG OF THE SIRENS

Edward Lucas Wright

I first caught sight of him as he sat on the wharf. He was seated on a rather large seaman's chest, painted green and very much battered. He wore gray, his shirt was navy-blue flannel, his necktie a flaring red bandana handkerchief knotted loosely under the ill-fitting lop-sided collar, his hat was soft, gray felt and he held it in his hands on his knees. His hair was fine, straight and lightish, his eyes china-blue, his nose straight, his skin tanned. His features were those of an intelligent face, but there was in it no expression of intelligence, in fact no expression at all. It was this absence of expression that caught my eye. His face was blank, not with the blankness of vacuity, but with the insensibility of abstraction. He sat there amid the voluble negro loafers, the hurrying stevedores, the shouting wharf-hands, the clattering tackles, the creaking shears and all the hurry and bustle of unloading or loading four vessels, as imperturbable as a bronze statue of Buddha in meditation. His gaze was fixed un varyingly straight before him and he seemed to notice and observe more distant objects; the larger panorama of moving craft in the harbor, the fussy haste of the scuttling tugboats tugging nothing, the sullen reluctance of the urged scows, the outgoing and incoming pungies and schooners, the interwoven pattern they all formed together, the break in it now and again from the dignified passage of a towed bark or ship or from the stately progress of a big steamer. Of all this he seemed aware, but of what went on about him he seemed not only unaware but unconscious, with an impassivity not as if intentionally aloof nor absorbingly preoccupied but as if utterly unconscious or totally insensible to it all. During my long, fidgety wait that first morning I watched him at intervals a good part of the time. Once a pimply, bloated boarding-master, patrolling the wharf, stopped full in front of him, caught his eye and exchanged a few words with him, otherwise no one seemed to notice him, and he scarcely moved, bare-headed all the while in the June sunlight. When I was at last notified that the *Medorus* would not sail that day, went over her side, and left the pier, I saw him sitting as when I first caught sight of him.

Next morning I found him in almost the same spot, in precisely the same attitude, and with the same demeanor. He might have been there all night.

Soon after I reached the *Medorus* the second morning the bloated boarding-master came on board with that rarity, a native American seaman. I was sitting on the cabin-deck by the saloon-skylight, Griswold on one side of me and Mr. Collins on the other. Captain Benson, puffy, pasty-faced and shifty-eyed, was sitting on the booby-hatch, whistling in an exasperatingly monotonous, tuneless and meaningless fashion. As soon as the Yankee came up the companion-ladder he halted, turned to the boarding master who was following him and blurted out.

"What! Beast Benson! Me ship with Beast Benson!" And back he went down the ladder and off up the pier.

Benson said never a word, but recommenced his whistling. It was part of his undignified shiftlessness that he aired his shame on deck. Almost any captain, fool or knave or both, would have kept his cabin or sat by his saloon table. Benson advertised his helplessness to crew, loafers and passers by alike.

The boarding master walked up to Mr. Collins and said:

"You see, Sir. I can't do anything. You're lucky enough to be only two hands short for a crew and luckier to have gotten a second mate to sign. Wilson's the best I can do for first mate. He's willing and he's the only man I can get. Not another boarding-master will so much as try for you."

Mr. Collins kept his irritating set smile, his mean little eyes peering out of his narrow face, his stubby scrubbing-brush pepper-and-salt mustache bristling against his nose. He made no reply to the boarding-master but turned to Griswold.

"You're a doctor, aren't you?" he queried.

"Not yet," Griswold replied.

"Well," said Mr. Collins impatiently, "you know pretty much what doctors know?"

"Pretty much, I trust," Griswold answered cheerfully.

"Can you tell whether a man is deaf or not?" Mr. Collins pursued.

"I fancy I could," Griswold declared, gaily.

"Would you mind testing that man over there for me?" Mr. Collins jerked his thumb toward the impassive figure on the seaman's chest.

Griswold stared.

"He looks deaf enough from here," he asserted.

"Try him nearer," Mr. Collins insisted.

Griswold swung off the cabin deck, lounged over to the companion ladder, went down it leisurely and sauntered toward the seated mariner. Griswold had a taking way with him, a jaunty manner, an agreeable smile, a charming demeanor and plenty of self-confidence. He usually got on immediately with strangers. So now you could see him win at once the confidence of the man. He looked up at him with a sentient and interested personal glance. They talked some little time and then Griswold sauntered back. He did not speak but seated himself by me as before, lit a fresh cigarette and smoked reflectively.

"Is he deaf?" Mr. Collins inquired.

"Deaf is no word for it," Griswold declared, "an adder is nothing to him. I'll bet he has neither tympanum, malleus, incus nor stapes in either ear, and that both cochleas are totally ossified; that the middle ear is annihilated and the inner ear obliterated on both sides of his head. His hearing is not defective, it is abolished, non-existent. I never saw or heard of a man who impressed me as being so totally deaf."

"What did I tell you?" broke in Captain Benson from the booby-hatch.

"Benson, shut up," said Mr. Collins. Benson took it without any change of expression or attitude.

"You seemed to talk to him," Mr. Collins said to Griswold.

"He can read lips cleverly," Griswold replied. "Only once did I have to repeat anything."

"Did you ask him if he was deaf?" Mr. Collins inquired.

"I did," said Griswold, "and he told the truth instanter."

"Impressed you as truthful, did he?" Mr. Collins queried.

"Notably," Griswold said. "There is a gentlemanly something about him. He is the kind of man you respect from the first, and truthful as possible."

"You hear that, Benson?" Mr. Collins asked.

"What's truthfulness of a pitch-dark night in a gale of wind!" Benson snorted. "The man's stone deaf."

Mr. Collins flared up.

"You may take your choice of three ways," he said, "the *Medorus* tows out at noon. If you can find a first-mate to suit you by then, or if you take Wilson as first-mate, you take her out. If not, I'll find another master for her and you can find another ship."

Benson lumbered off the booby-hatch and disappeared down the cabin companion-way. The cabin-boy came up whistling, went briskly over the side, and scampered some little distance up the pier to where three boarding-masters stood chatting. One of them came back with him, three or four half sober sailors tagging after him. These he left by the deaf man's sea-chest. Its owner came aboard with him and together they went down into the cabin.

"Look here, Mr. Collins," I said, "I've half a mind to back out of this and stay ashore."

"Why?" he queried, his little gray eyes like slits in his face.

"I hear this captain called Beast Benson, I see he has difficulty in getting a crew and before me you force him to take a deaf mate. An unwilling crew, a defective officer and an unpopular captain seem to me to make a risky combination."

"All combinations are risky at sea, as far as that goes," said Mr. Collins easily. "Most crews are unwilling and few captains popular. Benson is not half a bad captain. He always has bother getting a crew because he is economical of food with them. But you'll find good eating in the cabin. He has never had any trouble with a crew, once at sea. He is cautious, takes better care of his sails, rigging and tackle than any man I know, is a natural genius at seamanship, humoring his ship, coaxing the wind and all that. And he is a precious sharp hand to sell flour and buy coffee, I can tell you. You'll be safe with him. I should feel perfectly safe with him. I'm sorry I can't go, I can tell you."

"But the deaf mate," I persisted.

"He has good discharges," said Mr. Collins, "and is well spoken of. He's all right."

At that moment the boarding-master came out of the cabin and went over the side. Two of the sailors picked up the first-mate's chest and it was soon aboard. The two men went down into the cabin to sign articles. As they went down and as they came up I had a good look at them. One was a Mecklenburger, a lout of a hulking boy, with an ugly face made uglier by loathsome swellings under his chin. The other was a big, stout Irishman, his curly hair tousled, his fat face flushed, his eyes wild and rolling with the after-effects of a shore debauch. His eyes were notable, one bright enamel-blue, the other skinned-over with an opaque, white, film. He lurched against the companion-hatch, as he came up, and half-rolled, half-stumbled forward. He was still three-quarters drunk.

The *Medorus* towed out at noon. Mr. Collins and Griswold stayed aboard till the tug cast loose, about dusk. After that we worked down the bay under our own sail. Even in the bay I was seasick and for some days I took little interest in anything. I had made some attempt to eat, but beyond calling the first-mate Mr. Wilson and the second mate Mr. Olsen, my brief stays at table had profited me little. I had brought a steamer-chair with me and lolled in it most of the daylight, too limp to notice much of anything.

I couldn't help noticing Captain Benson's undignified behavior. A merchant captain, beyond taking the sun each morning and noon and being waked at midnight by the mate just off watch to hear his report, plotting his course on his chart and keeping his log, concerns himself not at all with the management of his ship, except when he takes the wheel at the critical moment of tacking, or of box-hauling, if the wind changes suddenly, or when a dangerous storm makes it incumbent upon him to take charge continually. Otherwise he leaves all routine matters to the mate on watch. Benson transgressed sea-etiquette continually in this respect. He was forever nosing about and interfering with one or the other mate in respect to matters too small for a self-respecting captain's notice. His mates' contempt for him was plain enough, but was discreetly veiled behind silent lips, expressionless faces and far-off eyes. The men were more open and exchanged sneering glances. The captain would sit on the edge of the cabin-deck, his feet dangling over the poop-deck, and continually nag the steersman, keeping it up for hours.

"Keep her up to the wind," he would say, "keep that royal lifting."

"Aye, aye, Sir," would come from the man at the wheel.

Next moment the captain would call out:

"Let her go off, you damn fool. You'll have her aback!"

"Let her go off, Sir," the victim would reply.

Presently again Benson would snarl:

"Where are you lettin' her go to? Keep her up to the wind."

"Keep her up to the wind, Sir," would come the reply and so on in maddening reiteration.

A day or two after we cleared the capes the big one-eyed Irishman had the wheel. His name, I found afterwards, was Terence Burke and he was from Five Rivers, Canada. He had been a mariner all his life; knew most of the seas and ports of the world. He was especially proud of having been in the United States Navy and of his Civil War record. He had been one of the seamen on the *Congress* or the *Cumberland*, I forget which, and graphic were his descriptions of his sensations while the *Merrimac's* shells were tearing through the helpless ship, the men lying flat in rows on the farther side of the decks, and the six-foot live-oak splinters, deadly as the bits of shell themselves, flying murderously about as each shell burst; of how they took to their boats after dark, and reached the shore, expecting to be captured every moment; of how they saw the *Ericsson's* lights (Burke always called the *Monitor* the *Ericsson*) coming in from the sea, and took heart. Burke was justly proud that he had been one of the men detailed, as biggest and strongest, to work the Ericsson's guns, and that he had helped fight her big turret guns in her famous first battle.

All this about Burke I did not learn till many days later. But it was plain to be seen, even by a sea-sick land-lubber, that he was an able seaman, seasoned, competent and self-respecting. All that was manifest all over him as he stood at the wheel. Likewise it was plain that he had brought liquor aboard with him, for he was still half-drunk, and quarrelsome drunk. Even I could see that in his attitude, in his florid face, in his boiled eye. But Captain Benson did not see it when presently he came on deck and seated himself on the edge of the cabin-deck. He cocked his eye up the main-mast and presently growled.

"Let her go off."

Burke shifted the wheel a quarter of a spoke, his jaws clenched, his lips tight shut.

Benson chewed on his big quid and kept his eye aloft. Again he growled:

"Keep her up to the wind."

Burke shifted the wheel back a quarter of a spoke, again without any word.

"I'll learn ye sea-manners," Benson snarled, "I'll learn ye to repeat after me what I say. Do ye hear me?"

"Aye, aye, Sor," Burke replied, smartly enough.

Shortly Benson came at him again.

"Let her go off, you damn fool."

"Let her go off, you damn fool, Sor," Burke sang out in a rasping Celtic roar which carried to the jibboom.

It was Olsen's watch and the big Norseman was standing by the weather-rigging, his hand on one of the main shrouds. He grinned broadly, full in Captain Benson's face and then looked away to windward. Burke was clutching the spokes as if he were ready to tear them out of the wheel. He looked fighting mad all over. Captain Benson looked aft at him, looked forward, looked aloft, and then rose and went below without a word. Henceforward he worried the steersman no more, unless it were Dutch Charlie, the big loutish boy with the ulcerated chin, or Pomeranian Emil, a timid Baltic waif. Burke and the other full-grown men he let alone.

Next day Burke looked drunker and more belligerent than ever. I noted it, even in my half-daze of flabby nauseated weakness, which subdued me so totally that not even a beautiful and novel spectacle revived me. It was just before noon. The captain and the first-mate had come on deck with their sextants to determine our latitude. The day was fine with a gentle steady breeze, a clear sky and unclouded sunlight, over all the white-capped blue waters. Smoke sighted a little before turned out to be that of a British man-of-war. Just as the captain told the man at the wheel to make it eight-bells, the man-of-war crossed our bows, all white paint and gilding, her ensign spread, flags everywhere, her band playing and her crew manning the yards. The cabin-boy said it was an English bank-holiday, and that she was bound for Bermuda. I was too flaccid to ask further or to care. I made no attempt to go below for the noon meal. I lay at length in my chair. While the captain and mates were at their dinner I could hear loud voices from the forecastle, or perhaps round the galley door. Presently the first-mate came on deck. He walked to starboard, which was to windward, and stood staring after the far off smoke of the vanished man-of-war. He was a tall, clean-built square-shouldered man, English in every detail of movement, attitude and demeanor. He interested me, for in spite of his expressionless face he looked far too intelligent for his calling. I was watching him when I was aware of Burke puffing and snorting aft along the main deck. He puffed and snorted up the port companion-ladder to the poop-deck. His face was redder than ever and his eyes redder than his face. He carried a pan of scouse or biscuit-hash or some such mess. He approached the first-mate from behind and hailed him.

"Luke at thot, Sor," he said, "uz thot fit fude fur min?"

The mate, unaware of his presence, did not move or speak.

"Luke at thot Oi say," Burke roared, "uz thot fit to fade min on?"

The mate remained immobile.

Burke gave a sort of snarling howl, hurled at the mate the pannikin, which hit him on the back of the head, its contents going all over his neck and down his collar. As he threw it Burke leaped at the officer. He whirled round before he was seized and met the attack with a short, right-hand jab on Burke's jaw. There was not enough swing in the blow to down the sailor. He clutched both lapels of the mate's open pea-jacket and pulled him forward. The force the mate had put into the blow, and the impetus it had imparted to Burke, besides his sideways wrench, took the mate half off his feet. He got in a second jab, this time with his left hand, but again too short to be effective. Both men lurched toward the booby-hatch and the inside breast-pockets of the mate's jolted jacket cascaded a shower of letters upon the deck, which blew hither and thither to port. My chair was on the cabin-deck just above the port companion-ladder. The booky man's instinct to save written paper shook me out of my lethargy. In an instant I was out of my chair, down the ladder and picking up the scattered envelopes. Not one, I think, went over-board. I saved three by the port rail and a half a dozen more further inboard. As I scrambled about from one to the other I glanced again and again at the men struggling on the other side of the booby-hatch. The mate had not lost his footing. His short-arm jabs had pushed Burke back till he lost hold of the pea-jacket. The Irishman gathered himself for a rush, the mate squared off, in perfect form, met the rush with a left-hand upper cut on the seaman's chin, calculated his swing and planted a terribly accurate right-hand drive full in Burke's face. He went backward over the starboard companion-ladder down into the main deck.

Paying no more attention to him the mate turned to pick up his letters. He found several on the deck against the booby-hatch, and one by the break of the cabin. Then he looked about for more. I stepped unsteadily toward him and handed him those I had gathered up. In gathering them it had been impossible for me to help noting the address, and the stamps and the postmarks, which on several were English, on two or three French, on two Italian, on one German, on one Egyptian and on one Australian. The address the same on all, was:

> *Geoffrey Cecil, Esq.*
> c.o. Alexander Brown & Son
> Baltimore, Maryland,
> U. S. A.

Instinctively I turned the packet face down as I handed it to him. He took it gracefully and in his totally toneless voice said:

"Thank you very much."

As he said the words Captain Benson appeared in the cabin companion-way, his revolver in his hands. The mate in the act of stowing with his left hand the letters in his inner breast-pocket, pointed his extended index finger at the pistol.

"Put that thing away!" he commanded.

The voice was as toneless as before, but far otherwise than the blurred British evenness of his acknowledgment to me, these words rang hard and sharp. Benson took the rebuke as if he had been the mate and the other his captain, turned and shuffled fumblingly back down the companion-way. As he passed the pantry door the cabin-boy whipped out of it and popped up the companion-way to see, and the big Norse mate emerged deliberately behind him.

By this time the fat negro steward and most of the crew had come aft and gathered about the prostrate Burke.

The first-mate cleared the scouse from his neck and collar, took some tarred marline from an outside pocket of his pea-jacket, and in a leisurely way went down into the waist. He had the men turn Burke over and tie his hands behind him and his ankles together. Then he had buckets of sea-water dashed over him. Burke soon regained consciousness.

"Carry him forward and put him in his bunk," the mate commanded. "When he says he will behave cut him loose."

Captain Benson had come on deck and was standing by the booby-hatch.

"That man ought to be put in irons," he said as the mate turned.

The mate's eyes were on his face as he said it.

"He needs no irons," he retorted crisply. "Why make a mountain out of a mole-hill."

I had been hoping that I was getting used to the sea, for I was only passively uncomfortable and mildly wretched. But sometime that night it came on to blow fresh and I waked acutely sea-sick and suffering violently from horrible surging qualms in every joint. I clambered out of my bunk, struggled into some clothes and crawled across the cabin and up the after companion-way to the wheel-deck. There I collapsed at full length into four inches of warm rain water against the lee-rail. At first the baffling breeze was comforting after the stuffy cabin, smelling of stale coffee, damp sea-biscuit, prunes, oilskins and what not. But I was soon too cold, for I was vestless and coatless, and before long my teeth were chattering and I had a general chill to add to my misery. It was the first-mate's watch and coming aft on his eternal round he found me there. He at once went below and brought me not only vest and jacket but my mackintosh also. I was wet to the skin all over, but the mackintosh was gratefully warm. Forgetting that he could not hear I thanked him inarticulately, and relapsed into my shifting pond, where I slipped into oblivion, my head on the outer timber, the tearing dawn-wind across my face.

Sometime before noon I was again in my chair, as on the day before, and it was again the first-mate's watch. Again I saw Burke come aft. He was not puffing and snorting this time, but very silent. His florid face was a sort of gray-brown. His head was tied up and the bandage tilted sideways over his bad eye. He came up to port companion ladder half way from the waist of the poop-deck. There he stood holding on to the top of the rail, looking very humble and abashed. It was some time before the first-mate noticed him or deigned to notice him. In that interval Burke said a score of times:

"Mr. Willson, Sor."

Each time he realized that he was ignored he waited meekly for a chance to try again. Finally the mate saw him speak and asked:

"What is it, Burke?"

Burke began to pour out a torrent of speech.

"Come here," said the mate.

When Burke was close to him he said:

"Speak slow."

"Shure Sor," he said, "ye wudn't go fur to call ut mut'ny whan a man's droonk an' makes a fule of himsilf?"

"Perhaps not," the mate replied, his steady eyes on Burke's face.

"Ye, wudn't, I know," Burke went on confidently. "Ye see, Sor, Oi was half droonk whan Oi cum aboord. An' Oi had licker tu, more fule Oi. Mr. Olsen, he cum forrard in the dog-watch afther ye'd taat me me place, and he routed ut out an' hove ut overboord. Oi'm sobered now Sor, with the facer ye giv me an' the cowld wather an' the slape, Oi'm sobered, an' Oi'm sobered for the voyage, Sor. Ye'll foind me quoite and rispectful Sor. Oi was droonk Sor, an' the scouse misloiked me, an' Oi made a fule ov mesilf. Ye'll foind me quoite and rispectful, Sor, indade ye wull. Ye wudn't go for to log me for mut'ny for makin' a fule ov mesilf Sor, wud ye now, Sor?"

"No, Burke," said the mate. "I shall not log you. Go forward."

Burke went.

Some days later I was forward on the forecastle deck, ensconced against the big canvas-covered anchor, leaning over the side and watching the foam about the cut-water and the upspurted coveys of sudden flying fish, darting out of the waves, at the edge of the bark's shadows and veering erratically in their unpredictable flights. Burke, barefoot and chewing a large quid, was going about with a tar-bucket, swabbing mats and other such devices. He approached me.

"Mr. Ferris, Sor," he said, "ye wudn't have a bit of washin' a man cud du for ye? Ye'll be strange loike aboord ship, an' this yer foorst voyge, an' ye the only passenger, an' this a sailin' ship, tu. Ye'll be thinkin' ov a hotel, Mr. Ferris, Sor. An' there's no wan to du washin' here fur ye, Sor. The naygur cuke is no manner ov use

tu ye. Ye giv me anny bits ye want washed an Oi'll wash 'em nate
fur ye. A man-o-war's man knows a dale ov washin' an' ye'll pay
me wut ye loike. Thin I'll not be set ashore in Rio wudout a cint,
Sor."

"You'll have your wages," I hazarded.

"Not with Beast Benson," he replied, "little duh ye know Beast
Benson. Oi know um. Wut didn't go into me advances ull go into
the shlop-chest. Oi may have a millrace or maybe tu at Rio, divil a
cint moor."

This was the beginning of many chats with Burke. He told me
of Five Rivers, of his life on men-of-war, of his participation in the
battle between the *Merrimac* and the *Ericsson*, as he called the
Monitor, of unholy adventures in a hundred ports, of countless
officers he had served under.

"An' niyer wan uz foine a gintlemin uz Mr. Willson," he would
wind up. "Niver wan ov them all. Shure, he's no Willson. He ships
as John Willson, Liverpool. Now all the seas knows John Willson
ov Liverpool. There's thousands ov him. He's afloat all over the
wurruld. He's always the same, short and curly-headed, black-
haired and dark-faced, ivery John Willson is loike ivery other wan.
Ivery Liverpool Portugee uz John Willson whin he cooms to soign
articles. But Mr. Willson's no Dago, no Liverpool man at all. He's
a gintlemin, British all over, an' a midlander at thot an' no seaman
be naature at all. But he's the gintlemin. Ye saa him down me. He's
the foine gintlemin. Not a midshipman or liftenant did iver Oi see
a foiner gintlemin than him, and how sinsible he uz. Haff the
officers Oi've served under wuz lunies, sinsible on this or thot, but
half luny on most things and luny all over on this or thot. But luke
at Mr. Willson. Sinsible all over he uz, sinsible all thru. Luke at
the discipline he huz. An' no wunder. Luke at huz oi! He cudn't du
a mane thing av he wanted tu, he cudn't tell a loi av he throid,
thrust me Soi, Oi know, the min knows. It's loike byes at skule wid
a tacher, or min in the army wid their orficers. You can't fule thim,
they knows, an' wull they knows a man whin they say wan. Oi'd
thrust Mr. Willson annywhere and annyhow. So wud any other
sailor man or anny man. Deef he uz, deef as an anchor fouled on a

rock bottom. But he hears wid huz eyes, wid huz fingers, wid the hull skin av him. He's all sinse an' trewth an' koindness."

Not any other of the sailors besides Burke did I find sociable or communicative or capable, apparently, of intelligent intercourse. Of the captain I saw and heard enough, and more than enough, at meal times. He deserved his nickname and I avoided him with detestation.

The second mate, a big Norwegian named Olaf Olsen, was a kindly soul, but dull and uncommunicative. He had a companionable eye, but felt neither any need of converse nor any promptings toward it. Speech he never volunteered, questions he answered monosyllabically. One Sunday indeed he so far unbent as to ask if he might borrow one of my books. I told him I doubted if any would please him. He looked them over disappointedly.

"Have you any books of Doomuses?" he queried.

"Doomus?" I repeated after him reflectively.

"You're a scholar, aren't you?" he demanded.

"I aim to be," I said.

"How do you pronounce, D-u-m-a-s?" he inquired.

"I am no Frenchman," I told him, "but Dumas is pretty close to it."

"That's what I said," he shouted, "and they all laughed at me and said 'Doomus, ye damn fool.' Have you any of his books?"

"No," I confessed and he ceased to regard me as worth borrowing from.

Not so Mr. Wilson. Before we ran into the doldrums I had found my sea-legs and exhausted the diversion of learning the name of every bit of rope, metal and wood on the bark, and also the amusement of climbing the rigging. I settled down to luxurious days of reading. The first Sunday afterwards Mr. Wilson asked for a book. I took him into my cabin and showed him my stock, one-volume poets mostly, the Iliad, the Odyssey, the Greek Anthology, Dante, Carducci, Goethe, Heine, Shakespeare, Milton, Shelley, Keats, Tennyson, Browning, Swinburne and Rosetti, and a dozen volumes of Hugo's lyrics. I watched him as he conned them over and thought I saw his eyes light over the Greek volumes, thought I saw in them both desire and resignation. He took Milton to begin on and afterwards borrowed my English books in series. I believe he read each entire, certainly he read much during his watches below.

At first I felt equal only to the English myself. But after we entered the glorious south-east trades, I read first Faust, then the Divina Commedia, then the Iliad, and, as our voyage neared its end gave myself up to the delights of the Odyssey.

Meanwhile I had come to feel very well acquainted with the deaf mate. Generally we had spent part of each fair Sunday in conversation. He read lips so instantly and accurately that if I faced the sun and he was close to me we talked almost as easily as if he had heard perfectly. The conversations were all of his making. He was not a man whom one would question, whereas he questioned me freely after he had made sure, but very delicately managed tentative beginnings, that I did not at all object to being questioned. He was a little stiff at first, half timid, half wary. When he found in me no disposition to intrude upon his reserve, and felt my manner untinged by either condescension, which I did not feel, or curiosity, which I sedulously repressed, he surrendered himself somewhat to the pleasure of exchanging ideas as an equal with a man of his own kind. We came to an unspoken understanding and talked openly on a level footing as two men of education, as two aspirants after culture. He relaxed his caution sufficiently to discard any concealment of his attainments and we discussed freely not only my books which he had borrowed but also whatever I had in hand. He never let slip anything which could tell me whether his spiritual background had been Oxford or Cambridge, yet I knew that only at one or the other could he have developed the mind he revealed.

Toward the end of the voyage our day-time chats usually began with his asking what I was reading. Even in the midst of the steady routine of his unremitting seamanly diligence he often paused by my chair on a week-day and delighted me with a brief talk which I enjoyed as much as he. Our Sunday talks came to take up much of his deck-watches. But what most delighted me was to listen to his monologues at night. Monologues they were, for I could neither interrupt nor reply. He would begin his watch by a double turn round the bark, twice speaking to the steersman, twice to the lookout. Then he would pace the poop-deck, just aft of the break, from rail to rail. As he turned by the lee rail he would throw a comprehensive glance over the whole spread of the bark's canvas, so he turned by the weather rail he would stoop down, peer out under the mainsail and sweep his eyes along the horizon on our lee bow. In the early part of our voyage I had watched him night after night keep this up for an entire watch, evenly as an automaton, breaking it only by three rounds of the vessel made precisely on the hours. After we grew to know each other he would patrol the deck only at intervals, spending most of his watch seated on the cabin-deck at the break, on the rail or on the booby-hatch, according to the position of my chair. He mostly began.

"Have you ever read —?" Or,

"Did you ever read —?"

Sometimes I had read the book, oftener I had not. In either case I was fascinated by his sane, cool judgment, equally trenchant and subtle, and by the even flow of his well-chosen words.

Our voyage neared its end sooner than I had anticipated. The south-east trades had been almost head winds for us and we had tacked through them close-hauled, a long leg on the port tack and a short leg on the starboard. Then the proximity of the land blurred the unalterable perpetuity of the trade winds and on a Sunday morning the wind came fair. It was my first experience of running before the wind and it intoxicated me with elation. We were out of sight of land, even of its loom, yet no longer in blue water, but over that enormous sixty-fathom shelf which juts out more than a hundred miles into the Atlantic between Bahia and Rio de Janiero, or to be more precise, between Cannavieiras and Itapemirim. The day was bright and the sky sufficiently diversified with clouds to vary pleasingly its insistent blue, the sea a pale, golden green all torn by racing white-caps and dappled with the scurrying shadows of the clouds. The bark leapt joyously, the combers overtaking her charged in smothers of foam past each counter, the delight of merely living in such a glorious day infected even the crew.

I had my chair amidships by the break of the deck, just abaft the booby-hatch. There I was reading the Odyssey. The mate came and sat down by me on the booby-hatch.

"What are you reading?" he asked as usual.

"About the Sirens," I answered.

The strangest alteration came over his expression.

"Did you ever notice," he asked, "how little Homer really tells about them?"

"I was meditating on just that," I replied. "He tells only that there were two of them and that they sang. I was wondering where the popular notions of their appearance came from."

"What is your idea of the popular notions of their appearance?" he demanded.

"I have a very vague idea," I confessed. "They are generally supposed to have had bird's feet. It seems to me I have seen figures of them as so depicted on Greek tombs and coins. And there is Boecklin's picture."

"Boecklin?" he ruminated. "The Munich man? The morbid man?"

"If you choose to call him so?" I assented. "I shouldn't call him morbid."

"His ugly idea is a mere personal conception," he said.

"I grant you that," I agreed, "as far as the age and the ugliness go. But the birds' feet of some kind are in the general conception."

"The general conception is wrong," he asserted, with something more like an approach to heat than anything I had seen in him.

"You seem to feel very sure," I replied.

"I do not feel," he answered, "I know."

"How do you know?" I inquired.

"I have seen them," he asserted.

"Seen them?" I puzzled.

"Yes, seen them," he asseverated. "Seen the twain Sirens under the golden sun, under the silver moon, under the countless stars; watched them singing as they are singing now!"

"What?" I exclaimed.

My face must have painted my amazement, my tone must have betrayed my startled bewilderment.

His face went scarlet and then pale. He sprang up and strode off to the weather rail. There he stood for a long time. Presently he wheeled, crossed the deck, the booby-hatch between us, and plunged down the cabin companion-way without looking at me.

He did not once meet my eye during the remaining days of the voyage, let alone approach me. He was again the impassive, inscrutable figure I had first seen him on the wharf at Baltimore.

We drew near Rio harbor, late of a perfect tropic September day, just too late to enter before sunset. In the brief tropic dusk we anchored under the black beetling shoulder of Itaipu inside the little islands of Mai and Pai. There we lay wobbling at anchor, there I watched the cloudless sky fill with the infinite multitudes of tropic stars, and gazed at the lights of the city, plainly visible through the harbor mouth between Morro de Sao Joao and the Sugar Loaf, twinkling brighter than the stars, not three miles away.

It must have been somewhere toward midnight when he approached me. My chair was by the rail on which he half sat, leaning down to me. So placed he began such a monologue as I had often heard from him, a monologue I could neither question nor modify, which I must listen to entire or break off completely.

"You were astonished," he said, "when I told you I had seen the Sirens, but I have. It was about six years ago, in 1879. I was in New York and I had my usual difficulty getting a ship on account of my deafness. My boarding-master tried a Captain George Andrews of the *Joyous Castle*. Andrews looked me over and said he liked me. Then he talked to me alone.

"'We are bound on an adventure,' he said, 'and I want a man who will obey orders and keep his mouth shut.'

"I told him I was his man for whatever risk. With a light mixed cargo, hardly more than half a cargo, hardly more than ballast, we cleared for Guam and a market. I was second mate. The first mate was a big Swede named Gustave Obrink. The very first meal I ever sat down to with him he made an impression on me as one of the greediest men I had ever seen. He not only ate enormously, but he

seemed more than half unsatisfied after he had stuffed himself with
an amazing quantity of food. He seemed to possess an unbluntable
zest in the act of swallowing, an ever fresh gusto for any and every
food flavor. I never saw a man relish his food so. He was an equally
inordinate drinker, the quantity of coffee he could swill at one meal
was amazing. Between meals he was always thirsty and drank
incredible quantities of water. He was forever going to the butt by
the galley door and drinking from it. And he would smack his lips
over it and enjoy it as a connoisseur would a rare wine.

"When we came to choose watches Captain Andrews told us to
choose a bo'sun for each watch. Obrink wanted to know why.

"The captain told him it was none of his business to ask
questions. The Swede assented and backed down. We chose each
an Irishman. Obrink, a tall, loose-jointed man named Pat Ryan and
I, a compact stocky fellow named Mike Leary. Next day the captain
had the boatswains shift their dunnage and bunk and mess aft. They
were nearly as great gluttons as Obrink. They fed like animals and
the subject of food and drink was the backbone of their conversation.

"The crew were hearty eaters as well and Captain Andrews
catered to their likings. The *Joyous Castle* was amazingly well
found, the cabin fare very abundant and varied, the forecastle food
plenty and good.

"Soon after Captain Andrews was sure that the crew had entirely
sobered up from their shore-drinking he called them aft one noon
and announced that the steward was to serve grog daily until
further notice. Naturally they cheered. After that we had a good,
cheap wine daily in the cabin. When Captain Andrews had made
up his mind that both mates and both boatswains were sober men
he had a bottle of whisky placed on the rack over the table and
kept filled. It was a curiosity to watch Obrink, Ryan and Leary
patronize that bottle. Not one of the three but was cautious, not
one of the three but could have drunk three times as much as he
did. But the way they savored every drop they took, the affectionate
satisfaction they exhibited over each nip, their eager anticipation
of the next made a spectacle.

"Captain Andrews kept good discipline, we crossed the line and rounded the cape of Good Hope without any event.

"When we were off Madagascar, Obrink, going below to get his sextant, missed it from its place. The ship was searched and Captain Andrews held an inquisition. But the sextant was never found, nor any light thrown on how it had disappeared. After that the captain alone took the observations.

"Then began a series of erratic changes of our course. We kept on dodging about for six weeks, until the crew talked of nothing else and openly said the captain was trying to lose us; certainly not one of us except the captain could have designated our position. We knew we were south of the line, not ten degrees south of it, and between 50 and 110 east longitude, but within those limits we might be almost anywhere.

"We had had nothing that could be called a storm since we left New York. When a storm struck us it was a storm indeed. When it blew over it left us making water fast. After a day and a night at the pumps, we took to our boats. Captain Andrews had the cook and the cabin boy in his boat, gave each boatswain a dory and two men, and directed us to steer north by east. When Obrink and I asked for our latitude and longitude he said that was his business. He had had the boats provisioned while we pumped and they were well supplied. We left the ship under a clear sky, the wind light after the storm, the ground-swell running heavy and slow. We lowered near sunset.

"Next morning the Captain's boat had vanished, and there we were, two whale boats, two dories, twenty men in all and no idea of our position.

"The third day we sighted land. It was a low atoll, not much more than a mile across, nearly circular as far as we could make out, with the usual cocoa palms all along its ring, the surf breaking on interrupted reefs off shore, and, as we drew nearer, a channel into the lagoon facing us; as we threaded it we saw about the center of the lagoon a steep, narrow, pinkish crag, maybe fifty feet high, with a bit of flat island showing behind it. Otherwise the lagoon was unbroken. We made a landing on the atoll near the channel where we had entered, found good water, cocoanuts in abundance and hogs running wild all about, but no traces of human beings. I shot a hog and the men roasted it at once. As they ate they talked of nothing but the short rations they had had in the boats. They were all docile enough and good natured, but I believe every man of them said a dozen times how much he missed his grog and, Obrink, who had kept himself and his boat-load well in hand, said a score of times how much he would like to serve out grog, but must take care of his small supply. They talked a great deal of their hunger in the boats and of their relish for the pork; they ate an astonishing number of cocoanuts. It seemed to me that they were as greedy a set of men as could be met with.

"We cut down five palm-trees, and on supports made of the others set one horizontally as a ridge pole. Over this we stretched the sails of the whale-boats. So we camped on the sandbeach of the lagoon. I slept utterly. But when I waked I understood the men one and all to complain of light and broken sleep, of dreams, of dreaming they heard a queer noise like music, of seeming to continue to hear it after they woke. They breakfasted on another hog and on more cocoanuts.

"Then Obrink told me to take charge of the camp. I agreed. He had everything removed from his whale-boat and into it piled all the men, except a little Frenchman who went by no name save 'Frenchy,' a New Englander named Peddicord, a short red-headed Irishman named Mullen, Ryan, my boatswain and myself. Those of my watch who wanted to go I let go. They rowed off, across the lagoon toward the pink crag.

"After Obrink and the men were gone I meant to take stock of our stores. I sent Ryan with Frenchy around the atoll in one direction and Peddicord, who had sense for a foremast hand, with Mullen in the other direction. I then went over the stores. Fairly promising for twenty men they were, even a random boat-voyage in the Indian Ocean. With unlimited cocoanuts and abundant hogs they were a handsome provision, and need only be safeguarded from the omnipresent rats.

"Very shortly my four men returned, the two parties nearly at the same time. It was nearly noon, and no sign of Obrink or the boat. I had followed the whale-boat with my glass till it rounded the pink crag, a short half mile away, and had disappeared. Ryan asked my permission to take one dory and go join the rest on the crag. I readily agreed, for I had not yet cached the spirits. They rowed off as the others had.

"I made use of their welcome absence to conceal the liquor in four different places, carefully writing, in my note-book, the marks by which I was to find the caches again. I did the like with most of the ammunition. I had no idea of trying to get the upper hand of Obrink. I meant to tell him of my proceedings and expected him to approve.

"I expected the men back about two hours before sunset. No sign of them appeared. No sign of them near sunset, nor at sunset. Of course I had waited inactive till it was too late for me to venture alone on the unknown lagoon at night, and there would have been no sense in one man going to look for nineteen anyhow. Moreover I must protect our stores from hogs and rats. I turned over in my mind a thousand conjectures and slept little.

"Next morning I slung what I could of our stores from our jury-ridge-pole, out of the reach of hogs and rats, made sure that the remaining whale-boat would not get adrift, prepared the remaining dory with cocoanuts, biscuits, a keg of water, liquor, some miscellaneous stores, medicine, ammunition, repeating rifle, my glass and my compass. I carried two revolvers. I knew by this time something was wrong and I rowed warily across the placid lagoon toward the pink crag.

"As I approached it I could not but remark the peacefulness and beauty of my surroundings. The sky was deep tropic blue, the sun not an hour high, the wind a mild breeze, hardly more than rippling the lagoon, my horizon was all the tops of palms on the atoll except the one glimpse of white surf on the reef beyond the channel where we had entered.

"I rowed slowly, for the dory was heavy, and kept looking over my shoulder.

"The crag rose sheer out of deep water. It might have been granite, but I could not tell what sort of stone it was. It was very pink and nothing grew on it, not anything whatever. It was just sheer naked rock. As I rounded it I could see the flattish island beyond. There was not a tree on it and I could see nothing but the even beach of it rising some six or eight feet above high water mark. Nothing was visible beyond the crest of the beach. I knew our men had meant to land on it and I stopped and considered. Then I rowed round the base of the crag. Facing the flat islet was a sort of a shelf of the pink rock, half submerged, half out of the water, sloping very gently and just the place to make a landing. I rowed the dory carefully till its bottom grated on the flat top of this shelf, the bow in say a foot of water, the stern over water may be sixty fathom deep, for I could see no bottom to its limpid blue. I stepped out and drew the dory well up on the shelf. Then I essayed to climb the crag. I succeeded at once, but it was none too easy and I had no leisure to look behind me till I reached the top. Once on the fairly flat top, which might have been thirty feet across, I turned and looked over the islet.

"Then I sat down heavily and took out my flask. I took a big drink, shut my eyes, said a prayer, I think, and looked again. I saw just what I had seen before.

"There was about a ship's-length of water between the crag and the islet, which might have been four ships-lengths across and was nearly circular. All round it was a white beach of clean coral-sand sloping evenly and rising perhaps ten feet at most above high-water mark. The rest of the island was a meadow, nearly level but cupping ever so little from the crest of the beach. It was covered with short, soft-looking grass, of a bright pale green, a green like that of an English lawn in Spring. In the center of the island and of the meadow was an oval slab of pinkish stone, the same stone, apparently, as made up the crag on which I sat. On it were two shapes of living creatures, but shapes which I rubbed my eyes to look at. Midway between the slab and the crest of the beach a long windrow heap of something white swept in a circle round the slab, maybe ten fathom from it. I did not surely make out what the windrow was composed of until I took my glasses to it.

"But it needed no glass to see our men, all nineteen of them, all sitting, some just inside the white windrow, some just outside of it, some on it or in it. Their faces were turned to the slab.

"I took my glass out of my pocket, trembling so I could hardly adjust it. With it I saw clearly, the windrow as I had guessed, the shapes on the slab as I had seemed to see them with my unaided eyes.

"The windrow was all of human bones. I could see them clearly through the glass.

"The two creatures on the slab were shaped like full-bodied young women. Except their faces nothing of their flesh was visible. They were clad in something close-fitting, and pearly gray, which clung to every part of them, and revealed every curve of their forms; as it were a tight-fitting envelopment of fine mole-skin or chinchilla. But it shimmered in the sunlight more like eider-down.

"And their hair! I rubbed my eyes. I took out my handkerchief and rubbed the lenses of my glasses. I looked again. I saw as before. Their hair was abundant, and fell in curly waves to their hips. But it seemed a deep dark blue, or a dull intense shot-green or both at once or both together. I could not see it any other way.

"And their faces!

"Their faces were those of white women, of European women, of young handsome gentlewomen.

"One of them lay on the slab half on her side, her knees a little drawn up, her head on one bent arm, her face toward me, as if asleep. The other sat, supporting herself by one straight arm. Her mouth was open, her lips moved, her face was the face of a woman singing. I dared not look any more. It was so real and so incredible.

"I scanned our men through my glass. I could see their shoulders heave as they breathed, otherwise not one moved a muscle, while I looked him.

"I shut my glass and put it in my pocket. I shouted. Not a man turned. I fixed my gaze so as to observe the whole group at once. I shouted again. Not a man moved. I took my revolver from its holster and fired in the air. Not a man turned.

"Then I started to clamber down the crag. I had to turn my back on the islet, regard the far horizon, fix my gaze on the camp, discernible by the white patch, where the white sails were stretched over the palm trunk and try to realize the reality of things before I could gather myself together to climb down.

"I made it, but I nearly lost my hold a dozen times.

"I pushed off the dory, rowed to the islet, and beached the dory between the other and the whale-boat. Both were half adrift and I hauled them up as well as I could.

"Then I went up the beach. When I came to its crest and saw the backs of our men I shouted again. Not a man turned his head. I approached them, their faces were set immovably towards the rock and the two appearances on it.

"Peddicord was nearest to me, the windrow of bones in front of him was not wide nor high. He stared across it. I caught him by the shoulders and shook him, then he did turn his head and look up at me, just a glance, the glance of a peevish, protesting child disturbed at some absorbing play, an unintelligent vacuous glance, unrecognizing and uncomprehending.

"The glance startled me enough, for Peddicord had been a hard-headed, sensible Yankee. But the change in his face, since yesterday, startled me more. Of a sudden I realized that Peddicord, Ryan, Mullen and Frenchy had been without food or water since I last saw them, that they had been just where I found them since soon after they left me, had been exposed the day before to a tropical sun for some six hours, had sat all night also without moving, or sleeping. At the same instant I realized that the rest had been in the same state for some hours longer, some hours of a burning, morning tropical sun. The realization of it lost my head completely. I ran from man to man, I yelled, I pulled them, I struck them.

"Not one struck back, or answered, or looked at me twice. Each shook me off impatiently and, relapsed into his intent posture, even Obrink.

"Obrink, it is true, partially opened his mouth, as if to speak.

"I saw his tongue!

"I ran to the boat, took a handful of ship-biscuit and a pan of water, with these I returned to the men.

"Not one would notice the biscuit, not one showed any interest in the water, not one looked at it as if he saw it when I held it before his face, not one tried to drink, not one would drink when I tried to force it on him.

"I emptied my flask into the water, with that I went from man to man. Not even the smell of the whisky roused them. Each pushed the pan from before his face, each resisted me, each shoved me away.

"I went back to the boat, filled a tin cup with raw whisky and went the round with that. Not one would regard it, much less swallow it.

"Then I myself turned to the slab of stone.

"There sat the sirens. Well I recognized now what they were. Both were awake now and both singing. What I had seen through the glass was visible more clearly, more intelligibly. They were indeed shaped like young, healthy women; like well-matured Caucasian women. They were covered all over with close, soft plumage, like the breast of a dove, colored like the breast of a dove, a pale, delicate, iridescent, pinkish gray. As a woman's long hair might trail to her hips, there trailed from their heads a mass of long, dark strands. Imagine single strands of ostrich feathers, a yard long or more, curling spirally or at random, colored the deep, shot, blue-green of the eye of a peacock feather, or of a gamecock's shackles. That was what grew from their heads, as I seemed to see it.

"I stepped over the windrow of bones. Some were mere dust; some leached gray by sun, wind and rain; some white. Skulls were there, five or six I saw in as many yards of the windrow near me and more beyond. In some places the windrow was ten feet wide and three feet deep in the middle. It was made up of the skeletons of hundreds of thousands of victims.

"I took out my other revolver, spun the cylinder, and strode toward the slab.

"Forty feet from it I stopped. I was determined to abolish the superhuman monsters. I was resolute. I was not afraid. But I stopped. Again and again I strove to go nearer, I braced my resolutions. I tried to go nearer. I could not.

"Then I tried to go sideways. I was able to step. I made the circuit of the slab, some forty feet from it. Nearer I could not go. It was as if a glass wall were between me and the sirens.

"Standing at my distance, once I found I could go no nearer, I essayed to aim my revolver at them. My muscles, my nerves refused to obey me. I tried in various ways. I might have been paralyzed. I tried other movements, I was capable of any other movement. But aim at them I could not.

"I regarded them. Especially their faces, their wonderful faces.

"Their investiture of opalescent plumelets covered their throats. Between it and the deep, dark chevelure above, their faces showed ivory-smooth, delicately tinted. I could see their ears too, shell-like ears, entirely human in form, peeping from under the glossy shade of their miraculous tresses.

"They were as like each other as any twin sisters.

"Their faces were oval, their features small, clean-cut, regular and shapely, their foreheads were wide and low, their brows were separate, arched, penciled and definite, not of hair, but of tiny feathers, of gold-shot, black, blue-green, like the color of their ringlets, but far darker. I took out my binoculars and conned their brows. Their eyes were dark blue-gray, bright and young, their noses were small and straight, low between the eyes, neither wide nor narrow, and with molded nostrils, rolled and fine. Their upper lips were short, both lips crimson red and curved about their small mouths, their teeth were very white, their chins round and babyish. They were beautiful and the act of singing did not mar their beauty. Their mouths did not strain open, but their lips parted easily into an opening. Their throats seemed to ripple like the throat of a trilling canary-bird. They sang with zest and the zest made them all the more beautiful. But it was not so much their beauty that impressed me, it was the nobility of their faces.

"Some years before I had been an officer on the private steam-yacht of a very wealthy nobleman. He was of a family fanatically devoted to the church of Rome and all its interests. Some Austrian nuns, of an order made up exclusively of noblewomen, were about to go to Rome for an audience with the Pope. My employer placed his yacht at their disposal and we took them on at Trieste. They several times sat on deck during the voyage and the return. I watched them as much as I could, for I never had seen such human faces, and I had seen many sorts. Their faces seemed to tell of a long lineage of men all brave and honorable, women gentle and pure. There was not a trace on their faces of any sort of evil in themselves or in anything that had ever really influenced them. They were really saintly faces, the faces of ideal nuns.

"Well, the sirens' faces were like that, only more ineffably perfect. There was no guile or cruelty in them, no delight in the exercise of their power, no consciousness of it, no consciousness of my proximity, or of the spell-bound men, or of the uncountable skeletons of their myriad victims. Their faces expressed but one emotion: utter absorption in the ecstasy of singing, the infinite preoccupation of artists in their art.

"I walked all round them, gazing now with all my eyes, now through my short-focused glass. Their coat of feathers was as if very short and close like seal-skin fur and covered them entirely from the throat down, to the ends of their fingers and the soles of their feet. They did not move except to sit up to sing or lie down to sleep. Sometimes both sang together, sometimes alternately, but if one slept the other sang on and on without ceasing.

"I of course could not hear their music, but the mere sight of them fascinated me so that I forgot my weariness from anxiety and loss of sleep, forgot the vertical sun, forgot food and drink, forgot my shipmates, forgot everything.

"But as I could not hear this state was transitory. I began to look elsewhere than at the sirens. My gaze turned again upon the men. Again I made futile efforts to reach the sirens, to shoot at them, to aim at them. I could not.

"I returned to my dory and drank a great deal of water. I ate a ship-biscuit or two. I then made the round of the men, and tried on each food, water and spirits. They were oblivious to everything except the longing to listen, to listen, to listen.

"I walked round the windrow of bones. With the skulls and collapsing rib-arches I found leather boots, several leather belts, case-knives, kreeses, guns of various patterns, pistols, watches, gold and jeweled finger rings and coins, many coins, copper, silver and gold. The grass was short, not three inches deep and the earth under it smooth as a rolled lawn.

"The bones were of various ages, but all old, except two skeletons, entire, side by side, just beyond the windrow at the portion opposite where the men sat. There was long fine golden hair on one skull. Women too!

"I went back to the dory, rowed to the camp, shot a hog, roasted it, wrapped the steaming meat in fresh leaves and rowed back to the islet. It was not far from sunset.

"Not a man heeded the savory meat, still warm. They just sat and gazed and listened.

"I was free of the spell. I could do them no good by staying. I rowed back to camp before sunset and slept, yes I slept all night long.

"The sun woke me. I shot and cooked another hog, took every bit of rope or marline I could find and rowed back to the islet.

"You are to understand that the men had by then been more than forty hours, all of them, without moving or swallowing anything. If I was to save any it must be done quickly.

"I found them as they had been, but with an appalling change in themselves. The day before they had been uncannily unaware of their sufferings, to-day they were hideously conscious of them.

"Once I had a pet terrier, a neat, trim, intelligent, little beast. He ran under a moving train and had both his hind legs cut off. He dragged himself to me, and the appealing gaze of his eyes expressed at once his inability to comprehend what had happened to him, his bewilderment at pain, the first really excruciating pain he had ever known in all his little life, and his dumb wonder that I did not help him, that it could be possible he could be with me and his trouble continue.

"Once I had the misfortune to see a lovely child, a beautiful little girl, not six years old, frightfully burned. Her look haunted me with the like incomprehension of what had befallen her, the like incredulity at the violence of her suffering, the like amazement at our failure to relieve her.

"Well, out of the staring, blood-shot eyes of those bewitched men I saw the same look of helpless wonderment and mute appeal.

"Strange, but I never thought of knocking them senseless. I had an idea of tying them one by one, carrying or dragging them to the dory and ferrying my captives to camp.

"I began on Frenchy, he was nearest the boat and smallest.

"He fought like a demon. After all that sleeplessness and fasting he was stronger than I. Our tussle wore me out, but moved him not at all.

"I tried them with the warm juicy, savory pork. They paid no heed to it and pushed me away. I tried them with biscuit, water and liquor. Not one heeded. I tried Obrink particularly. Again he opened his lips. His tongue was black, hard, and swelled till it filled his mouth.

"Then I lost count of time, of what I did, of what happened. I do not know whether it was on that day or the next that the first man died. He was Jack Register, a New York wharf-rat. The next died a few hours later, a Philadelphia seaman he was, named Tom Smith.

"They putrefied with a rapidity surpassing anything I ever saw, even in a horse dropped dead of over-driving.

"The rest sat there by the carrion of their comrades, rocking with weakness, crazed by sleeplessness, racked by tortures inexpressible, the gray of death deepening on their faces, listening, listening, listening.

"As I said, I had lost consciousness of time. I do not know how many days Obrink lived, and he was the last to die. I do not know how long it was after his death before I came to myself.

"I made one last effort to put an end to the enchantresses. The same spell possessed me. I could not aim, much less pull trigger; I could not approach nearer than before.

"When I was myself I made haste to leave the accursed isle. I made ready the second whaleboat with all the best stores she could carry and spare sails. I stepped the mast and steered across the lagoon, for the wind was southerly and there was a wider channel at the north of the atoll.

"As I passed the islet, I could see nothing but the white sand beach that ringed it. For all my horror I could not resist landing once more for one last look.

"Under the afternoon sun I saw the green meadow, the white curve of bones, the rotting corpses, the pink slab, the feathered sirens, their sweet serene faces uplifted, singing on in a rapt trance.

"I took but one look. I fled. The whale-boat passed the outlet of the lagoon. North by east I steered.

"Parts of the Indian Ocean are almost free of storms. The atoll was apparently in one of those parts. I soon passed out of it. Three storms blew me about, I lost my dead-reckoning, I lost count of the days. Between the storms I lashed the tiller amidships, double-reefed the sail and slept as I needed sleep. Through the storms I bailed furiously, the whale-boat riding at a sea-anchor of oars and sails. I had been at sea alone for all of twenty-one days when I was rescued, not three hundred miles from Ceylon, by a tramp steamer out of Colombo bound for Adelaide."

Here he broke off, stood up and for the rest of the watch maintained his sentry-go by the break of the poop.

Next day we towed into the harbor of Rio de Janeiro, then still the capital of an Empire, and mildly enthusiastic for Dom Pedro. I hastened to go ashore. When my boat was ready the deaf mate was forward, superintending the sealing of the hatches.

After some days of discomfort at the Hotel des Etrangers and of worse at Young's Hotel I found a harborage with five jolly bachelors housekeeping in a delightful villa up on Rua dos Jonquillos on Santa Theresa. The *Nipsic* was in the harbor and I thought I knew a lieutenant on her and went off one day to visit her. After my visit my boatman landed me at the Red Steps. As I trod up the steps a man came down. He was English all over, irreproachably shod, trousered, coated, gloved, hatted and monocled. Behind him two porters carried big, new portmanteaux. I recognized the man whom I had known as John Wilson of Liverpool, second mate of the *Medorus*, the man who had seen the Sirens.

Not only did I recognize him, but he recognized me. He gave me no far off British stare. His eyes lit, even the monocled eye. He held out his hand.

"I am going home," he said, nodding toward a steamer at anchor, "I am glad we met. I enjoyed our talks. Perhaps we may meet again."

He shook hands without any more words. I stood at the top of the steps and watched his boat put off, watched it as it receded. As I watched a bit of paper on a lower step caught my eye. I went down and picked it up. It was an empty envelope, with an English stamp and postmark, addressed:

> *Geoffrey Cecil, Esq.,*
>   C.O. Swanwick & Co.,
>   54 Rua de Alfandega,
>   Rio de Janeiro, Brazil.

I looked after the distant boat, I could barely make him out as he sat in the stern. I never saw him again.

Naturally I asked every Englishman I ever met if he had ever heard of a deaf man named Geoffrey Cecil. For more than ten years I elicited no response. Then at lunch, in the Hotel Victoria at Interlaken, I happened to be seated opposite a stout, elderly Briton. He perceived that I was an American and became affable and agreeable. I never saw him after that lunch and never learned his name. But through our brief meal together we conversed freely.

At a suitable opportunity I put my usual query.

"Geoffrey Cecil?" he said. "Deaf Geoffrey Cecil? Of course I know of him. Knew him too. He was or is Earl of Aldersmere."

"Was or is?" I queried.

"It was this way," my interlocutor explained. "The ninth Earl of Aldersmere had three sons. All predeceased him and each left one son. Geoffrey was the heir. He had wanted to go into the Navy, but his deafness cut him off from that. When he quarreled with his father he naturally ran away to sea. Track of him was lost. He was supposed dead. That was years before his father's death. When his father died nothing had been heard of him for ten years. But when his grandfather died and his cousin Roger supposed himself Earl, some firm of solicitors interposed, claiming that Geoffrey was alive. That was in 1885. It was a full six months before Geoffrey turned up. Roger was no end disappointed. Geoffrey paid no attention to anything but buying or chartering a steam-yacht. She sailed as soon as possible, passed the canal, touched at Aden, and has never been heard of since. That was nine years ago."

"Is Roger Cecil alive?" I asked.

"Very much alive," affirmed my informant.

"You may tell him from me," I declared, "that he is now the Eleventh Earl of Aldersmere."

The Thing that Smelt

Christopher Blayre

To the Zoologists of twenty-five years ago the name of Augustine Black—Austin Black he called himself—was uncomfortably familiar. He was a patient and keen observer of animal life, and his photographs of beasts and birds made under all kinds of critical conditions were greatly and justly admired. But there was another and an extraordinary side to the man. He was a semi-professional spiritualist, and reaped a rich harvest, it was said, from that curiously constituted segment of humanity whose vanity leads them to seek for evidence of a personal life after death, who 'sit' with obscurely disreputable 'mediums' in lower middle-class parlours in doubtful neighbourhoods, and accept the suggestions of the managers of such séances that the raucous cacklings of uneducated persons through tubes of brown paper are 'communications' from their dear ones who, in the cant phrase of the profession, 'have passed over.' They even welcome the futile familiarities of 'John King,' whose Arab face glowers over the 'circle'—and incidentally may be bought for a few shillings from any reputable purveyor of conjurors' accessories.

Austin Black's success in this branch of industry resulted from the fact that he ran his séances in his studio at Tulse Hill on more highly sophisticated lines. He had an admirable chamber-organ and employed a professional string-quartet to play behind impermeable curtains, what time 'materializations' took place, of High Church Dignitaries whose Latin would disgrace a fourth form schoolboy, and of eminent Scientists whose scientific observations were startling in their puerility and ignorance.

At the same time it must be confessed that there were occasions upon which the phenomena exhibited in return for the guineas of his 'sitters' (for his were not the normal five-shilling entertainments) were, though futile, quite inexplicable to an ordinary observer—and a new patron had to be introduced by a convinced dupe, and the keen scrutiny of Austin Black, and his few well-chosen remarks and questions to the newcomer, made it clear that none but ordinary observers were privileged to get their money's worth. If Black was not satisfied as to gullibility, or suspected a plot to expose the modus operandi, the spirits 'lay doggo' and would not perform. He would explain that there was 'an inimical Influence' present, and when the séance was given up the habitués regarded and treated the stranger in such a manner as to convey to him that they considered that he had not only spoilt their evening, but had meanly swindled them out of the fees for that séance—and that stranger was never introduced again.

I frequently met Austin Black at the scientific meetings of the Zoological Society, and in spite of his over-florid courtesy he was to me as Dr. Fell of pious memory. It was therefore with mixed feelings that I yielded to my friend Mark Shelton's pressing invitation to assist at one of Black's séances in company with him and his friend George Carver.

"No doubt he does help out his séances with tricks," explained Mark, "but things do happen there that I cannot explain in any way whatever. I do wish you would come, once at least."

"What sort of things?" I asked.

"Oh! little things—generally of no importance, which have little or nothing to do with the 'show.' But at least twice there has been a sort of snarling in the room, and when this happens Black stops the séance—says the Controls are getting angry, or out of hand; and then, when the lights go up, he is a sight to see. Horrible! He seems to have worked himself up to such a pitch that he is white and sweating with terror. He bundles us all out as quickly as he can."

I confess that this interested me. Shelton was an extraordinarily prosaic and clear-minded man, an idle man-about-town, with ample means and a beautiful apartment in the Albany. He did not believe in 'spiritualism' as such, but confessed that the manifestations interested and, on occasion, thrilled him. He never missed a good conjuring show at a Variety Theatre, and admitted that he loved to be taken in, and to see tricks and 'phenomena' that passed his comprehension.

Well—I went. Black had small piercing dark eyes and a little waxed moustache, and I found him a very different person from the obsequious Black I had avoided becoming accustomed to. He put me through a short but highly efficient cross-examination as to my experience of séances, and my object in assisting at this one; but I managed to convey an impression of imbecility, and to place in his hands my guilty secret that, in spite of my position as Professor of Zoology in the University of Cosmopoli, I was a dabbler in metaphysics, and prepared to admit the existence of super-physical forces which I did not understand but viewed with respect.

The solidity of my introduction, however, it was, that secured my admission to the 'Circle'; but Black was obviously on his guard, and nothing called for astonishment or remark in the perform-ance—unless it was a 'materialization' of Pope Innocent the Third, who welcomed and blessed us in a mixture of elementary school Latin and atrocious modern Italian. A Cardinal was in attendance upon him who wore a long beard. I commented, foolishly, upon this, and Black quickly explained that he was a Franciscan Cardinal, which entirely satisfied the 'Circle' but put our ecclesiastical visitors to flight.

"What did you think of it?" asked Shelton as we walked down to the main road. 'I didn't think of it," I replied.

"But I can't help thinking of Black—poor chap."

"Why 'poor chap?' "

"Don't you see how it has got hold of him? He is clearly a char-latan, but he is afraid of himself. Have you never seen a child who is afraid of the dark experimenting with mock-bravery? Going into a dark cupboard of which he controls the door handle—he is not really in the dark. Black's tricks are the dark cupboard of which he holds the door handle. I'll bet you he doesn't hold séances by himself."

"I wonder!" replied Shelton. He was curiously silent all the way back to town.

A few weeks later I noticed casually in the *Daily Telegraph* the announcement of the death of Augustine Black, F.Z.S., at his house on Tulse Hill.

It was about three weeks or a month after this that Mark Shelton rang me up on the telephone. The telephone was not then the universal blessing (or curse) that it is now, and installations were few and far between, a sort of scientific toy for the chosen few, and I could have counted on my fingers the friends who had them in their houses. Shelton's voice sounded grave and subdued, in answer to my cheery greeting.

"I want you to dine with me tonight," he said.

"Can't possibly—I am dining out."

"Oh! but you must," he answered; "I want you particularly. It's most important."

"But I tell you I can't. Who else is coming?

"No one—I want you, and you must come. Put your other party off. Tell them it's a matter of life and death."

"But, I say—"

"Don't say anything," he interrupted. "I'm telling you the truth. I've got something to tell you, which must be told here; and it is a matter of life and death. If you don't come, I shall not be alive in the morning."

By this time his voice was quivering, and I realized that something very serious was the matter. So I answered curtly:

"Oh! all right. I'll come, but don't talk bosh; and buck up. What have you been doing with Yourself?"

"Nothing. I haven't left my rooms for three weeks."

All right," I replied; "I'll come and dig you out."

I got to the Albany at half-past seven, and was let in by his man, the imperturbable Bates.

"How is Mr. Shelton?" I asked him casually, as I put down my hat and coat.

"I don't know, sir," replied Bates; "I can't make him out. Seems to be brooding all the time. Never goes out, and doesn't eat anything to speak of."

I went into Shelton's sitting-room, which was stiflingly hot. Though it was a fine May day he had a large fire, and all the curtains were closely drawn. Mark was sitting before the fire in his day clothes, doing nothing.

"Good heavens!" I said. "What an atmosphere! No wonder you are nervy. Got any windows open?"

"No—and don't open them. I've a reason. Is the air very beastly?"

"Not beastly," I said; "but intolerably hot."

"Not foul and stuffy?"

"No."

"Don't you notice a queer smell?"

"No—what sort of smell?"

"Well"—he hesitated a moment, and then said— "like the Small Cat House at the Zoo."

"Not in the least," I replied.

"What ever is the matter with you?"

"I don't know. I want you to tell me."

I looked at him critically. Was he—the sane and athletic Shelton—going mad? The phrase 'olfactory delusions' came into my mind.

"Tell me all you can about it," I said.

"Presently," he replied, "after dinner." So with that, for the moment, I had to be content. We went in to dinner. As usual it was exquisite. Shelton could, and did, afford a perfect cook, and on this occasion she had surpassed herself. Shelton tasted everything and sent his plate away practically untouched. At every dish he said:

"Pah! beastly. Don't you notice a filthy taste in this?"

"No—it's excellent. What kind of taste?"

"Well"—and again the hesitation— "like the Small Cat House at the Zoo."

It seemed to be a mania. I told him he should consult X. the great nose and ear specialist. He only shook his head wearily.

After dinner he consented to have a window open, and to let the fire die down. He told me he had 'got up a frowst' so that I should get It in all its force—but he accepted, doubtfully, my assurance that the air was perfectly clean.

He brought me a volume of Japanese engravings he wanted me to see, and as he leaned over me, he said:

"Don't you mind my leaning over you?" and he looked searchingly into my eyes.

"Not in the least. Why on earth should I?"

"Good God, man! don't you notice that I stink?"

"Not at all. What do you imagine you stink of? The Small Cat House again?"

"Yes—that's it. It's ghastly. I can never get away from it."

"Tell me," I said quietly. "When and how did this begin?"

And he told me a most amazing and horrible story.

"You remember Austin Black—the Spiritualist Zoologist? Yes, we took you, Carver and I, to one of his séances. You may have seen that he is dead. Carver and I were there when he died; there was no inquest, for his domestic G. P. certified the ever-ready heart disease of long standing.

"There was a séance, only four of us and Black and his Medium. Black was awfully strung up that night—he told us the conditions could not be more favourable. It wasn't a 'show night,' and there was no music and no tricks—but queer, uncomfortable things happened. A spreading light over the table—and a leg of my chair suddenly snapped off. We turned up the lights—it seemed to have been bitten through. I wanted to stop, but Black, though he looked ghastly, wouldn't hear of it. He said: "I want to see this thing through—I want to 'down' it"—and we started the séance again. Almost immediately I heard that snarling I told you about, and Black, who was on my right, got up in the dark and left the table. We heard a sort of scuffling, and then a choking noise in the corner of the room. We switched on the light and saw Black lying on his back by the wall, his tongue out, and blue in the face, struggling violently with nothing. We rushed at him and tried to pick him up.

There was Something that we could not see, between us and him, pinning him down. We could feel it though—it was soft and pulpy, with a surface not furry, but like a mouse or a mole—and huge! And it stank like the Small Cat House at the Zoo. We could not free him of it, and we saw him die; choked before our eyes, whilst we clawed at that soft pulpy Nothing. We could not move it. When he was quite still, the Thing got up of its own accord. Carver and I were crouched close together, and the Thing forced its way between us, and so away. How it stank! It seemed to leave a greasy smear of smell all over us. We called his wife—a queer woman—she did not seem badly shocked, or to care much. Carver said afterwards that she seemed to him to he intensely relieved at something. All she said was: "I expected this—it has happened before"—she evidently did not realize that he was dead— "please go away at once. I will send for his doctor—he is close by." We went. The other two—strangers—and the Medium had bolted directly we turned up the lights. As Carver and I walked down the hill he said: "It's awful—it's awful. How it stank! and I can't get rid of the stink." No more could I. Carver and I parted at Vauxhall. I never saw him again. I enquired a day or two later and heard he was ill; a week later I heard he had had a stroke, and was in a private mad-house. I had baths—Turkish baths—I changed my clothes half a dozen times a day—I always smelt of that Thing—I do still—I can't bear it. I shall go mad like Carver. Everything I touch smells of it, everything I try to eat tastes of it. I've tried to get over it and I can't. That's why at last I sent for you, and closed up everything and lit a fire, to give you the fullest chance.

"Now I know that I can't do anything. It's in me and part of me—I shall never be free of it. That Thing is here with me! It's prowling round all the time, but only I can smell it. God help me!"

To say that I was horrified is to use a miserably inadequate term; but before I left Mark Shelton that night I had arranged with him to go in three days to Norway, fishing. We settled everything—when to start, where to go, and what to take. I left him, still rather dazed, but much easier in my mind.

That night at about 1 a.m. Mark Shelton blew out his brains.

Negotium Perambulans

E. F. Benson

The casual tourist in West Cornwall may just possibly have noticed, as he bowled along over the bare high plateau between Penzance and the Land's End, a dilapidated signpost pointing down a steep lane and bearing on its battered finger the faded inscription "Polearn 2 miles," but probably very few have had the curiosity to traverse those two miles in order to see a place to which their guidebooks award so cursory a notice. It is described there, in a couple of unattractive lines, as a small fishing village with a church of no particular interest except for certain carved and painted wooden panels (originally belonging to an earlier edifice) which form an altar-rail. But the church at St. Creed (the tourist is reminded) has a similar decoration far superior in point of preservation and interest, and thus even the ecclesiastically disposed are not lured to Polearn. So meagre a bait is scarce worth swallowing, and a glance at the very steep lane which in dry weather presents a carpet of sharp-pointed stones, and after rain a muddy watercourse, will almost certainly decide him not to expose his motor or his bicycle to risks like these in so sparsely populated a district. Hardly a house has met his eye since he left Penzance, and the possible trundling of a punctured bicycle for half a dozen weary miles seems a high price to pay for the sight of a few painted panels.

Polearn, therefore, even in the high noon of the tourist season, is little liable to invasion, and for the rest of the year I do not suppose that a couple of folk a day traverse those two miles (long ones at that) of steep and stony gradient. I am not forgetting the postman in this exiguous estimate, for the days are few when, leaving his pony and cart at the top of the hill, he goes as far as the village, since but a few hundred yards down the lane there stands a large white box, like a sea-trunk, by the side of the road, with a slit for letters and a locked door. Should he have in his wallet a registered letter or be the bearer of a parcel too large for insertion in the square lips of the sea-trunk, he must needs trudge down the hill and deliver the troublesome missive, leaving it in person on the owner, and receiving some small reward of coin or refreshment for his kindness. But such occasions are rare, and his general routine is to take out of the box such letters as may have been deposited there, and insert in their place such letters as he has brought. These will be called for, perhaps that day or perhaps the next, by an emissary from the Polearn post-office. As for the fishermen of the place, who, in their export trade, constitute the chief link of movement between Polearn and the outside world, they would not dream of taking their catch up the steep lane and so, with six miles farther of travel, to the market at Penzance. The sea route is shorter and easier, and they deliver their wares to the pier-head. Thus, though the sole industry of Polearn is sea-fishing, you will get no fish there unless you have bespoken your requirements to one of the fishermen. Back come the trawlers as empty as a haunted house, while their spoils are in the fish-train that is speeding to London.

Such isolation of a little community, continued, as it has been, for centuries, produces isolation in the individual as well, and nowhere will you find greater independence of character than among the people of Polearn. But they are linked together, so it has always seemed to me, by some mysterious comprehension: it is as if they had all been initiated into some ancient rite, inspired and framed by forces visible and invisible. The winter storms that batter the coast, the vernal spell of the spring, the hot, still summers, the season of rains and autumnal decay, have made a spell which, line by line, has been communicated to them, concerning the powers, evil and good, that rule the world, and manifest themselves in ways benignant or terrible . . .

I came to Polearn first at the age of ten, a small boy, weak and sickly, and threatened with pulmonary trouble. My father's business kept him in London, while for me abundance of fresh air and a mild climate were considered essential conditions if I was to grow to manhood. His sister had married the vicar of Polearn, Richard Bolitho, himself native to the place, and so it came about that I spent three years, as a paying guest, with my relations. Richard Bolitho owned a fine house in the place, which he inhabited in preference to the vicarage, which he let to a young artist, John Evans, on whom the spell of Polearn had fallen for from year's beginning to year's end he never let it. There was a solid roofed shelter, open on one side to the air, built for me in the garden, and here I lived and slept, passing scarcely one hour out of the twenty-four behind walls and windows. I was out on the bay with the fisher-folk, or wandering along the gorse-clad cliffs that climbed steeply to right and left of the deep combe where the village lay, or pottering about on the pier-head, or bird's-nesting in the bushes with the boys of the village. Except on Sunday and for the few daily hours of my lessons, I might do what I pleased so long as I remained in the open air. About the lessons there was nothing formidable; my uncle conducted me through flowering bypaths among the thickets of arithmetic, and made pleasant excursions into the elements of Latin grammar, and above all, he made me daily give him an account, in clear and grammatical sentences, of what had been occupying my mind or my movements. Should I select to tell him about a walk along the cliffs, my speech must be orderly, not vague, slip-shod notes of what I had observed. In this way, too, he trained my observation, for he would bid me tell him what flowers were in bloom, and what birds hovered fishing over the sea or were building in the bushes. For that I owe him a perennial gratitude, for to observe and to express my thoughts in the clear spoken word became my life's profession.

But far more formidable than my weekday tasks was the prescribed routine for Sunday. Some dark embers compounded of Calvinism and mysticism smouldered in my uncle's soul, and made it a day of terror. His sermon in the morning scorched us with a foretaste of the eternal fires reserved for unrepentant sinners, and he was hardly less terrifying at the children's service in the afternoon. Well do I remember his exposition of the doctrine of guardian angels. A child, he said, might think himself secure in such angelic care, but let him beware of committing any of those numerous offences which would cause his guardian to turn his face from him, for as sure as there were angels to protect us, there were also evil and awful presences which were ready to pounce; and on them he dwelt with peculiar gusto. Well, too, do I remember in the morning sermon his commentary on the carved panels of the altar-rails to which I have already alluded. There was the angel of the Annunciation there, and the angel of the Resurrection, but not less was there the witch of Endor, and, on the fourth panel, a scene that concerned me most of all. This fourth panel (he came down from his pulpit to trace its time-worn features) represented the lych-gate of the church-yard at Polearn itself, and indeed the resemblance when thus pointed out was remarkable. In the entry stood the figure of a robed priest holding up a Cross, with which he faced a terrible creature like a gigantic slug, that reared itself up in front of him. That, so ran my uncle's interpretation, was some evil agency, such as he had spoken about to us children, of almost infinite malignity and power, which could alone be combated by firm faith and a pure heart. Below ran the legend "Negotium perambulans in tenebris" from the ninety-first Psalm. We should find it translated there, "the pestilence that walketh in darkness," which but feebly rendered the Latin. It was more deadly to the soul than any pestilence that can only kill the body: it was the Thing, the Creature, the Business that trafficked in the outer Darkness, a minister of God's wrath on the unrighteous. . . .

I could see, as he spoke, the looks which the congregation exchanged with each other, and knew that his words were evoking a surmise, a remembrance. Nods and whispers passed between them, they understood to what he alluded, and with the inquisitiveness of boyhood I could not rest till I had wormed the story out of my friends among the fisher-boys, as, next morning, we sat basking and naked in the sun after our bathe. One knew one bit of it, one another, but it pieced together into a truly alarming legend. In bald outline it was as follows: A church far more ancient than that in which my uncle terrified us every Sunday had once stood not three hundred yards away, on the shelf of level ground below the quarry from which its stones were hewn. The owner of the land had pulled this down, and erected for himself a house on the same site out of these materials, keeping, in a very ecstasy of wickedness, the altar, and on this he dined and played dice afterwards. But as he grew old some black melancholy seized him, and he would have lights burning there all night, for he had deadly fear of the darkness. On one winter evening there sprang up such a gale as was never before known, which broke in the windows of the room where he had supped, and extinguished the lamps. Yells of terror brought in his servants, who found him lying on the floor with the blood streaming from his throat. As they entered some huge black shadow seemed to move away from him, crawled across the floor and up the wall and out of the broken window.

"There he lay a-dying," said the last of my informants, "and him that had been a great burly man was withered to a bag o' skin, for the critter had drained all the blood from him. His last breath was a scream, and he hollered out the same words as passon read off the screen."

"Negotium perambulans in tenebris," I suggested eagerly.

"Thereabouts. Latin anyhow."

"And after that?" I asked.

"Nobody would go near the place, and the old house rotted and fell in ruins till three years ago, when along comes Mr. Dooliss from Penzance, and built the half of it up again. But he don't care much about such critters, nor about Latin neither. He takes his bottle of whisky a day and gets drunk's a lord in the evening. Eh, I'm gwine home to my dinner."

Whatever the authenticity of the legend, I had certainly heard the truth about Mr. Dooliss from Penzance, who from that day became an object of keen curiosity on my part, the more so because the quarry-house adjoined my uncle's garden. The Thing that walked in the dark failed to stir my imagination, and already I was so used to sleeping alone in my shelter that the night had no terrors for me. But it would be intensely exciting to wake at some timeless hour and hear Mr. Dooliss yelling, and conjecture that the Thing had got him.

But by degrees the whole story faded from my mind, overscored by the more vivid interests of the day, and, for the last two years of my out-door life in the vicarage garden, I seldom thought about Mr. Dooliss and the possible fate that might await him for his temerity in living in the place where that Thing of darkness had done business. Occasionally I saw him over the garden fence, a great yellow lump of a man, with slow and staggering gait, but never did I set eyes on him outside his gate, either in the village street or down on the beach. He interfered with none, and no one interfered with him. If he wanted to run the risk of being the prey of the legendary nocturnal monster, or quietly drink himself to death, it was his affair. My uncle, so I gathered, had made several attempts to see him when first he came to live at Polearn, but Mr. Dooliss appeared to have no use for parsons, but said he was not at home and never returned the call.

After three years of sun, wind, and rain, I had completely outgrown my early symptoms and had become a tough, strapping youngster of thirteen. I was sent to Eton and Cambridge, and in due course ate my dinners and became a barrister. In twenty years from that time I was earning a yearly income of five figures, and had already laid by in sound securities a sum that brought me dividends which would, for one of my simple tastes and frugal habits, supply me with all the material comforts I needed on this side of the grave. The great prizes of my profession were already within my reach, but I had no ambition beckoning me on, nor did I want a wife and children, being, I must suppose, a natural celibate. In fact there was only one ambition which through these busy years had held the lure of blue and far-off hills to me, and that was to get back to Polearn, and live once more isolated from the world with the sea and the gorse-clad hills for play-fellows, and the secrets that lurked there for exploration. The spell of it had been woven about my heart, and I can truly say that there had hardly passed a day in all those years in which the thought of it and the desire for it had been wholly absent from my mind. Though I had been in frequent communication with my uncle there during his lifetime, and, after his death, with his widow who still lived there, I had never been back to it since I embarked on my profession, for I knew that if I went there, it would be a wrench beyond my power to tear myself away again. But I had made up my mind that when once I had provided for my own independence, I would go back there not to leave it again. And yet I did leave it again, and now nothing in the world would induce me to turn down the lane from the road that leads from Penzance to the Land's End, and see the sides of the combe rise steep above the roofs of the village and hear the gulls chiding as they fish in the bay. One of the things invisible, of the dark powers, leaped into light, and I saw it with my eyes.

The house where I had spent those three years of boyhood had been left for life to my aunt, and when I made known to her my intention of coming back to Polearn, she suggested that, till I found a suitable house or found her proposal unsuitable, I should come to live with her.

"The house is too big for a lone old woman," she wrote, "and I have often thought of quitting and taking a little cottage sufficient for me and my requirements. But come and share it, my dear, and if you find me troublesome, you or I can go. You may want solitude . . . most people in Polearn do . . . and will leave me. Or else I will leave you: one of the main reasons of my stopping here all these years was a feeling that I must not let the old house starve. Houses starve, you know, if they are not lived in. They die a lingering death; the spirit in them grows weaker and weaker, and at last fades out of them. Isn't this nonsense to your London notions? . . ." Naturally I accepted with warmth this tentative arrangement, and on an evening in June found myself at the head of the lane leading down to Polearn, and once more I descended into the steep valley between the hills. Time had stood still apparently for the combe, the dilapidated signpost (or its successor) pointed a rickety finger

down the lane, and a few hundred yards farther on was the white
box for the exchange of letters. Point after remembered point met
my eye, and what I saw was not shrunk, as is often the case with
the revisited scenes of childhood, into a smaller scale. There stood
the post-office, and there the church und close beside it the
vicarage, and beyond, the tall shrubberies which separated the
house for which I was bound from the road, and beyond that again
the grey roofs of the quarry-house damp and shining with the moist
evening wind from the sea. All was exactly as I remembered it, and,
above all, that sense of seclusion and isolation. Somewhere above
the tree-tops climbed the lane which joined the main road to
Penzance, but all that had become immeasurably distant. The years
that had passed since last I turned in at the well-known gate faded
like a frosty breath, and vanished in this warm, soft air. There were
law-courts somewhere in memory's dull book which, if I cared to
turn the pages, would tell me that I had made a name and a great
income there. But the dull book was closed now, for I was back in
Polearn, and the spell was woven around me again.

And if Polearn was unchanged, so too was Aunt Hester, who
met me at the door. Dainty and china-white she had always been,
and the years had not aged but only refined her. As we sat and
talked after dinner she spoke of all that had happened in Polearn
in that score of years, and yet somehow the changes of which she
spoke seemed but to confirm the immutability of it all. As the
recollection of names came back to me, I asked her about the
quarry-house and Mr. Dooliss, and her face gloomed a little as with
the shadow of a cloud on a spring day.

"Yes, Mr. Dooliss," she said, "poor Mr. Dooliss, how well I
remember him, though it must be ten years and more since he died.
I never wrote to you about it, for it was all very dreadful, my dear,
and I did not want to darken your memories of Polearn. Your uncle
always thought that something of the sort might happen if he went
on in his wicked, drunken ways, and worse than that, and though
nobody knew exactly what took place, it was the sort of thing that
might have been anticipated."

"But what more or less happened, Aunt Hester?" I asked.

"Well, of course I can't tell you everything, for no one knew it. But he was a very sinful man, and the scandal about him at Newlyn was shocking. And then he lived, too, in the quarry-house. . . . I wonder if by any chance you remember a sermon of your uncle's when he got out of the pulpit and explained that panel in the altar-rails, the one, I mean, with the horrible creature rearing itself up outside the lych-gate?"

"Yes, I remember perfectly," said I.

"Ah. It made an impression on you, I suppose, and so it did on all who heard him, and that impression got stamped and branded on us all when the catastrophe occurred. Somehow Mr. Dooliss got to hear about your uncle's sermon, and in some drunken fit he broke into the church and smashed the panel to atoms. He seems to have thought that there was some magic in it, and that if he destroyed that he would get rid of the terrible fate that was threatening him. For I must tell you that before he committed that dreadful sacrilege he had been a haunted man: he hated and feared darkness, for he thought that the creature on the panel was on his track, but that as long as he kept lights burning it could not touch him. But the panel, to his disordered mind, was the root of his terror, and so, as I said, he broke into the church and attempted . . . you will see why I said 'attempted' . . . to destroy it. It certainly was found in splinters next morning, when your uncle went into church for matins, and knowing Mr. Dooliss's fear of the panel, he went across to the quarry-house afterwards and taxed him with its destruction. The man never denied it; he boasted of what he had done. There he sat, though it was early morning, drinking his whisky.

"'I've settled your Thing for you,' he said, 'and your sermon too. A fig for such superstitions.'

"Your uncle left him without answering his blasphemy, meaning to go straight into Penzance and give information to the police about this outrage to the church, but on his way back from the quarry-house he went into the church again, in order to be able to give details about the damage, and there in the screen was the panel, untouched and uninjured. And yet he had himself seen it smashed, and Mr. Dooliss had confessed that the destruction of it was his work. But there it was, and whether the power of God had mended it or some other power, who knows?" This was Polearn indeed, and it was the spirit of Polearn that made me accept all Aunt Hester was telling me as attested fact. It had happened like that. She went on in her quiet voice.

"Your uncle recognised that some power beyond police was at work, and he did not go to Penzance or give informations about the outrage, for the evidence of it had vanished."

A sudden spate of scepticism swept over me.

"There must have been some mistake," I said. "It hadn't been broken. . . ."

She smiled.

"Yes, my dear, but you have been in London so long," she said. "Let me, anyhow, tell you the rest of my story. That night, for some reason, I could not sleep. It was very hot and airless; I dare say you will think that the sultry conditions accounted for my wakefulness. Once and again, as I went to the window to see if I could not admit more air, I could see from it the quarry-house, and I noticed the first time that I left my bed that it was blazing with lights. But the second time I saw that it was all in darkness, and as I wondered at that, I heard a terrible scream, and the moment afterwards the steps of someone coming at full speed down the road outside the gate. He yelled as he ran; 'Light, light!' he called out. 'Give me light, or it will catch me!' It was very terrible to hear that, and I went to rouse my husband, who was sleeping in the dressing-room across the passage. He wasted no time, but by now the whole village was aroused by the screams, and when he got down to the pier he found that all was over. The tide was low, and on the rocks at its foot was lying the body of Mr. Dooliss. He must have cut some artery when he fell on those sharp edges of stone, for he had bled to death, they thought, and though he was a big burly man, his corpse was but skin and bones. Yet there was no pool of blood round him, such as you would have expected. Just skin and bones as if every drop of blood in his body had been sucked out of him!"

She leaned forward.

"You and I, my dear, know what happened," she said, "or at least can guess. God has His instruments of vengeance on those who bring wickedness into places that have been holy. Dark and mysterious are His ways."

Now what I should-have thought of such a story if it had been told me in London I can easily imagine. There was such an obvious explanation: the man in question had been a drunkard, what wonder if the demons of delirium pursued him? But here in Polearn it was different.

"And who is in the quarry-house now?" I asked. "Years ago the fisher-boys told me the story of the man who first built it and of his horrible end. And now again it has happened. Surely no one has ventured to inhabit it once more?"

I saw in her face, even before I asked that question, that somebody had done so.

"Yes, it is lived in again," said she, "for there is no end to the blindness. . . . I don't know if you remember him. He was tenant of the vicarage many years ago."

"John Evans," said I.

"Yes. Such a nice fellow he was too. Your uncle was pleased to get so good a tenant. And now. . . ."

She rose.

"Aunt Hester, you shouldn't leave your sentences unfinished," I said.

She shook her head.

"My dear, that sentence will finish itself," she said. "But what a time of night! I must go to bed, and you too, or they will think we have to keep lights burning here through the dark hours."

Before getting into bed I drew my curtains wide and opened all the windows to the warm tide of the sea air that flowed softly in. Looking out into the garden I could see in the moonlight the roof of the shelter, in which for three years I had lived, gleaming with dew. That, as much as anything, brought back the old days to which I had now returned, and they seemed of one piece with the present, as if no gap of more than twenty years sundered them. The two flowed into one like globules of mercury uniting into a softly shining globe, of mysterious lights and reflections. Then, raising my eyes a little, I saw against the black hill-side the windows of the quarry-house still alight.

Morning, as is so often the case, brought no shattering of my illusion. As I began to regain consciousness, I fancied that I was a boy again waking up in the shelter in the garden, and though, as I grew more widely awake, I smiled at the impression, that on which it was based I found to be indeed true. It was sufficient now as then to be here, to wander again on the cliffs, and hear the popping of the ripened seed-pods on the gorse-bushes; to stray along the shore to the bathing-cove, to float and drift and swim in the warm tide, and bask on the sand, and watch the gulls fishing, to lounge on the pier-head with the fisher-folk, to see in their eyes and hear in their quiet speech the evidence of secret things not so much known to them as part of their instincts and their very being. There were powers and presences about me; the white poplars that stood by the stream that babbled down the valley knew of them, and showed a glimpse of their knowledge sometimes, like the gleam of their white underleaves; the very cobbles that paved the street were soaked in it.

All that I wanted was to lie there and grow soaked in it too; unconsciously, as a boy, I had done that, but now the process must be conscious. I must know what stir of forces, fruitful and mysterious, seethed along the hill-side at noon, and sparkled at night on the sea. They could be known, they could even be controlled by those who were masters of the spell, but never could they be spoken of, for they were dwellers in the innermost, grafted into the eternal life of the world. There were dark secrets as well as these clear, kindly powers, and to these no doubt belonged the *negotium perambulans in tenebris* which, though of deadly malignity, might be regarded not only as evil, but as the avenger of sacrilegious and impious deeds. . . . All this was part of the spell of Polearn, of which the seeds had long lain dormant in me. But now they were sprouting, and who knew what strange flower would unfold on their stems?

It was not long before I came across John Evans. One morning, as I lay on the beach, there came shambling across the sand a man stout and middle-aged with the face of Silenus. He paused as he drew near and regarded me from narrow eyes.

"Why, you're the little chap that used to live in the parson's garden," he said. "Don't you recognise me?"

I saw who it was when he spoke: his voice, I think, instructed me, and recognising it, I could see the features of the strong, alert young man in this gross caricature.

"Yes, you're John Evans," I said. "You used to be very kind to me: you used to draw pictures for me."

"So I did, and I'll draw you some more. Been bathing? That's a risky performance. You never know what lives in the sea, nor what lives on the land for that matter. Not that I heed them. I stick to work and whisky. God! I've learned to paint since I saw you, and drink too for that matter. I live in the quarry-house, you know, and it's a powerful thirsty place. Come and have a look at my things if you're passing. Staying with your aunt, are you? I could do a wonderful portrait of her. Interesting face; she knows a lot. People who live at Polearn get to know a lot, though I don't take much stock in that sort of knowledge myself."

I do not know when I have been at once so repelled and interested. Behind the mere grossness of his face there lurked something which, while it appalled, yet fascinated me. His thick lisping speech had the same quality. And his paintings, what would they be like? . . .

"I was just going home," I said. "I'll gladly come in, if you'll allow me."

He took me through the untended and overgrown garden into the house which I had never yet entered. A great grey cat was sunning itself in the window, and an old woman was laying lunch in a corner of the cool hall into which the door opened. It was built of stone, and the carved mouldings let into the walls, the fragments of gargoyles and sculptured images, bore testimony to the truth of its having been built out of the demolished church. In one corner was an oblong and carved wooden table littered with a painter's apparatus and stacks of canvases leaned against the walls.

He jerked his thumb towards a head of an angel that was built into the mantelpiece and giggled.

"Quite a sanctified air," he said, "so we tone it down for the purposes of ordinary life by a different sort of art. Have a drink? No? Well, turn over some of my pictures while I put myself to rights."

He was justified in his own estimate of his skill: he could paint (and apparently he could paint anything), but never have I seen pictures so inexplicably hellish. There were exquisite studies of trees, and you knew that something lurked in the flickering shadows. There was a drawing of his cat sunning itself in the window, even as I had just now seen it, and yet it was no cat but some beast of awful malignity. There was a boy stretched naked on the sands, not human, but some evil thing which had come out of the sea. Above all there were pictures of his garden overgrown and jungle-like, and you knew that in the bushes were presences ready to spring out on you. . . .

"Well, do you like my style?" he said as he came up, glass in hand. (The tumbler of spirits that he held had not been diluted.) "I try to paint the essence of what I see, not the mere husk and skin of it, but its nature, where it comes from and what gave it birth. There's much in common between a cat and a fuchsia-bush if you look at them closely enough. Everything came out of the slime of the pit, and it's all going back there. I should like to do a picture of you some day. I'd hold the mirror up to Nature, as that old lunatic said."

After this first meeting I saw him occasionally throughout the months of that wonderful summer. Often he kept to his house and to his painting for days together, and then perhaps some evening I would find him lounging on the pier, always alone, and every time we met thus the repulsion and interest grew, for every time he seemed to have gone farther along a path of secret knowledge towards some evil shrine where complete initiation awaited him. . . . And then suddenly the end came.

I had met him thus one evening on the cliffs while the October sunset still burned in the sky, but over it with amazing rapidity there spread from the west a great blackness of cloud such as I have never seen for denseness. The light was sucked from the sky, the dusk fell in ever thicker layers. He suddenly became conscious of this.

"I must get back as quick as I can," he said. "It will be dark in a few minutes, and my servant is out. The lamps will not be lit."

He stepped out with extraordinary briskness for one who shambled and could scarcely lift his feet, and soon broke out into a stumbling run. In the gathering darkness I could see that his face was moist with the dew of some unspoken terror.

"You must come with me," he panted, "for so we shall get the lights burning the sooner. I cannot do without light."

I had to exert myself to the full to keep up with him, for terror winged him, and even so I fell behind, so that when I came to the garden gate, he was already half-way up the path to the house. I saw him enter, leaving the door wide, and found him fumbling with matches. But his hand so trembled that he could not transfer the light to the wick of the lamp.

"But what's the hurry about?" I asked.

Suddenly his eyes focused themselves on the open door behind me, and he jumped from his seat beside the table which had once been the altar of God, with a gasp and a scream.

"No, no!" he cried. "Keep it off! . . ."

I turned and saw what he had seen. The Thing had entered and now was swiftly sliding across the floor towards him, like some gigantic caterpillar. A stale phosphorescent light came from it, for though the dusk had grown to blackness outside, I could see it quite distinctly in the awful light of its own presence. From it too there came an odour of corruption and decay, as from slime that has long lain below water. It seemed to have no head, but on the front of it was an orifice of puckered skin which opened and shut and slavered at the edges. It was hairless, and slug-like in shape and in texture. As it advanced its fore-part reared itself from the ground, like a snake about to strike, and it fastened on him. . . .

At that sight, and with the yells of his agony in my ears, the panic which had struck me relaxed into a hopeless courage, and with palsied, impotent hands I tried to lay hold of the Thing. But I could not: though something material was there, it was impossible to grasp it; my hands sunk in it as in thick mud. It was like wrestling with a nightmare.

I think that but a few seconds elapsed before all was over. The screams of the wretched man sank to moans and mutterings as the Thing fell on him: he panted once or twice and was still. For a moment longer there came gurglings and sucking noises, and then it slid out even as it had entered. I lit the lamp which he had fumbled with, and there on the floor he lay, no more than a rind of skin in loose folds over projecting bones.

The Ghoul

Sir Hugh Charles Clifford

We had been sitting late upon the veranda of my bungalow at Kuâla Lîpis, which, from the top of a low hill covered with coarse grass, overlooked the long, narrow reach formed by the combined waters of the Lîpis and the Jelai. The moon had risen some hours earlier, and the river ran white between the black masses of forest, which seemed to shut it in on all sides, giving to it the appearance of an isolated tarn. The roughly cleared compound, with the tennis ground which had never got beyond the stage of being dug over and weeded, and the rank growths beyond the bamboo fence, were flooded by the soft light, every tattered detail of their ugliness standing revealed as relentlessly as though it were noon. The night was very still, but the heavy, scented air was cool after the fierce heat of the day.

I had been holding forth to the handful of men who had been dining with me on the subject of Malay superstitions, while they manfully stifled their yawns. When a man has a working knowledge of anything which is not commonly known to his neighbours, he is apt to presuppose their interest in it when a chance to descant upon it occurs, and in those days it was only at long intervals that I had an opportunity of forgathering with other white men. Therefore, I had made the most of it, and looking back, I fear that I had occupied the rostrum during the greater part of that evening. I had told my audience of the *pen-anggal*—the "Undone One"—that horrible wraith of a woman who has died in childbirth, who comes to torment and prey upon small children in the guise of a ghastly face and bust, with a comet's tail of blood-stained entrails flying in her wake; of the *mâti-ânak*, the weird little white animal which makes beast noises round the graves of children, and is supposed to have absorbed their souls; and of the *pôlong*, or familiar spirits, which men bind to their service by raising them up from the corpses of babies that have been stillborn, the tips of whose tongues they bite off and swallow after the infant has been brought to life by magic agencies. It was at this point that young Middleton began to pluck up his ears; and I, finding that one of my hearers was at last showing signs of being interested, launched out with renewed vigour, until my sorely tried companions, one by one, went off to bed, each to his own quarters.

Middleton was staying with me at the time, and he and I sat for a while in silence, after the others had gone, looking at the moonlight on the river. Middleton was the first to speak.

"That was a curious myth you were telling us about the *pôlong*," he said. "There is an incident connected with it which I have never spoken of before, and have always sworn that I would keep to myself; but I have a good mind to tell you about it, because you are the only man I know who will not write me down a liar if I do."

"That's all right. Fire away," I said.

"Well," said Middleton. "It was like this. You remember Juggins, of course? He was a naturalist, you know, dead nuts upon becoming an F. R. S. and all that sort of thing, and he came to stay with me during the close season* last year. He was hunting for bugs and orchids and things, and spoke of himself as an anthropologist and a botanist and a zoologist, and Heaven knows what besides; and he used to fill his bedroom with all sorts of creeping, crawling things, kept in very indifferent custody, and my veranda with all kinds of trash and rotting green trade that he brought in from the jungle. He stopped with me for about ten days, and when he heard

* "Close season," *i. e.* from the beginning of November to the end of February, during which time the rivers on the eastern seaboard of the Malay Peninsula used to be closed to traffic on account of the North East Monsoon.

that duty was taking me upriver into the Sâkai country, he asked me to let him come, too. I was rather bored, for the tribesmen are mighty shy of strangers and were only just getting used to me; but he was awfully keen, and a decent beggar enough, in spite of his dirty ways, so I couldn't very well say 'No.' When we had poled upstream for about a week, and had got well up into the Sâkai country, we had to leave our boats behind at the foot of the big rapids, and leg it for the rest of the time. It was very rough going, wading up and down streams when one wasn't clambering up a hillside or sliding down the opposite slope—you know the sort of thing—and the leeches were worse than I have ever seen them—thousands of them, swarming up your back, and fastening in clusters on to your neck, even when you had defeated those which made a frontal attack. I had not enough men with me to do more than hump the camp-kit and a few clothes, so we had to live on the country, which doesn't yield much up among the Sâkai except yams and tapioca roots and a little Indian corn, and soft stuff of that sort. It was all new to Juggins, and gave him fits; but he stuck to it like a man.

"Well, one evening when the night was shutting down pretty fast and rain was beginning to fall, Juggins and I struck a fairly large Sâkai camp in the middle of a clearing. As soon as we came out of the jungle, and began tight-roping along the felled timber, the Sâkai sighted us and bolted for covert *en masse*. By the time we reached the huts it was pelting in earnest, and as my men were pretty well fagged out, I decided to spend the night in the camp, and not to make them put up temporary shelters for us. Sâkai huts are uncleanly places at best, and any port has to do in a storm.

"We went into the largest of the hovels, and there we found a woman lying by the side of her dead child. She had apparently felt too sick to bolt with the rest of her tribe. The kid was as stiff as Herod, and had not been born many hours, I should say. The mother seemed pretty bad, and I went to her, thinking I might be able to do something for her; but she did not seem to see it, and bit and snarled at me like a wounded animal, clutching at the dead child the while, as though she feared I should take it from her. I therefore left her alone; and Juggins and I took up our quarters in a smaller hut nearby, which was fairly new and not so filthy dirty as most Sâkai lairs.

"Presently, when the beggars who had run away found out that I was the intruder, they began to come back again. You know their way. First a couple of men came and peeped at us, and vanished as soon as they saw they were observed. Then they came a trifle nearer, bobbed up suddenly, and peeped at us again. I called to them in Sê-noi*, which always reassures them, and when they at last summoned up courage to approach, gave them each a handful of tobacco. Then they went back into the jungle and fetched the others, and very soon the place was crawling with Sâkai of both sexes and all ages.

"We got a meal of sorts, and settled down for the night as best we could; but it wasn't a restful business. Juggins swore with eloquence at the uneven flooring, made of very roughly trimmed boughs, which is an infernally uncomfortable thing to lie down upon, and makes one's bones ache as though they were coming out at the joints, and the Sâkai are abominably restless bedfellows as you know. I suppose one ought to realize that they have as yet only partially emerged from the animal, and that, like the beasts, they are still naturally nocturnal. Anyway, they never sleep for long at a stretch, though from time to time they snuggle down and snore among the piles of warm wood ashes round the central fireplace, and whenever you wake, you will always see half a dozen of them squatting near the blazing logs, half hidden by the smoke, and jabbering like monkeys. It is a marvel to me what they find to yarn about: food, or rather the patent impossibility of ever getting enough to eat, and the stony-heartedness of Providence and of the

---

*Sê-noi—one of the two main branches into which the Sâkai are divided. The other is called Tê-mi-au by the Sê-noi. All the Sâkai dialects are variants of the languages spoken by these two principal tribes, which, though they have many words in common, differ from one another almost as much as, say, Italian from Spanish.

neighbouring Malays must furnish the principal topics, I should fancy, with an occasional respectful mention of beasts of prey and forest demons. That night they were more than ordinarily restless. The dead baby was enough to make them uneasy, and besides, they had got wet while hiding in the jungle after our arrival, and that always sets the skin disease, with which all Sâkai are smothered, itching like mad. Whenever I woke I could hear their nails going on their dirty hides; but I had had a hard day and was used to my hosts' little ways, so I contrived to sleep fairly sound. Juggins told me next morning that he had had *une nuit blanche*, and he nearly caused another stampede among the Sâkai by trying to get a specimen of the fungus or bacillus, or whatever it is, that occasions the skin disease. I do not know whether he succeeded. For my own part, I think it is probably due to chronic anaemia—the poor devils have never had more than a very occasional full meal for hundreds of generations. I have seen little brats, hardly able to stand, white with it, the skin peeling off in flakes, and I used to frighten Juggins out of his senses by telling him he had contracted it when his nose was flayed by the sun.

"Next morning I woke just in time to see the stillborn baby put into a hole in the ground. They fitted its body into a piece of bark, and stuck it in the grave they had dug for it at the edge of the clearing. They buried a flint and steel and a woodknife and some food, and a few other things with it, though no living baby could have had any use for most of them, let alone a dead one. Then the old medicine man of the tribe recited the ritual over the grave. I took the trouble to translate it once. It goes something like this:

"'O Thou, who hast gone forth from among those who dwell upon the surface of the earth, and hast taken for thy dwelling-place the land which is beneath the earth, flint and steel have we given thee to kindle thy fire, raiment to clothe thy nakedness, food to fill thy belly, and a woodknife to clear thy path. Go, then, and make unto thyself friends among those who dwell beneath the earth, and come back no more to trouble or molest those who dwell upon the surface of the earth.'

"It was short and to the point; and then they trampled down the soil, while the mother, who had got upon her feet by now, whimpered about the place like a cat that had lost its kittens. A mangy, half-starved dog came and smelt hungrily about the grave, until it was sent howling away by kicks from every human animal that could reach it; and a poor little brat, who chanced to set up a piping song a few minutes later, was kicked and cuffed and knocked about by all who could conveniently get at him with foot, hand, or missile. Abstinence from song and dance for a period of nine days is the Sâkai way of mourning the dead, and any breach, of this is held to give great offence to the spirit of the departed and to bring bad luck upon the tribe. It was considered necessary, therefore, to give the urchin who had done the wrong a fairly bad time of it in order to propitiate the implacable dead baby.

"Next the Sâkai set to work to pack all their household goods— not a very laborious business; and in about half an hour the last of the laden women, who was carrying so many cooking-pots, and babies and rattan bags and carved bamboo-boxes and things, that she looked like the outside of a gipsy's cart at home, had filed out of the clearing and disappeared in the forest. The Sâkai always shift camp, like that, when a death occurs, because they think the ghost of the dead haunts the place where the body died. When an epidemic breaks out among them they are so busy changing quarters, building new huts, and planting fresh catch crops that they have no time to procure proper food, and half those who are not used up by the disease die of semi-starvation. They are a queer lot.

"Well, Juggins and I were left alone, but my men needed a rest, so I decided to trek no farther that day, and Juggins and I spent our time trying to get a shot at a *sêlâdang**, but though we came upon great ploughed-up runs, which the herds had made going

* *Sêlâdang*: The gaur or wild buffalo. It is the same as the Indian variety, but in the Malay Peninsula attains to a greater size than in any other part of Asia.

down to water, we saw neither hoof nor horn, and returned at night to the deserted Sâkai camp, two of my Malays fairly staggering under the piles of rubbish which Juggins called his botanical specimens. The men we had left behind had contrived to catch some fish, and with that and yams we got a pretty decent meal, and I was lying on my mat reading by the aid of a *dâmar* torch, and thinking how lucky it was that the Sâkai had cleared out, when suddenly old Juggins sat up, with his eyes fairly snapping at me through his gig-lamps in his excitement.

"'I say,' he said. 'I must have that baby. It would make a unique and invaluable ethnological specimen.'

"'Rot,' I said. 'Go to sleep, old man. I want to read.'

"'No, but I'm serious,' said Juggins. 'You do not realize the unprecedented character of the opportunity. The Sâkai have gone away, so their susceptibilities would not be outraged. The potential gain to science is immense—simply immense. It would be criminal to neglect such a chance. I regard the thing in the light of a duty which I owe to human knowledge. I tell you straight, I mean to have that baby whether you like it or not, and that is flat.'

"Juggins was forever talking about human knowledge, as though he and it were partners in a business firm.

"'It is not only the Sâkai one has to consider,' I said. 'My Malays are sensitive about body snatching, too. One has to think about the effect upon them.'

"'I can't help that,' said Juggins resolutely. 'I am going out to dig it up now.'

"He had already put his boots on, and was sorting out his botanical tools in search of a trowel. I saw that there was no holding him.

"'Juggins,' I said sharply. 'Sit down. You are a lunatic, of course, but I was another when I allowed you to come up here with me, knowing as I did that you are the particular species of crank you are. However, I've done you as well as circumstances permitted, and as a mere matter of gratitude and decency, I think you might do what I wish.'

"'I am sorry,' said Juggins stiffly. 'I am extremely sorry not to be able to oblige you. My duty as a man of science, however, compels me to avail myself of this god-sent opportunity of enlarging our ethnological knowledge of a little-known people.'

"'I thought you did not believe in God,' I said sourly; for Juggins added a militant agnosticism to his other attractive qualities.

"'I believe in my duty to human knowledge,' he replied sententiously. 'And if you will not help me to perform it, I must discharge it unaided.'

"He had found his trowel, and again rose to his feet.

"'Don't be an ass, Juggins,' I said. 'Listen to me. I have forgotten more about the people and the country here than you will ever learn. If you go and dig up that dead baby, and my Malays see you, there will be the devil to pay. They do not hold with exhumed corpses, and have no liking for or sympathy with people who go fooling about with such things. They have not yet been educated up to the pitch of interest in the secrets of science which has made of you a potential criminal, and if they could understand our talk, they would be convinced that you needed the kid's body for some devilry or witchcraft business, and ten to one they would clear out and leave us in the lurch. Then who would carry your precious botanical specimens back to the boats for you, and just think how the loss of them would knock the bottom out of human knowledge for good and all.'

"'The skeleton of the child is more valuable still,' replied Juggins. 'It is well that you should understand that in this matter—which for me is a question of my duty—I am not to be moved from my purpose either by arguments or threats.'

"He was as obstinate as a mule, and I was pretty sick with him; but I saw that if I left him to himself he would do the thing so clumsily that my fellows would get wind of it, and if that happened I was afraid that they might desert us. The tracks in that Sâkai country are abominably confusing, and quite apart from the fear of losing all our camp-kit, which we could not hump for ourselves, I was by no means certain that I could find my own way back to civilization unaided. Making a virtue of necessity, therefore, I decided that I would let Juggins have his beastly specimen, provided that he would consent to be guided entirely by me in all details connected with the exhumation.

"'You are a rotter of the first water,' I said frankly. 'And if I ever get you back to my station, I'll have nothing more to do with you as long as I live. All the same, I am to blame for having brought you up here, and I suppose I must see you through.'

"'You're a brick,' said Juggins, quite unmoved by my insults. 'Come on.'

"'Wait,' I replied repressively. 'This thing cannot be done until my people are all asleep. Lie down on your mat and keep quiet. When it is safe, I'll give you the word.'

"Juggins groaned, and tried to persuade me to let him go at once; but I swore that nothing would induce me to move before midnight, and with that I rolled over on my side and lay reading and smoking, while Juggins fumed and fretted as he watched the slow hands of his watch creeping round the dial.

"I always take books with me into the jungle, and the more completely incongruous they are to my immediate surroundings the more refreshing I find them. That evening, I remember, I happened to be rereading Miss Florence Montgomery's *Misunderstood* with the tears running down my nose; and by the time my Malays were all asleep, this incidental wallowing in sentimentality had made me more sick with Juggins and his disgusting project than ever.

"I never felt so like a criminal as I did that night, as Juggins and I gingerly picked our way out of the hut across the prostrate forms of my sleeping Malays; nor had I realized before what a difficult job it is to walk without noise on an openwork flooring of uneven boughs. We got out of the place and down the crazy stair-ladder at last, without waking any of my fellows, and we then began to creep along the edge of the jungle that hedged the clearing about. Why did we think it necessary to creep? I don't know. Partly we did not want to be seen by the Malays, if any of them happened to wake; but besides that, the long wait and the uncanny sort of work we were after had set our nerves going a bit, I expect.

"The night was as still as most nights are in real, *pukka* jungle. That is to say, that it was as full of noises—little, quiet, half-heard beast and tree noises—as an egg is full of meat; and every occasional louder sound made me jump almost out of my skin. There was not a breath astir in the clearing, but miles up above our heads the clouds were racing across the moon, which looked as though it were scudding through them in the opposite direction at a tremendous rate, like a great white fire balloon. It was pitch dark along the edge of the clearing, for the jungle threw a heavy shadow; and Juggins kept knocking those great clumsy feet of his against the stumps, and swearing softly under his breath.

"Just as we were getting near the child's grave the clouds obscuring the moon became a trifle thinner, and the slightly increased light showed me something that caused me to clutch Juggins by the arm.

"'Hold hard!' I whispered, squatting down instinctively in the shadow, and dragging him after me. 'What's that on the grave?'

"Juggins hauled out his six-shooter with a tug, and looking at his face, I saw that he was as pale as death and more than a little shaky. He was pressing up against me, too, as he squatted, a bit closer, I fancied, than he would have thought necessary at any other time, and it seemed to me that he was trembling. I whispered to him, telling him not to shoot; and we sat there for nearly a minute, I should think, peering through the uncertain light, and trying to make out what the creature might be which was crouching above the grave and making a strange scratching noise.

"Then the moon came out suddenly into a patch of open sky, and we could see clearly at last, and what it revealed did not make me, for one, feel any better. The thing we had been looking at was kneeling on the grave, facing us. It, or rather she, was an old, old Sâkai hag. She was stark naked, and in the brilliant light of the moon I could see her long, pendulous breasts swaying about like an ox's dewlap, and the creases and wrinkles with which her withered hide was criss-crossed, and the discoloured patches of foul skin disease. Her hair hung about her face in great matted locks, falling forward as she bent above the grave, and her eyes glinted through the tangle like those of some unclean and shaggy animal. Her long fingers, which had nails like claws, were tearing at the dirt of the grave, and her body was drenched with sweat, so that it glistened in the moonlight.

"'It looks as though some one else wanted your precious baby for a specimen, Juggins,' I whispered; and a spirit of emulation set him floundering on to his feet, till I pulled him back. 'Keep still, man,' I added. 'Let us see what the old hag is up to. It isn't the brat's mother, is it?'

"'No,' panted Juggins. 'This is a much older woman. Great God! What a ghoul it is!'

"Then we were silent again. Where we squatted we were hidden from the hag by a few tufts of rank *lâlang* grass, and the shadow of the jungle also covered us. Even if we had been in the open, however, I question whether the old woman would have seen us, she was so eagerly intent upon her work. For full five minutes, as near as I can guess, we squatted there watching her scrape and tear and scratch at the earth of the grave, with a sort of frenzy of energy; and all the while her lips kept going like a shivering man's teeth, though no sound that I could hear came from them.

"At length she got down to the corpse, and I saw her lift the bark wrapper out of the grave, and draw the baby's body from it. Then she sat back upon her heels, threw up her head, just like a dog, and bayed at the moon. She did this three times, and I do not know what there was about those long-drawn howls that jangled up one's nerves, but each time the sound became more insistent and intolerable, and as I listened, my hair fairly lifted. Then, very carefully she laid the child's body down in a position that seemed to have some connection with the points of the compass, for she took a long time, and consulted the moon and the shadows repeatedly before she was satisfied with the orientation of the thing's head and feet.

"Then she got up, and began very slowly to dance round and round the grave. It was not a reassuring sight, out there in the awful loneliness of the night, miles away from every one and everything, to watch that abominable old beldam capering uncleanly in the moonlight, while those restless lips of hers called noiselessly upon all the devils in hell, with words that we could not hear. Juggins pressed up against me harder than ever, and his hand on my arm gripped tighter and tighter. He was shaking like a leaf, and I do not fancy that I was much steadier. It does not sound very terrible, as I tell it to you here in comparatively civilized surroundings; but at the time, the sight of that obscure figure dancing silently in the moonlight with its ungainly shadow scared me badly.

"She capered like that for some minutes, setting to the dead baby as though she were inviting it to join her, and the intent purposefulness of her made me feel sick. If anybody had told me that morning that I was capable of being frightened out of my wits by an old woman, I should have laughed; but I saw nothing outlandish in the idea while that grotesque dancing lasted.

"Her movements, which had been very slow at first, became gradually faster and faster, till every atom of her was in violent motion, and her body and limbs were swaying this way and that, like the boughs of a tree in a tornado. Then, all of a sudden, she collapsed on the ground, with her back toward us, and seized the baby's body. She seemed to nurse it, as a mother might nurse her child; and as she swayed from side to side, I could see first the curve of the creature's head, resting on her thin left arm, and then its feet near the crook of her right elbow. And now she was crooning to it in a cracked falsetto chant that might have been a lullaby or perhaps some incantation.

"She rocked the child slowly at first, but very rapidly the pace quickened, until her body was swaying to and fro from the hips, and from side to side, at such a rate that, to me, she looked as though she were falling all ways at once. And simultaneously her shrill chanting became faster and faster, and every instant more nerve-sawing.

"Next she suddenly changed the motion. She gripped the thing she was nursing by its arms, and began to dance it up and down, still moving with incredible agility, and crooning more damnably than ever. I could see the small, puckered face of the thing above her head every time she danced it up, and then, as she brought it down again, I lost sight of it for a second, until she danced it up once more. I kept my eyes fixed upon the thing's face every time it came into view, and I swear it was not an optical illusion—*it began to be alive*. Its eyes were open and moving, and its mouth was working, like that of a child which tries to laugh but is too young to do it properly. Its face ceased to be like that of a newborn baby at all. It was distorted by a horrible animation. It was the most unearthly sight.

"Juggins saw it, too, for I could hear him drawing his breath harder and shorter than a healthy man should.

"Then, all in a moment, the hag did something. I did not see clearly precisely what it was; but it looked to me as though she bent forward and kissed it; and at that very instant a cry went up like the wail of a lost soul. It may have been something in the jungle, but I know my Malayan forests pretty thoroughly, and I have never heard any cry like it before nor since. The next thing we knew was that the old hag had thrown the body back into the grave, and was dumping down the earth and jumping on it, while that strange cry grew fainter and fainter. It all happened so quickly that I had not had time to think or move before I was startled back into full consciousness by the sharp crack of Juggins's revolver fired close to my ear.

"'She's burying it alive!' he cried.

"It was a queer thing for a man to say, who had seen the child lying stark and dead more than thirty hours earlier; but the same thought was in my mind, too, as we both started forward at a run. The hag had vanished into the jungle as silently as a shadow. Juggins had missed her, of course. He was always a rotten bad shot. However, we had no thought for her. We just flung ourselves upon the grave, and dug at the earth with our hands, until the baby lay in my arms. It was cold and stiff, and putrefaction had already begun its work. I forced open its mouth, and saw something that I had expected. The tip of its tongue was missing. It looked as though it had been bitten off by a set of shocking bad teeth, for the edge left behind was like a saw.

"'The thing's quite dead,' I said to Juggins.

"'But it cried—it cried!' whimpered Juggins. 'I can hear it now. To think that we let that horrible creature murder it.'

"He sat down with his head in his hands. He was utterly unmanned.

"Now that the fright was over, I was beginning to be quite brave again. It is a way I have.

"'Rot,' I said. 'The thing's been dead for hours, and anyway, here's your precious specimen if you want it.'

"I had put it down, and now pointed at it from a distance. Its proximity was not pleasant. Juggins, however, only shuddered.

"'Bury it, in Heaven's name,' he said, his voice broken by sobs. 'I would not have it for the world. Besides, it *was* alive. I saw and heard it.'

"Well, I put it back in its grave, and next day we left the Sâkai country. Juggins had a whacking dose of fever, and anyway we had had about enough of the Sâkai and of all their engaging habits to last us for a bit.

"We swore one another to secrecy as Juggins, when he got his nerve back, said that the accuracy of our observations was not susceptible of scientific proof, which, I understand, was the rock his religion had gone to pieces on; and I did not fancy being told that I was drunk or that I was lying. You, however, know something of the uncanny things of the East, so to-night I have broken our vow. Now I'm going to turn in. Don't give me away."

Young Middleton died of fever and dysentery, somewhere upcountry, a year or two later. His name was not Middleton, of course; so I am not really "giving him away," as he called it, even now. As for his companion, though when I last heard of him he was still alive and a shining light in the scientific world, I have named him Juggins, and as the family is a large one, he will run no great risk of being identified.

THE CUBE

Charles Loring Jackson

Plashkill, like so many other Hudson River towns, dozes peacefully between the river and the creek, from which it takes its name; and there lived in a pleasant old house on the outskirts of the village the girl, who was the victim of this strange experience.

One hot day toward the end of September, now many years ago, she started for a morning's fishing, and after five minutes' walk on the dusty road was glad to turn into the woods beside the creek, where it was cool enough to be pleasant, though still too warm for anything but leisurely sauntering. It was some time, therefore, before she came to the fishing place she liked best, a flat mossy rock jutting out into a more than usually tranquil reach of the stream, and so completely shaded by trees that they almost dipped their branches into the water. Here she established herself comfortably and was soon dreamily watching her float, since even in this shade it was too hot to take a lively interest in anything.

The morning slipped away pleasantly in lazy meditation, now and then perhaps even in dozing, and the fishes seemed to be as languid as she, for not even a nibble disturbed her float.

At length the noon bells from the distant village warned her that dinner time was approaching, and she thought with comical dismay of the shower of chaff which would burst upon her, if she came home empty handed after her boasts at the breakfast table of the number of fish she was going to catch. But, if the fish would not bite, what could she do? All she could think of was to allow herself ten minutes more, when at last it was time to start for home; and, after these had brought nothing, two minutes more for luck.

These passed too, and she was just pulling in her line to go home, when a tremendous bite dragged the float deep under the water, and nearly jerked the pole out of her hands. In an instant she was all alive to land this fish, which must be large enough to make up for bringing home no others. After a short but fierce struggle she managed to pull her hook to the surface, but it flew out of the water with such a bounce that she thought she had lost him; and, indeed, at first the hook seemed empty, but when she looked more carefully, she saw on it what appeared to be a little square of flesh.

It was about half an inch across and certainly could not have pulled so tremendously. This made her examine it with a good deal of curiosity, and she found it was an irregular cube of what looked like raw meat, except on one side, which was covered with an unhealthy yellowish skin; the others were rough with projecting fibres like a piece of tough beef cut with a dull knife; and the worst of it was, the disgusting thing was alive. The fibres were vibrating with a slow waving motion, which seemed to reach out for some prey, and every now and then the whole mass was shaken with a convulsive jerk, as if it were trying to open and shut like some of the larger jelly-fishes.

Altogether it was so inexpressibly loathsome, that she could not bring herself to touch it, but tried to rub it off her hook upon the rock; and, when this failed, pried and pushed at it with a stick; and at last, when she could not get rid of it, utterly overcome with disgust, she threw into the creek hook, line, rod and all, and hurried away from this unclean spot.

After leaving it well behind, she sank down on the pine-needles breathless and thoroughly unstrung; but soon the soft warm air, and the green quiet of the woods soothed her jangled nerves enough for her to start for home; and, before she got out of the woods, she had so far recovered her usual cheerful serenity that she began thinking what a good story she could make out of her adventure.

Just beyond the woods she caught sight of a belated water-lily growing in the creek so near a log, which reached out into the stream, that she could pick it easily; and, as it was an uncommonly fine one, she decided to bring it home with her, as it would at least be something to show for her morning. Accordingly she rolled up her sleeve, and cautiously ventured out to the end of the slippery log. Then to get the longest possible stem she plunged her arm under water nearly to the shoulder, and, just as her fingers closed about the cool smooth stem, she felt on her upper arm a prick like the bite of a leech, and drawing it out quickly there was the cube clinging to it, as a shell-fish sucks itself on to a rock.

It was a mercy that she did not tumble off the log! And only by the use of the utmost self-control could she manage to totter back to the shore. There, although she shrank in every fibre from the loathsome thing, she seized it and tried to wrench it off her arm, but her fiercest struggles did not even stir it. Next she scraped at it feverishly with a sharp piece of slate, but with no success; so that at last she was obliged to pull down her sleeve over it and go home.

During this short hot walk she shuddered at herself, for she could not help feeling disgraced by the presence of this unclean thing upon her arm; and it was a very flushed, unstrung girl who sneaked into the house, and crept up to her room. Here she rolled up her sleeve again, almost hoping to find nothing, as it seemed too horrible to be true, but there it was still clinging to her arm, and it was the very cube she had caught further upstream, for she saw the mark of her hook in its yellow mottled skin.

This time she was bound to get it off, but she pulled, pushed and tore at it in vain, even when she grasped it with a towel to get a firmer hold on its slimy surface; and, when the dinner bell rang, she had to pull her sleeve over it once more, and go down to the table.

There, as her brothers had heard she brought home no fish, the expected chaff broke loose.

"Soup? No thank you!" said one; "I will wait for Daphne's fish."

"It must have been an awfully big haul," said the other. "See how heated she got carrying such a pile home."

"I hope we shan't get perfectly sick of fish, before we get them all eaten up."

Instead of, as usual, meeting this feeble teasing with a lively crushing answer, Daphne, to the dismay of all, burst into tears, and hurried out of the room.

In her chamber she locked the doors, and attacked the cube once more, and when she found again she could not stir it, tried her best to cut it off with a knife but could not make even the slightest impression on its tough surface. Then, thoroughly desperate, she made up her mind to cut out of her arm the piece of flesh, to which it was clinging, but the first cut bled so much that she grew frightened, and dared go no further. In fact, she found it no easy matter to stop the blood.

When at last she succeeded, she had hardly collapsed a limp, hopeless mass of wretchedness on the couch, when her mother came knocking at the door, and asked tenderly what was the matter. It was hard not to throw herself on her lap, and tell her everything, but the loathsome thing stood between them like some secret too shameful to be confessed even to her mother, and all she could do was to sob on her shoulder, and say she was very miserable.

After soothing her as best she could, her mother left her trying to go to sleep, and hoped that the next day would bring Daphne back to her old wholesome self, but it did not. Nor the one after that, nor many days to come.

The shrinking consciousness of her loathsome parasite was always with her, and oppressed her with a sense of disgrace, as if she were guilty of some shameful crime; for, unreasonable as it was, she could not get rid of the feeling that in some way she was to blame. Under this strain her health gave way rapidly. A nervous, anxious look never left her face, and she grew so thin and pale that they feared she was going into a decline. Her appetite, however, instead of falling off, as would have been natural, actually increased, until she was eating enough for two, so that one of her brothers indulged in the time-worn joke that, if she had consumption, it was only consumption of food. The doctor when summoned could find no disease, spoke of a nervous shock, and was plainly puzzled.

As the weeks dragged into months, her health continued to run down, for, instead of getting accustomed to the cube upon her arm, her hatred and disgust for it increased. This terrible repulsion, however, was the only cause of her sufferings, since the cube gave no physical pain, in fact, she would not have known it was there, had it not been for an occasional slight suction on her arm.

Meanwhile, its appearance changed but little. Toward the end of the third month the red parts had grown more purple, and the whole, although its size was unaltered, had taken on a bloated overfed look, a change, slight as it was, which made it even more repulsive than before, if that were possible.

One day not long before Christmas an errand took her to the village, and, as she reached the bottom of the hill on which her house stood, she felt suddenly a most intense relief, a cheerful buoyancy unknown to her for months. Full of a wild hope she turned into a retired lane that ran along the foot of the hill, and hastening down it, until she was out of sight of the road, rolled up her sleeve and—she was not deceived. The cube was gone!

All the way to the village she walked on air, greeting the acquaintances she met with all her old time vivacity, and started for home briskly, as she was anxious to look at her arm again, and make sure the good news was really true.

On her way home at the foot of the hill she met a girl, whom she did not know, which was strange, as the village was so small that she must have heard, if any guest from out of town was staying in it. This girl, too, looked curiously familiar, although she could not remember where she had seen her before, but this puzzle was driven out of her head by the excitement of reaching home, when she flew to her room, rolled up her sleeve, and it was true; The cube was really gone. It had dropped off, leaving a barely perceptible scar.

She went down to dinner overflowing with the wildest of spirits. To the delight of every one it was the real Daphne again, in place of the silent, dejected wraith of the last three months; and the rest of the day was a little triumphal celebration of her return to herself.

It was later than usual, therefore, when at last she sat before the glass in her room combing out her hair for the night, and happily thinking over the great deliverance of the day.—And then in the glass she saw the door behind her slowly pushed open, and wondered, who could be coming to her room at this time of night. Very slowly it opened wider and wider, until at last a girl dressed in white with a comb in her hand stood in the doorway, peering into the room. It was the stranger, she had met in the morning, and now she saw why it had looked so familiar.

It was herself!

Herself even to the least detail.

Slowly the thing crept toward her, while she, paralyzed with terror, sat watching it in the glass.

Nearer it crept and nearer, until close behind her it crouched to spring at her. Then the spell was broken. Her courage came back in a flood, and springing to her feet she turned, and faced it—and it went. She never could tell how, whether it vanished, or ran from the room, but it went.

This was too much for her over-strained nerves, and running into her sister's room, she said she must sleep with her.

"What is the matter?" said her sister. "Have you seen a ghost?"

"No! (rather doubtfully). But I am frightened, terribly frightened."

Her sister laughed at her for being afraid of nothing, but was quite willing to take her in for the night.

What a relief it was to take refuge under her sister's wing! And when at last she nestled down in bed be side her, she felt entirely safe, although still too excited and shaken to go to sleep for a long time.

In the early dawn she started broad awake in quivering horror, and, as her eyes opened, they met the cruel glare of that hateful thing, which with its face almost touching hers was kneeling on her chest, while its smooth slender fingers felt for her throat. With a wild shriek she grasped her sister's arm, and it went.

After this it was always near her. She soon found that it never ventured to come in, unless she was alone, but, if she was alone even for a minute, in it peered through the window, or slowly the door began to open, and she felt it was there, so she had to make sure that some one was with her all the time. This was hard to manage, but it had to be, as the slightest gap in her watchfulness showed her the double close at hand lying in wait for her.

Although constant vigilance saved her from an actual clash with her follower, she found this so trying that often she was tempted to meet it face to face, and dare it to do its worst, but each time the mysterious uncanny horror which enveloped it was too much for her courage.

At first the nights were times of terror, but a long and wearing trial at last proved to her that sleeping with her sister was a complete protection, in spite of her horrible experience the first night.

Even with quiet nights, however, this last state was much worse than the three months, when she was nourishing the cube upon her arm. Then shame and disgust were all she had to endure. Now it was a gnawing suspense and an always threatening danger. Her anxious worried expression became very painful, her nerves were completely out of tune, and she grew even more thin and pale.

Her mother, thoroughly alarmed, was at her wits' end to find some way to help her, and, when early in the winter Plashkill was excited by the prospect of a party, urged Daphne to go, hoping that the change might do her good. At first she would not hear of it; but on thinking it over she realized that, as the cube appeared only when she was alone, a crowded party would be the safest place possible, and so agreed to go and even looked forward to it with a good deal of pleasure.

When the evening came she enjoyed herself so thoroughly that she almost forgot her hated double. For one thing, she was dancing the German with John, which was happiness enough, and beside, as she was very popular, she was taken out much of the time.

In one of the figures, which resembled a quadrille, she started forward in ladies' chain looking back over her shoulder to throw some lively remark at her partner, when, as her hand met that of the other girl, she felt those long smooth, slender fingers, which had once fumbled for her throat, and looking around met the mocking gaze of the Thing. She was actually hand in hand with it! With a convulsive shudder she tried to tear her hand away from those dreadful fingers, but they clung like a shellfish to its rock; and, when at last they reluctantly drew themselves off, they left her so shaken that she could hardly force herself to keep on dancing.

On her return, when she passed the Thing once more, she took the best of care to keep her hand well out of its reach, for she could not have borne its touch a second time.

As she got back to her place, she began to wonder how the Cube had found a partner, and looking across saw it was dancing with Eben Trissell, the most able and successful young man in the village, and so attractive and lively that even his goodness was forgiven. Evidently, too, this was no chance meeting, for they were chatting and laughing together with the intimacy of an old friendship. Then she saw the Cube draw his attention to her, and both looked at her with a strange hungry eagerness, which was really terrible.

All this time Daphne had been holding herself up only by sheer force of will. She kept saying to herself: "I won't give way! I won't! I won't!"

And for a few minutes more she managed to totter through her part of the dance, but then it became too much for her, and she grew so faint, that she had to ask her partner to take her back to her seat.

This broke up the set. The music stopped, and her friends crowded around her full of sympathy and clumsy attempts to help her. Foremost among them was the Cube, and it was actually offering to stroke her forehead. This was too much! She could not have endured the touch of those loathsome fingers with their veiled suggestion of slimy horrors, and staggering to her feet asked to be taken home at once. John was more than ready to escort her, and, after she had refused to drag her sister from the half-finished party, they were soon on their way.

The sharp, crisp air and the winter moonlight lying on the fresh snow quieted her nerves, and presently she began to wonder what the Cube had looked like to other people, and so asked John:

"Who was it dancing with Eben Trissell?"

John began to answer—then stopped puzzled, and after a little hesitation said:

"Bless me, if I know! It is queer too, as I thought I noticed especially, but now I can only remember it was a pretty girl."

Daphne smiled at the unconscious compliment, but was not surprised at the vagueness of John's impression of the Cube; and, when in the next few days she took occasion to ask several of the girls the same question, all of them either had forgotten who danced with Eben Trissell, or, if they named his partner, it was a girl who had danced with some one else.

After this no more parties, as, instead of proving the safest of places, this one had exposed her to the Cube so cruelly.

The winter dragged its slow length wearily along, and her health sank lower and lower under the incessant strain, with her enemy always just out of sight on the watch to pounce on her; until, as February drew to an end, her condition grew so alarming that her mother bitterly regretted her inability to send her to a warmer climate, and could only hope for an improvement when Spring had fairly come at last.

Daphne, by constant brooding on this murderous persecution, gradually came to understand that the Cube, while clinging to her arm, had absorbed enough of her nature to take on her bodily appearance and perhaps even her character, and now it was lying in wait to kill her, so that by appropriating her soul it could take her place in the world, condemning her to utter extinction. The thought of this loathsome thing taking her place with her mother, or with John stiffened her weakening courage, and she vowed, if she must succumb, it should be only after fighting to the last fibre of her strength and endurance.

One bright day late in March, John came to invite her to go with him and see the breaking-up of the ice, which was being driven out of the creek by a heavy freshet. She accepted this attractive invitation gladly, because there was not the least chance that John would leave her alone.

The day was sunny, and, although blustering—as March should be—very pleasant, especially as the sun and wind of the morning had dried the ground, making excellent walking, in spite of the heavy rains of the last two days.

After a brisk walk of a mile and a half they reached an ideal place for seeing the flood, for here a low but precipitous hill jutted out into the stream, which swept in a wide curve around its base, brawling through a narrow valley, that might fairly be called a gorge.

They stood here for some time, watching the cakes of ice sailing down the stream above, until reaching the narrow throat of the gorge they were jostled, and thrown together, grinding against, or over each other, and piling up on the farther shore of the bend, or elbowing their way past, and then fighting savagely for a passage through the constantly narrowing channel. It was a most thrilling sight, more like a battle of fierce barbarians, than the crash of inanimate ice.

The flood evidently had been very bad farther up the creek, as now and then fence-rails, uprooted bushes, or even trees were whirled down amid the ice, and the rush of this great mass of water between the cramping banks would alone have been well worth seeing without the savage grinding and crashing of the great blocks of ice.

As they were watching this wonderful sight, they saw far up the stream something dark lying on one of the ice-cakes. The level rays of the sun were so dazzling that for some time they could not make out what it was; but, as it came nearer, there was even through the glare a suggestiveness about its shape that sent the blood from their cheeks.

Nearer it came and nearer, until at last they could see clearly that their worst anticipations were too true. It was a woman lying on her face apparently collapsed by terror. Daphne seized John's arm convulsively.

"Do something! We must do something!"

And John, whose mind had worked quickly, shouting, "I may catch her lower down!" started down the hill at the top of his speed, barely hearing Daphne's agonized cry of, "Go! Do go!"

It was the only chance of rescuing the poor woman, for by running across the hill John could strike the creek where it spread into the broader channel, before the cake of ice had time to get through the longer winding gorge; and in this quieter water there was a chance he might reach and save her, which it would have been madness to attempt amid the turmoil of the gorge.

If only there would be ice enough left to float her but, even before it had entered the gorge, great pieces had been broken from the cake, and Daphne shuddered, as she thought of it mauled and crushed by the frightful blows of the jostling cakes.

As she was straining her eyes to watch it, suddenly the woman sat up and smiled at her! Then she knew her hour had come. There was no escape! John was far out of hearing, and flight was impossible.

For an instant the thought of what was before her turned her almost faint, and she sank down on a log to gather up her scattered courage.

Presently she heard footsteps rustling through the withered leaves of the oak wood, and looking up there it was, standing on the edge of the wood. But now she was more than ready. Springing to her feet she advanced warily to meet it, and, when they were near enough, each sprang at the throat of the other.

Once more she felt those slender, cool, smooth fingers with their loathsome suggestion of uncanny sliminess, but this time they were clutching her throat, not merely fumbling at it; and, as her fingers sank into the throat of the Cube, the flesh, firm as it was, made her think of sinister depths of treacherous fresh water.

Then began a terrible battle. The two clung together, swaying with the fierceness of their struggles to choke each other, and the fingers of the Cube sank deeper and deeper into Daphne's flesh, while its eyes strove to force her eyes down before them with a fearful determined power, all the more ghastly because they were the very eyes she saw in her own face, whenever she looked in the glass.

And so they fought on, until at last Daphne's lids began to sink. They fell. She lost sight of her enemy, and felt it was all over, as the clutch on her throat tightened shutting off her breath. But just on the verge of the end the thought that this loathsome Thing was casting her down to annihilation stung her to one last supreme effort. Fiercely she labored to raise her heavy lids, weighed down by the gaze of the Cube. She fought with her whole heart, her whole strength. At first in vain, but at last, although with many pauses and sinkings-back, she slowly and painfully forced them up, and again met the intense purposeful glare of the Cube. Could she hold out against it, and be able to stand for another second that choking grip upon her throat?

It seemed hours that by mere force of will she held her eyelids up, and bent the whole energy of her being to forcing down those fearful eyes; but at last she saw a faint hint of doubt, almost of fear steal into them. Desperately she hung on, until there came a faint quiver of its eyelids. Were they falling? Yes! Slowly, as if weighed down by an irresistible power, they sank over its eyes, and, although at once they flew up again, this was enough. Wonderfully heartened she threw into her gaze reserves of power undreamed of before, and once more its eyelids fell; and down she held them in spite of its desperate struggles to lift them again.

Then—then at last she felt the clutch on her throat relaxing, and, as her strength returned, threw it all into the grip of her fingers, which each instant sank deeper into the flesh of the accursed Thing, while its grasp slackened, until its fingers dropped away from her throat.

Its face turned black. Its tongue protruded; and, when at length the death-rattle sounded in its throat, it was hanging a limp flaccid mass from her hands.

Then she fainted.

When John, hurrying up the hill, found her lying there he did all he could think of to bring her to herself, and succeeded at last with the help of some snow, that he found in the woods.

As she first opened her eyes, she cried out:

"Where is it?" looked around fearfully, and even tried to struggle to her feet, but when she caught sight of John she sank back with a sigh of relief, and her eyes closed once more.

In a few minutes she was able to sit up, and, as she was very thirsty, John ran down to the creek for some water, after she made him promise not to go out of sight. Then she noticed that her right hand was tightly clenched, and opening it found there a little dry shrivelled piece of flesh, and in this read a sure proof of her victory. She buried it under the dead leaves, and after she had stamped it well into the soft earth, the relief was so great that soon she felt well enough to start for home.

It was a long, hard walk for her, however, and she could barely drag herself along even with frequent rests and John's tender care and help; so he did not dare to tell her that the cake of ice was empty, when at last, it drifted out of the gorge, as he naturally supposed anxiety for the poor woman had caused Daphne's fainting-fit.

When at last they reached home, she was so exhausted that her mother put her to bed at once; but the long night's sleep brought a wonderful change in her; and a day of rest with, still more, the hope that her troubles were over made her so well that by evening she ventured on the experiment of being alone for a minute; and as this brought no sign of the double, the next day she passed a whole hour alone without being molested, and now that she was certain the Cube was gone, her health and spirits came back with a rush, and were even more buoyant and overflowing than ever before.

After Easter, when there was another party, she was eager to go, before her mother had even thought of urging it. As, early in the evening she was standing with a group of girls, she found herself shuddering violently, and felt there was something uncanny and sinister behind her. On turning she saw Eben Trissell coming toward her, and an unerring instinct told her he was a Cube. Then it flashed through her mind that three years ago Eben had suffered from a mysterious illness, which now she realized with horror was the attack of a cube, and in the struggle the true Eben must have succumbed, leaving the Cube in his place. As she shrank from the transformed Cube with loathing, his eyes grew full of terror, and he seemed to shrink together.

"You know me," he whispered. "I must go! I must go! For no Cube will ever dare to cross your path again."

He hurried from the room; and she heard later that the next day he had gone to Texas, and she never laid eyes on him again.

When she came to think over the Eben Trissell affair, the most surprising part of it was that the Cube did not differ from the original Eben Trissell in any respect, but during all those three years was the same excellent and desirable member of society, so that his real nature was revealed to her enlightened eyes alone.

It was not more than two months after this that Daphne and John were—. But this has nothing to do with the story.

COACHWHIP PUBLICATIONS

COACHWHIPBOOKS.COM

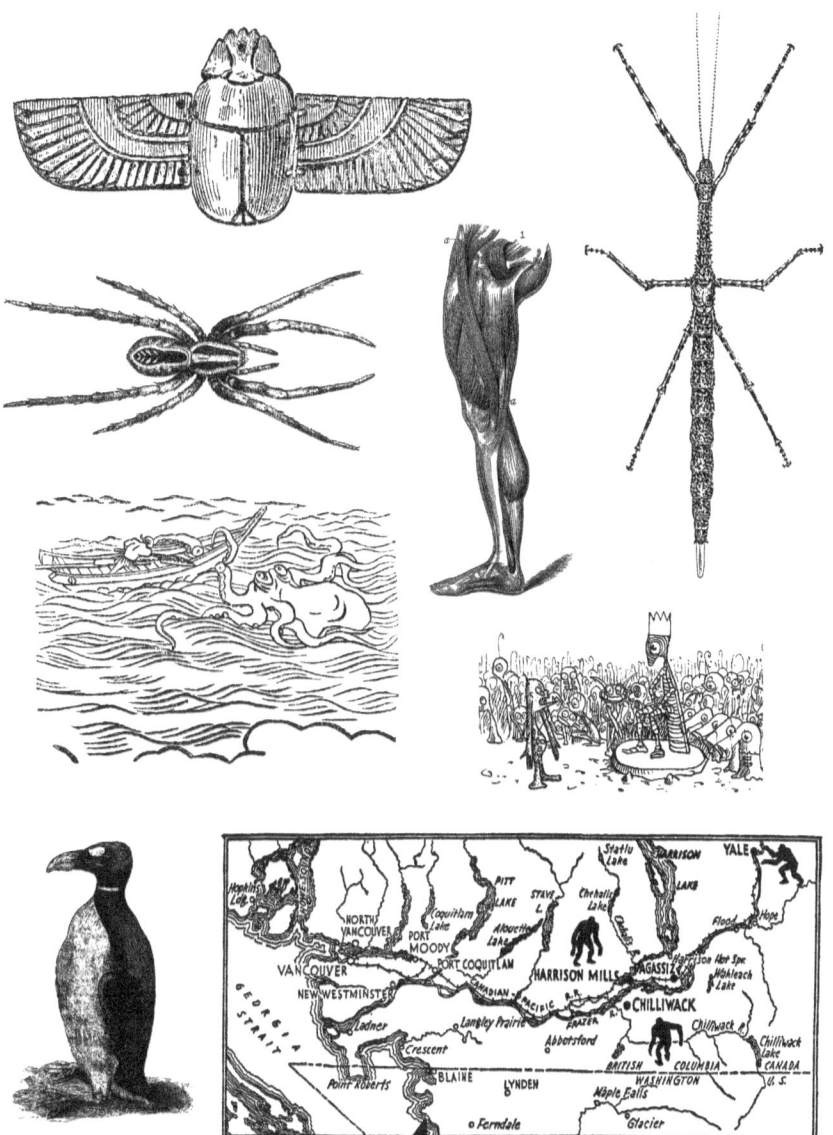

COACHWHIP PUBLICATIONS

COACHWHIPBOOKS.COM

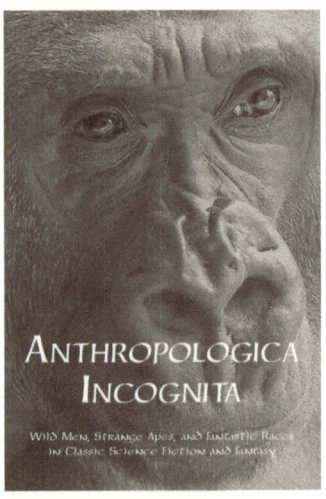

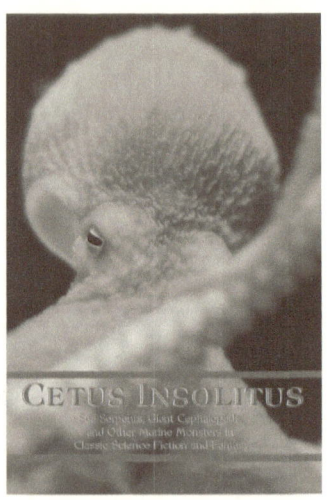

Unknown Creatures and Monstrous Beasts
in Classic Science Fiction and Fantasy

Flora Curiosa
ISBN 1-930585-56-X